KING

KING

SON OF NO MAN SERIES

BOOK 5

D. LAMBERT

To my kids.
May they love the world as much as I do.

Table of Contents

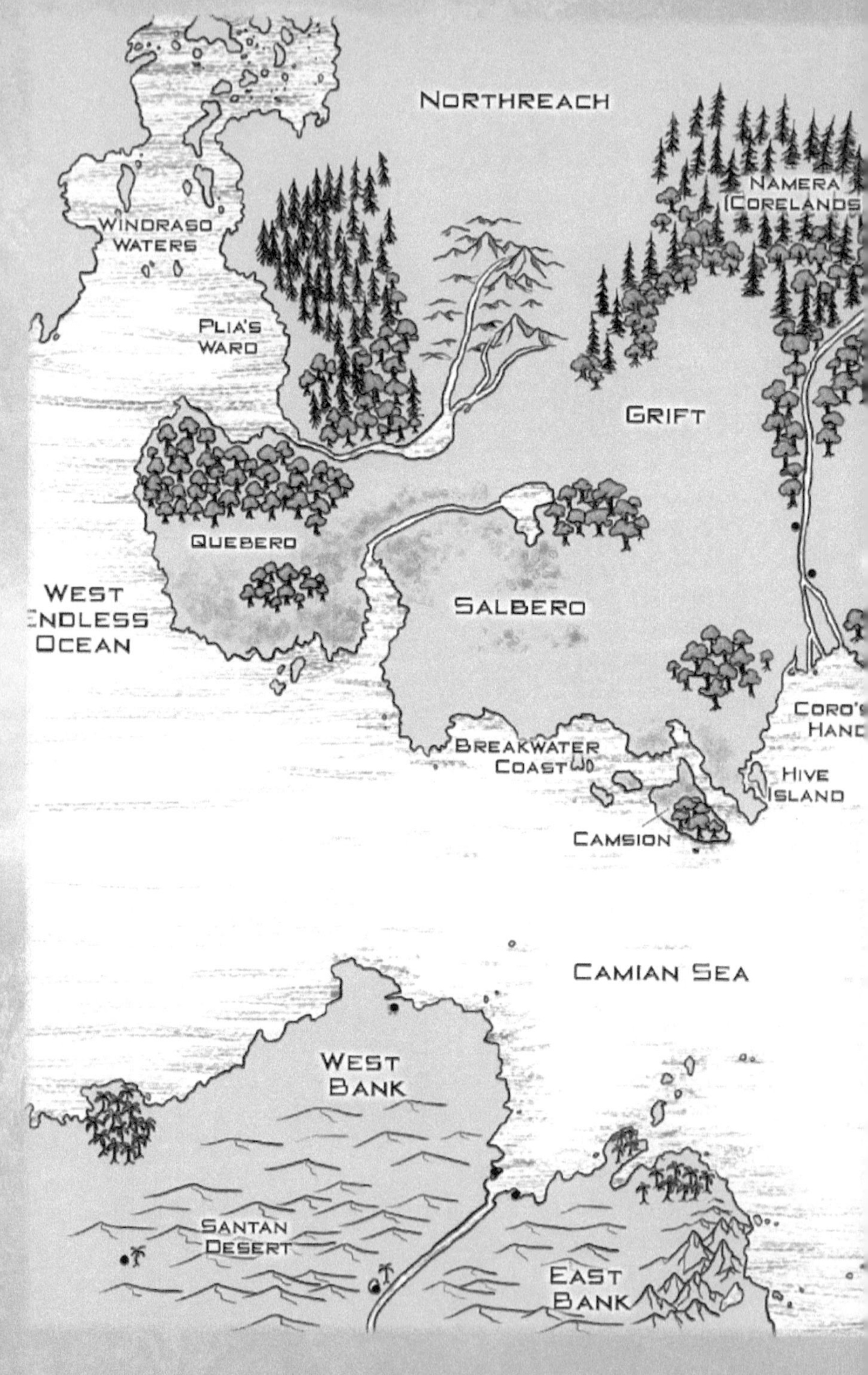

NORTHREACH
NAMERA (CORELANDS
WINDRASO WATERS
PLIA'S WARD
GRIFT
QUEBERO
WEST ENDLESS OCEAN
SALBERO
CORO'S HAND
BREAKWATER COAST
HIVE ISLAND
CAMSION
CAMIAN SEA
WEST BANK
SANTAN DESERT
EAST BANK

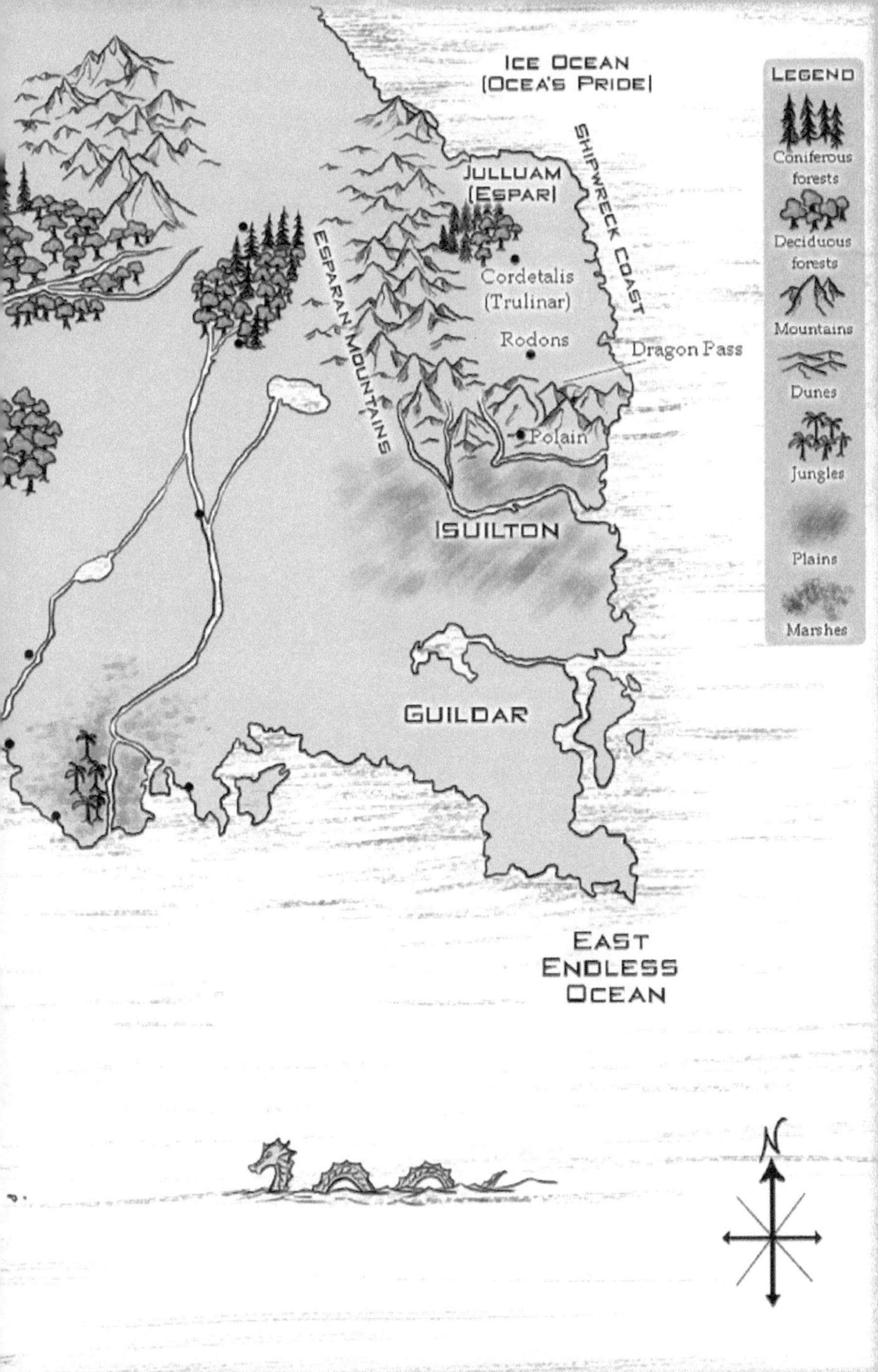

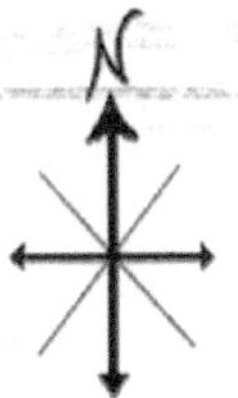

Ice Ocean
(Ocea's Pride)
Julluam
(Espar)
Shipwreck Coast
Cordetalis
(Trulinar)
Rodons
Dragon Pass
Polain
Esparan Mountains
Isuilton
Guildar
East Endless Ocean
Legend
Coniferous forests
Deciduous forests
Mountains
Dunes
Jungles
Plains
Marshes
N

"Judge a man lightly for his thoughts and judge him evenly for his words, but judge him harshly for his actions."

-Prince Kelland Trulin
of Trulin

Chapter 1

The tent set along a track in the northern reaches of Espar was more familiar than any hall or manor. After just under a year of marching through the countryside and wilderness, the green canvas and white ash wood shelter smelled of battlefields and smoke, which was home for Tohmas. It had survived the damp of river crossings, the ice of the Northland's tundra, and the wind of a hesitant spring. In the far north, the season was colder than he was accustomed to. Snow clung to the shadows of the countryside.

Victorious, the army's march headed south toward kinder weather. In thanks, Tohmas knelt before his altar of Inac, his sword SoulBurner reverently placed atop it. Despite the traditional prayer he recited, his mind remained elsewhere.

The army would reach the city of Narsol tomorrow. Prince Sol had gone ahead, and now messengers were wearing a new road through the hills connecting the army to Sol's manor in the walled city. Tonight, Sol's runner had reported the city ready for Prince Dragal's funeral.

The invitations Tohmas had asked Master Kitable to send to the many Princes of Espar had done their duty. All fourteen princedoms had a representative in a single location for the first time in known history. It was not always a region's ruling prince, but Tohmas was satisfied by the assortment of relatives or lords sent instead. The number of Princes of Espar was equally unprecedented.

Sol was humble in his letter, but Tohmas knew the prestige of hosting such an event was sure to be significant. They were there for a funeral, yet they would leave at the start of a new era or a new war, whichever Inac willed.

The dampness of the ground cut through his breeches as he knelt before the flickering flame of the altar, having insisted the servants keep the damn meeting table on the waggons and leave him be. He had no plans for formal conversations tonight. His soldiers knew the camp routine well enough to no longer require directions. Carsh, his brother by deed but not by blood, had gone down into the Rydan side of camp in search of company. Like most Rydans, Carsh was still celebrating the sacking of Arcott and the death of the Prince of Barlaby. The Rydans were looking forward to their next battle and would have grown restless should the rumors reach them that the war had ended.

Carsh's presence among his fellow Rydans had another purpose; he would beat down any suspicions of peace, just as Darknim DoomDragon did for the Northlanders. Keeping to themselves, the Esparans were the only ones yet to be told the truth. Tonight, they relaxed and looked forward to the prospect of real beds the next night.

Tohmas let them keep their illusion. Spies could not hide among the Rydans or the Northlanders, but a well-placed traitor among the main forces could learn too much from the Esparans. He had to wait before informing his Esparans of the grander plan.

Finishing the prayer, Tohmas leaned back and turned his attention to the three piles of painted stones arranged at his knees. The largest pile to his left did not require organization. The markers of the princedoms he knew and controlled were a heap. He'd laid out the other two piles, so each colored symbol faced him, ready for his consideration.

"Always so hard at work," an alto voice said from the other side of the tent.

Instinctually defensive, Tohmas tensed before fully recognizing the voice. He stayed his hand, leaving the sword on the altar, and turned respectfully to face her, still on his knees.

The Goddess of Fire lay sprawled on his bed, one hand draped comfortably over the edge. Her attire was one part elegant and one part scandalous, ranging from golden chainmail draping her upper arms to a skirt cut for riding but too shear to protect even her modesty. One hand was gold-tinted, but her other glinted like glass. She seemed thinner, her dark blond hair taking on a red hue in the candlelight. Her clothing was partially transparent, but he was grateful for even that slight cover. He had seen her without any coverings; no conversation was possible then.

He had come to expect the goddess' visits since they had left Arcott and would have been disappointed if she had failed to attend tonight. Before that, she had appeared to him sporadically, although most commonly after battle celebrations. With the frequency of her presence now, he had ceased worrying about being caught with her. Everyone, from Tohmas' brother to the princes who had marched with him in the Northlander War, knew that the candles after sunset were his time. They did not know why, but they knew not to intrude.

There were nights when she came as the Lady of Lust and others when she was the Bitch Goddess. Most visits were from the Warrior Queen aspect of the Goddess of Fire, although some elements of the Lady of Lust shone through all her manifestations.

He forced his stare away from her, feeling desire rise.

"Is this what you wish of me tonight?" he asked. The time was short to finish his plans for each princedom, but even a Prince of Espar obeyed his Goddess. She would know best how to utilize the time he had left.

She slid from the bed and onto gold-touched feet that made no sound despite the assortment of bangles decorating her ankles. She wore no sword tonight.

"No, no other plans, Champion," she cooed, her accent slipping from southern to strongly Lourite. The shift reminded Tohmas of his training with Chief Tamv when he had been coached to trade his Rydan accent for a Galanth one that better suited his Esparan blood.

Inac approached, and Tohmas lowered his head. When she touched his shoulder, her hand was frigid. It had burned before; perhaps it changed on her whim. He took the cold to mean he had to finish the matter at hand, not to be distracted by the increasing need her long, graceful legs stirred in him.

"Your allies number the greatest," she said softly, keeping him on task.

Tohmas' eyes went to the pile on his left, the stack representing the princedoms he had already brought under his control. Among them was a quartz stone he had selected as Darknim DoomDragon's marker. He had thrown aside the stones representing Barlaby, Meloch, and

Tanble, as Darknim had conquered those princedoms before Tohmas had brought the Northlander to his side.

"Show me," Inac said, the accent now nearly Rydan as she paused behind him.

He felt her gaze on his back, like a candle's heat behind him, as he gestured at the first pile. "The sons of Zayban are already mine."

"The three that live, yes," Inac replied. "But Sol and Barnon are not the force their brother Dragal was. And the third son is yoked to your blood by a dead marriage. The hold is brittle."

The word "marriage" was bitter. Her realm was lust, not the sweet love of her sister goddess, Ocea.

Tohmas' stare went to the brown and white stone representing his uncle-by-marriage. "Prince Deiton is a coward with no heart for fighting. He will follow where the sons of Zayban lead," Tohmas said.

Beside the stone was Dragal's blue and yellow stone. "Dragal's sons-in-law are taking his place, keeping the family strong. Sol says they will divide Clandac, but I have a better offer for them. This much is simple. We have the north and center of Espar between us six." The quartz stone in the pile was key. Darknim knew the offer Tohmas intended to make. He had already approved the plans for Dragal's heirs.

"You did right to finish off Prince Dragal," Inac said, her voice husky. "Now we can press on without interruption."

She knows. Of course she knows. Dragal had sought death, although he had never explicitly requested it from Tohmas. Still, Tohmas had provided it. He had been well within Rydan customs and laws, and he doubted the Northlanders minded, but the Esparans would be outraged if they knew he had stabbed an arrow into the back of a Prince of Espar. Princes did not kill princes. They did not see that illnesses needed purging. In their eyes, Tohmas had committed murder. He had no intention of telling any Esparan about it.

Inac was the Mistress of Justice; her approval freed him of all guilt.

"I am glad you approve. My uncles would damn me should they discover it," Tohmas said.

"Their hands are no less blood-stained. They were the death of Prince Marfaie. But he was a traitor to his title as a prince," Inac said. It was strange to hear the name spoken aloud; Rydan tradition insisted the names of the damned should never be spoken aloud. Tohmas presumed Inac did not care, being a goddess.

"You did right. And they did right. Vengeance can be just."

Vengeance, in the form of slow maiming and starvation, had left the corpse of Prince Marfaie at the border to Solta. Starvation was traditional for traitors in Espar.

He had slain four princes now, one by choosing not to act, one by poisoning, one by respecting the man's request for relief, and one by giving him over to his enemies. Only a mild sense of guilt remained for the first. None of the others upset him.

"Now, your enemies?" Inac asked, her hand siding behind his neck to rest on his left shoulder. The scar there tingled, bringing Prince Dorakon of Gaidol to the forefront of Tohmas' mind. His eyes went to the white stone with the blue center.

"Prince Dorakon hates me. I won the bet and made him look like a fool. He will fight me." Leaving Dorakon's stone where it lay, he picked up the green and yellow stone beside it. "Prince Neillen is tied closely to his brother, so I expect him to follow Dorakon and set Nothor against me. But Neillen did not come for the funeral. He sent an emissary, Lord Garmont, who will soon marry Prince Neillen's sister-in-law." He paused for his thoughts to coalesce. The connections between lords and ladies of Espar puzzled him. Instead of assessing a hierarchy of skill, as he had in the Outlands, he memorized bloodlines with little understanding of their importance.

Maybe he could find leverage somewhere in those connections. "And Damoria," he finished, listing the last stone in the right-hand pile, "has a feud with my princedom that goes back two generations. Prince Wevan has sent his son. Apparently, the last time the young Warrah and I met, I bloodied his nose, and he gave me a black eye." Tohmas smiled. Although he did not remember the encounter, he appreciated the simplicity of their relationship.

Inac lifted her hand from his shoulder. The chill lingered. "And the others?"

A yellow stone with a grey anvil for Lour, a blue stone with a red bird for Polthian, and the white stone with the brown horse for Trulin lay between the two piles, unassigned.

"We will see," he said.

She came around, standing before him. Like her feet, her legs were gold-tinged. He could see up to her hip through the long slit of her crimson skirt.

The chill left his shoulder, heat rising instead. It started in his chest and moved down suggestively like a lover's caress.

"You will suffer for this quest, but it will be for the best."

Since the first night he had seen her red dress in a Rydan *shella*, Tohmas had felt her will in everything he had done. Chief Tamv had presented the idea to go into Espar, but Tohmas had heard the echo of Inac's will in his voice. The time was ripe now, even it if was earlier than any of them had expected. That was because of her assistance. She was ready to lead him on. With her at his side, he could do anything.

When she beckoned, Tohmas came to his feet. Physically, she was a head shorter than him, but in her presence, he felt small.

"Give me SoulBurner," she commanded, and he immediately retrieved his enchanted blade from the altar and dropped to a kneeling position to present it to her. Although the sword would only glow red when held in his grip, its enchanted aura filled the tent when her hand wrapped around the hilt.

His soul stirred to see her standing with the green and silver blade flickering flames in hand. It marked the first time he had seen the sword from a distance, and he now found himself cowed by it. He felt like a brand had been laid on his soul.

"I have a final task for you," she announced, and he adjusted to a Rydan-ready stance with one leg bent and his knee not quite touching the ground. "Your undertaking must have an heir, Champion. This realm I created must stand. You must have a son."

Inac was goddess of war, fury, justice, and passion. He had not expected her to comment on matters of family.

"Is it not Ocea who would need to give her blessing?" he asked.

Inac tossed her hair in the firelight and sneered with a dismissing wave of her hand. "Fine, fine," she said indignantly. "Ask her permission. Fall in love, if you want, Champion, even marry. You will always belong to me."

He bowed his head in acceptance. Into the silence, he spoke the prayer of Inac.

CHAPTER 1

By the time he had finished, the blade lay on the ground, and the goddess was gone. The heat through his body dwindled and then vanished. A damp chill again filled the tent, his knees wet from kneeling and growing cold.

But his soul still felt bound to her, and his heart locked onto the command as he re-sheathed the sword.

He would have an heir. He had to have a son. If that were so, then, by Esparan, Rydan, and Northlander law, he had to marry. Only then would a son be his heir as well.

The thought confused him. He knew war well. Women were easy. *But a wife?*

He had come to no conclusion by the time he changed the light on Inac's altar and slept.

Lance stood when the dapple horse arrived, as did the crowd of protectors who had been waiting. The camp was being struck around them, the familiar motions of the well-traveled forces predictable. But before they made the final approach to the capital, the protectors would spar. That tradition began when the Prince of Galanth arrived on the sparring ground.

The emptied farmer field outside the camp defenses had been trampled flat by protectors, Tohmas' closest defenders, in the thin light of the late spring sun. So long had Solta been war, the field was fallow, if muddy. While it was an excellent sparring ring, the terrain also made a good breeding ground for flies. Clouds of the pests were emerging in the chill of the morning, leaving the protectors swatting and cursing.

Lance's blue and white tabard of Gaidol stood out starkly among the green and silver of Galanth, but he was at home with the protectors now. For a season, Lance and his Gaidolon guardsmen had fought side by side with the Galanth soldiers.

"You look unusually fresh and clean," Lance said, squinting up in the early light at Prince Tohmas. Having left Bolt, his horse, by the ring's edge, he had a long way up to meet Tohmas' eyes. Behind Tohmas, Prime Protector Carsh, perched atop his black warhorse Bashuran, snorted. He eyed Carsh's sour expression. "You haven't sparred with

Carsh this morning," Lance concluded. "The splint slowing him down? How much longer is he supposed to have it on?"

The prime protector's baldrics were filled with knives, but a splint held his right arm from the elbow to the fist. Despite the injury, in typical Rydan stubbornness, he carried a knife in his right hand and wrapped his grass bracelet over the splint. His rank rope, a jaunty new green and black combination, hung from his vest since he lacked armor to strap it to.

Carsh muttered Rydan curses in answer. Some of the protectors nearby cocked their heads in interest, although how much they understood was questionable. Having traveled with Rydans recently, Lance understood every word. The swearing was particularly vivid this morning.

"Darak says it'll be on for five quartercycles. Seven if Carsh doesn't stop using the arm in practice," Tohmas said.

"It's going to be seven, isn't it?" Lance replied, stepping back to let Tohmas dismount. Even though he was taller than Lance by two hands and weighed easily twice as much—and all muscle at that—Prince Tohmas had a long way to drop from Schlavarai's back. Thanks to his experience with Trulin warhorses, Lance felt he had a certain immunity to intimidation from the horse. Schlavarai seemed to know she could not phase Lance and never tried.

Bashuran, Carsh's horse, was a different matter. The black stallion puffed up his chest and stomped a foot at Lance's proximity, but Lance only gave the horse an unimpressed look. He knew Carsh would never allow the threat to be followed through.

"Probably," Tohmas answered. He swept the blanket off the horse's back and handed it blindly to the groom trailing him.

Carsh grimaced and spat.

"We reaching Narsol today?" Lance asked once Tohmas had released his horse. The mare took a place beside the ring and nuzzled the trampled grasses in search of new breakfast. When Carsh's horse tried to join her, she made to bite, and he respectfully decided to graze a little farther away.

Ready, Lance handed Tohmas a spare sword for the spars between the protectors. Leather coverings could not hold Tohmas' blade for practice. The enchanted edge cut anything, including metal.

"Prince Dragal's funeral is tomorrow," Tohmas replied, smirking. "We had better reach the capital to attend it, seeing as we have his ashes."

Lance joined him as they walked to the sparring area. Four of the protectors, smartly dressed in green tabards and bearing swords and shields, stood rigidly on duty at the corners of the space.

"Lots of nice dignitaries there, I expect," Lance goaded.

"I'm looking forward to meeting them."

"You hate politics. What are you looking forward to?"

Tohmas pressed his lips in a smothered smile. "I'll tell you more later. Narsol is going to be interesting. Now, shall we get on with this? We don't want to be late."

A short cheer answered from the protectors, cutting off further questions from Lance. They quickly selected their foes for the bout and took to the field.

He's up to something, Lance thought. If he did not wish to discuss something among the protectors—allies and friends Tohmas admitted he knew and trusted—Lance had to wait.

Besides, Lance was Gaidolon, no matter what relationship the Northlander War had forged between them. As they closed on the southern princedoms, Lance felt the weight of his blue and white tabard more and more.

It was temporary chaos as each pairing of protectors took to exchanging blows. The thud of covered weapons, interspersed by the clang of metal for those who had chosen bare blades, echoed over the cheering of onlookers. Lance accepted Protector Derry's challenge and started a spar, thankful he had stretched before the bout.

Before he or Derry landed a blow, Lance spotted a runner in Galanth colors reaching one of the on-duty protectors. They called Tohmas over in the next moment. After a discussion, the runner left again.

A covered sword slammed into Lance's shoulder. He staggered back, slipped, and landed in the mud. When the world re-stabilized, he was sitting in the wet, Protector Derry kindly reaching down to assist him to his feet.

"Sorry for the hit. I thought you had a block coming around. Would've pulled it if I'd known!" Derry said.

"Got distracted," Lance admitted, trying in vain to brush off the dirt and ending by smearing it down his leggings. He felt mud squelch against his ankle, the cold goo slipping down his boot. "Not an excuse," he amended. "I'm out."

Derry shrugged and went to seek another contender. He waved his hands as he walked away, having gone through a cloud of flies. On the other side, the protector found Prince Tohmas. In an instant, he had a new challenger.

Lance sat on a nearby waggon's bed and put his feet up, hoping to dry them out before the march. He picked up a chew of lavender and lemon from another defeated protector in the hopes of keeping the bugs at bay. Six more defeated protectors had joined him by the time new riders approached the grounds.

The tunics of the approaching riders were brown and white.

"Trulin? What, by the hells, are they doing here?" a protector shouted.

Although none of them would be pleased by uninvited dignitaries of high enough rank to be wearing a princedom's colors, Lance doubted the protectors shared his dread. Constant border skirmishes dominated Gaidol's northern border with Trulin. He had done his share of fighting on the border and had killed plenty of Trullers while they tried to kill him.

The clatter of weapons came to an abrupt halt, the joviality gone from the morning routine in a flicker. The last to finish was Prince Tohmas himself, who was still sparring.

Deciding he needed to avoid drawing attention, Lance whistled for Bolt, his stolen Trulin warhorse, and headed out. Sori would have the tent packed already, but he probably had time to swap into dry boots. It was best his Gaidolon blue and white were not seen if Trulin was about.

Chapter 2

Tohmas had won two spars by the time the new colors appeared among the protectors. Per his orders, a block of his men led the strangers; he could not trust them in his ranks without an escort, even if they proclaimed themselves neutral. When they arrived at the field, the lead rider stepped off his horses to converse with the protectors.

Greetings should have fallen to Carsh, for the prime protector was officially the commander of all the protectors, but the protectors all knew it was safer to do the talking themselves. The prime protector tended to offend people with his broken Esparan. Tohmas knew it was deliberate, and he was starting to suspect others had figured that out.

The colors were that of Trulin, the same colors as the stone he had left between the two piles, uncertain, the night before.

He decided he would first finish his match. Trulin would do well to see the strength of the Galanth forces without it being a threat to them.

The only annoying thing was how long it would take at this rate. His opponent's strike went wide enough to be aimed at the next person over.

"Just because you have an audience, Protector Derry, does not mean you have to act like an idiot," he scolded.

The next blow narrowly missed Tohmas' right ear, and the following hit grazed his shoulder through the fabric.

Tohmas grinned. "Much better!" It had taken him too long to get the protectors willing to fight with him in earnest. He was done with pretenses.

Naturally, he had to repay the hit, and so he used his shield arm—his strongest—to knock Derry back so that he could slip the training blade across the protector's leg. He bruised the thigh firmly.

In the flicker it took for him to regain the ground he had lost during the battering, Protector Derry laughed. "Maybe we should talk to Cutter Darak about this delight you have for pain."

They knocked shields, then swords, as Tohmas replied, "Nonsense. I hate pain. I just like knowing you're skilled enough to hit me."

Tohmas moved his bulk sharply left, dropped his shield, caught his protector's extended arm, and wheeled the man off his feet. Tall as he was, Derry lost his balance. By the time he could recover, Tohmas had a sword at his throat.

The man glared up at his patron. "That is the third time I have fallen to the whirl! Why do I never see that coming?"

"Because only an idiot drops his shield during a fight!" another protector said. Protector Linco swung his sword in tease at Tohmas' now-unprotected left side. The prince brought his sword around, met the blow, turned it, and twisted into a new ready stance facing the thickly-bearded protector.

"So long as the idiot can manage without one," Tohmas countered, "what's the problem?"

To test him, Linco followed through with a series of swings, but Tohmas' feet and sword kept him out of harm's way for all seven attacks. After the seventh, he even managed to get in an attack of his own under the protector's shield.

As they paused to acknowledge the winning blow, a light whistle sounded.

Tohmas immediately checked with Carsh, the source of the warning. The Rydan's stare was on the gathering of strangers who were, Tohmas cringed to realize, all staring at him. The protector with them raised his chin pointedly, telling the prince they needed him.

He had to change his mindset deliberately. He was accustomed to battle. This was different.

"I guess I am out of this running," he told Linco.

The protector saluted with a sword in hand and stepped back to let Tohmas go. Carsh slunk into Tohmas' shadow as soon as he moved, ready to defend him with two knives in hand. It was unlikely to be necessary, but the presence of the Rydan was a great comfort.

As Tohmas left the protectors to continue their contest, he assessed the visitor. He had been in the Esparan lands for most of a year, yet the Rydan instincts were still there. Who was stronger? Who would lead?

The lead rider was a fighter. He was tense, implying with his posture that he was not expecting trouble but would not be caught off guard. He seemed older at first because of his bald head and face, but a second moment revealed that the smooth scalp was shaved. Tohmas had never come across a man having the time, skill, and inclination to shave his head. Tohmas had a general apprehension toward letting anyone with a knife close to his head.

Beyond the man's hairlessness, the Truller was unremarkable. His shoulders were broad like those of a young Northlander, but he was lean like a Rydan. His height, even if it was only reaching Tohmas' nose, was tall for an Esparan.

"Prince Tohmas of Galanth," the Truller greeted when Tohmas was within easy hearing distance. "They said you inherited the height of your grandfather Zayban, yet you are shorter than I expected. The stories are calling you a giant of a man."

The stranger then nodded to Tohmas, a shortened version of a formal bow that would be more appropriate for a Prince of Espar. The man's gaze went to Carsh but returned swiftly to Tohmas with effort, politely ignoring the Rydan at Tohmas' back.

"I fear Prince Zayban has been dead for too many years for me to know whether the tales of his size were exaggerated. I know not the stories you have heard," Tohmas said, his Esparan deliberately formal. "I know many have been elaborated upon." He paused, waiting.

Into the awkward pause, the man in brown said, "I am Anga Trulin."

Tohmas was tempted to feign ignorance. The man was arrogant to give his name and assume it would be sufficient and equally arrogant to be informal with a prince, even if he was of Tohmas' generation. However, Tohmas did not yet know where the Princedom of Trulin would fall. He had to recognize the name if he wanted their interactions to be favorable.

"Son of Prince Kelland of Trulin," Tohmas recited, earning an approving nod. Anga's name had been one of many Tohmas had memorized in readiness for Prince Dragal's funeral, and he was glad he had. He suspected that failing to identify his guest now would have been an insult of the highest order. Should something happen to Prince Kelland of Trulin, Anga would become Tohmas' equal in more than age.

"Your timing is unfortunate," Tohmas said in the breath before Anga replied. "Had you waited another day, we could have met you in Narsol, and you need not have wasted your time traveling out to meet us."

"I heard you sparred every morning," the Truller replied with an eager smile. "Once in the city, I feared you would be too busy for a demonstration."

He wants to size me up before others do. It was a very Rydan thing to do; Tohmas approved.

Putting on the guise of the prince he was meant to be, Tohmas smiled. "Then you are welcome to join in. Covered swords or bare blades as you prefer. The victor progresses, and the loser sits down."

Before Tohmas could turn away, Anga said, "I would test myself against you, if you permit, good prince."

The nearest protectors tensed, but Carsh snorted derisively. The prime protector turned away, assuming the conversation had ended. He had confidence in Tohmas' abilities.

"I welcome the challenge," Tohmas answered, and the protectors stepped back as Carsh had. Despite his assessment of the man's prowess, Tohmas did not believe he would be outmatched. "I will need another blade," Tohmas added, glancing about.

Protector Derry, rising from his seat as a defeated warrior, presented his patron with his sword. He was not the nearest protector, but the men on duty seemed to think they would need theirs.

"I heard you had a sword of your own! Something special?" the Truller said with a hollow laugh.

Tohmas did not hesitate to pull SoulBurner from where he wore it. If the Truller wanted to see his strength, he would show it to him.

SoulBurner was a carbiron blade—a rare Lourite metal—so polished it glittered silver. Emeralds the size of plums decorated the cross guard, and a final fist-sized gem was set in the pommel. When Tohmas freed the sword of its sheath, the glitter of the green was lost in the fiery red aura that exploded around them. It was a fitting reminder of the creator and giver of the blade, the Goddess of Fire.

CHAPTER 2

Anga's expression became neutral. Tohmas recognized the man was concealing his emotions, but he could not see through the façade enough to know what the man truly felt. Envy? Fear? Interest?

"SoulBurner's edge," Tohmas informed his visitor, "cuts through stone and iron. No blade can stand against it, so I must use a spare when I do not want to cleave my opponent from nose to navel. Surely you do not wish it in my hand for a friendly match?"

Anga's face finally released, a false smile stretching across his wide cheeks. Although he could not say what the man was thinking, Tohmas was confident the friendliness was a lie.

"Of course not. As you like, good prince."

Tohmas slid the sword away and accepted the well-used sword from Derry. Having SoulBurner hanging on his belt would be a hindrance, but Tohmas would not be without his true weapon.

Someone else handed him a shield, which he looped over his arm. Although Lord Anga had his secured, Tohmas did not adjust the straps. He could hold it well enough for a short bout.

"Lord Anga," he invited, "at your leisure."

Although the protectors ostensibly resumed their spars, Tohmas felt eyes on him from all sides as he and the Truller faced off. No one was paying attention to anything besides this exchange. Tohmas waited, allowing the guest to strike first.

An overhead strike, but the man kept his shield positioned in defense, limiting Tohmas' options for retaliation. He brought up his sword to deflect his opponent's, then adjusted the angle when Anga immediately slashed down under the block. Instead of counting on the shield, Tohmas dropped his hilt across the blade and shouldered forward, knocking against the opponent's shield with his impressive bulk.

Anga did not shift but instead rolled the hit to one side. The Truller brought a knee up, and Tohmas was tossed off his feet.

He rolled swiftly to his feet, ready for the next blow. It became a rapid sword-shield-sword exchange, Tohmas matching the speed and ferocity of Lord Anga. On the third block, the Truller stepped back, pausing to reassess.

Anga had been trying to capitalize on Tohmas' imbalance, but the moment had passed. They were back on even footing.

Except this being my third bout, Tohmas realized. Fresh, Anga had an advantage. And he was showing his skill matched Tohmas'.

This time, Tohmas initiated the exchange, feinting a direct stab. The Truller did not knock it aside with his raised blade as Tohmas had expected. Instead, Anga used his shield, freeing his sword to slice down at Tohmas' head from an unusual high-guard position. The Prince of Galanth had to abandon his cut with the blade in favor of defense. After three strikes and blocks, they paused again for a breath, their swords held at the ready.

Anga moved into a high guard position while Tohmas kept his more familiarly low.

A voice reached them from the sidelines. "Just because you have an audience does not mean you have to act like an idiot!" The protectors watching from the sideline laughed.

Smiling and shaking his head, Tohmas rotated his left hand, freeing his shield. He had a few tricks left, and the protectors knew it. He had fooled them for most of a season, after all.

Lord Anga's expression faltered, his brow creased to lower his thin eyebrows together. "You take such insults from your own protectors?"

Tohmas, forgoing a reply, lurched forward as if using the shield to bash, but he released it as soon as it contacted his opponent. It hid Tohmas' left hand as it snatched a dagger from his belt, although his right hand still sliced at the Truller's shoulder as Tohmas moved around him. Anga blocked and faced him.

In the pause, Tohmas swapped hands. He fell into a more comfortable style with his sword in his more powerful left and his dagger in his right.

The exchange picked up speed, Tohmas no longer slowed by the cumbersome shield. The change flustered Lord Anga, who defaulted to more attacks than blocks and became increasingly aggressive. The swords were mirrored, a fact that Anga accommodated poorly. While he attempted to use the shield as a weapon, Tohmas' constant attacks, split between left and right, kept any blows from landing.

It was the best workout Tohmas had had in quartercycles!

"Enough!" a voice cried with enough authority that Tohmas pulled his attacks up short in surprise. He had not heard anyone give *him* an order in a very long time.

Lord Anga appeared to forget what he was doing and turned on the spot to regard the spectators. He dropped into a deep bow.

A new rider had arrived, surrounded by their obvious bodyguard and more Galanth soldiers. The speaker was garbed in perfect brown and white, but his attire went well beyond the utility of a soldier's attire. Tohmas assigned each visitor ranks based on the horse hair plumes of their helmets; all but one were brown-capped Truller riders, basic warriors. The exception, the speaker, wore a white plume that matched both the chain hung from the helmet across the nape of the neck and the white chainmail adorning his enormous warhorse. The horse, a brilliantly white warhorse, had its mane braided into battle knots.

The white plume meant "prince" among the Trullers.

Prince Kelland, Anga's father. Demons, Tohmas thought.

Reminding himself that he was a Prince of Espar, Tohmas did not bow. Instead, he and Prince Kelland stared at each other for a dozen heartbeats. He had no idea where to start. Was the Prince of Trulin upset with him, or Anga, or both?

Ultimately, Tohmas raised an eyebrow at Prince Kelland, prompting him.

"I trust Anga has not offended you, Prince Tohmas," the new arrival groused in a deep baritone.

Protectors moved in, retrieving the shield and the borrowed sword. Clearly, the bout was ended.

"I am hard to offend," Tohmas replied mildly, struggling to get an assessment of the prince facing him. He thought Kelland stoic, although he suspected the prince had let the pause linger to chastise his son. Anga still had not been given leave to stand from the bow.

Stern? Tohmas thought. The prince seemed passive, but something warned Tohmas not to take him lightly. It was not an overt physical threat, yet there was subtle danger here.

Tohmas was torn: help Anga and earn support from the next in line or focus on the current, older generation? He had not expected an opportunity to deal with Prince Kelland so soon.

"Have you come to join us?" Tohmas asked, leaving Anga where he was. "We will march to Narsol shortly. I am to attend Inac's service at noon."

"I came to retrieve my wayward son. Get up, Anga," the prince said as he dismounted.

The prince could have sent a messenger. Did he fear Anga would not heed the command? And why rush after his son at all? Was Anga a liability to him?

As Anga straightened, Tohmas realized that he had also misinterpreted Anga's zeal. Tohmas had enjoyed the bout, but Lord Anga's face was flushed and not from the exercise. The arrogance was gone, replaced with rage.

At being caught? Or because victory was not easily achieved?

Damned Esparan politics. Nothing is plain with these two!

The prince's son dragged his feet to his father's side, making Tohmas sure of one thing; had it not been for Prince Kelland's physical presence, the recall would not have been obeyed.

Prince Kelland looked hale enough to be commanding Trulin for many years to come. His opinion mattered the most for now.

Thinking to cheat slightly, Tohmas whistled for Schlavarai, then nodded to the prince and said, "Good Prince, your company would be most welcome. Will you ride with me?"

"We can make our own—"

"Demons from the depths!" Anga cried as Tohmas' dappled mare trotted up.

The Princedom of Trulin was known for its horses. Even the ranks in Trulin reflected their obsession: in place of the companions, wardens, and guardians used in any of the princedoms descended from Zayban, Trullers had riders, lancers, and chargers. People from all corners of Espar flocked to buy Trulin-bred warhorses, both for the prestige of the animal and for its unquestionable excellence in battle. Hailing from the far south, Tohmas had never seen a Trulin horse before Lance had introduced him to his stolen gelding Bolt.

Schlavarai was a Rydan horse, dappled like a riverbed stone and with four black hooves despite white fetlocks. Her face was dark like her dam's, but streaks of white tickled her cheeks on either side. Tohmas had known her since her birth, although that was over a decade ago. She was a friend in all ways and one of the few living beings he fully trusted.

To an outsider, her most impressive feature was her size. She was a little over eighteen hands and had the build of a runner. Regardless of their Trulin horses, no one could fail to find Schlavarai striking.

Unfortunately, she had rolled in the grasses while he sparred and was flecked with mud and grass.

Carsh finished the scene by whistling for Bashuran. The black stallion, of Schlavarai's build but a finger taller, marched to Carsh with a snort of disapproval at having been left out. He, too, was mud-crusted from a good roll.

"Schlavarai, *sta*," Tohmas told his horse. The mare squared her posture and lifted her head, a glob of mud reaching over her arching neck and matting her long mane. Tohmas picked a brush from the groom who had rushed after the horses. *Wise man,* Tohmas acknowledged. Since Tohmas had not introduced the groom to Schlavarai and had no intention of doing so, the groom had never touched the mare, yet he had his tools with him, just in case. Now he could pass them to Tohmas.

"That," the Prince of Trulin said through a choked throat, "is one hell of a horse."

"*Hee doh,*" Tohmas answered, and the warhorse lowered her head to allow Tohmas to brush out her head and ears. Tall as Tohmas, Schlavarai was impossible to groom if she did not cooperate.

"She is Schlavarai," Tohmas said, but he was careful not to give the horse the name of the human. Only allies were properly introduced to a Rydan horse. He gratefully applied a salve between her ears, trying to discourage the flies. *Probably why she rolled,* he mused. Mud was a decent fly repellent.

"These are Rydan horses," Anga stuttered, amazement replacing his irritation. There were a few hundred steeds with Tohmas' forces, all living with their riders in herds on the Rydan side of camp. Bashuran and Schlavarai had been taken from their herds, a fact neither horse resented so long as they were with their riders.

"My older horse, Honest Justice, was injured at Arcott and has been retired. I called upon Schlavarai as his replacement," Tohmas explained as he checked each of Schlavarai's hooves and swept dried mud from her legs.

The prince remained speechless for another breath before venturing, "I did not think they sold their horses."

Carsh growled, and Bashuran perked up his ears. Even if the horse did not understand the words, he understood his rider. It took Carsh's slap to scold the stallion into standing still. A particularly thick mud patch covered the horse's back, and Carsh was still fighting to release it from the glossy coat.

"No Rydan horse is ever sold," Tohmas explained. "I won Schlavarai over the years."

"What contest is it that parts men from their horses?"

I phrased it wrong, Tohmas realized. Even after the year of living in Espar, his Esparan was imperfect. He could practically hear Carsh laughing and muttering *yadder, yadder,* under his breath.

"I won her *over,* Prince Kelland. I worked with her for mooncycles, went away, returned, and so on. It took me three years, which was still faster than most!" He had cleared the mud from her back. Somehow, her tail remained clean. *Probably because she's flicking it constantly after the pests.*

There was a long silence as the Prince of Trulin stared ahead, pensive. He still wore a confused expression when he inquired, "Well if she is yours now, have you ever considered breeding her?"

It took Tohmas another breath to understand what the prince had meant.

"She finds a stallion when she chooses," Tohmas replied with a pat on her flank. She was not currently in foal; she was, in fact, in heat. She had rejected her herd's stallion, which made Tohmas suspect that she would join a different herd when he released her from the Esparan corrals. Then again, if Carvanshal was being rejected, it seemed likely the strongest of the bachelor herd would move in. The Rydan horses managed their own relationships.

The reply further confounded the Prince of Trulin. He rambled about the purity of blood and selection of qualities as Tohmas finished cleaning her.

"She recognizes a good stallion better than I do," Tohmas interrupted, "and would only permit breeding to an acceptable sire regardless of my opinion. Once the foal is born, it is hers to raise, not mine, and will leave her only once she and the foal are happy with the rider. If you want to turn your stallions loose with her, I will not object but expect her opinions to be stronger." It was the best concession he could offer.

CHAPTER 2

The groom handed Tohmas a blanket.

The Prince of Trulin was still staring, taking in every detail of the horse.

She had no bit—it was not a concept Rydans had ever discovered—and no saddle for the same reason. Convincing any Rydan horse to wear Esparan equipment was a laughable idea. Training was all they needed.

"Perhaps you would consider riding with us, after all. It seems we have something in common," Tohmas offered, ready to mount.

Although he did not trust the look in Prince Kelland's eye, Tohmas accepted the nod. With a wave, a rider brought up Kelland's stallion and Anga's gelding in their brown and silver tack, complete with a breastplate that bore the crest of the princedom: a horse.

The stallion snickered at Schlavarai in greeting and invitation. Schlavarai gave an unequivocal snort of refusal and took to ignoring the stallion.

"Shall we?" Tohmas invited.

Prince Kelland's riders came up and offered the prince the leg up he would need to get onto his posturing stallion. Once in the saddle, the prince gathered the reins and turned the stallion sharply. Bashuran was taking offense, but a word from Carsh redirected the irate stallion.

"I am impressed," Kelland said once they were underway, the crowd around them parting to give them a path. "I have never known an Esparan to ride a Rydan steed."

On Tohmas' left, the protectors formed up. On Kelland's right, his riders did the same. Carsh rode Bashuran slightly to Tohmas' right but stayed far enough back to avoid any kicks, whether from Schlavarai or Kelland's stallion. In a similar position, Anga's smaller gelding had to trot every sixth pace to keep up on his father's right side.

"I understand Trulin has been trying to negotiate with the Rydans regarding horseflesh for years," Tohmas tentatively agreed, avoiding the topic of his ties to the Outlands and the Rydans there. These men considered him Esparan. That was still for the best. He needed to know more about where Trulin stood in the following affairs.

"Of course," Kelland replied, his eyes forward. The train of Tohmas' army trickled down the road ahead, the ranks already moving. The protectors, with their horses, would quickly overtake them, so they kept to a serene walk. Tohmas did not need to check the positions of the various ranks. They knew their duty well by now.

The pause lingered until the Truller added, "Prince Deiton claims he speaks with the Second Clan amicably, but even he has been unable to free a horse from their corrals. Prince Polthian claims no Rydan will ever part with a horse." The Prince of Trulin examined Tohmas again. "Yet here you are, with just such a steed. So it can be done."

Tohmas faced the road once more. "Trade with the Rydans is certainly possible. You have to forget the idea of currency; otherwise, it is mutually beneficial. Trade horses, though? I doubt it." He paused, not wanting to make a promise that would never be fulfilled. He could convince Rydans to trade almost everything, but the horses were a permanent exception.

And there was no Second Clan to deal with anyway. Since the conquest of the Outlands by Chief Tamv and his sons, only the First Clan remained. It was their fault if they didn't know as much.

They rode on for a half dozen steps before the Prince of Trulin asked, "Tell me, Prince Tohmas, what do you make of Prince Deiton?"

Deiton? Tohmas had not given his uncle-by-marriage much thought in cycles. But the questions made imminent sense from Kelland. When Tohmas had last seen Prince Deiton, he had been, as the Prince of Forsinth, entertaining dignified guests from Trulin, specifically Lady Arnika Trulin, Prince Kelland's only daughter. Deiton had made no effort to hide his interest in the Lady of Trulin. Dining with the pair had clearly shown what the lady thought of the potential arrangements, but if Prince Kelland was asking about the match now, Lady Arnika had failed to communicate her despair to her father.

The Princedom of Forsinth shared a border, albeit a short one that spanned a river, with the Outlands and her Rydans.

"Why ask me?" Tohmas answered with a shrug. "I hardly know the man."

"He is your uncle. I understand his loyalty to the sons of Zayban remains despite the passing of his wife."

At a loss, Tohmas allowed the silence to persist. He had nothing good to say about the bookkeeper-like Prince of Forsinth, who could not defend the lands he had inherited through marriage. He thought the man useless.

"Did you not meet with him when my Arnika was present?" Kelland pressed. "Surprisingly, your reputation paints you as a remarkably honest person. So, what do you think of Prince Deiton?"

It was a type of test, Tohmas guessed. He preferred to have Kelland Trulin on his side when his plans for Espar came to light. So what was the reply that would endear him to the Prince of Trulin?

"Prince Deiton has done very well with the land Zayban gave him," Tohmas diplomatically said. "With their pottery, he could do even better through new trade north, particularly with the Northlands now open." He waited but got no reply. Pushing on, Tohmas added, "Having the princedoms able to cooperate has benefited him heavily. And with our improved relationship with the Rydans, he stands to gain much, as we all do."

"Northlanders. Rotten barbarians," Anga cursed behind him.

Another test.

"Smarter than many Esparan I know," Tohmas replied. "The Northlanders and Rydan see the benefit of trade and common terms." His next words were for Kelland alone. "Would you like to meet Darknim DoomDragon and discuss it with him? You share a border. I would offer a conversation with the Rydans, but their Leader is not a talkative type."

Prince Kelland's smile was smug. "No, he is not. Burlotak has never been friendly. But DoomDragon, yes, I would be delighted to meet him. We must get to know our new neighbors." He nodded as if having come to a conclusion he had no intention of sharing. "And I would meet with you again, Prince Tohmas, once you are settled in Narsol. For now, I must take my leave. I am needed in Narsol promptly."

Tohmas did not miss that Kelland had just named the Rydan Leader who traveled with him. He heeded it as a warning; spies kept Kelland informed about Tohmas' forces. But he had not named Chief Tamv, so there were things Kelland did not yet know.

Anga kicked on his gelding to follow when Prince Kelland brought his horse to a trot, then to a canter. It was the kind of gait warhorses could maintain for a candle of time and finish with a devastating charge.

Carsh pulled Bashuran into the emptied place as the protectors reformed their ranks to create a complete circle around them, watching the strangers and their escort depart.

"Not sure," Tohmas said, anticipating Carsh's question. "We'll have to see where the next conversation goes. Maybe? Regardless, we will have to watch him." If Kelland knew of Tohmas' true plans, he might oppose him with formidable strength. But if Tohmas could keep him believing the padded truth—that peace was possible—there was hope Trulin would place its banner with Tohmas'.

He thought back to the spar. "Just be grateful it is Kelland we will deal with, not his son."

Relief flooded over Kitable to see Prince Tohmas' enormous mare finally ride over the cobblestones of Narsol, heading for the temple. Late as the prince was, there was no chance to catch up before the service. Although even Tohmas publicly insisted all four gods should be acknowledged equally, Kitable knew Tohmas had a distinctive preference for Inac. It would not do for the prince to miss the noon service.

Tohmas' arrival allowed Kitable to excuse himself from the conversation with two ladies of Trulin where their questions had pinned him. The two young ladies had recognized his robes that marked him as a wizard and had already told him at least five tall tales about casters. He only felt slightly guilty about leaving in the middle of Lady Altana's sentence.

However, by the time Tohmas dismounted, Kitable was at his side.

"All eight copies are ready and waiting, copied onto the finest vellum available, word for word," Kitable confirmed without preamble.

"What about BookKeeper Olmer?" Tohmas asked as he pulled the blanket from the horse and turned Schlavarai loose. Bashuran followed. They took up a place nearby, uncontested, in the crowd.

"He's working with Lord Hurtz, apparently for old-time sake, but he's sick and getting worse."

Tohmas cocked one eyebrow as they followed the line of people toward the temple entrance. Despite the block of protectors that made a path, they were surrounded by a crowd, but Kitable did not fear being overheard. The roar of the crowd's conversations was as effective as a Wind Barrier. Kitable did not need to activate a spell to provide privacy.

"Sickness like...?"

"Could be Prince Dragal's cough, yes," Kitable said. "BookKeeper Olmer certainly spent enough time with his old patron." There had been talk at one point of enlisting BookKeeper Olmer to Tohmas' service, but if the man had caught Dragal's blood-coughing illness, that possibility died. The best thing they could do was send the man home to Clandac and wish him well.

It was for the best; Kitable was certain. He had worked with other wizards before, but the encounters tended to leave him disappointed or dueling to the death. Other wizards were a problem, and Kitable would not be displeased to see the Clandacanese man go elsewhere.

There were only a few more steps before the temple door. Kitable had to finish quickly.

"The sons of Dragal offer a meeting after the service. I said you would be available." A nod was all he got, but since he still had one step before his prince vanished into the temple with only his prime protector, he added, "And send a runner next time! My feet hurt!"

The prince chuckled as he disappeared into the dim light of the temple to the four Esparan gods. Kitable could have attended the service. He was still the Master Wizard of Galanth, although the Rydans called him "wisavi" instead of "master wizard." But Kitable had little interest in religious services.

The ladies, however, were expected within. Everyone of note was within the temple now, leaving Kitable in the masses outside.

He found a seat with his back to the temple, happy to stay in a corner where people would not spot his robes and trinkets. He was not yet old enough to grow a long white beard, but he was otherwise a prominent wizard and thus a rarity.

With Olmer out, Kitable was once more the only wizard in Tohmas' army sworn to anyone, but he was not the only person capable of casting spells. The city of Narsol would see its share soon enough.

Dust and Shimmer Weaver—a father-daughter pair of apothecaries, alchemists, performers, and casters—were still in the assorted rabble known as Fixer City that followed and serviced the people of Tohmas' army. The daughter of the pair had sought Kitable out a few times since they had left Arcott, where she had saved him, but Kitable pointedly ignored her as much as possible. She was a distraction he did not need.

He had already thanked her, and it was not as if he had never assisted her. They were even as far as he was concerned.

The only other casters were the Northlander Circle, which was now fragmented. Without the complete gathering of seven, the Circle was just a group of elders, each with a distinctive gift for a given domain or element of magic. Their experience in using those gifts outside of the Circle was minimal; Kitable thought he would see his waggon driver Colt casting first.

Except for Elder Tril, Kitable admitted. After enough late-night conversations, Elder Tril had somehow wormed his way into being a friend to Kitable. The Northlander's domain was divination, but the powers wielded by the elder were now a curse. Northlander magic was intuitive, not structured like Kitable's magic, and thus controlled by more instinct than training. Tril had reached a state where he was bombarded by divinations almost perpetually, and since usage increased usage, he was in a spiral downward into insanity. Kitable had helped slow it by sharing training tips, but he could not stop the progression of the power without cutting Tril entirely off from his powers.

There had to be a way. Kitable sat by the wall, working through the code in his mind. He would find it.

Being alone was a relief; he did not have to worry about other magic users for now. He could focus on his projects.

But Tohmas' plans meant it would not last. That thought loomed over all his contemplations.

<h1 style="text-align:center">Chapter 3</h1>

Prince Sol's manor in Narsol was not large enough to house all the visitors to the capital. Many princes and their entourages were given houses in the city, ostensibly to provide more independence but also to permit a buffer between dignitaries who would otherwise be in conflict. It forced Tohmas to formally request conferences with people instead of seeking them out or allowing conversations to flow more organically. There was no choice; he had to play the formal prince now.

In preparation for the many guests who would attend, the usual furniture in the manor's main hall had been pushed against its soot-coated walls, freeing space for mingling. The large central table, a mainstay in every hall in Espar, was removed to an unknown location, but the chandeliers still hung low over its expected location. It must have taken days to sweep out the thrush and days more to wash out the last of winter's mud from the stone floor. The interlocking bricks were spotless underfoot as Tohmas made his way into the ample space.

Cooking was happening in an outside oven today, leaving the vast fireplace built up but unlit at the far end of the hall. As he had requested, chairs formed a circle at the center of the room, too far from the walls to tempt eavesdroppers. It was almost as good as being outside but more acceptable to those he had invited; his cousins.

His uncles, Prince Sol and Prince Barnon, took their seats as if they were at the war table again. They had already accepted Tohmas' offer without knowing Chief Tamv's plans for Espar. But Tohmas knew he could control them. Sol had quiet confidence now, built over the long siege to his princedoms and brief imprisonment. Barnon remained inexperienced, despite being two decades Tohmas' senior. Even if the two brothers disagreed with Tohmas, they were no threat. For now, they believed him their kin, and he could trust them to be predictable. Not feeling ready to settle until the rest of his guests arrived, Tohmas stood by, his hands on the irregular wood of an empty armchair.

The two couples, Tohmas' cousins, arrived together, all four wearing the blue and gold of the Princedom of Clandac, their homeland and, now, inheritance.

One pair was in their early thirties, while the other was sorely uneven; the man could have been one of Tohmas' uncles, but the woman was young enough to be Tohmas' little sister.

"Uncle Sol! Uncle Barnon!" The young woman rushed ahead of the others and grabbed Sol in a hug as he sat on his thick oak chair. She quickly repeated the gesture and embraced Barnon, nearly knocking the man's chair over with her enthusiasm. Chittering laughter, she stepped back and blinked up at Tohmas, unconcerned but reserved.

Lady Sarilai, Tohmas identified. He had no memory of their meeting before, but she was Prince Dragal's youngest daughter.

Her husband arrived behind Sarilai, his hand possessively on her shoulder. In stark contrast, Lord Hurtz was taller than the other three and carried a head of grey like a trophy kill. Judging by the man's square stance and weathered hands, Tohmas was almost surprised not to see a blade or two on the man's belt. Lord Hurtz had been a protector for Prince Dragal for more than fifteen years before he married Sarilai Galanth, Tohmas recalled.

"Hello, cousin," the little woman said. She curtsied prettily. "I am Sarilai. This is my husband, Courion Hurtz."

The other two arrived, the taller woman stately. The man had a bookish appearance, his reading glasses low on his nose and his eyes beady. "And this is my sister Elsiene and *her* husband, Talbit Darmac," Lady Sarilai introduced with a sweeping hand. Her delicate fingers were pale.

Tohmas focused on the husband. Lord Darmac had initially been an ambassador to Clandac from the metal-making Princedom of Lour. That post had been due to family connections: Talbit Darmac was the nephew of the current Prince of Lour. If Tohmas could bring Talbit and his wife to his cause, Tohmas would also have sway in Lour.

The once-ambassador—young for his post or was that a result of blood ties?—bowed his head.

Lady Sarilai shifted her weight as Tohmas nodded his head respectfully. "I am pleased to meet—" He was interrupted when the young woman skipped onto the armchair in front of Tohmas and threw her arms around him in a surprisingly crushing embrace. She tittered as she released him.

"Sarilai, come sit," Lady Elsiene called, taking a proper seat on the positioned chairs. She sat straight, her hands folded formally on her lap. As Dragal's eldest, she would have had the most practice, Tohmas assumed.

Lady Sarilai skipped down from the chair and allowed herself to be led to her seat by her husband. Courion Hurtz shot Tohmas a glare over his shoulder, and Tohmas consciously looked away from the pretty young wife Lord Hurtz seemed to feel the need to protect. The youngest of Dragal's daughters smiled brightly as she settled, but she did not release her husband's hand even once seated. She outshone her sister, Tohmas noted. Her long golden hair flowed freely, giving her a spritely appearance, while Elsiene's was braided tightly like a stern matron.

Tohmas went to the center of the circle of chairs and placed a grey egg-shaped stone on the stone floor.

"Privacy, Tohmas?" Sol asked, clearly having recognized the magic stone.

"If we keep our voices down, we can be assured no one will overhear. The stone," he explained to the newcomers, "will turn red if magic intrudes on this region. It is Master Kitable's contribution."

His assessments done, Tohmas took his seat. He left the largest armchair still open.

Elsiene lifted her chin, looking down her nose at each attendant in turn. "Well then, since we have the place to ourselves, shall we get awkward questions out of the way?" She turned her head sharply and stared at Tohmas. "Is it true that you carry a sword from Inac's hand?"

SoulBurner was on Tohmas' belt.

"She stood in front of my entire camp in a burning waggon to give it to me," Tohmas confirmed. "It was indeed quite a sight."

"It was quite a spectacle," Barnon added.

Elsiene nodded at Barnon in acknowledgment, then turned her pale blue stare back to Tohmas. The severity of the gaze made Tohmas worry she was seeking falsehoods. "And is it true your goddess moved a dragon from your path so that your march north would not be hindered?" Elsiene raised one perfectly-plucked eyebrow at him.

"Carsh and I asked the dragon to move," Tohmas corrected, "and the Goddess allowed it to understand and obey." Tohmas did not know why the dragon had moved without trying to eat them, but he happily blamed and thanked Inac for the event.

"And is it true you can now control fire and keep it from harming you by your Goddess' will?"

Tohmas laughed. "Now you are getting into the fantastical. I burn just as easily as anyone."

"So your scars prove," Prince Dragal's oldest daughter said poignantly.

Inwardly, Tohmas smiled to hear the rumor spreading. Out loud, he put on airs of humility and grumbled, "News travels fast."

"Well, you did ride out of Arcott barefooted," Talbit Darmac pointed out in support of his wife. He scowled low enough to dip his glasses low. "Why were you not wearing shoes if you did not mean to have people notice your brand?" It could have been an accusation, but the indifferent tone made it seem more like a casual observation. The man sat in a similar straight-backed position as his wife, forcibly formal.

At the age of eleven, while sitting on the roof of his father's *shella*, Tohmas stepped on a smoldering log and burned the sole of his foot. The scar resembled a pair of vertical waves and had meant nothing to the Rydans. Upon his arrival to Espar, Tohmas realized they matched the symbol of the Goddess Inac exactly. For the next year, he kept the scars hidden, but with the victory over Prince Marfaie and their triumphant departure, he had completely forgotten about the brand on his foot.

The brand on his foot lent credence to his status as a Champion of Inac. He assumed Inac had intended it as such.

"My shoes," Tohmas said, smiling as sincerely as he could, "had become a hindrance." The confrontation with Marfaie and all his magic manifestations did not merit going into.

"Regardless," Elsiene said, using her husband's stern tone of voice, "if there is to be a Champion of Inac in Espar, I suppose we must be grateful it has come to our family. You will always be welcome in the Princedom of Clandac, cousin."

It seemed odd to hear the woman offer him the welcome when her husband, easily the more suited, sat beside her, but the word that most surprised Tohmas was "cousin." Being the children of Tohmas' uncle did indeed mean they were related, even if it did not feel like it.

Rather than question her authority, Tohmas said, "Is it my turn for a question?"

Elsiene titled her head in concession. Her beaded headband glittered with the movement.

"What becomes of Clandac now? Prince Dragal once mentioned that he had spoken to you all about succession, but he never said what the agreement had been." Theirs was an unfortunate position. By Esparan tradition, the eldest son ruled upon the father's death, but Dragal had only ever had daughters. Which son-in-law should inherit? The eldest was Courion Hurtz, but he was married to the youngest daughter, and if the title could not go to the eldest son, should it not go to the eldest daughter, meaning Elsiene and her husband?

The four exchanged looks. Elsiene seemed to take a vote from each of them before declaring, "We have maps drawn of the division. Clandac is to become two territories."

"I take it you knew Father was ill," Sarilai added, sorrow filling her voice. Her bright blue eyes were doe-like as they peered up at Tohmas.

At no point had Tohmas considered the poor health of Prince Dragal any more than a perceived secret, but he had let Prince Dragal keep his illusions, and he would let his children keep theirs.

"He spoke to the princes about it," Tohmas said. Sol and Barnon nodded in agreement, glazing over the fact that Tohmas had not been included in those conversations in truth. But he had known. How he knew didn't matter.

Elsiene's words came out as an accusation: "Is that why you requested a meeting? To ascertain the status of the family?"

This was delicate. Too aggressive, and he would be refused. Helpful, but not eager. Kind but not presumptuous.

Damn Esparan politics.

Tohmas was slow with his words. "I have pondered the fate of Clandac. If my counsel might be welcome, I have an idea."

Again, they shared a look. Elsiene sat straighter, her chin lifted again, making it seem she had picked the highest chair. "We are willing to hear it."

"Well, it is not just me who needs your time," Tohmas said, rising. "It is him."

At the side door, Tohmas knocked to signal Darknim DoomDragon, then opened the servant entrance.

The wide Northlander had to turn to slip through the doorway, despite his signature axe missing over his shoulders.

Crossing the room with long strides as smooth as a hunter, Darknim took the armchair Tohmas had left empty. Broad as he was with the armor, it was the only chair that would have fit him comfortably.

Darknim took his seat with poise Tohmas admired, a piece of folded papyrus in hand. His presence had been distilled over decades; every action, from the subtle lean into the chair to the spacing of his feet on the floor, appeared deliberate. He proudly wore furs announcing his heritage as Northlander, a new bear pelt draping his shoulders as a replacement for the one lost fighting, by all accounts, an actual demon. The man's face on one side was slightly less wrinkled, a fact only noticeable when he met someone face on.

Their reactions were mixed. Sarilai jumped in her seat, glancing at the other three for an indication of how to respond to the sight of the Northlander. Elsiene, who Tohmas was confident knew about the Northlanders' position in his army, looked on tepidly, her head tilted to match her husband as if she too had to look through glasses to see the intruder well. Courion tensed, a hand reaching across as if for a blade, even though no sword lay on his hip now.

"Thank you for hearing me out," Darknim said in his gravel voice.

"We have a proposition for you," Tohmas added. He pulled out the vellum sheets he had hidden beneath the chair and passed them around. Sol and Barnon did not require a copy, a fact that Tohmas was certain bolstered his case in the eyes of his cousins.

They sat and read in the dim light of the hall for long moments. Tohmas refused to fidget, knowing it would make him appear impatient. He tried to emulate Darknim's calm; this would work.

Each couple spoke amongst themselves. Sarilai appeared to need it explained to her by her husband. At length, Courion and Elsiene, the spokesperson for each couple, met stares across the circle. Perhaps optimistically, Tohmas thought he saw Courion nod.

He had the most to gain. Without the treaty, many could contest his claim to any of Prince Dragal's land.

"These lands, as their borders stood before the Northlander invasions?" Elsiene clarified.

"I mapped it out for you," Darknim offered, unfolding the paper he had in hand. An old map, probably stolen from Tanble before they left their conquest, unfurled onto the stones between the chairs. Darknim had industriously crossed out the names of the princedoms he had conquered but had left the border lines.

Seeing her interest in the map, Darknim passed it over. Talbit, Courion, and Elsiene mulled over it, asking specifics about the borders. Darknim, familiar with the territory, easily answered their questions.

"Cousin," Sarilai's soft voice whispered suddenly from over Tohmas' shoulder, "how did my father die?"

She had no stake in the talks, Tohmas saw. Sarilai had no interest in governing. Besides, they had come for a funeral, their father's funeral. It was not unreasonable for her to ask about him.

"An arrow," Tohmas said before detailing the truth with lies. "He was shot in the back through a window when we were chasing the Prince of Tanble."

Her crystal eyes filled with tears. "Did he suffer?"

I made it quick, Tohmas thought, but aloud he only said, "He had suffered for so long, I think it came as a relief to him." He resisted the urge to place a hand on her shoulder, knowing Courion would be jealous. He could feel the old protector's eyes on them, even if he was too far away to hear the words.

The truth, Tohmas thought, *fair Lady, is that I stabbed him with that arrow so he would stop spreading illness and getting in my way.*

For the briefest instance, Tohmas felt grief. He did not regret his actions at all. The flicker of grief he felt was for the girl beside him who, under her husband's watch, forced back tears of mourning.

He was surprised to feel anything at all, so he pushed the thought out of his mind. He did not know this girl, ties of family be damned.

Elsiene's alto voice interrupted the thought. "We will converse on this, but I think it has great potential, Prince Tohmas." She met and held Tohmas' stare meaningfully.

Darknim couldn't govern all the land he had conquered. And if they could assign people who liked him to do so, that suited Tohmas all the more.

There was new life to come out of Dragal's death. The world Tohmas was creating would dwarf any Dragal had planned for his daughters.

Prince Loritat Naygan had been ruling Lour for thirty years of peace. Iron and copper from Lour's mines kept the rest of the princedoms happy and deferential. No prince dared disrupt their metal trade by fighting with the provider. It was a good position to be in, one Loritat had become accustomed to.

The closest he had come to war had been skirmishes in the north when the Northlanders had failed on Lour's borders. The closest he had come to political upset had been bargaining with Prince Dragal, and that had been because someone had suggested Loritat's nephew marry Dragal's daughter. He still did not know whose idea it had been, but both sides had come to appreciate the usefulness of the marriage.

His nephew Talbit was now a problem. Loritat had respected him enough to appoint him as the ambassador to the once-hostile princedom of Clandac. The man had done marvelously, as his marriage to Elsiene Galanth testified, and Loritat had been extremely happy with him. He had thus been entirely blind-sided by Talbit's visit to his assigned house in Narsol, a sheet of vellum in hand and a bizarre proposition on offer.

In fairness to his nephew, Talbit was not changing loyalties. He had been added to Prince Dragal's family by marriage and was merely accepting an alternative inheritance from his deceased father-in-law. But it felt like Talbit was abandoning Lour. Loritat was also concerned by what his sister, Talbit's mother, was going to say about the situation.

Talbit was Lady Loria's third boy, and Loritat's sister was a protective mother. Talbit and Loritat had both fought for Talbit to even be allowed to leave Lour for Clandac. The marriage had been quite the upset. What would she do when she heard about *this*?

CHAPTER 3

There was no doubt Lour could fight if they had to. They lacked Trulin's horses, but they were expert weapon and armor smiths, and every smith knew how to use their creations. Every boy in Lour was trained. If it came to war, Lour was better prepared than most.

But Loritat had faith in Talbit. If Talbit was allying with Prince Tohmas, there had to be a reason.

The reason now stood in front of him. In a dark room, before the dawn of the 27th day of the 2nd cycle, Tohmas Galanth and his Rydan prime protector stood before the Prince of Lour.

As the prime protector wandered distractedly through the room, Prince Tohmas of Galanth claimed the seat Loritat had been offered at the small table. Plates lay before them, a breaking of fasts that Loritat hoped would keep the meeting informal.

"Have you faith in your guards? My words are for you alone," Prince Tohmas said, his voice mild despite the depth of the words. Attempting to be polite, Loritat had reduced his company of heart guards, recognizable by the gold of one of the sword shards strung across their chest, to a meager two. It had the advantage of reducing the risk of rumors as well. Loritat had no idea where the conversation with Prince Tohmas would lead, but he was confident discretion would be prudent.

"Of course," Loritat replied, trying to control his tone. With only two guards, his stomach felt sour with unease. He'd heard about Prime Protector Carsh's prowess, and Prince Tohmas was said to have bested a dragon. Loritat had never been a warrior and knew he was outmatched physically. But he had other strengths. He held Lour and the greatest supply of iron in Espar.

The sheet of vellum sat on the table, the words turned down against the rough wood. Loritat considered it a wall between them. The prince would do nothing so long as that writing lay between them.

As he took a strawberry from the stack before him, Loritat said, "You must understand our position. Traditionally, we avoid involvement."

"So you can sell metals to both sides with impunity," Prince Tohmas replied, but his smile remained, and he did not seem offended. "I understand, but you can probably see why I do not want that happening."

Accepting a cup, Tohmas tasted the wine and then laid the cup on the table. Although Loritat had provided it, wine was not something he usually drank. His first wife had hated the taste of wine, and he had gotten out of the habit because of her. This wine tasted vaguely like the wild blackberries that grew on the rocks outside his capital. The single sip slithered into his gut and made it rumble further.

The stress did not aid in his digestion, nor did the wine. He glared at the bottle and noted it was from the Princedom of Forsinth. Forsinth stood with the sons of Zayban already. Combined with DoomDragon, those loyal to Tohmas held a large part of Espar. Most notably, between the family, they controlled every one of Lour's borders.

If it came to fighting, which Loritat suspected it might, he would be alone. Gaidol had Nothor nearby. Trulin was their neighbor, another possible enemy of Tohmas. Even if Polthian pushed against Tohmas and his treaty, he had help in the north with Nothor.

Lour, in contrast, would be isolated.

Talbit was probably right. The agreement written on the sheet between them may be the better solution. Lour did not have the stomach for fighting a doomed war against a man chosen by the Goddess of War and Victory.

With that thought, Loritat examined the younger man across the table. Legends were forming now. He did not understand faith or magic, but he knew weapons.

"I have heard things about your blade. Might I see it?"

It was a noticeable change of topic, but one the Prince of Galanth seemed ready to accommodate. Rather than draw the blade openly, perhaps with respect to the sanity of the heart guards behind Loritat, Prince Tohmas released the knot that held the scabbard and presented the sheathed weapon to Loritat. He was careful not to touch the handle.

SoulBurner was rumored to produce a magic-killing aura in Tohmas' grip. Loritat had four magic items on him that provided physical and magical defenses. He presumed Prince Tohmas was similarly defended. His careful handling avoided destroying those enchantments with SoulBurner's aura.

The workmanship of the blade was unmistakable. SoulBurner was made of carbiron, a fusion of iron and coal, a uniquely Lourite construction. Further, the use of the bronzed flame as the support to the hilt was distinctive. It was eerily similar to Loritat's sword, RoyalCourt, for which the board game had been named.

CHAPTER 3

"Master Gandon's work," he identified, pulling RoyalCourts absently. Like Tohmas had, Loritat undid the knot and passed it to his guest. His blade was a much older representation of Master Gandon's abilities, for it had been forged more than forty years prior, and even the master had learned a great deal since then. The flame on the hilt was the same.

The Prince of Galanth examined the gold and silver sword in silence, taking particular interest in the words "From the heart of the earth" engraved along the blade. Prince Tohmas' sword read "A blade for the war that brings peace to Espar" in the same script.

What a strange concept, to fight a war for peace. The stories had it that the blade had been given to Tohmas during his fights with DoomDragon. Had this plot for the conquest of Espar been in the works even then?

Loritat cleared his throat and replaced SoulBurner into its sheath carefully. "You are fortunate to have some of Master Gandon's works. He passed away last winter. That may be the last blade he made."

"SoulBurner," Tohmas said as he reattached his blade to his right hip, another gesture to make Loritat pause, "was given to me by Inac's hand. Beyond that, I do not know its origin."

Loritat had heard the stories, but stories were stories. A crowd could believe a goddess had walked the earth, but one did not expect the same of princes.

Yet there was nothing deceptive in Prince Tohmas' voice, and his tale matched what Loritat had heard.

The world was being conquered, Loritat reminded himself. Maybe goddesses were wandering around too.

Was that really what was happening?

"You believe Inac stands with you," Loritat said.

Prince Tohmas again smiled, but it was more baring teeth this time. "Without a doubt."

"They call you Champion of Fire."

"They call me many things."

It was a surprisingly honest reply.

Loritat's voice lost volume as he asked the question he truly feared to say aloud. His stomach turned over like a tortured demon within. "What will become of Lour?"

The smile lessened when the Prince of Galanth sat forward.

"Even portion, even contribution. Everyone is together in this."

Loritat had read as much in the treaty Talbit had delivered. "We will not get involved against the others," he objected.

"There can be no neutrals, Prince Loritat," Prince Tohmas replied. "If you asked me here to pledge neutrality, I cannot accept."

"Lour does not take sides."

"If we do not all stand together, we lose the benefits of unity. I cannot permit it." The words were flat, and although they said all the correct, polite things, they sounded like a threat.

Silence hung between them like tattered sails. The word "permit" knocked Loritat hard. He was a Prince of Espar. He required no one's permission.

His gut churned now, and the spring's fruit lost all appeal. He felt the weight of Prince Tohmas' words and understood Talbit's recommendation all the better.

This man was taking over the known world, and the gods themselves would have to come down to stop him. Loritat could spare the soldiers. He had a few names to volunteer that would cause him no grief if the war did not go in Tohmas' favor.

I had it backward, Loritat realized. He had considered Lour alone, but the separation from the others meant Lour was far from the fighting. His isolation would be a blessing, too far away to bother with. And, when the dust settled, everyone needed metal. He could declare a side and remain unaffected.

"Once I have evidence of the agreement from the others," Loritat decided, "I will join this enterprise." Loritat glared at the younger prince, hoping he did not see how little Loritat's promise meant.

The Prince of Galanth offered a fist across the table, and Loritat stood. He was reminded of the eight shards across his chest as he moved, the weight of his office. The mark of a Prince of Lour for the last two generations. Would it mean anything if Prince Tohmas took Espar?

"Then we agree," Tohmas said.

Loritat knocked his fist against Prince Tohmas' in finality.

It would do.

Chapter 4

 hen Tohmas left the company of Prince Loritat, Prince Kelland of Trulin was waiting for him. The protectors had kept the crowds away, yet Prince Kelland stood facing the home, leaning against his warhorse. He had swapped formal armor and plumed helm for fine tunic and overcoat, exposing his bald head. Now Tohmas understood why Anga had shaved his head; the similarity between father and son was now striking.

Tohmas wondered if any of the protectors had tried to move the prince. If they had, none had succeeded despite Tohmas' request for discretion. This prince continued to arrive when Tohmas did not expect. Perhaps that much was deliberate, a means of putting Tohmas off balance.

"Busy morning?" Prince Kelland asked, standing tall from his place against his horse. The riders with him were still mounted, and Tohmas spied the prince's disgruntled son among them. Anga's forehead seemed likely to gain new wrinkles, so profoundly did his glowers crease his scalp.

Ignoring the heir to Trulin, Tohmas bowed his head respectfully to the prince. "Prince Kelland, have I kept you waiting?"

"I figured I would save you the time of seeking me out. I assume you wish to talk."

Like flexing muscles, Kelland demonstrated his prowess by revealing how much he knew. This appeared to be a ploy the Esparans used as much as the Rydans did, if less literally.

So he knew Tohmas was gathering people to his side. How much did he know?

"I would be delighted if you would join me. I am heading for the pyre, of course," Tohmas invited. All the princes were due at the funeral pyre. Sol and Barnon were already there, Sol claiming his direct supervision was required to ensure preparations were immaculate. If Tohmas did not hurry, he would be late.

The Truller fell into step beside Tohmas, and the enormous warhorse followed, although no lead rope bound him. They were led, Soltan runners ahead of them, through the busy streets. In the city, his entourage was limited to four, plus Carsh. Prince Kelland was similarly defended, although Tohmas noted both of them were armed again.

"How did your conversation with Prince Deiton go?" Tohmas asked his visitor, willing to show his reconnaissance.

Kelland made a face, his beard creasing along the corners. "I knew he would tell you about it eventually," he admitted. "Earlier than I expected."

Tohmas let the thought sit between them unanswered. There had been no time for Prince Deiton to speak to Tohmas, nor did Tohmas believe his uncle would have volunteered the information. Spies had served Tohmas in this, and it should not take much for Kelland to realize as much. Although Tohmas had no intention of letting Kelland know, Deiton's ties to Tohmas' family were fast failing.

"Deiton's weak," Kelland said flatly as they turned a corner, passing through a courtyard. "He was given everything, never earning it, never defending it. Zayban gifted him land. Zayban's allies kept it for him. He is feeble." The bustle of people went on as they passed, the protectors and riders creating a path for the princes and Kelland's horse. The townsfolk occasionally looked up, then swiftly looked away and decided on a different path. The well at the center of the courtyard was swiftly being abandoned.

"Does that make him a good or poor match for your daughter?" Tohmas asked. "You could expand your influence over his lands if he lacks the gall to oppose you. But then, the association might embarrass your princedom if others feel as you do." Tohmas ducked a low-hanging sign by the wall. The little shopkeeper stepping out of his store thought better of venturing out when a protector glared at him. The short man scuttled back and shut the door.

"He was the only suitable candidate until recently," Kelland replied evasively.

Inside, Tohmas' stomach tensed, but he kept his expression neutral, his eyes on the milling crowd. He had not needed to play the part of a prince, only a warlord, for the last year. The conversation was slipping out of his grip.

He decided on a personable approach, trying to find a balance between respectful and friendly. "Now, that's not fair," Tohmas said with a smile. "If I presume you mean me, I am challenging Prince Deiton's bid for your daughter, allowing you to assume I have no loyalty to my family. And if I am not supporting the family, can I be trusted at all? And if I deny such inferences, I risk insulting Lady Arnika and, by association, you by my lack of interest."

Kelland paused, a small smile sneaking through his thick beard, his ruse detected.

Coming to an unexpected halt as they passed the well, the Prince of Trulin sat on the lip, and the riders formed up, pushing aside the other people until the well was clear. The bucket was full, the woman who had drawn it forced to leave by one of Kelland's soldiers. The protectors, in contrast, stayed behind Tohmas, respectfully a full pace distant. Carsh, with a subtle shake of his head, told them to hold their positions. This was not a competition they needed to enter.

"I am not so easily offended," Prince Kelland replied as he drank from the ladle. He wiped his hands on his breeches and, for a moment, stared down the well as he waited for Tohmas' response to the echoing sentiment.

"You're driving my spies mad by lingering here," Tohmas said after a pause. "They were expecting you at the temple."

Sure enough, Kelland smiled, and it became far more sincere. He ran his hands over the carvings on the edge of the well, a blessing meant to attract the gods' attention and keep the well from drying up, as he pushed himself back to his feet.

"Being unpredictable is why my enemies hate me," the Prince of Trulin replied. "My spies, on the other hand, have the morning off. Late night, you see." He grinned wider, a broken tooth just left of center gleaming. It had been patched with gold.

"And did they earn their rest?"

"They didn't get me a copy of whatever you showed Loritat."

"Maybe they don't deserve a day off then," Tohmas replied, turning from the other prince. Sol's guide had waited at the edge of the courtyard for them. The young boy was prancing on his feet, checking the sky. Dawn was passing. The pyre would be lit soon.

Tohmas reached the guide and then looked back. The Prince of Trulin stood by the well, peering at Tohmas indecisively.

Tohmas gestured down the road. This would be his last chance to speak with Kelland before the evening's meal. They both needed to decide where they stood.

Dragging his feet slightly, Kelland joined Tohmas once more. Carsh moved aside to allow the Prince of Trulin to walk at Tohmas' side once more as they re-entered the cluttered streets on the guide's heels. Closer to the river, the roads were choked with sacks and barrels, leftovers of the army not yet disbanded. The soil waggon had finished only half of this road, and it smelled potently in the rising morning heat.

Around one more corner, they were ushered through a crowd. The temple came into view across a large field, the grounds between Tohmas and the building filled with people. A platform stood near the four-armed building, the pennants of each prince currently in Narsol hanging drably from posts in front of it.

Kelland reached the raised platform, fitted with chairs and canopy for the princes, and waited for Tohmas. The canopy above them did little to keep heat in but cast a cloudlike shadow, making the details of the people under it difficult to see.

Once on the stage, the pyre for Prince Dragal came into view at the center of the enormous temple's grounds. No one stood between the princes and the pyre. The crowd formed up on the other three sides in muddled ranks. Many mourners were soldiers in blue tabards, but all attendees wore the blue mourning band over their arms.

Upon his arrival on the stage, Tohmas accepted an embrace from Sol and Barnon, who then re-took their seats. When Tohmas sat in the third chair, Sol to his right, Kelland took the chair directly on Tohmas' left.

CHAPTER 4

Leaning over, Tohmas asked, "Tell me, Prince Kelland, do you believe the princes should cooperate more?"

"Of course," Kelland replied. The prince placed an elbow on his right knee and leaned over. "But I've been forced to defend my southern border from Gaidol since I took my title. Dorakon wants the north shore."

"I suspect Prince Sol would be happy if you relinquished your claim to the west side of Barrow Hills, especially as you can't access it for eight quartercycles of the year," Tohmas replied. To Tohmas' delight, the Prince of Trulin did not immediately balk. He considered his words.

Sol's gaze flicked over to them, but the Prince of Solta seemed to recognize the conversation did not require him and returned to supervising the unlit pyre from his seat. He called over Celebrant Sedgan to provide directions. The lamp of Inac's holy light hung from the celebrant's wrists in readiness.

The cold would not be a problem shortly, Tohmas knew. The pyre, perfected by Sol, would burn hot soon.

At length, Kelland cleared his throat. "Alliances can be useful. You have the advantage of family ties binding your princedoms. I was afforded no such luxury."

"What if you needed no blood ties?"

The silence fell heavily between them. Tohmas suspected every word he had spoken, both the day before and since they had met outside the manor this morning, was being reconsidered. Tohmas took it to mean he had judged the man well. Kelland sought stability. That was something Tohmas could offer in exchange for cooperation.

"It could benefit many," Kelland admitted.

Satisfied, Tohmas reached into his coat and retrieved his copy of the treaty. "Then tell me what you think," he said, handing Kelland the vellum.

While the Prince of Trulin read, the remaining representatives arrived and took their places on the platform. Tohmas noticed Anga Trulin watching from the crowd beside the platform. His gaze was suspicious, so Tohmas made a point of not acknowledging it.

Tohmas was content that Kelland kept the words of the treaty turned away from others, preventing anyone from reading over his

shoulder. Unsurprisingly, Warrah of Damoria sat on the end nearest the stairs and farthest from Tohmas.

The Princedom of Damoria was a lost cause. Nothing he did would convince Galanth's traditional enemy to change its position. Prince Wevan was probably planning an invasion of Galanth even now. Perhaps that was why he had sent his son Warrah to the funeral in his stead. Tohmas had been forced to send forces back to Galanth earlier that year to keep his territory defended from such incursions.

Prince Dorakon of Gaidol arrived and took a seat with Lord Garmont of Nothor. That was a firm alliance, even without the presence of Prince Neillen of Nothor himself. Lord Garmont was courting Prince Neillen's sister-in-law, who had also come up to Narsol for the funeral. Political opportunities appeared to be well for Garmont if he was trusted to represent his prince so far from home. The would-be wife must have been with the rest of the dignitaries beside the pavilion, but Tohmas could not guess which of the milling nobles she could be. No one in the crowd appeared to be wearing Nothor's colors.

Dorakon refused to meet Tohmas' stare, but Tohmas spotted the Prince of Gaidol glancing at Kelland. The angle prevented him from seeing any of the treaty, though.

Another lost cause, Tohmas knew. Dorakon's attempts at blocking Tohmas' march north had been thwarted, leaving the prince embarrassed.

Dragal's family had central seats on the pavilion, but only Sarilai greeted Tohmas with a wave. The others nodded at him, noted what Kelland was reading, and quickly took their seats without interrupting.

When Kelland finished, he held the vellum in his hand for a long moment. His eyes were on the pyre as it was lit, Celebrant Sedgan presiding over the use of the blessed flame to ignite the wood. It caught instantly and burst with fire, the flames running over the kindling like a perverted waterfall, then climbing into the sky.

The crowd gasped loudly, but Kelland appeared too engrossed in his thoughts to see the blaze abruptly reaching over the temple's rooftops.

Prince Dragal's pyre promised to be short if it burned so hotly. The ashes lay in a box atop the pyre, and the thick chest was already catching on the corners.

The celebrants led, and the crowd chanted the prayers, although none on the pavilion joined. The noise was enough to hide Prince

CHAPTER 4

Kelland's voice from eavesdroppers when he leaned over and said, "You know there are those who will fight this."

"Gaidol, Nothor, Damoria," Tohmas recited. He left out Polthian. As squeezed as it was against the borders with the Outlands, he still held hope of its agreement. Although Prince Polthian, the one prince who shared his first name with his princedom, had not come to Narsol, he had sent a High Guardsman by the name of Ranth Prem. Unlike Tohmas and Prince Polthian, who had not met or parted as friends during his march, Carsh and High Guardsman Prem had gotten on remarkably well. Carsh was due to visit the High Guardsman this afternoon.

"You left Lour and Polthian off the list," Kelland said soberly.

"Yes, I did."

The Prince of Trulin sat back, pensive. When Tohmas put out his hand, Kelland placed the vellum into it. Tohmas tucked the sheet away.

"You've got nine," the Prince of Trulin said softly.

"Or more." Tohmas left it there, giving the prayers time to rise to deafening volumes, then end. The Celebrants of Totho now appeared, burning incense and twirling the smoke in spinners. The prayer of Totho was always whispered, yet with the many voices, the sound became a steady hiss.

The fire was already dimming.

"It's a good idea. Hells, you might even be able to do it."

Was that admiration he heard in Kelland's voice?

He took one final chance. "The formal announcement is tonight," Tohmas said. "Combining our forces against Gaidol means it cannot hold, and Nothor will fold without Gaidol. The Rydans fight with us; your wealth can reach them. I deal with Damoria. You join, and there's hardly a fight."

Kelland nodded slowly. "I think we can make this work," he said, although he seemed distracted as he spoke. "It is the way this world is going."

They said nothing further on the matter. When the pyre died, they parted ways, although Tohmas still felt Anga watch him leave.

It was shaping up to be easier than he had expected. Tamv would be proud. Once all of Espar fell under Tohmas' banner, the Chief's influence would be felt from the southern marshes to the IceOcean itself in the north.

Ten princedoms were committed. Only four remained, and as he had told Kelland, they could not stand against the combined forces of the rest.

All too easy.

After lighting the pyre, Celebrant Sedgan had no further duties. Acolytes were more than capable of maintaining the fire. The piles of dry wood he had supervised earlier that day would last until nightfall. Celebrant Loni had even provided a few alchemical "miracles" to ensure the flames caught and burned appropriately. It became a spectacle in Narsol, which satisfied Sedgan.

A part of him was bothered by the use of tricks to make the fire catch. What had Prince Dragal done in life that might cause the gods to snuff the pyre? And would the gods not overcome the alchemical mixes Loni had provided? Did the gods care enough to be paying attention?

Although once Sedgan would have argued that Loni's tricks were not required, he now doubted. The last "miracles" he had witnessed had been falsified. Now he found it difficult to believe any of them had been real. Loni, the harlot masquerading as a Celebrant among the rabble, was not a wizard. She had no powers except being untouchable and thus immune to magic. But she played a crowd expertly and used her knowledge of alchemical mixes to profound effect.

Still, it would not do to have the holy fire going out at an inopportune moment, regardless of what those omens may mean. Sedgan had hidden omens from the population before and suspected he would again. It was for their good.

While his home was the Galanth Temple waggons, Loni's was in Fixer City, encamped outside the walls. Her tagalong group would be expecting a noon service. Another service would be held in the city, but the local celebrants presided there. The privilege of lighting the dead prince's pyre was the extent of Sedgan's duties. He was pleased that someone else could cater to the soldiers and lovers who called Inac their patron. Quiet moments had been precious few of late.

Chapter 4

He watched Loni depart, wondering if he should follow. The brand of insanity hid under her glittering sleeve, but he never forgot it was there, not anymore. Her power over the rabble was extensive and dangerous. Her madness had cost lives before.

For now, he let her go. He would check on her after the noon service once the gathering had dispersed. The fewer people who saw him at her fire, the better.

The city streets were packed, people choking the cobblestones and gutters. He passed four inns during his walk, each with the lamps over their signage extinguished, indicating they were full. Tents occupied every available corner, the detritus piling up in the less accessible nooks of the roadways. Every warden in Narsol appeared to be on duty, their red and gold uniforms tattered and stained already. Work parties roamed under their watch. Slaves and criminals worked side by side to gather as much garbage as possible into the slave-pulled carts.

His long robes, marked by the undulating lines of Inac, identified him and his acolytes to passerbys, who called out for alms, charity, or blessings in equal measure. His acolytes dealt with most, although he ensured they gave out more blessings than coins.

At length, he reached the Temple waggons arranged in a slightly-cramped city square within Narsol. The three waggons faced each other although there was no common campfire this time. In the tight spaces, Sedgan could have hopped from the steps of one waggon to the next easily.

Celebrant Calanor, wearing his usual long robes of white with tassels and scarves, sat on the steps of the Temple waggon to Totho. Celebrant Darak completed their trio, sitting in a chair beside the waggon of Pari. The thought of the title made Sedgan sigh in defeat. Calling Darak "celebrant" was a bit like calling the man's dog Stitches a pedigree hound. Instead of a half-lifetime of apprenticeship to a celebrant, Darak had only ever been a cutter, a mere religious fragment. Suddenly promoted by Prince Tohmas, Darak had stumbled into the rank of celebrant, a position the man neither deserved nor wanted. The works of the earth god Pari were now maintained by an unofficial council of healing mother facets, headed and spoken for by a farmer's son whose first interest was patients of a four-legged nature.

At least Darak was easy to get along with. They had needed a Celebrant of Pari after Celebrant Barga's death.

When Sedgan sat down on the steps of his waggon, his acolytes headed in for chores and left him alone with his fellow celebrants. Calanor only ever had his single acolyte, Timon, present, but now an assortment of boys and girls milled around Darak's wooden chair. They had a rotten log between them, something they must have carried into the city. One was writing, but Sedgan could not make sense of their babbling.

"I challenged them to find a spotted dancing beetle," Darak explained when Sedgan's raised an eyebrow at the group. Lowering his voice, Darak added, "They have the right habitat, but the spotted dancing beetle is only found farther south. They may be a while."

Sedgan nodded in understanding. He could name a dozen similar tasks he had assigned his acolytes over the years. There were hidden lessons in each challenge, but mostly, they were reprieves for the attending celebrant.

With Calanor in some meditation and Darak enjoying the temporary peace he had won for himself, Sedgan settled into the comfortable silence. Three days from now, on the first of the quartercycle, the celebrants would meet formally to discuss business. For now, nothing was required of them.

It lasted only a breath.

"I seek Calanor Blow. Might any of you direct me?" a female voice interrupted.

A tall woman stepped into the Temple waggon's circle. Dressed in a flowing dress of blue decorated with drops of silver and shells from seemingly every beach in Espar, she identified herself as a Celebrant of Ocea. But she was not Galanth, and her attire was too ornate to be the city's celebrant.

Sedgan rose, but Calanor was faster. The Celebrant of Totho leaped off his step seat as if he had been shoved, his swirling robes temporarily blinding Darak and Timon. Sedgan expected the Celebrant of Totho to greet her but remembered belatedly that Calanor, thanks to DoomDragon's mercy over the winter, was mute. After Calanor had taken refuge with the then-enemy of Galanth, DoomDragon had been commanded to kill the celebrant. In defiance, DoomDragon had instead taken the celebrant's tongue and hands and dropped him in a pile of snow to be found by Galanth soldiers. Sedgan was still uncertain if Celebrant Calanor begrudged the Northlander that treatment, as all other reports hinted that the two men remained friends.

It was still possible for the Celebrant of Totho to speak through his acolyte, but even Timon was silent.

Although Sedgan could only see Calanor's eyes visible over his scarf, he was shocked to see recognition in those eyes. Further, the woman seemed to recognize Calanor.

Her expression melted into a mix of relief and sorrow. The woman swept toward him, halting as Calanor froze. Delicately, she placed a hand on his chest.

The Celebrant of Totho eased into the touch, and the woman's smile glowed. Her hand dropped to reach for his, but when her fingers caught his wrist, Calanor pulled his arm away sharply.

"Oh, Calanor," the woman whispered as she drew against him, "I heard the stories, but I did not want to believe them. What has happened to you?"

With a bejeweled hand, the woman pulled aside the scarf. It was hard to tell if Calanor closed his grey eyes to block fresh tears or to savor the kiss the woman planted on his lips.

Of all the celebrants, Sedgan had known Calanor the longest. He had served Totho since a young age and had been ordained at twenty, the youngest possible. He had been the Celebrant of Totho for the Princedom of Galanth for the last six years and had not left the princedom to Sedgan's knowledge during that time. How did Calanor know this woman well enough to have a kiss—and not a casual peck either—laid on him in greeting?

"Corolys."

Hearing the child's voice beside the celebrant, the woman released the tender hold she had wrapped around Calanor. She seemed to disbelieve her eyes.

"Timon!" she whispered, collapsing to her knees and throwing her arms around the boy. She buried her face against his thin neck, the teardrop painted at the corner of her right eye flicking to a deeper blue with her tears. "I heard only one acolyte had lived," she muttered through gentle weeping. "I knew it had to be you! I knew your father would keep you safe!" Slowly, she released the child and held him at arm's length. "I expect you do not recognize me."

"You are Celebrant Corolys of Nothor," came the timid voice of the acolyte. "You are my mother."

"You know me?" The blue-garbed woman breathed the words. Tentatively, as if fearing the gesture would be rejected, she hugged the child again. Celebrants of Ocea, thanks to their goddess' purpose in family and mothering, exemplified the sincerest love. Her tears, Sedgan recognized, were tears of joy. After Inac's purging flames, three Temple waggons had been lost. This woman had not known if her child had survived.

He felt a sharp jab of guilt. How many mothers were grieving now because of the flames Sedgan had secretly lit that night?

She finished the hug with a kiss atop Timon's head, releasing him.

"He told me," Timon explained to his mother, no doubt with the celebrant's permission. "When he speaks, I hear."

"How—?" was all the mother had time to say.

Her face showed shock, and her eyes went blank. The extent of Calanor's new abilities had just been explained to her fully, Sedgan assumed. When he desired, Calanor could speak directly into minds, a feat understandably unnerving for those unaccustomed to it.

"Ocea preserve us," she whispered. Then, with a shake of her pearl-adorned hair, she encompassed both worshippers in her embrace and said, "You must tell me everything, especially you, Timon. My time here is disgracefully short thanks to my patron, but I want to hear all about you..."

The word "patron" snagged Sedgan's curiosity. Being sworn to their gods first and foremost, celebrants only took patrons in one circumstance: princes. Like the three celebrants gathered here, she was the celebrant of a princedom.

Turning toward the Temple waggon of Totho, the woman suddenly seemed to realize she had an audience. A weak smile graced her elegant face upon spotting Darak's gaping mouth.

Her voice returned to its previous strength. "I apologize for the disturbance, good celebrants."

"A disturbance as lovely as yours is welcome in any camp," Darak replied. Sedgan had to curse the man's speed and wondered if the slack jaw, now corrected pointedly, had been because of the woman's behavior or appearance. She was undoubtedly beautiful.

The Celebrant of Ocea sighed as though she was reading a love letter. Her ring-adorned fingers did not leave Timon and Calanor. "You are kind. I shall disturb you no longer." She glanced at Sedgan, but her eyes lingered on the exposed scar on his chest.

"You could stay, you know," Darak said, and Sedgan fought the urge to slap the Celebrant of Pari. "We are a broken group," Darak added. "None here worship Ocea. You could stay. We could be a completed four."

Sedgan had lived through a broken circle long before fires had slain Barga and Glorian and chased Calanor away. How could he explain to Darak that an alliance of lovers in the circle was just as bad, if not worse, than an incomplete circle? An unbalanced circle gave the illusion of equality. At least an incomplete circle knew it was uneven.

Her voice was sweet and light as honey candies. "I fear I am only a visitor, and I do not know your prince, but your offer is kind."

Sedgan cleared his voice nosily and falsely declared, "I should be prepping the altar." Seeing Darak still gaping, Sedgan added, "Pari's voice, would you be so kind as to join me? Someone dislodged one of the insets. You know metallurgy better than I do."

Darak moaned loud enough for his dog Stitches to sit up abruptly. "Of all Pari's blessings, I know squat about—"

"Get over here, Darak," Sedgan snapped, "and get your brats to give these three a moment alone."

It took some chasing, but soon enough, the brown-clad children had scampered into the waggon of Pari, and Darak followed Sedgan obediently into Inac's waggon.

The last thing Sedgan saw was the grateful smile on Corolys' face.

By the time night fell, the box containing the ashes of Prince Dragal of Clandac was a pile of embers. Ocea's acolytes wept mourning tears as Totho's worshipers prayed to open the path to the stars. Then, with as much ceremony as could be crammed into a quartercandle walk, the remains were buried by a Celebrant of Pari, and the prince was officially laid to rest for the second time.

It was a calmer affair than Prince Rairn's funeral had been by far. There were no magic ghosts to insult Tohmas this time and no tornados to tear apart their seating. Carsh arrived as it ended to report High Guardsman Prem had approved their plan. Although he could not officially pledge Polthian, he would highly recommend the agreement to the prince. Trulin's support had swayed Polthian heavily, for it pinned Gaidol and Nothor.

As a final homage to their host's brother, the dignitaries met for dinner in the grand hall. Only the princes and their representatives were invited, leaving out attendants, wives, and bodyguards. Sol touted it as a symbol of trust among these men of rank, for they all believed sternly that—as Tohmas had heard recited almost daily since taking Prince Habal's seat—princes did not kill princes.

Even if the mantra saw the princes gather without their defenders, it was not enough for them to arrive unarmed.

Tohmas took the seat at Darknim's side and received a friendly pat on his arm. Darknim was meeting many of these princes and nobles for the first time; Tohmas knew how important it was for the Northlander to be considered an equal among them.

To Tohmas' surprise, Darknim was fidgeting. When Tohmas raised an eyebrow at the Northlander, he said, "Tiki has started her..." He paused in search of a word. Tohmas sympathized. He worked around difficult words to hide his occasional slip. Esparan was not his first language, although it was best none of the others knew as much.

"When a child is to be born, the woman strains."

"Labor," Lord Talbit happily supplemented as he joined Darknim at the table. "She is in labor."

"Labor?" The Northlander laughed. "How apt! Yes, Tiki is in labor, and so my Layla is to be born soon. It is early, but I am eager to return to her."

Talbit handed over a mug to the Northlander. "He won't be given leave to speak until the end, I fear." Darknim made a face but drank from his cup instead of saying what he thought about the useless formalities.

Tohmas noticed eyes watching the exchange. Good.

The guests ate and talked about nothing to people they did not care about with false sincerity and a thinly veiled lack of interest over the meal. Tohmas ended up in conversation with Polthian's High

Guardsman Prem. Although they did not speak about the treaty or Carsh's visit, Prem discussed their southern borders with the Rydans. Since it was, the High Guardsman asserted, not Tohmas' problem, they did not speak on it long. It was to the High Guardsman's misfortune, as Tohmas had more insight into those minor disturbances than Polthian's spies, scouts, and philosophers combined.

After dinner ended, Sol thanked his guests, then gave Tohmas the leave he had requested to address the room.

He felt like he was back in Homestead over a year and a half ago, meeting his uncles for the first time to bring news they did not want to hear. This time, most of the room already knew about his news. The only people he would offend were those who already hated him. He felt the fire at his back as he had in Homestead, the lights shadowing the older faces around him as they judged him as closely as he judged them.

The future would depend on how he presented himself now. It was no small weight on his shoulder now.

Tohmas stood. A performance was required, an Esparan one.

The room stilled, the importance of his words registering.

"Over the last year, I have traveled through Espar from one end to the other. As you all know, my march north crossed through as many princedoms as possible to raise awareness of the Northlander threat."

Tohmas did not mention how his rally had been met, for it was already known that crossings had been progressively more difficult. Gaidol, the last princedom, had been traversed only by wagering and winning against Prince Dorakon himself. Even the peaceful crossings had left a sour taste in many of their mouths. All the princes resented losing their soldiers to Tohmas' cause. Their goodwill and congratulations at his victory now probably stemmed from the misguided assumption that, now that threat in the north had ended, he would give their men back.

"During my travels," Tohmas continued, "I saw many people and crossed many borders. What I saw, to be frank, disappoints me."

He had expected objections, but these men were too unaccustomed to being spoken to in this manner. Only silence resounded. Into it, Tohmas pressed, "You bicker. You squabble and pick at each other like malnourished chickens. Your borders are held out of fear, for you neither like nor trust your neighbors. Because of this, Espar suffers."

"Are your borders any different, boy?" Prince Dorakon of Gaidol groused.

"My borders are held by the sword against Damoria," Tohmas confessed, "because my family has been fighting his family," he indicated Prince Damoria's son Warrah, "since Zayban first claimed the land." He pointed at Polthian and Nothor next. "And his border is guarded against him for the same reason, just as Trulin fears Gaidol and Gaidol fears Clandac. You all go in circles arguing and lose all the benefits of a possible alliance."

The word "alliance," when spoken in a statement so close to the names of their enemies, sparked fury. Prince Dorakon and young Warrah Damoria leaped to their feet.

Tohmas hid his smile. Driving them to anger worked in his favor. If they were angry, they were not thinking straight.

"Sit down! We're not finished," Sol barked at the two offenders. Barnon joined, driving Dorakon to pound his fist against the table and shout louder. The din rendered both sides incomprehensible.

It was almost as if, Tohmas mused, *they were already at war.*

Tohmas lowered his voice. "Kit, if you would."

There was no flash of light or poof of smoke, but a piece of vellum appeared, hovering, over every place setting.

The commotion trickled away as, one by one, the princes and their representatives noticed the off-white sheet.

"I have a solution," Tohmas said in the silence. "I am weary of fighting border wars and wasting resources because of neighbors that are either neutral or hostile to me. I am equally weary of sending my warriors to die guarding borders without purpose. I have been a Prince of Espar for less than two years and am already tired of it. You have been fighting each other for decades. Are you not also weary?"

All of them had taken up the vellum. Even those who had pledged themselves seemed determined to verify the details in this, the final moments. The only one who left the vellum on the table was Darknim, who was still eyeing the door. Tohmas took that to mean "hurry up."

"I offer you each the chance to join me in this better future," Tohmas finalized.

Reading kept them silent for moments more. Warrah eventually gave voice to the disbelief beginning to show on the other faces in the room. "You lay claim to all of Espar!" The words were choked by outrage.

"Do not be so surprised," came a clear voice from the end of the table. "It is not such a bad idea."

When Chief Tamv had asked for an account, Tohmas listed the princedoms he confidently believed would join him. Trulin had not been among them. Now, Prince Kelland's agreement would solidify his power in Espar.

Once they came under Tohmas' control, he could pass them to Tamv. The Chief would have the Esparans under his command by the following year. His presentation was not entirely a lie, after all. Under one Chief, Espar would do better.

Tohmas nodded gratefully to the prince with the shaven head, but the Prince of Trulin did not seem to have anything further to say.

"I am offering complete cooperation," Tohmas explained to some and reminded others. "Borders can be opened for trade. Merchants can travel without bribing border guards. The kingsmen will have the same duties as princes have now, including overseeing the judicial needs of their region. But they will have someone to turn to if any need is unmet. A king."

The word "koeng" was Northlander in origin, for there was no such concept in Esparan, and it meant the "Chief of the Chiefs." It was a weighty claim but one both he and Darknim thought appropriate.

"This king will coordinate interactions between provinces and defend Espar as a whole. Borders will be set, *as they stand now*," he insisted, "and will not change. No more fighting for scraps of land you never use. We will have peace!"

He had seen the peace Chief Tamv had brought to the Outlands by eliminating the Second and Third Clans of Rydans. With one clan, wars had been eliminated. It could be done in Espar as well.

Of course, the First Clans had defeated the other clans to prove the point. Tohmas had higher hopes for the people of Espar.

"Under you!" snapped Warrah, jumping to his feet once more and reaching for his sword. They were too far apart for the threat to be real, but Tohmas' hand itched for SoulBurner in response. "You as this 'king?' Your control will be complete."

"Something must change for Espar to be free of petty squabbling," Tohmas retorted, resisting the blade's call. An open threat would boil the confrontation over. "Someone has to stand. I rose to the challenge of the Northlanders and brought that to a close. I stand now for this."

Sol, seated as host at the head of the table, stood, and the eyes of the guests turned to him. For a second time, Tohmas thought of Homestead, where Dragal had once confronted him on his father's death. Sol was now the eldest of the sons of Zayban, and he seemed to have inherited some of Dragal's strength with the title. When he stared at Warrah, the Damorian slowly lowered himself back into his seat and took his hand off his sword.

Tohmas did not sit, for he was not finished.

When Sol spoke, it was with the presence of a prince, one Tohmas had seen Sol use precious little.

"Tohmas, you have saved my life twice—once by providing the resources for my rescue from Marfaie…" Tohmas cringed to hear the name of a condemned spirit. Perhaps all Esparans failed to grasp the need to forget defeated evil. "…and once by bringing the dead prince's deception to light. I have fought by your side this last year. I hope by now, I have earned your respect. You have certainly earned mine. Solta stands with you."

Prince Barnon, Zayban's youngest, lifted his cup and declared, "Rabarch stands with you as well! You are family, after all! Call me your kingsman!"

By the time the cup was lowered, Lord Darmac of Clandac had adjusted his spectacles and risen to his feet to address the table in a calmer voice that had probably been forged in service to Lour.

"As of this morning, the land of Clandac officially passed into the hands of Lord Hurtz and me, as per Prince Dragal's wishes. I have rescinded my claim to southern Clandac and offer the princedom in its entirety to my brother-in-law."

He sat in time for Lord Hurtz to raise his cup to Tohmas as Barnon had done.

"Clandac swears to join Galanth's purpose!" the grizzled protector declared.

The murmurs of discontent grew with each passing promise. Still, they ceased utterly when Darknim DoomDragon, the Dragon of the

Northlanders and current Chief of all the north, stood and rested his callused palms on the table. Axe handles reached out over both his shoulders like arrows to draw their attention. He had come armed this time.

"None of you," the Northlander began in booming Esparan, "have contested my claim to the Princedoms of Meloch, Tanble, and Barlaby. Any who would, do so now." None of the princes or representatives moved. Warrah seemed to consider it, but something stopped him long enough for the Northlander to continue, "I am no prince and have no desire to be, but these lands need governance, and so I offer the land of Barlaby to Lord Darmac in King Tohmas' name."

"Thank you, Darknim," Talbit answered from his seat, a sigh releasing the last of his hidden doubt. "Consider me your kingsman as well, Tohmas."

"Aye," said DoomDragon as he sat down. "Me too."

"There," Tohmas said, nodding to those who had already offered their service. "You have a perfect demonstration of what I mean. Dragal left two men capable of governing but land for one. Darknim had land for many. No battles. No marches of armies. Not even a hard word. Now they each have what they need."

Complete silence reigned at the table. The onlookers were not stupid; they had been quietly counting and had realized that, of the fourteen princedoms, Tohmas now had the open support of seven. Talbit's rule in Barlaby was new, and DoomDragon could not defend Meloch and Tanble, but the count was still too high for anyone to be comfortable. And there were still the Rydans to consider, an entire people rallying to Tohmas.

Into that silence, Tohmas' unexpected ally stood.

Prince Kelland placed the vellum smoothly on the table, his stare gliding from one person to the next around the table. He reminded Tohmas of Prince Dragal, a man chiseled out of stone decades ago, still strong despite the weathering of years. His voice was crisp.

"I agree that this ambitious proposition of yours could be done, hells, even that it should be done, Tohmas." He paused, and doubt made itself known in Tohmas' gut.

"But I have one requirement before I commit myself or my princedom to this cause of peace," Kelland finished. He, as Darknim had, laid both hands on the table and leaned heavily toward Tohmas. "Choose another to lead. If this is about making peace, then prove it by naming another king."

D'aems, Tohmas cursed within.

Tohmas met the stare of the Truller across the table, spinning possible answers in his mind. But there was no alternative, no way to redirect the argument. The man was correct; if it *had* been about peace, another would suffice, but this was about conquest in Tamv's name. Conquest with as little bloodshed as possible, but still conquest. Tamv had sent him to take Espar for the First Clan.

For long moments, Tohmas tried every combination he could think of, but despite his best efforts, the answer remained unchanged. He searched for the words to make his reply less suspicious.

"I cannot. No other can shoulder this burden."

"Many of us have been princes for longer than you have lived!" shouted Prince Dorakon from his seat, tossing his hand and spilling his wine across the table. No one moved to right the glass. "What makes you the only choice? I agree with Prince Kelland! This is a grab for power!"

"The Rydans," Tohmas said with a defeated shake of his head, "will not follow another. I am the only person who can bring all three parts of Espar together. They will not—"

"Rydans," the High Guardsman of Polthian cut in, "only follow Rydans. Why do they follow you?"

D'aems, he cursed again within. Would he lose Polthian because Trulin had wavered?

Tohmas reviewed possible answers, all lies. Would they have accepted if he claimed the Rydans followed his prime protector? But then, why would Carsh follow him? The lies were too blatant.

For his answer to bear the weight of the suspicions, he needed a half-truth. If he could convince them of his sincerity, perhaps the situation could be salvaged.

"Because to them, I am Rydan," he confessed.

He had tried to avoid the topic at Tamv's request, for the Chief of the Outlands did not want men of Espar to know just how close Tohmas' ties were to the Outlands. Still, Tohmas knew it had to be explained eventually. The usual story, with some embellishments, would suffice.

"I was hidden from Damoria for fifteen years," he explained. "For that time, I lived with the Rydans. They know me. I know their ways. They will not follow any of you, but they will follow me." His stare sought the glower from the Prince of Trulin as he finished, "I am sorry, Prince Kelland. I hope you can see that one—"

Kelland shook his head. "Trulin stands against you, Prince Tohmas," he calmly declared. "I will not have my princedom conquered by you."

With that, he left the table, leaving Tohmas to sit back down, feeling a mix of anger and disappointment. He had liked the Prince of Trulin. He did not want to come to blows with Trulin for several reasons.

But Prince Kelland had lied to him. *Or did I let myself be misled?* Tohmas wondered. Had he wanted to hear something and refused to acknowledge anything else?

"Nor will I!" Dorakon declared. Warrah did not bother speaking—perhaps he found himself speechless—but followed Dorakon out of the hall. Lord Garmont slunk out behind them, muttering excuses about needing to bring the proposal to Prince Neillen's attention. He smiled snidely as he stopped in the doorway. "Although I doubt he will look favorably upon such a proposal," he said. He retreated down the corridor in the next blink, denying them a rebuttal.

High Guardsman Prem of Polthian lingered for a short while but then rose and took the vellum with him, promising to send word to Polthian for his decision. With the loss of Trulin's support, Tohmas suspected he knew what that answer would be.

Of the remaining princedoms, only Loritat took the vellum and approached Tohmas. The old warrior placed the treaty before Tohmas, the shards over his chest clanging as he slammed it down.

"You going to kill them?" Loritat asked.

The silence deepened, the entire table awaiting his answer.

"On the battlefield," Tohmas said. He looked up at Loritat. "Satisfied?"

"I am," the Prince of Lour said. "I'll swear the oath. Perhaps this is merely East versus West in the end, but I know where my interests lie. Perhaps they will see it in time." He lifted his hand from the treaty, revealing the marked bottom, stamped with Lour's anvil sign.

"I hope so," Tohmas replied, seeing the many empty chairs at the table.

There was much to do.

Chapter 5

For the first time in six years, Corolys put her son to bed. Timon, too old to need tucking in, accepted her ministrations with patience, as silent as his father but just as tentatively loving.

Once alone, she sat with Calanor and told him about the years apart. Calanor had never been verbose, making his silence almost normal. When he felt the need, his power reached out and spoke into her mind like the brush of a feather. Although it was strange, his thoughts were as gentle as his touch.

Words were insufficient anyway. By gaze alone, he roused the lover within her. Nothing in her life had ever been as sweet as lying with him again. Calanor shared her tears as they spilled in ecstasy. After passion had been satisfied, she rested her head on his chest and listened to his heart. His embrace lay softly around her shoulders.

She felt his presence after a time, a stirring in the back of her mind. Love reached out without words, surrounding her with sincere, deep joy. She drifted contently with him long into the night.

Ocea's moonlight found Corolys still with him a candle after the midnight service. Despite her negligence of the service, she did not think her goddess would be angry with her. The goddess smiled at a lover's joy. Corolys felt her love in the moonlight that shone through Totho's stars, carved through the waggon's wall.

Corolys watched Calanor in the moonlight, fighting the urge to kiss him again, worried she would wake him from the desperately needed slumber. The lover within her would not be satisfied by a single night. She wanted him a dozen times, and her tears also fell for that.

He had aged more in six years than she had expected. His expression was tired even in sleep. Her heart stung for him. Was he hiding his face with the scarf to disguise these signs of pain? He lay now without robes, scarves, or hood, and she could see the damage DoomDragon had done. Arms blackened by either fire or ice, nothing was below his wrists. He had not spoken about the injury and used the stumps well enough to show they did not actively pain him, but she still did not know if she should touch them. Although it had not mattered to her the night before, dawn's light brought uncertainty.

With her doubt, the memory of her oath to her patron intruded. Corolys rose, doing her utmost not to disturb either dozing wind worshippers. She had to return to Lord Garmont. They were due back in Nothor by the first of the mooncycle.

She wondered if Calanor had seen the departure buried in the back of her mind when they connected. She could not bring herself to wake him, unable to bear another farewell. The Princedom of Nothor had always been her home, but as she slipped her clothing back on, she found herself cursing it. *Six years!* For six years, she had scraped by, her thoughts on Timon and his father, wondering where they were and what they were doing. For six years, she had been denied access to her son. How could Ocea, goddess of children and mothers, approve?

The goddess, Corolys decided with an aching heart, must object. Corolys had come to Narsol for a funeral, dragged along with her suitor to represent the princedom when Prince Neillen could not. She had not expected to find Calanor or Timon. Ocea had guided her here, Corolys was certain. The goddess wanted her celebrant to find her love.

Six years, her soul cried again, for what, one night? Was that it? Would she go another six before feeling his touch again? Would Timon be shaving by the time she next ruffled his hair? She already thought it was too late; he was growing so quickly. How could she be a mother with her child so far from her?

Yet as her heart, mind, and soul pleaded their impossible questions to her goddess, Corolys donned her fine jewelry, fastened her hair, and made ready to leave. She paused over Timon's hammock. He looked so much like his father, it pained her.

As much as she longed to get to know him, he was safer here than he would be in Nothor.

She crept by, leaving him to sleep. When her hands touched the latch of the waggon, fresh tears welled in her eyes.

Her life was in Nothor, as it always had been. But her heart was with Calanor and Timon. She would embody the Weeping Goddess aspect of Ocea once more. She saw no choice.

She slipped out, closing the latch behind her as softly as possible. "Morning!"

The cheery call jolted Corolys out of her contemplation. The three Temple waggons faced each other in a courtyard, and she had walked into the central area. The Celebrant of Pari, with a group of six boys around him, waved in greeting, his smile broad through his untrimmed beard.

He finished his conversation with his acolytes, "Well done! Whoever painted the spots did a glorious job too!" He returned a freckled insect to the nearest boy's hand. "Go get cleaned up."

As he faced her again, the boys rushed back into the waggon behind the celebrant. He beamed at her, bowed, and said, "I don't think we were introduced last night. I am Darak Degree. If you see a bay horse limping around untethered, that's Justice, and this here is Stitches." A mongrel dog, lying by the cooking fire made of broken waggon parts and a chair, lifted its lopsided head and wagged its tri-colored tail. Corolys tried to smile, but she knew it was strained. Animals were not her favorite aspect of any god, even Ocea. Of course, Ocea's beasts were not known for being endearing; most were fish.

"I would offer you breakfast," Celebrant Darak continued, "but Stitches ate the rest of it." Again, the dog wagged her tail but seemed disinclined to move even her head this time. The dog's belly was bulging, likely from the stolen breakfast. Darak had not specified exactly how much "the rest of it" had entailed.

He almost seemed to expect Corolys to sit, but time was already short. She did not have enough left for pleasantries or a slobbering mutt.

"I must be on my way."

His smile lost some enthusiasm. "I hope you enjoyed your visit. Calanor is not usually up this early. I can give him a message if you want. I wouldn't be up, but I picked the wrong deity."

His reply stunned her. Darak was the highest-ranked Celebrant of Pari in all Galanth. She had never heard a celebrant, any celebrant, be so flippant about their devotions.

She was torn for a moment, wondering if she should leave a message. She could not bring herself to go through another goodbye—the last one had broken her heart—but was leaving nothing not worse?

It all crashed in on her. She was leaving, without a farewell, without even a note.

While her heart debated, her feet carried her to a seat by the fire. The Celebrant of Pari handed her something to drink, but she could only hold the hot cup. Everything in her froze from her lungs to her ever-knowing feet.

Her life in Nothor was comfortable and safe. People knew her. She was successful and influential in the temples. She had everything most people died trying to achieve. Was she truly considering turning her back on it?

But a celebrant to Ocea lacking love was no use to anyone. Her love was sleeping in the waggon of Totho.

Celebrant Darak busied himself around the fire as she mulled. In her musing, she found the words the Darak had said the night before: *You could stay, you know.*

"What is Prince Tohmas like?" Corolys asked, not knowing where the thought was leading.

The celebrant and his hound smiled. Rolling over, the dog rose and sauntered over to lean a happy head against Corolys' knee.

"Tohmas?" Celebrant Darak said with enough energy to distract her from the dog's attention. "Tohmas is a huge man." He procured a bladed instrument from a pocket, one she usually saw cutters use. As he spoke, he cleaned, trimmed, and polished his nails. "He has a huge presence, huge strength, and huge prowess. Further, that man has a huge intelligence and," he finished with a wink at a joke she did not get, "huge ideas."

It took Darak another moment to realize she had missed his jest. He exploded into laughter. "Of course! I don't imagine you went to the midnight service, did you? And I know you were not at today's morning service. You don't know!"

The mutt was sniffing at her cup; Corolys pulled it back. "Know what?"

Celebrant Darak leaped to his feet and flared his robes out grandly. "Last night, my esteemed patron, Prince Tohmas of Galanth, declared all of Espar, in its vast entirety, at peace!"

His enthusiasm baffled her. No one could declare peace in Espar. Even with wizards bringing communication between the princes, she could not imagine *all* of the princes agreeing on anything. This was insanity. "The other princes..."

"Well, seven of them agreed," Darak informed her with a skip. "Who knows about the others, so we are, rather paradoxically, going to war for peace."

Prince Tohmas had made the declaration without the consent of the other Princes of Espar.

"But that means..." The scope of the news dawned on her, and she forgot the cup, dropping it. Stitches' head shot off her lap to clean up the spill.

"Conquest," Celebrant Sedgan's authoritative voice filled in. The Celebrant of Inac now stood atop the stairs to his waggon, latching the door behind him as he emerged. His robes were parted across his chest, the double S of Inac's fire visibly branded onto his sternum. "It means he is taking on every princedom that has not agreed to his proposition. Whatever the end, we are at war again."

Corolys hardly heard the celebrant, her mind whirling. It was unlikely that Nothor was among Prince Tohmas' supporters. Even if Prince Neillen could be convinced, Prince Dorakon would never forget the bet he had rigged and still lost, and the brothers could not be divided. Prince Neillen had lost over three hundred men to Tohmas' march, opening him to his traditional enemy, Polthian in the south. He had plenty of reason to hate Prince Tohmas. Mercifully, Polthian had made no attack.

Her decision had been hard enough when the choice had been between two relatively peaceful princedoms, but how could she justify leaving Nothor for what was so clearly now her enemy?

The goddess did not care if she was in Nothor or Galanth, she reasoned. They would be traveling. She could spread Ocea's word. She could support the Galanth, who had been without a Celebrant of Ocea.

And she could be with Calanor.

CHAPTER 5

"Do you want to meet Tohmas?" Somehow, the little Celebrant of Pari seemed able to read her thoughts.

If she were considering staying, she would have to forsake her oath to Prince Neillen. She could take one in Tohmas' name to hold onto her status.

What would her family think? The answer was evident: they would be appalled that she was even considering it. There were circumstances when celebrants stepped down, usually for illness or inability to perform their duties, but she knew of none who had forsaken their post. Did a broken heart count?

"He is a little busy at the moment, Darak," Sedgan warned, taking a seat at the fire and helping himself to the same hot drink Darak had shared with Corolys.

Darak grinned mischievously. "I *am* still his cutter, Sedgan." Celebrant Darak lifted an eyebrow at Corolys. "I can get you an audience." Stitches finished lapping up the spilled drink and cocked her head.

Corolys' decision solidified. She would meet Prince Tohmas. If what she learned pulled her along this path, so be it. If not, she could still ride with Lord Garmont and return to Nothor.

Corolys brushed the dirt that had come with the dog off her lap. "I would meet this man," she declared.

The Celebrant of Pari gave the other celebrant a told-you-so look better suited to an acolyte. "This way, fair Lady! This way!" he said, laughing as he led her out of the courtyard.

Summoned at dusk, Lance spent a miserable night dozing in a chair outside Prince Dorakon's temporary rooms in the Manor of Narsol. Prevented from leaving, "in case you are required," Lance organized the Fyrd of Arrow from a distance. When Lance finally met with his prince, Dorakon recalled all the Gaidolon forces he had loaned Tohmas. The news was not a surprise, and it should not have taken so many candles to relay. Under the command to organize his men and march out promptly with Dorakon, Lance was finally released to attend to his duties in person.

Dorakon had been delaying him, but he did not know why until he returned to his tent.

His guardsmen first ambushed him with the news; Galanth had allied with most of the princedoms and intended to conquer the rest. The forces that had been about to disperse were being reassigned instead.

Explains the recall, Lance admitted, although he had been expecting it. The Northlander War was over. The excuse Lance had used to leave Gaidol was gone.

Prince Tohmas' messenger was waiting for Lance at his tent. The message was short: Prince Tohmas of Galanth requested his presence. The runner handed Lance a token to prove it.

With no time to sleep or change, Lance followed the runner back into Narsol, his mind in chaos.

His assistance to Tohmas had always been a temporary arrangement, born of desperation to distance himself from Dorakon before Lance made a fatal mistake. Unlike the majority of Tohmas' army, who had left their home princedoms and sworn oaths to the Prince of Galanth, the Gaidolons under Lance had never abandoned their oaths to Prince Dorakon.

But something stirred in him hearing the news of Tohmas' new venture. Although he could not settle on the idea, Lance thought an opportunity was hidden in the upheaval being forced upon Espar.

He followed the messenger back into the city, trying to sort through his thoughts. He had expected to be going home to Gaidol. Valia was waiting. Even if Dorakon had no intention of changing his mind about his daughter's hand, Lance knew his patron could tell how much the distance was wearing on him. Even if he went back to the little border city of Varidee where Dorakon had stationed him, he would be closer to her, which would help.

But Lance had made a promise he could not keep. The vow was whispered in his ear as home became a tangible mirage in the distance. *When I come back*, he had said, after the forbidden kiss he and Valia had shared, *I swear I will marry you.*

He should never have made the promise. With Dorakon ruling Gaidol, it was a promise that could never be fulfilled. It hurt to accept that simple fact, but he could not escape it.

He was two blocks from the manor when a boy stepped into his path. "Message for you, Lance Carraway," the boy said.

Thinking another pointless order from Dorakon was to follow, Lance waved Tohmas' escort to halt. It took an extra moment for Lance to recognize that the messenger had not called him "High Guardsman" as appropriate. Nor was the boy in Dorakon's blue and yellow.

He blinked in disbelief as he finished assessing the boy.

His niece Lydia was dressed as a novice rider, complete with a dagger on her belt. Like most Carraway family members, she was tall and lean. Her baggy breeches and top hid her gender well. *A disguise?* Lance's entire family was watched by Dorakon's men, with the greatest attention devoted to Lance's brothers and their sons. Their daughters, however, had more freedom.

This was no message from Dorakon. This was from his family.

He snapped to attention. He could practically hear his father scolding him for taking so long.

"I have been summoned," Lance replied formally, erasing recognition from his face and making a point of being abrupt. Around the manor, too many people milled to guarantee no eavesdroppers. "Speak your message and be on your way."

"Do what you must," Lydia said, every word no doubt precisely that which Lance's father had spoken. "He cannot reach us."

Lydia presented her hand, and Lance had to rummage to find a coin for her. He wanted to say something else, make her promise to stay safe, but dared not draw attention to her now. She smartly walked away without a word more.

The niggling hope he had first felt upon learning of Prince Tohmas' plans rose to the front of Lance's mind as he and the escort moved onward.

Lance's father had preached obedience to Prince Dorakon over his sons' cradles, desperate to keep them from offending the Prince of Gaidol and endangering the family. Four sons had even become guardsmen to allay Dorakon's suspicion, although it never made a difference. Lance had always believed that to err in his loyalty to Dorakon, no matter how much it chaffed him to cater to the brute, was to damn his family. From birth, his every move had been monitored and critiqued.

The only time he had heard his father Hiron speak directly about "him" to the family with intolerance in his voice had been upon Lance's departure to follow Tohmas. Things were changing. Assuaging Dorakon was no longer an option.

Lydia's message became clear: Hiron expected repercussions and had made ready. The family was safe.

Lance dragged his feet forward, still lost in thoughts. He had spent the night planning the recall to Gaidol, but now everything spun on its head. If Dorakon could not reach the family, what did Hiron expect Lance to do? What *could* he do?

Prince Tohmas and Prince Dorakon were at odds in this endeavor to unite Espar. If Lance sided with one, he was an enemy of the other. But he was already Dorakon's enemy. He had been since being born into the family that had once ruled Gaidol.

If Dorakon lost control of Gaidol, Lance's family could, finally, be free. That was the distant, desperate hope that was nagging him.

He would have to break his oath to Dorakon. In doing that, he was also letting go of the promise he had made to Valia. Dorakon would never permit him to marry his daughter. How could Valia love him then?

Lance looked up and realized he had stopped. He was among Galanth protectors now, facing a door. The protector nearest cocked his head at Lance, sufficiently familiar with him to be unconcerned by his presence but awaiting an explanation.

Without a word, Lance showed the protector Prince Tohmas' token.

"You know," the protector said knowingly as he opened the door for Lance, "you'd look better in green."

The room beyond the door was an ornate bedroom, although the canopy bed and feather mattress looked unused. The fire burned low in the dawn, its light replaced by sunlight and spring air.

Prince Tohmas leaned over the round table that had awkwardly been crammed into the corner, its surface spattered with tokens, parchments, and a cluster of colored stones. Lance recognized the color combinations on the rocks as belonging to the princedoms. They were even arranged by their rough positions in the world, although he noted some were in pairs, like Gaidol and Nothor.

Beneath the tokens and scraps, it was the same table that had been carted around all the north during the Northlander War, now pitted and dented with stories. The most prominent damage was a stain of near-black wildwater that reached across the table like a tree growing from splattered roots, caused when a poison had been detected in Tohmas' waterskin. The crest that Tohmas occasionally wore on his chest was a barren tree that matched the stained surface.

"So," Lance said as he tossed the token onto the table and pulled out a chair to sit across from the prince, "I hear you're taking over the world."

Tohmas caught his token reflexively. Carsh, dropping from his perch atop a nearby chair, put a cup of wildwater into Lance's outstretched hand. It was a tiny cup, Lance gratefully acknowledged.

Leaving the table's mess as it lay, Tohmas took a seat and picked up his cup. He, for a rare moment, seemed apologetic. "I tried to tell you last night, but no one could find you."

Lance took a mouthful of wildwater and choked down the burning dirt taste. It was potent enough to cleanse wounds and start fires, the prime protector had once confided, which made Lance wonder who had ever decided to drink it, but he accepted the courtesy for what it was. He always swallowed at least some of it when visiting the prince or the prime protector.

"You can thank Dorakon for my absence. We were recalled, all of us, of course."

"Did he tell you why?" Tohmas asked.

"Of course not," Lance replied, swallowing the rest of the cup. Courtesy or not, no one sipped wildwater. Two mouthfuls were all that he could stand anyway.

Carsh took back the cup, nodding in approval.

Tohmas stood solemnly. "Lance, you are one hell of a fighter and have been a good friend ⎯"

"Sit down, you fool," Lance grumbled. "You're not getting rid of me so easily."

Tohmas paused, his hands spread on the table.

"I'm not sure I've ever seen you speechless before," Lance quipped.

Carsh grinned wide enough to show teeth. "Tol' ya," he said to Tohmas, who was self-consciously breaking into a smile.

"I didn't expect that! You're not sick, are you, Lance?" Tohmas said with a laugh.

"I changed my mind on the way here, so don't slow me down, or I might regret it," Lance said, the words running together. "I spent all night thinking I was heading home. But things changed. Most of the Fyrd of Arrow probably wants to stick with you anyway. They left Gaidol not expecting it to be temporary. Besides, you fought with them. You brought them victory. And you have that damned 'Champion' thing, so the fanatics are yours no matter what I do. Half of my guardsmen would run after you right now. But whether they do or not, I plan to, if you'll have me."

Tohmas' expression fell, worry reaching across his features. "You're a loyal man. What, by the hells, did Dorakon do to you to make you leave?"

The truth hurt, but Lance didn't dare stop now. The decision was made.

"Dorakon has broken too many promises. He hates me and always has. Hates my family too. I can't go back. For their sake, I want Dorakon to lose Gaidol."

Tohmas leaned away, reluctant. "And what if he signs my treaty? What if I do not replace him in Gaidol?"

Lance let out a breath and suddenly wished he *had* drunk more wildwater. "Then I want him held accountable. I want to stop being scared of losing my head every day for no reason. Or having my family wiped out because I make a mistake. He needs someone to judge him."

"So you'll fight against Gaidol?" Tohmas asked pointedly.

"I'll fight *for* Gaidol," Lance corrected. "But not *his* Gaidol. I fight to let Gaidol be free."

Tohmas fell into silent contemplation, his hand on his beard. *Speechless*, Lance thought, *for a second time.*

"Why do you even hesitate?" Lance demanded, feeling himself flush. "He lied to you! He cheated, and his tricks *killed* people. Why defend him?"

"It's not him I worry about," the Prince of Galanth replied. "It's you. You are an honorable man, Lance. I was convinced you would never forsake an oath. But if you will forsake an oath, what does your oath mean to me?"

The comment sobered Lance's ire like a bucket of cold water. He sat back, his mind clearing. He had knocked the stones on the table, pushing Trulin's brown and white stone off the edge of the table in his haste. He felt foolish.

Taking a deep breath, he retrieved the fallen stone.

"My oath," he said slowly, "was to Gaidol first, her prince second. In this, I am looking out for Gaidol. We need a judge to preside above him, take him to task. I believe you, as King of Espar, can do that." As he replaced the stone in the pattern, he finished, "And if, in the end, a judge believes I have acted wrongly, then I will face my punishment. But this is where my heart leads me. For Gaidol, I will break my oath to her prince."

They held each other's stares for long moments, and Lance suspected Tohmas' thoughts were just as harried as his own. He was being judged anew. Lance did not know if Tohmas would like what he saw.

Carsh slammed a cup down in front of Lance, breaking the gaze. "*Tatim*, drink!" the prime protector declared. "Drink *a'wa* serious!"

Lance left the cup on the table until Tohmas picked up his own. With a quick tip, the Prince of Galanth, soon-to-be King of Espar, downed the contents. Lance did the same for his wildwater. He felt flushed again, the alcohol rushing to his head.

"Still half a story," Tohmas said once they had drunk. "Tell me the rest when you think I should know it. But welcome back, Lance. How would you like to be a guardian?"

The prime protector tossed Lance a red rope for his rank marker, and Lance pulled the beaded rank headband of Gaidol off his brow for the last time. He placed it on the table delicately and took up the Galanth rope.

"A braid?" Although the Galanth soldiers had always used a shoulder rope of color as a rank marker, this rope was braided.

Tohmas shrugged. "Three parts. Northlander, Rydan, and Esparans, all unified."

"And stronger by being together. Clever."

"I thought you'd like it. Let me know when you are ready to make your oath. I'll leave you to sort through Arrow's fyrd too."

Lance shrugged. "Most of that rabble left Gaidol looking for a fight. Some will go home to their trades and farms, but the rest will hang on. They like you for some reason. There was a goddess involved or something. And something about a dragon? I don't know. Weird, if you ask me."

The Prince of Galanth had a legend surrounding him now. Many would march on solely because the Champion of Inac told them to.

They clasped arms before parting. Tohmas leaned in, and Lance heard the first heartfelt "Thank you" he had in over three years. It was a good feeling, but it was not enough to overrule the knot of fear in his stomach that he'd never see Valia again.

Sometimes, he told himself determinedly, *it's just time to move on.*

Passing through the streets of Narsol in the early morning made Corolys feel squeezed. It reminded her of Leviathan, the port city of Nothor, where every corner was lined with carts and every street was choked by sailors. Her status as Celebrant of Ocea usually earned her instant respect from any who depended on the sea. None of them would dare offend her goddess by getting in her way, but sometimes there was just no room.

But here, Darak's elbows made the path for them, their robes too unremarkable for the busy press of people to note. Once they reached the Manor of Narsol proper, the crowds thinned to uniformed soldiers who were inherently more deferential to celebrants. They seemed to notice Celebrant Darak the most, which made sense; any of these warriors could expect to end up in one of Pari's Healing waggons at any time. When they did, it would behoove them to be in good standing with the God of Healing.

Darak navigated the corridors of the manor rapidly, stopping in a seemingly random corridor near the center of the complex. A man dressed in Gaidol's white and blue exited the room as they reached it. Corolys spotted the smile and nod the stranger gave the Celebrant of Pari. Everyone in Galanth, Corolys was beginning to suspect, knew Celebrant Darak.

Darak spoke briefly to a protector and was as good as his word; he was given leave to enter Prince Tohmas' chambers. Feeling out of place, Corolys waited at the entrance for a moment before following in.

She had seen Prince Tohmas of Galanth during social gatherings in Narsol, and his size did not intimidate her. She knew he was a worshipper of Inac officially, but she had seen little enough of him to

CHAPTER 5

understand what that meant in practice. Most princes favored one god or another, but in her experience, princes and their ilk expected all the advantages of a god with none of the responsibilities. It was an annoying double standard.

This prince sat at a huge table strewn with colored stones, tokens, and parchment sheets. The parchments were all different sizes and weights, unlike the finer ones Corolys was accustomed to. All stacks stood on tilted angles. It looked like a child had thrown the objects across the table randomly.

Prime Protector Carsh, whom she had never met, was unmistakably the Rydan with the prince. Sitting atop a chair's back, he was decorated with more knives than she had shells and fiddled with one as she watched. Grass bracelets encircled both wrists, including his splinted arm, and rattled as he rotated his blade from one hand to another. It was hard to say how badly his arm was injured as the use of both hands was fluid.

"I've not got much time, Darak," the prince rumbled without looking up from whatever he was writing, "and I know there is nothing wrong with my health, so be quick."

His words were abrupt, but his voice was soft enough for the orders to be mere requests. The way he absently flipped a scrap of food to the healer's dog made even Corolys smile. *This is the man who is taking over Espar?* He seemed less and less prince-like.

"Look what I found wandering around the Temple waggons!" Darak said, gesturing for Corolys to enter.

The prince looked up and, with a glance, assessed her.

The silence in the room hung like an anchor. His lack of immediate response struck her as odd; what prince hesitated to make known their opinion?

"Are you looking for a job, Celebrant?" he asked after the pause.

Her first fear had been that he would not want a Celebrant of Ocea. If he was truly devoted to Inac, he might view another goddess' celebrant as competition for the Gathering of Inac. Or did he not care that much for Inac?

"No, but I may accept one," she replied honestly.

He took his hands off the writs and tokens laid out before him. "Congratulations, Darak, you have just won a quartercandle of my non-existent free time."

"I give it," Celebrant Darak said with a twirl of his long robes, "to the lovely Celebrant Corolys. Enjoy!" He twirled his way out of the room and left, his dog in tow.

Even after her many years in Nothor, Prince Neillen had always been surrounded by low and high defenders and guardsmen when Corolys met with him. Corolys' heart jumped into her throat when she realized she was alone with the Prince of Galanth except for his single defender.

But then, this prince was in the middle of organizing the takeover of the world. He was clearly in a hurry. She accepted the lack of an audience as practicality, not special treatment.

Corolys put on a soft smile. "Celebrant Darak certainly thinks highly of you, good prince."

The prince sat back and laughed while the prime protector cracked a tooth-filled grin that made Corolys shiver.

"Really? I thought he was still mad at me for having promoted him." Seeing her at a loss, he continued, "But I guess Darak, like all us Galanth, are more like Stitches than we care to admit. When things get tight, you can count on us to put our heads down and bear whatever the world tosses our way. We'll even wag our tails while we do it because we can. But what about you?" Prince Tohmas pressed without a pause. "Why exactly is a Celebrant of Ocea, and no minor Celebrant of Ocea I may add, not looking for a job but ready to accept one?"

"I had heard," she started, "of Galanth's lack of celebrant. I felt it necessary to correct the oversight. This is especially important in light of your newest endeavors. You will need all four gods."

Until that moment, she had found no reason to be ill at ease with the man who had declared himself ruler of Espar, so long as she ignored the presence of the hovering Rydan. But as she spoke, his eyes narrowed, and she felt her skin prickle in goosebumps. She felt naked in front of him.

"I may utterly destroy any possible relationship between us by saying this," the prince said in a more formal tone, "but I believe you have just lied to me. It is bad form to lie to possible patrons."

She fell silent. He was right, and now she could think of nothing to say. Miserably, the man did not speak to fill the gap, instead watched her, waiting.

When she opened her mouth, she surprised herself. "I am in love with Celebrant Calanor. I have been for eight years, only two of which I have spent with him. You need a celebrant. I—"

A voice, heavily accented in a manner she did not think she had ever heard before, interrupted from just outside the door. "You want an axe up your ass? Just keep getting in my way, you—"

"Let him through!" Prince Tohmas shouted, clearly knowing the intruder and not feeling threatened. Corolys received an apologetic smile. "Pardon me, fair lady. Just a moment."

The man through the door was the same size as Tohmas. His long beard, parted and braided, reached to his belt. A mat of hair worked as a cowl surrounding his wrinkled face. Axes hung off his belt, which he had thankfully not drawn despite his threat.

He was a Northlander, the first Corolys had seen this close, and obvious about his heritage.

"Sorry, Tohmas," the man said, "but it's about Layla, and I just—"

"Do not worry," the prince assured the intruder with a soothing gesture. "How is Tiki doing?"

Corolys, though oblivious to the names, knew the answer before it was spoken.

"Difficulties. I have told Layla that I will claim her as my daughter and give her all she requires, but she still does not wish to enter this world. I thought perhaps all the changes have frightened her. I figured you would be able to help."

There was no hesitation from the Prince of Galanth, which spoke well of his sincerity. "Anything you need, Darknim."

The rest of the Northlander's name was evident: Darknim DoomDragon. Most people would know him as the leader of the Northlanders and current ruler of Meloch and Tanble, but Corolys knew him most as the man who had maimed her lover.

For the last ten years, she had heard rumors of Solta and the war with the Northlanders, and every story had warned about the prowess of Darknim DoomDragon. Years had passed, and Espar had been battered. DoomDragon had slaughtered Esparans from Arcott to the north of Solta until Prince Tohmas had brought him to heel.

This fidgeting mammoth of a man was not what she had imagined.

"Well," DoomDragon stammered, "would you be Layla's eldafather?"

"If you tell me what it means, I will gladly," the prince vowed.

Again, the Northlander shifted on his feet and tugged at his beard with his thick hands. "You would help her in her life, but most importantly, if anything were to happen to me, you would become her father in my place. This way, she would be..."

Like her, the prince seemed to recognize that the man would likely ramble on in his anxiousness. DoomDragon was less imposing with every antsy moment. In his evident nervousness, he had failed to notice Corolys at all.

"I will happily be Layla's eldafather," Prince Tohmas promised.

DoomDragon settled and gestured to the door. "You will come? Declare it to her?"

The prince was already standing and nodding, but he, unlike his guest, was aware of his visitor. She could not tell if he was going to dismiss or welcome her, but she dared not take the chance that it would be dismissal. Her curiosity was too powerful now. She wanted to see what came of this, to judge Tohmas' character, and to gauge the force that was DoomDragon. This was Ocea's message, she was sure.

"I may be able to help," she said.

"Celebrant of Ocea?" came the surprised exclamation from the Northlander. The wrinkled face lit up. "You would be most welcome."

"Of course," Prince Tohmas added, leading her toward the exit. "We can finish our conversation afterward."

She felt guilty following them out. A child was being born, and she was not immediately thinking of how to bring it into the world safely. Ocea would be ashamed.

Still, she reasoned, *DoomDragon had cut off Calanor's hands and sliced out his tongue.* How could Ocea bless anyone who was so cruel? Or was this difficult birth punishment? Why would the woman be punished?

They left the room at a hasty pace, protectors crowding to follow as expected. Without clear instruction, the protectors surrounded the prince and his guests and created a path from the city. Soon the prince, the Northlander, and Corolys were outside the walls, walking through trails of puddles and mud between the tents of the remaining army.

The newly assigned army, Corolys reminded herself.

With the city's press behind them, she could be heard now. Sidling over to the Northlander, she asked, "Is this your first child, DoomDragon?"

Her question drew the Northlander out of contemplation. He distractedly replied, "Ah, no, no, definitely not." He seemed to gather his senses as he spoke, like a man waking from dreams.

"You seem nervous."

He shook his head. "I... I have had fifteen... no, it is seventeen now. I have had seventeen boys over these years, but Layla is the first daughter, so I am..." The sentence trailed off, forgotten.

"Why have I never met your sons, Darknim?" Prince Tohmas asked as if trying to help Corolys distract the Northlander. They walked so briskly, Corolys had to nearly jog to keep pace with their long strides.

Again, DoomDragon seemed forcibly drawn out by the conversation, but when he shrugged and sighed, it was sad.

"Winter is hard in the north, and the war was harder still. Of all my children, only my seventh son reached the age of thirteen. Elder Tril claims I have two sons I have not yet met—aged six and eight, I understand—but the rest are in the stars with many of their mothers."

While the mother's heart within her panged, Corolys tried to overrule the instinct. This was a murderer. Father or not, he had hurt Calanor, nearly killed him. And he *had* slain Esparans as he had invaded the three northern princedoms.

He said "stars," she realized. He had recognized her as a Celebrant of Ocea. She knew nothing of Northlanders, but she had never thought they worshipped as the Esparans did. Did he know Esparan lore well, or did they share religion between them?

"I am sorry for your losses, Darknim," Prince Tohmas quietly said as if he was somehow responsible.

The Northlander shrugged and increased their pace around what were now pelt tents. He smiled wistfully at the prince.

"You or Carsh a father yet, Tohmas?" The prince shook his head for them both. The Rydan said nothing from his place, following closely on their heels. "It is good to have children," the Northlander said. "Even if you lose them, it is worth caring for them, raising them, and seeing what they can do. I will find my other two boys soon, and Layla…" The recollection of the daughter who was in danger darkened the brightened face immediately.

"She will be fine, my friend," the prince said, and DoomDragon nodded.

"Of course, she will," DoomDragon said, glancing at Corolys. "Now we have a Celebrant of the Holy Mother with us as well."

Torn, Corolys did not meet the man's stare.

Thankfully, all the coming and going of Fixer City meant the Double Blades' vardo slipped in without drawing attention. They arrived at dusk, saving Maybel from another lonely night on the road. Sitting beside Tostig on the waggon's driver seat, Maybel watched the disorganized group. So many were coming and going since the news of Tohmas' march had reached the masses. Easy to fit right in with the changes.

Despite the dampness, the return to the road was overall welcomed for Maybel. Dancing—as much fun as it was to see the boys blush—in Cainton was boring. Even the capital of Trulin did not have enough men to keep Maybel entertained after the dancing was done. Staying meant seeing the same man more than once, maybe becoming a favorite to some dull, yet powerful, lout. Once they got possessive, it annoyed her.

Tostig brought the vardo to a halt. The ground was soggy under the wheels outside the city, but it would be better not to seek the best spot so early in their tenure in Fixer City. Once they knew the hierarchies, they could establish their place.

"What a dank place," Maybel heard Mapan grumble as he dismounted from his horse, having ridden beside the waggon protectively. He had spent his savings on food for his new horse before leaving Cainton, but Maybel still did not expect Mapan to keep the steed longer than a few mooncycles. The horse, dubbed "Too jumpy," or T.J., was a novelty that would lose its appeal soon. Like Maybel, Mapan had a short attention span.

"It's a camp," Tostig pointed out as he stepped down the waggon's ladder. At his tallest, Tostig still just reached Maybel's mid-thigh, but neither Maybel nor Mapan dared bring attention to Tostig's diminutive size. Maybel also used the steps to come down from the driver's seat although she could have done it in a single stride. She held the hem of her dancing dress high above the mud, displaying her long legs deliberately for onlookers. Her fake-gold bangles tinkled but were soon drowned out by the squelch of mud underfoot.

Like an alley behind a theater in Cainton. More musk but less urine.

Mapan took the bridle and saddle off T.J., and Tostig saw to the mules. It had been years since Tostig had expected her to help with animals.

Maybel turned her attention to the clearing they had found among the waggons and tents of the unmarked section of the army. Fixer City was a haven for merchants and tradespeople who wanted to supply the thousands on the march, but it came with its share of thieves and pimps. Who had noticed them so far?

Ostensibly, she collected the tinder from the back of the waggon, arranged it in the middle of their clearing, then spoke the activation word to make the wood light. She watched her new neighbors closely as she went through the motions.

They met at the flames created by Tostig's enchanted kindling. She nibbled on leftovers from breakfast and promised to explore Fixer City to find something better, preferably with better company.

"They will be moving first thing in the morning," Tostig warned as he found a stone to pull up to the fire and sat down. He had a new trinket—some spoon with an ornate handle—and was already tinkering with the tip of it. "Do not forget why we are here."

She smiled at him sweetly, but his attention was on the spoon, and she was certain her performance was missed.

Mapan, on the other hand, was snickering as he pulled out a knife. He held one low at his side in readiness, then drew another and flipped it over his fingers in a continuous loop. The message was clear; between the enchanted wood and the finesse of their fighter, the Double Blades were no easy target for pimps or thieves who were watching.

The oddest thing about Mapan's display was that their real power was not visible, Maybel mused. The one person the onlookers likely ignored was the important one, the second blade in their "double blades."

"Do not stay out too late," Tostig added.

"I will not be long. I just want to get to know the area," she assured her patron.

"Get to know some young Esparan fighter is more like it," Mapan quipped from his crouch in the dirt.

"I just got tired of you, Mapan," she replied.

Tostig chuckled as indignantly Mapan rose from his crouch. "Well goaded," he said. "Sit down, Mapan, and ignore her. Baiting, I can allow, but I will not have open conflict."

She watched the debate in Mapan's eyes, but Tostig's word was law when they were working. Mapan returned to his crouch.

Maybel flashed another smile to the fighter before tossing her golden locks over one exposed shoulder and sauntering off. Another city, another show, another mission. Someone would want warm company tonight. The more knowledgeable the person, the better. It may take a few days, but she would find the needed informants. One *last* job, she hoped.

Once they had collected the bounty on Master Kitable, she would never have to tolerate squelching mud soaking her sandals, the stink of animals in her nostrils, or Mapan's teasing again.

Chapter 6

As Darknim drew back the flap to the birthing tent, a strong iron scent hit Carsh. Within, three women crouched around a fourth, who lay against a heap of furs. The blood had soaked through their garments and deep into the ground around the birthing mother. They had feral looks in their eyes, like cornered fighters. Although she hardly moved, the central woman still had life in her.

Like Carsh, it visibly took Tohmas a moment to gather himself at the gruesome sight.

With Darknim's prompting, Tohmas spoke to the unborn child, somehow not sneering at the absurd thought of conversing with an infant. The woman nodded gratefully when Tohmas finished pledging his status as Layla's eldafather.

Fresh contractions hit the woman. At her screams, her attendants went back to work.

Carsh felt unusually helpless. He had never attended a birth before and had not expected them to be so bloody. As a knife dancer, he could kill a magic-using flyer with a single knife from a hundred paces away, but he had no idea what to do with a baby. He and his brother were both childless. The assorted women who visited Tohmas and left before nightfall were never prospective mothers. Carsh knew the protectors—and Kitable more recently, to Carsh's amusement—were tracking the women, watching for babies to be born. None of Tohmas' lovers, to Tohmas' relief, had ever become pregnant. That was deliberate.

The Esparans did not know Tohmas' heart was Rydan. To have a child of his born to a woman he had not claimed implied the woman had power over him and had the right to keep the child. It would be slander against him.

But the Esparans believed in blood rights. Bastards were not ideal, but they might be better than nothing.

As Carsh watched the struggling mother, one attending woman stood abruptly up. "The head's in place! Push!"

A final shudder coursed over the mother, every muscle down to those between the ribs contracting. The mother's screech was savage, sending a shiver down Carsh's spine.

But a red-covered infant dropped into the hands of one of the attending women, an elder Carsh knew belonged among the Circle of the Raven. Although the snowy-owl-aspected leader was a caster in her own right, Carsh felt no magic on her as she placed the baby on her knee and felt the tiny chest. A long chord of red and purple tethered the slimy child to its mother still.

Babies were meant to cry, weren't they? Why was Layla silent?

"The heart beats," the elder said in a squawking croak. Another of the attending women had swiftly tied a hide strip in an elaborate double knot around the cord. She sliced between the knots with a swift gesture, releasing the infant.

The good cheer at finding a heartbeat was short-lived. Blood poured anew from between the mother's legs around the tied cord.

With pale eyes almost as yellowed as the woman's teeth, the elder extended the child, no bigger than a hawk, to the celebrant who had followed Tohmas in. "Care for child, Celebrant. We care for mother."

"Tie these behind my neck," came the immediate response from the celebrant as she produced two strips of material from her sleeves. Tohmas was quick to obey her. The straps pulled her sleeves back and exposed her hands. She accepted the child and started clearing the fluid from its face with soft hide.

Layla did not move.

The celebrant alternated between swinging the infant and clearing the nose and mouth while chanting prayers. Carsh watched, wondering what he could do. Darknim was nearly ashen. Tohmas held a hand on the Northlander's shoulder in support. They were all helpless, the child's fate in the hands of the celebrant with them. The woman was a Celebrant of the Loving Mother Ocea. It was the best help they could have asked for.

As Carsh fidgeted, his knife playing over his fingers, he heard his bracelets rattle.

The knucklebones of Carsh's dead friends accompanied him in the grass bunches around his wrists. Each knucklebone was an anchor for one of those passed souls, carried to provide guidance and protection for the bearer. They spoke to him now.

He pulled off the grass from his splint and, in the middle of one of the celebrant's swings, slipped it over the ankle of the newborn.

The spirits of his friends were with him through every endeavor, working tirelessly to defend both him and his cause. Darknim was a friend. If the spirits were willing, they could extend their blessing to the Northlander and his new daughter.

Unable to do more, Carsh paced the tent's perimeter, feeling too restless to stand still.

The celebrant noticed the grass but did not change what she was doing until, after four swings and several washes of the child's face, she pinched the toe, and the child cried out.

DoomDragon's face lit up. A grin split his thick beard, the likes of which Carsh never expected to see again. After a final check of the infant, the celebrant passed her to Darknim, who coddled her tenderly, wrapping her in warm furs.

The mother was unconscious, but the elder and her women were still working away with bandages and honey as Carsh circled them. The woman lived yet.

Carsh heard Tohmas excuse himself from the company of the new father, and he hastened to join his brother. They needed to be easy to find as the army prepared for departure. They had told no one where they had gone. Their brief reprise from the politics of Espar was over. Layla had accepted Tohmas as her eldafather. She had joined the world after all.

Darknim thanked Carsh for the help and then knowingly handed back the bracelet. Its duty was done. The grasses had a tinge of red on them now, and Carsh dared not don the bracelet until he could clean it, lest he be accused of wearing the Chief's red.

"What is that?" the celebrant asked in a tired voice as they left the birthing tent. She pointed at his bracelet.

She had saved Darknim's baby. He was confident the blessings of Ocea were with her. "*SohlCahger*," he replied.

"A soul catcher?" she echoed, surprising him by correctly translating the Rydan. "What purpose does such a thing have on an infant? What were you doing with that child's soul?"

As Wisavi Kitable often reminded Carsh, the soul was the domain of celebrants. The wisavi was very powerful, but he could never touch a soul. Celebrants, on the other hand, specialized in just that.

"*Nawd' er sohl*," Carsh corrected. "*Id be sohls o me fawllowa.*"

Thankfully, he had confused her, and Tohmas got to take over the conversation. There were advantages to avoiding their language.

"The bones in the SoulCatcher," the Prince of Galanth said in proper Esparan, "focus the spirits of dead friends so they can guide and protect the living. He was transferring the attention of those spirits to the child to guide her soul, not to harm her."

They passed through the last of the Northlander pelt and whalebone tents, transitioning through the barren space between the city and the Northlanders. Carsh eyed the soldiers watching them from the defenses, but they looked lazy and uninterested in Carsh or his brother.

The woman did not seem to like the answer, for a frown wrinkled her otherwise pretty face.

"You should not have let me near DoomDragon's child," she said in a voice that reminded Carsh of his mother.

His brother raised an eyebrow at her tone. Tohmas was probably thinking the same as Carsh was. They often did.

"I told you how I feel about Calanor," the woman explained.

She could see their confusion, which spoke well of her.

"Surely you know what DoomDragon did to Calanor!" she exclaimed in protest.

"Saved his life," Tohmas calmly replied. "Twice."

She was so surprised that she stopped walking. The prince was forced to pause in the space between, now beyond the Northlanders but not quite at Narsol. The land between had been packed by the passage of feet, footprints deep enough to make puddles of their own.

"Saved his life?" she snapped in the same commanding voice. This time, Carsh smiled to hear it. Strong women were fun.

Tohmas' firm voice matched her. "Celebrant Corolys, Calanor was chased out of our camp by a mob. DoomDragon took him in despite knowing the man was sworn to Galanth. Darknim then disobeyed his patron's order to kill Calanor and instead turned him loose near our camp so we could recover him. Yes, he cut off his hands and pulled out his tongue. We were at war! He could hardly release a prisoner he had treated as a guest in his tent without at least trying to ensure they did not provide us with reconnaissance."

She said nothing but started moving once more. The way she chewed her bottom lip showed she was still thinking.

"I suggest you talk it over with Calanor and Darknim. I understand they play Royal Courts regularly," Tohmas said.

They arrived at the looming gates. The day had taken off, the people bustling with animals and goods. A steady line of merchants headed out into the camp, restocking supplies before the departure.

"Prince Tohmas," she decided, pulling them to another halt before crossing into the city. "I would join you if you allow."

It would come down to whether Tohmas believed her to be a true celebrant, Carsh reckoned. Putting a false celebrant in charge of a gathering in their midst would do nothing to help their purpose; that was a mistake they had made before. Tohmas had to be confident Ocea's favor was with Corolys before he allowed her to join the celebrants he had assembled in the wake of the purge.

"Why?" Tohmas asked.

"Because..." She glanced across the gap to the Northlander camp in hesitation that made Carsh doubt her despite the strength of her words. "Because, whether you realize it or not, you are bridging three worlds in this army of yours. Religion is the one thing all three sides have in common. If you want to use that, you must avoid the cursed three and move to a blessed four. Yes, I will be with Calanor, but I want to be a part of what you have started. You need a balanced circle of four gods. Prince Tohmas, you need me."

The look in Tohmas' eyes—the look that made him look like a younger boy in search of worms to chase the girls with—gave Carsh the answer.

"King," Carsh corrected her. When he got her baffled stare, he justified, "'Ee be king, naw prince."

"If you can bring yourself to swear an oath to the *King* of Espar in front of your goddess, I welcome you," Tohmas agreed.

It was nice to be back south. The dancing kept Shimmer warm, but her flimsy garb had left her chilly before and after performances. With summer inching in and their lives driven south with Fixer City, she could finally shed her heavy cloak.

Her father came up behind her to fasten the clasp of her dress, then laid two ribbons down the length of her back. He was abnormally quiet as they prepared the show against Narsol's smooth stone walls.

She knew he disapproved of this night's performance. Their audience was dwindling. With the war over, the wandering tradespeople, merchants, tailors, and blacksmiths of Fixer City headed back to more lucrative regions. It was easy to understand. Fixer City consisted of people seizing a short-term opportunity. They were returning home to their families now. She did not begrudge them that.

Dust argued that even the population within Narsol that was slowly sticking their heads outside of their city were too few to warrant a performance. Her regulars had a new city to explore and might not bother with her show. But the Rydans, who shied from the city, would attend her dances and happily throw away the useless coins they had accumulated. Shimmer was certain that they were the real reason Dust was nervous.

Shimmer had no fear of Rydans, for Sabian always chaperoned their presence. The boy had yet to miss or fail to resolve any altercation. Further, Shimmer had no less than a dozen defensive spells hovering around her, along with a half-dozen offensive ones. She could handle anyone's advances, and her father knew it. She wasn't sure how a Rydan would take her casting, knowing they were aggressively fearful of magic, but she was confident she could protect herself.

Working to undermine Dust's comfort further, rumors had reached them that a Rydan woman had been asking after Shimmer for two nights.

No one seemed to know anything about the woman except that she was one of only a handful of women ever seen outside the Rydan camp.

The strange Rydan woman was only one piece of news in the busy day. The camp was dividing, people quickly packing up while others prepared for another long march. The official announcement had not been made yet, but rumors abounded in the dusky evening.

Prince Tohmas planned to conquer all of Espar. Any who suspected they were allied to the wrong side quickly cleared out.

By nightfall, only a quarter of Fixer City remained.

A proper performer was never seen before the show, but Dust's speculations about dwindling attendance saw Shimmer peeking out from behind the Match and Mixer waggon to check on the crowd. The wall of Narsol rose at her back.

The typical gathering of Rydans, with their patched hide clothes and grass-and-bone bracelets, milled around the fire in the company of both known and unknown Esparans. Sabian perched in his customary place on a nearby waggon's canopy, but to her surprise, Prime Protector Carsh sat with him. Carsh had attended dances before but infrequently. She had to wonder why the Rydan, whose sole duty was to defend the prince, was not at Tohmas' side.

By Carsh's anxious fidgeting on the canopy and his constant glances toward the city walls, he seemed to be wondering the same thing. The prime protector only left Prince Tohmas at Tohmas' specific request. Perhaps, Shimmer mused, Sabian had dragged the Rydan out to the dance to distract him, but it seemed unlikely to work. She had never seen the prime protector so agitated.

As she watched him, Carsh went uncharacteristically still. Following his riveted gaze into the crowd, Shimmer saw new arrivals.

The woman at the head of the group was taller than Shimmer by a hand, which put her only slightly under Carsh's towering frame. She was undoubtedly Rydan with her lean features and high cheekbones, her long blond hair worn in a braid around her head. Her attire was not modest: two strips of hide crossed her chest to cover her, and her skirt was two flaps, one in the front and one behind. Her muscled arms bore no grass bracelets, but none of the women following her wore them either. Shimmer assumed them to be a man's tradition.

The woman's entourage dispersed as she advanced, seeming to assign themselves to Rydans in Shimmer's crowd randomly. The lead woman selected a Rydan bearing a wildcat tattoo over his chest, but the man turned away from her. Around her, the other women were accepted by every man they approached, settling into places on the laps of their chosen suitor. Only the lead woman was left standing alone, and that fact, for a moment, seemed to confuse her.

She checked her surroundings suspiciously.

Carsh dropped from the overhang and stalked toward her. Seeing him changed the woman's confusion to anger. The Rydan woman stiffened as Carsh circled her, his posture low and poised.

He spoke, but Shimmer was too far away to hear what was said. The woman took it all in stride until Carsh touched her.

Her hand shot out to slap the tips of his fingers from her shoulder, but the knife dancer was faster. Even with only one arm readily available—the other trapped in a splint—he caught both her hands. With a smile that made Shimmer shiver even from twenty paces away, Carsh placed a gentle, almost sweet, kiss on the side of the woman's neck.

The stranger recoiled and spat something in Rydan. The prime protector released his hold.

The woman drew her knife, and Carsh smirked, unfazed. As she endured the steady stare of the best fighter in Espar, the woman deliberately lowered her blade. Without fear, the prime protector turned his back and strolled back to Sabian.

There was silence around the campfire.

After a pause to gather herself, the woman squared her shoulders and approached the Match and Mixer.

Shimmer ducked back behind the waggon, suddenly conscious of her appearance. She had quietly acknowledged her eighteenth birthday early that spring and looked precisely her age. Hard work kept her body fit and fed. Her toned muscles made her appear strong, although she carried no weapon. She would look like a child next to the woman! Rydans understood only one thing: strength. If she wished to be taken seriously, she would need to perform to compensate for her physical inequalities. But she could not use her magic. Rydans hated magic and casters with a fanatic fervor. If Shimmer were seen as a caster, a "flyer" as they called them, she would be hunted and killed. Even the best caster feared a mob.

CHAPTER 6

"Papa!" Shimmer said, grabbing Dust and spinning him around. "That's the woman looking for me! Invite her back here!"

"Now?" Dust choked out.

"Yes, quickly! Our space. Our terms."

They had no time to discuss it.

He followed her lead. Erasing the concern from his face, Dust swept out from behind the waggon. Shimmer waited, chewing on a lock of her hair anxiously. She yanked the hair aside when Dust returned, his brightly colored garb a sharp contrast to the skin and hide of the woman who followed him. A flesh-tone necklace with the bones woven through it caught the lamplight of Match and Mixer, forming a lattice over the woman's neck.

For the four paces she took to advance, Shimmer felt the Rydan examining her. She wondered belatedly if this Rydan could feel magic like Carsh could. Little tricks could be explained as sleights of hand or misdirection, but any real magic would bring about fierce retribution from the magic-hating people, and Shimmer had dozens of invisible spells around her, awaiting an activation word.

When the woman did not immediately draw her blade, Shimmer assumed she was, like most of the population, blind to magic.

"Ya be Shimmer," the woman declared.

Shimmer bowed deeply in a profoundly Esparan manner. It was polite, and she suspected the woman would know as much.

"I hear you have been looking for me. How may I be of service?" She kept her voice diplomatic but her stance confident. It helped to know her magic would defend her should she require it.

"Teach us," the woman said in a heavy accent, "dance like ya."

Knowing that if she agreed too quickly, she would label herself as the servant and never again be seen as an equal, Shimmer sidled back and examined her visitor as the woman had examined her. "Why would I teach you or your women?" she retorted in a voice made strong by practice. "If you all learn to dance like me, your men will no longer come to watch my shows. No, if I teach you to dance, you must come dance with me here, at my fire."

No others in Fixer City could boast Rydans as part of their shows. She could double her audience with curious Esparans, in addition to keeping the regular Rydans interested. Perhaps they would find ways to incorporate more traditional Rydan forms. This was an unprecedented opportunity if she could convince the woman to join her.

The silence that followed was as deep as Lour's mines and as heavy as the walls of Narsol. Shimmer waited with her arms crossed and willed her gooseflesh away. The weather was warm, but the woman's stare was the Ice Ocean atop the highest peak of the DragonTail mountains.

For the second time, the woman examined Shimmer. The second scrutiny took longer than the first as if Shimmer's words had rendered the previous assessment invalid.

"*Evry nyed ta much. Tree nyed a kardercyke.*"

The accent was tricky, but Shimmer understood her well enough. Three nights a quartercycle.

Her heart skipped into her throat. She was bargaining with a Rydan. Days spent tending the shop had taught Shimmer a thing or two about haggling. "Three nights?" she considered aloud. "Not worth my time. To do a proper job of teaching, you must commit seven nights a quartercycle."

The Rydan slipped into to same hip-cocked position Shimmer held. She even crossed her arms as she said, "*Foh nyeds.*"

"Five at the least," Shimmer immediately countered, and the Rydan nodded concession. Shimmer let herself smile. "Good. Come by before midday for your lessons. I will determine when you or any of your ladies are fit to perform publicly. Take your seat tonight, and pay attention. My audience awaits."

With a victorious grin—a sure sign the Rydan had gotten what she wanted—the woman took several steps back, then returned to the audience in front of the waggon.

Shimmer let out a long, slow breath. Her nerves sagged. She would need to hide for a few moments and call it preparations just so her knees did not quake when she tried to dance.

"Impressive," a young voice said.

Shimmer had not noticed that Sabian had snuck around the waggon to watch but found him behind her, hidden in the lee of Match and Mixer. By his position, she suspected he had been ready to get involved, maybe even defend her, if things with the stranger went badly. Shimmer had once done that for him, and both recognized the debt that was due.

Sabian was about the same age as Shimmer—nearly seventeen. He could not grow a beard yet, and his hair was cut short in a Rydan style, complete with grease to hold it back. Despite his appearance, he was Esparan by blood. He had been taken under Carsh's tutelage and could fight like a Rydan, but he was still Esparan.

But now that the woman had moved off, the expression on Sabian's face was disbelief. Since he typically kept his countenance neutral, the obvious display warranted a raised eyebrow from her. To her amazement, he explained.

"Darcina is the most powerful woman in the Outlands," he said. "You were brave to bargain with her. Only Tamv, Tohmas, and Carsh outrank her, even here."

"So that was what Carsh was doing?" Shimmer replied. "Outranking her?"

Sabian's broadened shoulders shrugged under his non-descript tunic. Unlike most soldiers, who wore their green tabards religiously, Sabian was never seen in green anymore. He was not sworn to Tohmas' army any longer. Sabian belonged to Carsh.

"She must remember her place," he finished with a glance to where Darcina had passed. "I should not have been so surprised," he said to himself as he headed back to his canopy vantage point. "You are one of the most powerful women in this army. She saw that." He disappeared around the side of the shop waggon.

Dust stepped into Sabian's place, handing Shimmer charmed loop earrings. His hands were shaking as well, another one of her defenders who had been at the ready, she suspected.

Shimmer unconsciously fastened the earrings in place, her thoughts elsewhere. "Papa, do you think I am powerful?"

Dust scoffed lovingly. "Shim, you have gleaned more from our rotten books than I ever could. Even Wisavi Kitable—"

"Not magic," she corrected. "Sabian said I was one of the most powerful women in the camp. Do you think that's true?"

As a finishing touch, he tied black and gold ribbons into her crimson hair. "I suppose so," he said. "I mean, can you think of anyone who could force you to do anything you did not want to do?"

Carsh could, Shimmer thought. She had seen him in action against casters and knew he could withstand almost anything she could conjure.

Worse, he would kill her for using magic on him. So long as she kept Prince Tohmas among her allies, she was somewhat protected. The only other person capable of contending with her was Master Kitable.

The thought of the Master Wizard of Galanth made her smile.

Her father saw her wistful expression and chuckled. "Now go dance, oh sovereign of the slums, and enjoy yourself."

It was impossible not to when she danced, especially with Kitable in her thoughts.

With renewed spring in her step, Shimmer sauntered to her waiting audience. As she came into view, a cheer went up.

Let the performance begin.

Maybel sat inside at the low table instead of at a fire outside, the waggon as warm as a summer's day thanks to Tostig's enchantments. She enjoyed listening to the drip from a blocked gutter outside when the door opened, and a gust of damp air flooded in. Tostig stood in the doorway, his mohawk flat with the wet.

"Let's go!" he said.

"Now? We just got warmed up! And it's ugly out there!" Maybel snatched the teapot up and filled a cup, hoping enticing him with a hot drink would slow him down. She'd not even unpacked.

The Double Blade leader shrugged under his too-big coat, dropping a water flow onto the floor. "Doesn't matter. We have an opportunity. Let's go."

Abandoning the teacup, Maybel stood from the low table. "Just let me get dressed. I assume there is no reason to be in dancing clothes with no performance."

Tostig blinked at her in surprise, finally recognizing her attire was scandalous and should be adjusted. There was no talking him out of it, which was a shame. Maybel was accustomed to getting men to give her whatever she wanted when she wore the close-cut corsets of Inac's red and a ribbon skirt that showed off how little she was wearing underneath. But Tostig only ever paid attention to her when he wanted something.

CHAPTER 6

Maybel changed into a more traditional dress although it still had a plunging neckline. Advertising was an asset, even when off duty.

Retrieved her damp traveling cloak, she joined Tostig at the open door. "I thought I was meant to be winning over Master Kitable," she said.

"You are," Tostig said, turning from her and leaping off the middle step.

Maybel was suspicious. Tostig was usually more careful.

"Then why are you dragging me out into this evening when I've not prepared anything or researched anything?" she asked as she hastened to follow him.

He glanced back at her, his grin knowing. "Because I might not know where he is, but I know where he will be looking tonight! Unlike you, lounging around, I've been investigating. Come along!"

He briskly headed over the moldy-straw paths between the waggons. The rain had all but ceased, but a thick fog lingered, hiding the extensive camp set up the slope beyond the city walls, the army that could not fit within Narsol.

Mapan left his place under the awning to join them as they left the waggon; however, she didn't feel they would need him. Maybel had found Fixer City to be surprisingly safe. While there were pickpockets and thugs, most of Fixer City was tradespeople and merchants who had their society sorted out. It was fast becoming a village where everyone knew everyone. While they would not necessarily instantly trust someone, they were happy to make deals. That kept the crime down, at least the obvious kind.

The pounding drums reached her ears long before she saw the people. Once among the crowd, the source became obvious; a group of Esparans under the canopy of a colorful waggon beat out a primal rhythm for a dancer.

Tostig gestured. "There she is."

"She" was a young red-haired Esparan in a cut blouse that hung off her shoulders and ended above her navel. Jewelry sparkled from every surface—neck, ears, wrists, waist, and ankles—and the dampness made them shimmer further as she moved. Even the humidity could not make the curls of the long hair vanish. The transparent tunic and skirt showed tanned curves that gesticulated and flowed.

Tostig waited for a lull in the shouts of encouragement from the crowd. "She's called Shimmer Weaver. She dances most nights."

"She must make a fortune in her waggon after the shows," Maybel bemoaned.

Tostig shook his head. "As far as I can tell, no. She shares the waggon with her father, and even though he sometimes entertains without his daughter present, it never appears to be the other way around."

"Perhaps he has the waggon, and she goes on visits." That was Maybel's preference, as she never managed to keep both of her male companions out of the waggon when she was entertaining. Having either of the Double Blades walk in at the wrong moment was a proven disaster.

Tostig shrugged, his eyes still on the redhead. Maybel spotted the girl's father—he was among the drummers and identifiable by his matching red hair and bright, unmatched attire. He was a social creature, encouraging the drumming and chatting with the crowd equally. He had to be an entertainer, too, she surmised. By the billowing sleeves that were tightly cuffed, juggler and acrobat were her guesses.

When she looked back, Tostig's attention was still on Shimmer.

Perhaps the impervious Tostig has a flaw in his chain link yet.

"You know an awful lot about this dancer," Maybel teased. "Why all the attention?"

He scoffed. "For all my effort, you are still as dense as a log! Do not just look, Maybel! Feel! Pay attention!"

She felt nothing, even if she concentrated, but his inference was clear.

She mocked concentration, squinting at the woman. Then she leaned back with pretended surprise. "Magic," she said with hushed awe.

Her performance was wasted; Tostig rolled his eyes. "You sense nothing. You never do." He let out a theatrical sigh. "Yes, magic. Both the girl and her father."

"Wizards," she guessed, but Tostig shook his head again.

"Casters," a southern-accented voice interrupted, "like you."

By Mapan's startle, their bodyguard had not heard the stranger approach. The juggler spun with blades out. He took a quick step forward, placing himself between the new arrival and Tostig.

Maybel spun, too, then paused.

CHAPTER 6

The stranger was taller than Maybel, shorter than Mapan, and had a build that was fit but not built up. She guessed him around thirty, and his hair and beard were trimmed but not of a military style. There was nothing remarkable about him except the predominance of green and silver, Galanth colors, in every garment he wore. A belt with pouches made him look like a cutter, but there were not enough tools to make the comparison stick. Unlike the majority of people she dealt with, the man did not even carry a knife.

Maybel sat into one hip, let the traveling cloak drop off her shoulders, and flashed a smile. Except for the scowl on his face, he was a reasonably attractive man, and his colors identified him as loyal to Galanth. A useful contact?

Making a point of fiddling with her hair to draw his attention to her long locks of gold, Maybel said, "One should introduce oneself before intruding upon—"

Tostig shoved Mapan aside and placed himself in front of Maybel. "I apologize, Master Kitable," the leader of the Double Blades said. "I fear Maybel's beauty is her only asset." Maybel's patron was missing a tooth from the left side of his mouth, but the gap was only visible when he was grinning widely. Tonight she saw the hole, but the smile was still far from sincere.

She held her tongue against the insult and focused on the man she had almost dismissed as too ordinary to be of interest. Despite his physical appearance, he had to be formidable. Tostig must have been getting gooseflesh from standing so close to the wizard right now, for there must have been a hundred hovering spells and another dozen active defenses within only a stride of them. Tostig had succeeded in drawing out the elusive wizard after all.

"My face is not exactly well known," the master wizard agreed, "and it is evident she has no magic sense worth speaking of, so I will not fault her blindness."

Was that what he wanted? It made sense to avoid being a competition or threat; no magic was a good thing, as Tostig was implying. *A role to play,* Maybel decided.

Softening her expression, Maybel ostensibly checked him over, showing she was interested. A casual hand, disguised by flicking the loose curls over her shoulder, released the first knot of her blouse and let it hang farther down.

Kitable did not appear to notice. His gaze did not linger on her as she would have liked. Instead, he seemed to determine Tostig to be the leader and addressed him: "What is your business in Fixer City?"

"Oh, what concern is it of yours?" Maybel interrupted, sidling toward the caster.

"It is his business to monitor all magical things," Tostig pointed out calmly. The light tone of his correction indicated she was right to be drawing Kitable's attention as best she could.

Unfortunately, Master Kitable did not seem to agree. He did not flinch upon her approach, but the magic surrounding him made it unnecessary. She was stopped by a shield while still a stride from him.

Is there something about magic that neuters men? She knew Tostig was immune to her charms, but she had never expected a middle-aged single man to so easily dismiss her half-bare body and apparent advances.

"Our business," Tostig offered when Maybel was ignored, "is as performers and merchants. Mapan, the brute who gave you a sour look, is a well-established juggler, and I make and sell trinkets by order. Maybel..." He indicated her, trying to get the wizard to take a good look at her revealing outfit. "...dances and takes—"

"More dancers," the wizard cut in dismissively. "Just what we do not need."

Tostig's smile seeped with sincerity now, but Maybel still saw through it. She hoped Master Kitable would not be as perceptive.

"We shall endeavor to stay out of your way, Master Kitable," Tostig soothed. "Unless, of course, you would be interested in some of my work or exchanging notes or spells."

Even though his concentration was on Tostig, Master Kitable was still keeping one eye on both her and Mapan. She most noticed the glance when the colorful vision turned on her.

Her clothing showed plenty of skin, but she had not felt naked until his enchanted eyes ran over her. Life with Tostig allowed her to recognize Spell Sight by the scintillating, ever-changing colors that took over the wizard's eyes.

With a glance, his magic vision revealed every aura. Her entire collection of defensive trinkets was revealed.

Chapter 6

It would not be so for Tostig—he could mask some of his spells—but Master Kitable would still identify most of the magic surrounding him. The spell was rude, but neither she nor Tostig was in any position to argue with the Master Wizard of Galanth.

"You are wearing a Spell Sight," Kitable said once he had examined Tostig. "But there is no change to your eyes. Why do you hide it?"

Maybel's patron grinned. "I found the obvious colors a disadvantage when I wanted to observe subtly. I would be happy to provide the code, if you want, for a price of only—"

A single raised hand stopped the Double Blades leader cold. "I am not interested," Master Kitable flatly stated. With a sigh of annoyance, he added, "If you wish to stay in Fixer City, I will only interfere should you become a problem. Other than that, stay out of my way."

With a frown on her face, Maybel watched the man walk away into the shadows. Being rejected was terrible for her self-esteem. She would have to try again after a bit of research. Maybe he would like someone more intelligent, shier, more modest, or … something! She could become any person. She just needed to know what Master Kitable wanted.

Tostig should have shared her frown although for a different reason. Even if he had appeased the wizard, the sentiment had not been in any way genuine. But Tostig smiled his wide, incomplete smile, and headed back to the waggon, plans no doubt spinning in his mind now that he had met his target.

Maybel stayed to watch the redhead dance, Mapan on her shoulder protectively. It was surprisingly tricky to convince Mapan to leave, and Maybel promised she would have Tostig look over the juggler before sleep this night. The redhead was a caster, after all. Maybe she was using magic.

Chapter 7

Three days after presenting the treaty, Tohmas assembled his allies in the Soltan Hall once more. Lance wore his new green tabard and red braid to the assembly, having given his oath that afternoon forsaking Gaidol and pledging himself to Tohmas' purpose. Barnon helped Lance into a seat at the table in an ostentatious display of support.

One by one, the others arrived at the long table in the emptied stone hall, the fire blazing at the far end. Lord Darmac and Lord Hurtz took seats side by side, standing in as Clandac's support. DoomDragon's chair at Tohmas' right, marked by an axe, was notably empty; he was needed with his daughter and the weakened mother.

With Carsh representing the Rydans, he had delegates from the farther reaches of the north down the south borders along the DragonTail mountains. BookKeepers, fidgeting uncomfortably, sat on tiny stools along the closest wall, bundled in blankets. All had the squirrelly appearance Tohmas associated with the men who listened, memorized, and recorded history.

The eldest bookkeeper had a position on Tohmas' elbow. He continually sifted through his stack of letters, his skeletal fingers reorganizing them by touch. The man's stooped frame was layered with wrinkled skin and no muscle, making Tohmas wonder how the man remained upright. He squinted behind thick glasses.

"Let's hear it," Tohmas prompted once all the guests were settled.

Bookkeeper Telson smacked his lips and, without looking at the sheets in his hand, said, "Trulin sends their regrets via messenger, verified by a token. Prince Kelland has since departed Narsol, his son with him."

"Goh," Carsh said, grinning wide. "'Ee be fun ta fight."

Sol looked like a disapproving father when he frowned at Carsh. "You're looking forward to fighting the son of—"

"A challenge is always appreciated," Tohmas interrupted before they wasted time.

"The Rydans seemed restless over that decision," Lance added, his eyes on Carsh across the table. "He's here now. He's hardly protected. They thought he should fall now." Lance's tagalong Rydan cook had probably cautioned him about it.

The other assembled Esparans paled. That was not the Esparan way, but Tohmas understood, as did Lance. Usually, Lance knew such comments were better suited to private conversations, but the newest guardian had large bags under his eyes. Late nights?

"Tohmas be sayin' nah," Carsh replied helpfully, mocking an exaggerated pout.

"Of course, I let Anga leave. We need them to know we can be reasoned with." Tohmas let out a breath and faced the bookkeeper again. "What about Gaidol?"

Again without checking the sheets, BookKeeper Telson reported, "Prince Dorakon provided a written refusal, verified by a token. He was seen attending the oath of Guardian Lance Carraway but has since departed from Narsol." The glassy stare of the bookkeeper peered back at Tohmas. "Would you care to review the letter?"

Tohmas shook his head. "Nothor?" he asked instead.

The bookkeeper gave Tohmas a toothless smile. "A fairly identical letter was received from Lord Garmont just after the oath-taking. Confirmed by a token."

There was no point in dwelling on it. "Damoria?" Tohmas pressed.

Barnon snorted at the thought of Damoria and Galanth agreeing on anything. Sure enough, the bookkeeper shook his head.

"No message. Their refusal is assumed."

"Polthian?"

Telson pursed his pruned lips in a frown. Although Tohmas had not thought it impossible, the bookkeeper's face wrinkled further. "His letter, verified by token, professes neutrality," he said. Tohmas noticed the tokens on the table had been set in three piles, Polthian's standing alone by two other piles. Like him, Telson had been sorting the princedoms and had been unsure of the neutrality.

"Put him against us then. If he wants to think he is being ignored, all the better. Once the Rydans have stressed his borders enough, he'll change his mind. Forsinth?"

With a trembling hand, Telson meticulously moved Polithian's token onto the stack with Damoria, Trulin, and Nothor. He then cleared his throat. "Forsinth has agreed," he said with a rare smile. "No pledge of soldiers but terms are accepted.."

No soldiers was fine, Tohmas thought. Polthian's best warriors were sorely out of practice. It would be hard to integrate them. "At least we've got a buffer between Galanth and Polthian. Galanth?" Tohmas continued.

Telson eyed Kitable, who hung back from the table across from the other bookkeepers. "Master Kitable kindly sent the request to Guardian Vallant. He agrees to be Kingsman of Galanth but insists that I tell you he's not happy about it."

"About what I expected from Vallant," Tohmas said. "Lour?" He could already see the token bearing the anvil atop the stack of allies.

"Lour agrees. He has also pledged a seven-shard soldier and fourteen hundred men. Prince Loritat requests to return to Lour to assist with the transition."

"He knows he has to adopt our ranking system?" Tohmas knew the number of shards indicated skill, with the prince symbolically wearing eight, but that was the extent of his knowledge regarding the mountain men of Lour.

The bookkeeper nodded unsteadily. "This concludes the list. All princedoms have been accounted for." The toothless smile returned.

Nine with and five against. He had expected three against, but there was nothing more to be done. They had to move quickly.

"We march tomorrow," Tohmas declared. It was not a surprise to any assembled allies; they had been readying to march since the announcement. "You're dismissed to get organized. Lance, Sabian, and Kitable, stay. Rest of you, geddit."

The bookkeepers left first, filing out in order of age with Telson last. He took a long time to close the side door behind him. The princes-turned-kingsmen filed out through the main doors. Hurtz and Talbit were heading home shortly, the plan for their soldiers to join later. But marching immediately west was vital to prevent Tohmas' enemy from mobilizing.

War was inevitable. According to Rydan tradition, a war had to be started as it would end in celebration. He had no intention of telling the rest of his allies, but he made a few exceptions.

Sabian was a given and not Tohmas' problem. Since the opening bouts of the last war, the boy from Clandac had been following Carsh, and to Tohmas' surprise, the prime protector had accepted the Esparan knife thrower. Over the last while, Sabian had doubled his already-impressive skill and found an unexpected place among the Rydans. The last time Carsh had introduced Sabian, it had been as a Follower, the only Esparan Follower any Rydan acknowledged.

But tonight, that changed. Tonight, Tohmas intended to recognize the Followers he had made among the Esparans. With luck, they would be accepted as readily as Sabian had been.

Tohmas had been Kitable's patron since Prince Habal had died, but the new King of Espar had not considered the wizard a true Follower by Rydan standards until recently. He was prepared to take up the role of the Leader now; he would do all in his power to help Kitable achieve his goals, knowing he had the wizard's absolute fealty in return.

Lance had first become a friend, but with his abandonment of Gaidol in favor of Tohmas, Tohmas felt the relationship solid enough to accept the man as a Follower, whether Lance expected it or not.

The third Follower would be unable to attend. He had a new baby.

Once all eavesdropping bookkeepers were gone, Kitable finally sat down. Sabian, who had stood behind Carsh throughout the meeting, took the seat his Leader pointed at. He sat forward on his chair, attentive and wary.

Tohmas let himself relax. His first words were for Lance: "You look awful."

"Sorry. I was trying to hide it, but hey, I feel like demon shit, so I suppose I look it," Lance answered. "Nothing to do about it. It'll pass."

Besides fatigue, Tohmas could see nothing wrong with the man, so he took his Follower at his word. "Tonight might help. I asked you all to stay to invite you out."

"Out?" Lance replied blearily. "We are in a walled city. Where is out?'"

"Rydan camp," Kitable replied unexpectedly.

Tohmas was impressed. "You already knew, Kit? Carsh didn't tell you, did he?"

Kitable gave a slow shrug and avoided making eye contact. "Before you confessed the two protectors we thought were tutoring you in hiding died, my scrys had accidentally reflected on your life in the Outlands," Kitable admitted. "I know you were raised among them."

Tohmas forced down his unease. Chief Tamv would be furious that Tohmas' history was known, but it was unlikely the wisavi would be anywhere near Tamv. The Chief and his Followers had headed south before the winter war. Tohmas was safe enough; he trusted Kitable to keep the secret.

"I don't mind you knowing, but I'd rather the rest of Espar not think me barbaric if you don't mind."

Sure enough, Kitable shrugged again. "I have told no one else so far. Why would I start now? It has no bearing on current affairs."

"I appreciate your discretion. As for tonight," Tohmas continued, addressing Lance, "Rydans believe that wars end as they begin. So tonight is going to be fun."

Lance cocked his head, his expression confused.

"If you want to finish the war celebrating victory," Tohmas explained, "then you have to start the war celebrating victory. We are going to celebrate, Rydan style, and I want you two to come."

Rather abruptly, the wisavi looked as if his collar was too tight. "By the hells, why would I want—?"

"Because it's educational, Kit. Besides, you are considered my wisavi. They need to see you to respect you."

Kitable made a face. "What are the odds of running into the Pack Runner?"

Among the Rydans, knife dancers were trained to protect the Outlands from magic. There were only two knife dancers alive, and

Carsh was already familiar with Kitable. The other knife dancer was in the camp, a dozen hounds on his heel. He was a threat to everything magical.

At first, Tohmas thought it extremely unlikely—Crawthran had no interest in people, drink, or song and so would not attend—but he had to reconsider. They were going into the Rydan camp for the first time in mooncycles, which meant something unique to the Pack Runner. For the first time in years, the Hand, Arm, and Shoulder were all going to be together.

Only the Pack Runner would recognize the event, which was how Tohmas wanted it. Every First Clan Rydan knew that the sons of Tamv, Tohmas and Carsh, had been marked by the Pack Runner's blade and were now identified as Hand and Arm. The problem was the rank of Shoulder.

Out on a frozen lake before the last such celebration, Sabian had been invited to fight the Pack Runner in a private spar. To Tohmas' shock, the Pack Runner had been impressed enough to mark Sabian across his left shoulder. Although Sabian still appeared oblivious to the meaning of the cut, Tohmas and Carsh understood all too well.

Chief Tamv bore a scar across his shoulder, delivered by the previous Pack Runner's blade. Even now, Tohmas' adopted father was saluted as the Shoulder by the First Clan. Without divine intervention, Tohmas never intended to tell the chief that he had been replaced.

So long as the Rydans did not know, they were safe. But would the Pack Runner be interested in visiting all three of his marked men?

"Ya be wisavi," Carsh pointed out, and Tohmas agreed. He could not be sure they would not meet Crawthran, but the title they had bestowed on the wizard would keep him safe.

"But that does not—" Tohmas began to warn, but Kitable was already ahead of him.

"Every spell I have on me is subtle," he assured Tohmas. "Emotion controls, little deflections, and such. Mostly thought magic, so not overt enough to spook anyone. I know Rydans hate magic. I won't cast, at least not obviously, around them."

"Thought magic? Wasn't that abhorrent to you?" Tohmas teased when he realized his wizard had anticipated his plans for the evening.

"What I hate is domination thought magic. I cast creation thought magic. Big difference," Kitable corrected.

Knowing magic was not his region of expertise, Tohmas let it pass. "So, are you coming, Lance?" he asked instead.

When Lance nodded, Tohmas was not convinced the Gaidolon had any idea he was agreeing. He seemed surprised when Tohmas clapped him on the back and said, "Excellent! A couple of quick things. Since I don't know how many Esparans have figured this out, let me clarify." He pressed his right hand into his left palm in salute. "Right hand to palm is a salute to the Hand. That means me. If you get stuck, use it to say you are loyal to me above all else. Right hand to arm..." He showed the salute. "...is Carsh, but you shouldn't need it. Lastly, right hand to shoulder," he finished with the shoulder-slapping salute, "is to the Shoulder, Chief Tamv. If you are confronted by a salute to the Shoulder, copy it. Otherwise, use mine."

He briefly wondered if either man would figure out that the priority of Tamv's salute meant Tohmas himself was the Chief's inferior.

"You are my Followers among the Rydans," he continued, "and that means you are immediately protected and ought to find fast friends, but do not be afraid to stand up for yourself. They will want to test you. You will not get yourself killed so long as you show strength. Try to enjoy yourselves."

There was a contemplative silence, but he got two nods. He did not worry about how Kitable would show his strength without magic; the Rydans knew Kitable was his wisavi, which meant he was a wise man, not a fighter. Lance was a different matter, but he knew the man could handle it.

"Let's go," Tohmas finalized, leading them out.

The protectors begrudgingly obeyed when Tohmas sent them away and led the party into the Rydan camp.

The celebration was already underway when Lance entered the Rydan camp with Tohmas, Kitable, and Carsh. Sentries lined the fields they had claimed outside Narsol, a wide circle of hide-clad warriors on guard around the festivities and the horses grazing in herds beyond.

CHAPTER 7

The smoke rose hot and high from dozens of fires, each person's height. He had no idea where they had found so much firewood.

As they arrived, a gathering of Rydans rushed out, greeting them with the fist-in-palm salute Tohmas had called his own. Another group used the hand-to-arm salute to surround the prime protector. Sabian knew these fighters; he greeted them with teases and jokes in smooth Rydan. Sori had taught Lance various Rydan words, but her speech was quiet and deliberate, not this rambling, slurred version. As many Rydans spoke Esparan, Lance lowered his voice to ask Kitable, "Did you put up a Translation?"

The wizard smiled through his neat goatee. "Naturally. They may not like what I do, but only Carsh has shown an ability to detect things already in place." Kitable shrugged. "They are teasing Sabian, as near as I can tell. The others are running jibes at Carsh and Tohmas both. The king is holding his own."

As Kitable reassured Lance, Tohmas threw one of the Rydans over his shoulder in a dead man's carry. The entire group laughed at the unfortunate man. Tohmas flipped the man over his shoulder, and the Rydan rolled out of the toss, laughing the whole time.

Lance's fatigue had followed him through the fields, but it vanished when Tohmas pointed at Kitable and him. "Wisavi" was one word Lance understood. The rest was muddled except for his name. An introduction, he assumed.

Showing he was as fluent as Carsh, Tohmas rattled something more and headed farther into the camp.

Lance had to pause, surrounded by Tohmas' Rydans. The hairs on his neck rose. Rydans, as his dealings with Sori and Tanuka had taught him, believed in only one thing: strength. He had to prove himself.

A year ago, he would have been weak. Even now, he was not nearly as strong as some of them, but training with the protectors had improved his skills and, more importantly, given him confidence. He was fast enough to twist his arm aside when one of them, like a taunt, poked at him from the side.

There were chuckles but no words, making Kitable unhelpful.

The Rydans were armed—Lance was yet to see a Rydan who was not—but only one had drawn his weapon. The Rydan was the same age as Tohmas, a decade behind Lance, but had Carsh's rib-showing litheness. The man's chest tattoo depicted a fish with a long, sword-like nose in mid-jump, but Lance had no idea if the creature was one of myth or reality. The dagger, on the other hand, was real.

Tohmas had said to show strength.

The blade came at him directly. The Rydan was half as fast as Carsh; Lance found it surprisingly easy to catch the hand delivering the attack.

The Rydan's left hand was suddenly holding a knife. The second attack arched at Lance's chest. Lance immediately had his knife out—he did not have time for his sword—and deflected the attack with enough force to put himself into a comfortable fighting stance, ready for the next.

There, they paused, the other Rydans watching but not getting involved. After a twenty count, with a grin and a nod, the stranger slapped both blades away and placed his right hand into his left palm in salute to the Hand.

Lance surveyed the others before coming out of his fighting stance and putting away his knife. Uncertain, he copied the gesture of allegiance to Tohmas.

"I be Krahr," the Rydan introduced with a tooth-filled grin. "Ya be goh! I be lyhkin.'"

It was hard to tell if the man was speaking Esparan or Rydan, so Lance decided it was probably both. Letting the man put an arm around his shoulder, Lance relied on Kitable to translate the Rydan. Krahr was delighted to discover the wisavi could understand Rydan. Lance had, he discovered, been accepted. The show of a willingness to fight, along with a degree of competence, proved that Tohmas had chosen well. It came down to the same thing that had somehow convinced Lance to come down into the Rydan camp in the first place: trust. These men trusted Tohmas' judgment. They had to, by their own traditions, check, but it was a formality only.

Krahr assigned himself as Lance's guide and knew just enough Esparan to fill in blanks when Kitable was unavailable. No one tested the wisavi as they had Lance, but Lance understood from Krahr that no one could compete in matters of the mind. Tamv had taken his wisavis south and left his fighters. The Rydans here were for battle. They could not judge a wisavi.

They made their way between campfires and hovel-like shelters decorated with shells. The noise came in waves, at first a distant rumble, then a growing surge, and finally an all-encompassing roar. The music of drums and flutes followed the pattern, people cheering with horns lifted or wineskins tossed between them. Wildwater was shared readily. Between the smoke and the crowds, Lance lost all track of Tohmas and, ultimately, Kitable as well.

The dancing was impossible, the games challenging, and the conversations complex, but Lance did his best and was met with Krahr's encouragement at each turn. The Rydan even ensured Lance had a full cup, although Lance made a point of spilling it instead of drinking too much. But there were times he could not avoid joining someone for a drink, and his head was suitably swimming soon enough. Krahr paced him, handing him a muddy drink he did not know instead of more wildwater every few horns.

When the knot in his stomach loosened, Lance lost his trepidation. Wildwater seemed to chase out the heartache. And so the pain did not quite go away. Valia's tear-covered face still flashed into his mind throughout the evening, making him wince. He wasn't coming back. He had promised, and he was breaking that promise by walking away from Dorakon. He had failed her.

Lance downed another horn of wildwater, and the regret lessened again.

It wasn't his fault. Dorakon kept them apart. It had been a fantasy anyway. A prince's daughter? Lance had worked hard for his rank, but he was not what Dorakon wanted, regardless of his rank or family ties. *Perhaps despite my family ties*, he thought bitterly. Blood feuds were not easily dismissed.

Dorakon would find her a suitable husband. She would be married, run the manor, have children...

He felt sick and was filled with the desire to hit something. By the next time he saw her, she would be married to someone else. He was breaking her heart, just as he was breaking his own, all because Lance didn't want to play Dorakon's game anymore.

"Mo?" Krahr asked, taking Lance's empty horn. The pounding drum nearby forced the Rydan to shout the question.

"Hells yes," Lance replied. Valia's face tickled the edge of his mind through the blur of the drink, and his heart ached again.

While Krahr left to refill their cups, Lance sat on a stone. The world seemed to be gently tilting from side to side. Sitting was prudent.

His stone put him next to one of the bonfires, where a dozen men and women danced, leaping like deer around the raging fire. Three drum players sat clustered to his right while one, wearing a drum around his neck, spun around the fires with the dancers. Voices were raised in a kind of shouted song, but the words were utterly lost in the haze of his numbed skull.

Beyond the drummers, a Rydan man struck a woman across the face. She collapsed in the trampled scrub. The man grabbed her wrists and pulled her to her feet.

According to Tohmas' explanations earlier that year, every woman in the Rydan camp was married to one of the fighters, but that did not mean the man dragging this woman up was her husband. At the least, the husband must have given permission or been outranked for the woman to be treated so poorly. She could not retaliate without risking a worse beating. A wave of pity swelled in Lance. Poor girl. Poor ... Tanuka?

Lance shot off his stone in charge. He leaped the seated drummers and drove his shoulder into the man holding the Rydan woman he had once sheltered through a Northlander winter.

The Rydan rolled to the blow and spun quickly, his blades coming to bear, but Lance had his sword in hand. He placed himself between Tanuka and the attacker. "I will not have her treated like that!" he shouted.

For a flicker, the Rydan hesitated. The drums stopped, and into the pause, Lance heard a shout.

Krahr arrived at Lance's side, with a dozen other Rydans following him. Every Follower of the Hand heeded the call at a sprint, bone and iron blades brandished. Before the Rydan who had hit Tanuka could decide if he should attack the Esparan in front of him, Lance had a small army assembled around him. Tanuka cowered behind him, too surprised to move.

Sabian also appeared to one side, but he hovered at a distance instead of participating. Lance had lost track of Kitable long ago and had no idea where the wisavi was.

Protected indeed, Lance thought. A fight with one Hand's Follower became a fight with them all.

The Rydan put away his weapons and put out his hands in refusal, acknowledging that he was outranked.

Lance raised Tanuka up gently. By the time he faced the Rydan once more, the man had retreated into the masses, and the Followers were able to disperse.

Tanuka was bruised and scraped, and one scar, prominent on her left arm, looked like a burn, but nothing seemed permanently damaged. In seeing her injuries, Lance felt his rage rise again.

"Demons, Tanuka, I told you to watch out for yourself. How could you allow him to...?"

Lance let his curses fall off when he saw tears in her eyes. She threw her arms around his neck and collapsed against him, muttering words he did not understand.

"It's alright," he comforted, trying not to put any pressure on her injuries as he held her. "I won't let him hurt you."

The drums restarted, and the dancing resumed. Soon only Krahr remained on hand, and the crowd took to actively ignoring Lance.

"Sha be Trakn's wife," Krahr said. "Sha be belaw. Ya ken tak, bud dohn ged wid baybe." The broken Rydan and Esparan failed to make any sense.

Giving up, Lance looked to where he had seen Sabian.

"Sabe!" Sabian swiftly arrived at his side. "Please explain what the hell he just said. I have had way too much wildwater to be thinking."

Krahr repeated his explanations.

"He was telling you that Trakn is well below your rank, as you are a Follower of Tohmas. You can take her if you want but don't get her pregnant."

"Take her?" Lance stuttered, feeling like the Esparan made as little sense as the earlier Rydan.

Sabian looked back at him quizzically. "Rydans are not like Esparans—Esparan women always think they are owed something, or expect affection, or a favor or..." Sabian's expression soured "...a relationship. Rydans have no consequences like that. So long as you choose from those below you, there are no consequences here."

"Demon piss," Lance replied. "There are consequences. Look at her! Trakn is an ass if he's allowing her to be treated like this!"

Sabian cocked his head. "So you want to take her from her husband?"

Lance's mouth went dry. How could he explain that to Valia?

"I don't want her for myself. I just don't want him... was that her husband? I don't want him to have her. I don't want anyone to hurt her."

Sabian considered the distinction carefully, then nodded. "You're acting like a father; you don't mind her being married, but you don't want her married to him. Only the father can decide that."

"Can I adopt her or something?"

Sabian shrugged. "Never heard of it, but you've effectively done that by telling Trakn off and not taking her for yourself. You'll have to find her a better husband. So long as she finds someone above his rank, Trakn will have no recourse." Tanuka's sniffles had faded to shallow breathing as she stood huddled against Lance.

Krahr's face brightened. "I be havin'?" he delicately asked.

Tanuka's grip on Lance loosened.

Lance stared at Krahr, and the Rydan favored him with a wide grin and a shrug. "I naw be havin' wife. I be goh. I naw be hittin', promise."

Tanuka glanced out from Lance's chest to examine the suitor.

"I be lykin'," Krahr added.

"He's of equal rank to you, as a Follower of the Hand. It'll be a move up for her, too," Sabian agreed.

Tanuka turned out of Lance's grip, and Lance recognized her propositioning smile.

"She doesn't seem to object," Lance said, letting his grip fall from her entirely. She stepped forward to present herself to Krahr.

Krahr grinned enough for two men.

"If you ever hurt her, I'll hunt you down," Lance warned.

The wildwater must have been addling his brain; he would never have dared threaten a Rydan, yet the words came easily.

But Krahr only nodded and took Tanuka's hand. In his excitement, he did not say so much as a goodbye. Krahr disappeared under some kind of lean-to, Tanuka alongside him.

CHAPTER 7

Sabian watched them leave with a bemused expression. "I'm surprised you didn't keep her for yourself. She's pretty," he said, smirking slightly. "But then, you shared a fire with her for mooncycles. Maybe she's no good in bed."

Lance, his hackles still up, glared at the boy. "I never touched her or Sori, Sabian. Never would. So get those—"

"You want me to find you someone who knows what they're doing?"

"Don't bother. Kid, you worry me."

"And you confuse me, ex-High Guardsman Carraway," Sabian shot back. "You're shaken. We've all noticed it since your oath. Maybe you need a woman to relax you, as you apparently have no woman waiting for you in camp."

"I have one at home," Lance snapped.

The other Esparan raised an eyebrow, an expression he had picked up from Carsh. "Home? Gaidol? The place you just swore to fight? With the prince whose patronage you just forsook? That home?"

"Forget it. Just teach me to say 'no thank you,' and go away, Sabian."

Sabian stepped back, his frown disappointed. "'No' is 'naw.' There is no word for 'thank you.'"

"What do you mean there is no word for 'thank you'?"

"You never need 'thank you,' Lance. Everything you have, you either took or earned. Why thank anyone?"

"What about gifts?"

"No one gives things without wanting something in return."

Lance felt his age for the first time since walking into the Rydan camp. He had passed his thirty-second spring that year, had no children, and had never thought of himself as paternal but suddenly found himself protective of Sabian. The boy was several years shy of twenty. Even if he had done more in the last year than most did in a lifetime, Sabian was still a kid. The way he spoke made Lance wish he knew where his father was so that someone could cuff the boy. Since no one else would— Lance knew Sabian's only living relative had died early in the campaign last year—it fell to Lance. Because of Sabian's skill with the knife, Lance had to do it metaphorically instead of literally.

"People," Lance said in a voice he wished did not sound so preachy, "give things just for the sake of giving. That is the nature of goodwill and charity."

"When was the last time you got anything for nothing?" Sabian retorted. "Come on, Lance. I'm not young enough to believe in that dreck. You take what you can and fight to earn what you want in the real world."

For a long moment, Lance could not find the words to reply. The brief silence made his chest tighten in denial as he tried to disprove the logic that was too terribly true.

Through the haze of the wildwater, Valia answered. As he held her and savored the one kiss he had stolen from Dorakon, she slipped her hand into his. When she withdrew, she'd left a bracelet of pearls. The pearls now hung around his wrist.

"A year ago," Lance told the cynical Esparan, "I received a gift I didn't deserve. I'm sure there are others. The world is not about taking."

Carsh's Follower shrugged and turned away. "Prove it then."

Lance saw that as a challenge. He liked challenges ... if he remembered it come morning.

Sori heard Lance's return long before she saw the Rydans, their voices lilting in broken, drunken song and their usually steady steps staggering. The rest of the guardsmen had gone to their beds. Although they stuck their heads out at the commotion, they left her to meet the arrivals in the late night.

Unable to walk alone, Lance was half-carried by two Rydans. Tanuka followed along behind.

Seeing Tanuka's bruises made Sori's blood boil. Catching her eye, Tanuka shook her head subtly, telling Sori she was all right. Trusting Tanuka's decisions, Sori said and did nothing. Although it was brief, it was good to see Tanuka again after their mooncycles apart.

Sori held back the tent's flap, and the Rydans dropped Lance in. Without looking back, they left. One of them put out a hand, and Tanuka accepted it. The touch seemed soft, raising feelings of anger and envy. Tanuka had a new husband. She had become First Clan. She had hope for family and stability once more. That would make Tanuka happy.

CHAPTER 7

Although she envied the company Tanuka found so easily, Sori knew the First Clan would never accept her. A proper Rydan woman carried only a single shanye, but Sori had six blades even now. She would not give them up. She would not be controlled again. She would not be a proper Rydan woman.

Sori ducked into the tent and dropped the flap. After removing Lance's boots and placing them by the door, Sori pulled off his wet clothes for sleep. It had just started drizzling, but Lance's green overcoat was soaked. The new garment, given to him that day, was also stained with someone else's blood and smelled potently of wildwater. Had he tried to wash it?

He mumbled as she worked, but she paid it no mind until he was conscious enough to reach out a hand and touch her arm. "You look like her. Same eyes, same hair, same age..."

As much as she enjoyed the contact, the words set her on edge. Her. Sori hated it when he spoke about her. Lance was an unlucky man; he had fallen to foluv, the love that blurred reason and led men into foolish ruin.

Sori removed Lance's sword and knife and placed them in their customary place beside the cot, then added her six to the pile to allow her to crouch without stabbing herself.

"Your men be callin' fo' der wives," Sori said as she worked. "Will ya call fo' her?"

Lance flopped back onto the cot, letting his hand drop. "I can't. She can't. Gods know I be wandin' to, but her fatha'll never let her."

Sori stifled a laugh. Was that Rydan sneaking into his Esparan?

She sobered swiftly, realizing that his foluv and increasing connection to the Rydans endangered him. A woman manipulating him was dangerous, especially if the Rydans found out. He would be shamed, and his position diminished. No good Rydan man let a woman control him.

Zeken had. Sori's first husband had been accommodating to Sori in a way no other had before or since. He had trusted her more than a Follower and listened to her as if she was his wisavi. He had been a good Rydan man too.

But not like this. Not this blind, unrequited love. There had been an understanding between her and Zeken. To earn his approval, she had been an attentive lover, a creative cook, a hard-working seamstress, and more. The woman who held Lance's heart never did anything for Lance. She was not even here!

Perhaps it was time to break her power.

Sori would have generally stopped at his breeches—he could sleep even if wet—but she pressed on this time, and, in his drunkenness, Lance did not seem to notice. Once he was naked, Sori lay next to him.

"I ken be her," she whispered.

He rolled away, barely conscious, and pulled his arm from under her. "No one..."

Sori did not let him finish the thought. She spoke carefully, enunciating each syllable with as much of an Esparan accent as she could. "Use your eyes, not your head."

His back to her, averting his eyes, he tucked his knees up. She still had enough space to place an arm over him.

His voice was strained, as if he had to think every word through. "It's not my head, Sori. It's my heart."

She ran her hand down his side, trying to soothe the tension out of the muscles under her fingertips. He was older than her by at least fifteen years, but his muscles were tight. "Hearts mend," she said.

The hairs on his side and back stood on end at her light touch.

He let out a short breath. His voice was unsteady. "It's not broken. It's sitting in SwordWood by a window, crying, wishing it was dead. Sort of like me. Ya... you... you dohn understand. I love' er. I promised."

Sori was surprised. She had never seen a man weep, not even in pain. Was his hurt so deep?

A mooncycle before, Sori would have given up then, knowing Lance would never break any vow, but she had not seen his Gaidolon beaded rank band since he had taken Tohmas' braid of red. The once-immovable High Guardsman of Gaidol had forsaken the oath to his princedom. He might break another promise if given an incentive.

She continued stroking, but instead of bringing life back to him, Lance drifted off into restless sleep.

Chapter 8

Despite late spring rains, Tohmas' forces crossed Broken Mountain in three days.

As Tohmas checked the ranks at nightfall on their ninth day of travel, he regretted having pushed them through the grueling pass. The mountain had thinned Fixer City further. The fighters were worn. Illnesses had already started creeping in.

He could have led them around the hills, but that would have taken days longer and forced the army across DancingIce River. With the rains swelling the river, it would have been a treacherous crossing for an army five thousand strong, even with Kitable's aid. Tohmas had aimed to be in Trulin before Kelland could ready his army, yet that chance was slipping away despite his best efforts.

New people—a mix of soldiers and camp followers—had joined them at Narsol, encouraged by the glorified tales of the Northlander war. Now they discovered that the harsher truth of camp life was too bitter for their tastes. He could see the regret on their faces. It was better they break off now before he accepted their oaths and led them into battle. Now that the road could diverge out of the mountains, he had no doubt the forces would be hundreds fewer come morning.

After his inspection, Tohmas should have been sleeping. Instead, he stood outside his tent on a rise with the mountains at his back, haunted by those accusatory glares. BleakWater River cut through the hills to his right, and IceSerpant River traced a thinner line in the distance to his left. A thicket of trees edged BleakWater, the first trees he had seen in days. Now beyond the barren mountain trails, even the lowest ranked could gather enough firewood for a good fire. With the damp, the smoke was thick, but at least they could dry off.

The healing mothers were already expressing concerns; illness moved swiftly in the damp and chill. Tohmas had to provide medicines to his soldiers lest they become too sick to fight. And the terrain here was too soggy for horses or wagons, even if they kept north of rivers.

The road to the crossing of BleakWater River was impassable. Its broken bridge could be mended with enough time, but the summer heat was not yet upon them, and much of the terrain was marsh and swamp. Perhaps they could cross with magic, but then they were between Gaidol and Trulin, a fatal misstep. He could only go further north, keeping above IceSerpent River. Then the crossing would bring him into Trulin from a position backed by Darknim's land and support.

It was the only option.

He clutched his dagger's hilt. He hated having choices made for him.

Protector Derry emerged from the gloom and dropped a basket at Tohmas' side. "Supply of grann grass," he reported.

Chewing grann grass was Darak's suggestion as a way to combat leeches and ticks in the damp climate. The basket was smaller than Tohmas wanted it to be. It would not provide for all his forces.

"Take the grann grass to the Temple waggons," Tohmas commanded. "I want a dose in the hands of every warden. Tell Celebrant Darak to talk about its importance in his dawn service tomorrow morning." He needed the word out as swiftly as possible. It would spread from the service. Few people would miss a morning service when sickness threatened. Pari was known as the Healing Hands too.

Tohmas took a long breath, then added, "Make sure Celebrant Sedgan tells Loni about it. She can have her ladies inform the rest of the forces and start gathering it."

Protector Derry made a face, glancing down at the cut grass. "I assume a portion will be given to the kingsmen and their—"

"No," Tohmas interrupted, "they can handle themselves. Distribute all we have to the wardens." He held the protector's stare, wondering if the man would speak out, but Derry said nothing. "The wardens are responsible for getting their companions a daily dose. They don't get theirs until their charges have it. It is not to be sold, only given. They should work together to gather it as they march. But anyone hoarding it faces me."

Derry finally nodded. He took the basket as he left the rise, picking his way to the Temple waggons that had been assembled on the first flat spot on the mountain's side.

Finally feeling the pull of sleep, Tohmas retired into his tent.

A horn sounded before he could remove his boots. He rushed outside and paused, waiting for the second part of the signal: who had given it.

No second horn call came.

His guardians were better than that and had proven it in battle. How could they be so careless as to leave off their identification? How was he to know where the alarm had originated?

Carsh joined him, roused from sleeping in his tent a short distance away. Although he was missing a shirt, the Rydan had thrown two baldrics over his head by the time he reached Tohmas' side. The tattoo of the mountain cat on his chest seemed to wrap around the leather straps like claws for the cat.

The alarm call repeated, more obviously originating from the tree line along BleakWater River. Flystead's fyrd was camped closest, but the Rydans had taken lower grazing terrain next to the woods for their horses.

If a far crier could give the signal a second time, they could have given it correctly the first time! He still did not know which fyrd had sounded the warning of an attack.

A chill shot through him. His Esparans knew to identify themselves, but Rydans did not use identifications. All signs had indicated Prince Kelland had destroyed the bridge over BleakWater River and moved on. Could the saboteurs have waited at the obvious staging ground outside the mountains? The thick forest could easily conceal an attacker, but there was no sign of combat in the visible flatland. He could see the shadows of the horses stampeding away. There were no people but...

The horses. If the enemy attacked the Rydan's horses, it would cripple them. And the tactic put Tohmas' horse in danger, a thought that made his stomach drop.

Sprinting down the hill, Tohmas whistled for Schlavarai. Carsh followed an instant later with a call for Bashuran. Protectors rushed to follow Tohmas as he raced through a fyrd of Esparans, not knowing the threat but bound to follow where Tohmas went. They had not yet reached the Rydan's camp when a young Rydan, perched atop a filly, caught sight of him.

"T'steela!" the boy shouted. "Horses!"

His fear confirmed—a thief had come in and attacked the horses—Tohmas found a new burst of speed. Bashuran's whinny called out, the black stallion soon visible galloping up the hill to his master. But Tohmas heard nothing from his dappled mare.

The Rydans' low-lying shelters made of tangled bows of wood and blankets sprawled as far as he could see. The Rydans were already outside the shelters, crouched with their belongings.

Tohmas rushed along the edges of the camp, heading to the forest. He did not have time to call upon Rydan aid, not with Schlavarai in danger.

He whistled again.

Schlavarai's scream of protest and fury answered, coming from the river. Forgetting all else, Tohmas drew his sword and burst through the trees at a sprint.

As a prince, his protectors were his shadows, taking his disregard as permission to carry on. Tonight he was grateful for them. He had no idea how many followed him—he did not stop to count—and they matched him stride for stride through the forest, their path lit by the streaming, red glow of SoulBurner.

When the brief forest ended at BleakWater River, Tohmas searched up and down the slow-moving waters. Seeing nothing, he whistled. The answer, blessedly, sounded from downstream.

After only a few more strides, he heard a commotion in the water. He had never doubted that the Rydan mare would fight any trying to touch her. Tohmas feared that the thief would soon realize the futility and decide to end her struggle.

"Schlavarai!" he called as soon as he dared. "Lyh doh!"

The sounds of struggle ended with a thump. Tohmas crossed the river's shallows to circumvent the last of the rocks blocking his path at a full sprint. Rounding the bend, he spotted two men—the last two men, for there must have been more initially to rope the Rydan horse—turning from the downed mare. One carried a sputtering torch.

A knife outpaced Tohmas; Carsh's thrown blade took down one enemy. The dark and distance had been enough of a hindrance for Carsh to miss the killing blow he often delivered, instead taking the enemy in the shoulder. Tohmas had the pleasure of impaling the man through the sternum. Now illuminated fully by SoulBurner's aura, a second knife from Carsh caught the last attacker, who had turned to flee, through the ribs. With a truncated grunt, the Truller collapsed into the river face first and did not stir. His torch bounced from the stones, sputtered in the water, and went dark.

In only the aura of the enchanted sword, Tohmas spun to see to his horse. She was bleeding badly from her neck, three ropes deeply embedded in her muscles and making the bloody water look demonic. She had fought them fiercely despite that choke.

He took his knife to the rope as the protectors rushed beyond. She remained still under his touch, despite how the wound must have pained her.

"Demons," one protector muttered once he arrived at Tohmas' side. "How could anyone take out a horse that—"

"They are running. Should we pursue?" another interrupted. The other protectors had fanned out into a protective wall, searching the shadows of the trees but finding no more enemies. The wide water stretched to their right, the shallows ending in another pool. The woods beyond were dark, but there had to be others. Over the burbling waters, the crash of men through the underbrush was distancing itself.

Carsh answered for Tohmas, shaking his head. Anything beyond this mark could be an ambush, and Tohmas' allies were too few. There was no evidence that other horses had been attacked.

The rope released, and the Rydan horse coughed, bringing her dappled head up from the water. Her blue and brown eyes looked up at him, seeking permission.

"Schlavarai, uhp," Tohmas said, stepping back onto the rocky river bed.

She was slow coming to her feet, but at least she stood when he commanded her. Tohmas nearly wept in relief. The blood in the water was so thick that he had feared she might not be able to rise again.

"'Lyh doh,'" another protector grumbled. "Lie down. You told her to—"

"There was no way they could move her if she were lying down, and if she could keep her head flat, they would have a hard time getting to her windpipe or behind the arm for the…"

He stopped explaining. The words had come by habit, and he was not in the mood to entertain them. Schlavarai needed attention.

"I'll fetch Darak," yet another protector said, and Tohmas nodded absently. There was nothing the Celebrant of Pari could do directly, but Tohmas would take any advice Darak had to give. None of the mare's injuries were beyond what Tohmas had before stitched or bandaged, but the Celebrant of Pari had more healing experience than Tohmas.

"Trullers," said a voice from near the fallen men. "He has horse hairs on his helm. It looks like he was a rider."

This man had been a fighter, not a leader, and that meant whoever had led the attempted robbery had not been caught, Tohmas translated.

"Looks familiar," another protector said as Tohmas continued his thorough examination of Schlavarai. Someone had cut her heel, but it looked shallow. Still, the location worried him. He would have to bandage it. The other scrapes and bruises were superficial enough. One laceration behind the ear—

"Was with Lord Anga," another voice agreed. "I thought he looked like my cousin…"

Anga. Tohmas had known the Truller had lusted after Schlavarai, but he had certainly not expected the man to be brass enough to steal her. Was Prince Kelland's son out in the forest tonight? With minimal fighters? Tohmas would not waste such an opportunity.

"Horn," Tohmas commanded, and one of the protectors offered a signal horn for his use. A few blasts brought down a Rydan runner.

He gave his orders as they slowly traveled back to the camp, letting Schlavarai set the pace. Although the Esparans with him would not understand the distinction of "Hand Followers," they could undoubtedly recognize that his orders were to chase down the would-be thieves.

The Rydan runner saluted the Hand and ran off searching for Tohmas' friends. They would be riding in a matter of moments. By Rydan tradition, the thieves had just forfeited their lives and those of their families. Then his name would never be spoken again, doomed to anonymity.

And while his sense of vengeance agreed with the sentence, Tohmas wondered if it was extreme. In Espar, thieves were brought before a judge and a Celebrant of Inac. The sentence might be as little as a fine if the animal had been recovered. A brand would identify the thieves. Like any repeated crime, a second offense carried a death sentence, but even then, the execution would be swift.

He was setting the Rydans upon the thieves. His Esparan side objected it would compromise diplomacy and possibly offend Prince Kelland if Anga was involved, but he did not call the Rydans off. This time, he wanted Rydan justice. The insult had to be repaid.

Darak met Tohmas by the corral. The cutter never stepped within five strides of the horse; Schlavarai flattened her ears at his presence and threatened him with a glare that he wisely heeded. With Darak's guidance, Tohmas stitched the largest gashes without Schlavarai complaining. After dismissing the cutter, Tohmas sat up the rest of the night with her so that she could sleep. With feed and water, she rested deeply as Tohmas plotted vengeance.

Krahr was one of the first of the Hand's Followers to answer Tohmas' call. He was to pursue and punish the would-be horse thieves.

Tanuka made it possible. For the first time, Krahr left the job of packing to his wife. She even packaged food for him and grain for his horse, Vatnorish. Throwing his bags over his horse's back finished the preparations. Another of the Hand's Followers agreed to carry Tanuka with him until Krahr's return.

Krahr joined the others who had responded, and the chase was on. Despite the darkness, the Rydans found the tracks in the forest. The thieves did not even seem to make an effort to conceal their passage. Did they not believe they would be pursued?

They leap-frogged each other, one staying at the tracks and following while the others searched ahead, rushing to find where the enemy had left the forest. When they found a trail, the call went up, and they reconvened, then repeated the pattern. They moved at the fastest pace they could without losing the path.

Dagn shouted in the dawn. The Hand's Followers gathered, Krahr with them.

The tracks of several riders left the forest and headed south from the deer trail Dagn had found. Their quarry was on the fields now. A good opportunity, Krahr knew. Their horses would outpace the Esparan's on the flat.

With a whoop, Krahr led the run on Vatornish, the gathering of eager Rydans behind him. Their eager horses insisted on continuing through the dawn and into midday before slowing. Even slowed, they pressed on through the day, taking turns sleeping on horseback and taking short breaks to feed and water the horses. So long as one man was awake, the entire herd kept up the pursuit.

The trail remained obvious in the wet terrain even as night fell. Under the starlight of the wind god that granted them swiftness with each pounding hoof-beat, they caught sight of the fire their enemy had lit in a vale.

Rydans would never have failed to notice a hunt on their tail, but these were Esparans. Maybe they thought they were safe in their own lands or thought their horses could not be matched. Either way, the Hand's Followers did not take chances when chasing horse thieves. Although the enemy appeared oblivious, Dagn, one of their finest stalkers, was sent to investigate.

He reported that sleeping men in brown and white surrounded the campfire. There were sentries, but they were few.

The Rydans decided to make their run.

The enemy woke to the sound of hoofbeats, scrambling to get their weapons and horses as the Rydans descended upon them. Spears took them down from more than one side, preventing escape and swiftly cutting them down. They had no mercy for horse thieves.

Krahr came at the camp from the south, Vatornish trampling one enemy as the Esparan tried to get clear. Krahr dismounted in a bound, raking his hooknye through a dodging enemy's face. It was not fatal, but it blinded the Esparan warrior long enough for Krahr to cut the throat. The curved edge of the blade was perfect for hooking the side of the trachea and slicing across, through cartilage, vein, and finally, artery.

He spun in search of enemies. The other Rydans had fared well, although two had fallen from their horses and were cradling severe wounds, many more Esparans died. But as he turned, Krahr spotted horses and riders escaping out the far side of camp. Vathnan had failed to get to the enemy fast enough. His final spear throw glanced off a nearby tree, allowing a handful of Esparans to escape.

The Rydans split up immediately. Those closest to the enemy went to avenge the slight to their Leader. Those farther away dropped to the ground to help their fellow Followers. The one order a Rydan horse would accept from any man who had been introduced to them was "carry." The injured would be tended, then their horses could carry them back to the camp, even if the rider was unconscious.

Krahr's duty was to catch those who had evaded the raid. Atop Vatnorish, he rushed into the night on their tail.

To Krahr's surprise, the enemy's steeds matched the speed of the Rydan horses, pounding across the fields and keeping their lead in the shadows. There was only so long they could maintain the pace. Both groups ultimately slowed.

It seemed impossible. No Esparan horse could match a Rydan's, yet these stayed ahead. Krahr was baffled and, for once, impressed.

A tall, stone building appeared on a hill, lit in the darkness by enough torches to make it glow. Although they pushed the horses to charge in, the enemy did the same, and they did not sufficiently close the gap. The heavy metal grated door opened, and to Krahr's disappointment, the Esparans took refuge.

The Rydans pulled up to the enclosure, but the air became thick with little spears from the shelter. One of these short spears caught Dagn's horse in the shoulder, and a second went through Dagn's leg.

After getting out of range, Krahr packed the puncture and bound Dagn's leg. Together, the Rydans then assembled at a vantage point. Those who had gone to investigate reported no entrance into the shelter besides the metal gate their quarry had used.

Walls were an annoyance they did not often have to face. A chief's shella was the only structure like this in the Outlands. This shella was bigger but had many strange properties that made it stronger than any shella he had seen.

These walls were made of stones, although how the rocks had been found in such shapes, Krahr did not know. The roof was clay, not woven grass, and probably would not burn. There were also small gaps in the walls that the enemy's miniature spears could fit through but were too narrow for Krahr's spears. His enemy could hide behind the hole and attack while protected. The door, at least, was wooden, but he could see from his place on the hill that metal grates covered it. He did not like the idea of breaking through metal. Even the most basic bog iron used by Rydans, if ever they could forge it into such a shape, would be impossible to bend or shatter. And he already knew the Esparans had better metal works.

A shella could be defended by a few warriors and still not be breached. Someone had lit those torches. How large was the force inside?

The Rydans could not attack and expect to succeed. They had to wait. No rivers were visible, meaning they should run out of water soon, although Krahr knew the Esparans had ways of making water come out of the ground. Food would be another weakness, so long as the Rydan prevented the Esparans from coming out to hunt.

The Rydans separated, forming first a close square with a man at each corner and progressing to a circle containing the rest of the Rydans. One of the warriors who had slept rode back to Tohmas to give the report. Their Leader would be pleased by the many they had already killed, but until the thieves in the shella were dealt with, the Rydans would wait, their duty unfulfilled.

Chapter 9

Tandar felt distinctly out of place in the stuffy room overlooking the central courtyard of the Manor of Cainton. He had attended fire talks as a child with his sister, back when the woman in attendance had been Tandar's aunt Valiri, not his cousin Arnika. The sight of Arnika on the stool with them now made the situation feel entirely bizarre. Tandar better remembered Arnika for the games of hide and seek in the manor, but he had to admit she had stepped into her mother's position with surprising poise. She even knew how to sit like a proper lady while listening, her back straight and her hands folded. Despite turning seventeen earlier in the spring, it had been her mother's death that turned the girl into a woman.

Tandar's attendances at the fire talks—meetings of the ruler of Trulin— had ended five years ago, when Anga had been accepted into manhood and formally declared Prince Kelland's heir. It had been expected. Tandar had been excused, the nephew that the prince no longer needed.

But with Anga absent, his role fell to Tandar, and Tandar had many curt words to say to his cousin about the situation. An army had invaded Trulin. Anga, not Tandar, should have been at Prince Kelland's side. The prince and his finest warriors, the chargers, were now expecting Tandar to participate in Trulin's defense. The longer it continued, the more he found his memories of protocols and policies five years too far back.

The room smelled heavily of smoke, the nearby fireplace not drawing well in the still air of Cainton's valley. The benefit was that the smoke kept the bugs at bay. The windows had to be kept wide, which left Tandar either too hot sitting by the fire or too cold by the window. Outside, the clouds were low.

Although the gathering was called "fire talks," Tandar was certain the term had come from a reference to the Goddess Inac and her role in the war, not the presence of a physical fire.

"Tohmas marches with over ten-thousand Esparans," one of the nine chargers present said from by the fire. "Plus four-thousand, at least, Northlanders and three thousand Rydans. They will cross at Rimy Lake. Once through the fjord, nothing stands in their path to Cainton."

"The Rydan numbers might be the fewest, but their horses should not be underestimated," Charger Fawks added. Tandar knew the charger from his post in Cainton, but Fawks had come to Trulin from the far south, making him the only one among them to have met or seen Rydans.

Fawks had claimed Rydan horses matched Trulin warhorses, but Tandar wasn't sure he believed it. Not even the wind could outrun a Trulin horse at full gallop. Demonstrations of their strength had moved buildings and uprooted trees. How could the savages from the south, who knew nothing about documentation or planning, have bred steeds that could even come close?

"Lord Oranon," Prince Kelland said, snaring Tandar's attention, "what do you think of our invader? You dined with him in Forsinth during his march north."

Tandar snapped to attention, instinctually straightening on his stool by the fire, belatedly realizing his uncle wasn't looking at him and wouldn't notice. Prince Kelland leaned on the casement of the open window, his eyes on the courtyard below. Behind him, the sun broke through the clouds, brightening the smoky air.

Tandar cleared his throat to force out the lump. The room was filled with chargers, the highest-ranked soldiers in Trulin, and Tandar was by far their younger. He was not ranked; his family's business was horse breeding, not fighting. He feared having his voice squeak like a pubescent boy under the steady glares.

Damn Anga for getting himself trapped.

Hoping something he said would be helpful, he ventured, "Prince Tohmas speaks well. He will try to win people over instead of fighting them."

Kelland nodded but did not look into the room. "But he will fight," the prince said. "I saw his skill. He is not unfamiliar with a sword. We can expect no mercy." Prince Kelland leaned back into the room, meeting Tandar's stare. With no support behind him, Tandar's back and shoulders were tired of holding the straight posture, but he would not be seen slouching before his uncle.

Anga had complained about how the prince liked to involve him in the conversations, even when he had nothing to say. Taking over Anga's position meant taking lessons from the prince too, and Tandar wanted to curse his cousin again.

"What is his weakness?" Kelland prompted.

Tandar sorted through the information, from Kelland's description of Tohmas' dealings with Anga at Narsol to Tandar's own experience with the man in Forsinth. He repeated the numbers the chargers had reported and went through everything he knew about the relationship between the Rydans and Northlanders. He had the speed of Rydan horses helping him and the masses of Northlanders who knew the territory well. The Esparans loyal to him were fanatics, or so the prince had claimed.

Tohmas held three parts together, but Prince Marfaie of the north had tried to drive them apart and failed. That did not seem like a weakness.

Into Tandar's silence, Prince Kelland added, "What is the weakness of all large forces?"

"He will be spread too thin?" Tandar replied, confused. "But his army is not spread at..." The answer hit him with enough force to make him start. "His army may not be spread, but it should be. He's claimed seven princedoms. He can't defend all that."

Relief washed over him when Prince Kelland gave him a nod of approval.

"So where have I aimed my strike?"

The Princedom of Solta was nearby and weakened by a decade of war, but they had already fortified, and Northlanders were settling there, making even a straightforward march through farmland daunting. The farther north princedoms were equally populated by Northlanders. The Princedom of Forsinth to the south made a nice but useless target—there was no advantage to the land. There remained hope Prince Deiton would see reason and ally with Kelland, if ever they managed to agree on Arnika's hand. Tohmas may not even bother to defend it. And offending Deiton could be disastrous.

"Lour," Tandar decided. "Tohmas and Loritat have not fought together. They have no trust between them. It's also the farthest, making it hard for him to reach. If he can't defend the land he claims, support for him will break."

"Good boy," Kelland said, turning to face the chargers now that the lesson had ended. "We need only send a handful of men. We will destabilize Lour, force Prince Loritat to call for help, and Tohmas will either have to divide his forces or break his oath. The others will see how divided his loyalty is."

Facing Charger Fawks, Kelland continued. "Pull the people out of Cainton a handful at a time and move them into LandWater. If he reaches Cainton, I want it to be a pitiful prize. If he gets that far, we can attack from LandWater and pin his forces between the waterways."

The chargers nodded.

"The rest of the army is assembling now. In the meantime, we need to slow them. I want your riders on the move first thing tomorrow, Charger Grandon."

For a moment, Tandar didn't understand. Sending a group of a few hundred against Tohmas' thousands sounded like suicide. Surely no one deserved that!

But the rest of the chargers were not concerned; they were waiting.

"The only corner he doesn't watch is that gaggle behind him," Kelland continued. "Attack Fixer City, then pull out and run. Hit hard. Tostig tells me there's an opportunity if we time it properly."

Charger Grandon nodded gravely in acceptance. While the blow would be powerful, Truller casualties should be few if all went well.

And it would force Tohmas to defend Fixer City in the future, Tandar realized. The more sides he had to guard, the fewer men were left to enforce any given angle.

Tandar let out a small sigh of relief when the chargers stood as if to leave. They had all the information and their orders. The fire talk ended.

CHAPTER 9

"What of Lord Trulin?"

Arnika shrank from the gazes that fixed upon her, and the stares softened like those of understanding grandfathers. They'd all known her as a child, and Tandar suspected she would remain the child for a bit despite her entry into womanhood. The Lady of Trulin's sole duty was to keep the leaders from forgetting their hearts and families. Arnika was allowed to be defensive of her brother.

"A good question," Kelland replied. He turned his eyes, to Tandar's chagrin, back to Tandar.

Tandar avoided meeting Arnika's eyes as he answered the expectant stare of his uncle. "The needs of one man never outweigh that of the princedom," he recited. "Still, it would be poor for morale if we were to lose the heir. We should send a small group to investigate his situation. If assistance is possible, it should be considered, but we must know more first. He is too far south for us to reach easily. It would divide us when we cannot afford to be spread."

Prince Kelland's otherwise stern face cracked a wide grin. "Well said, Tandar. I take it you want off that stool."

The chargers burst into laughter, and Tandar finally felt safe letting himself slouch. "More than you can imagine, my prince."

The prince clapped Tandar on his shoulder hard enough to make him put his foot down, lest he lose his seat. "The way it should be!" Prince Kelland declared.

As the men dispersed, Tandar finally met Arnika's shy stare. "Sorry," he said as he passed her. He put a hand on his cousin's shoulder and squeezed in sympathy. "I now understand why you and Anga hate these things."

The hint of tears reflected in the corner of her eyes as she weakly smiled. "Anga was foolish," she said. "I just hope it does not cost my father his heir."

He helped her off the stool. "I couldn't agree more, cousin. I do not want to inherit the title of Lord Trulin, not ever."

The long dress threatened to trip her as she placed her hesitant foot down. "No offense, Tandar, but I hope you never have to inherit anything."

"Sounds fine to me," he agreed, finding his way into the hallways of the manor. He set his path toward the temple, thinking it was time he stopped wishing and started praying. At least prayers had a reputation of being heard, even sometimes answered.

In the temple, he avoided the corner of Inac pointedly.

Arriving at the Galanth camp set a smile on Fayela's face. A storm had broken, freezing her son's forces in their base for enough days to allow her to catch up. The looming mist thickened around the army camped by IceSerpent Run. The summer seasons had officially begun, but the weather kept the earth soggy. Fayela moved through tents pitched with stone anchors, there being insufficient earth for pegs on the rocky bank. At least the rain had stopped for now. Campfires were flickering to life throughout the wilderness camp the Esparans had set, lines drying out essentials over the flames.

Despite the few recent wars, Fayela remembered well the many days she had spent out in the field with her husband. The sight of the enormous green tent she had shared with Habal made her tear up. She shook aside the sentiments. The road had not been too rough. She had reached half a century but did not usually feel it. Habal's death had made the weight of her age fall on her. This trek out into the reaches of Trulin was her retaliation against the lingering threat of age. She was not old enough to stop being part of her princedom's fate.

She may have lost Habal, but she still had her son. The thought made her pause before approaching the tent.

Do I have Tohmas?

Vallant had suggested she join the army for Tohmas' education, as a woman's influence could soothe his fiery spirit, but Fayela had agreed for a very different reason. With Habal gone, she had come seeking the part of her husband that their son embodied. She wanted to see Tohmas, hoping it would convince herself thirty years of marriage had not been a fantasy.

She had come too far to go back now. Head held high, she approached the green tent with her escort.

The protectors bowed their heads and gave her leave to enter, but she was still standing outside it when she heard voices within. She paused to listen.

"They will kill Anga Trulin!" The voice belonged to Barnon, Habal's youngest brother. As the youngest, Barnon always sounded childish to her despite also having reached half a century and having several children of his own.

"Only if he leaves the fort, Barnon," another voice replied.

It took her another moment to recognize Tohmas' voice. They had spoken in Wayburn frequently before the march, but his arrival to Wayburn and then departure had been swift. She still thought of him as a child.

"He is the son of a prince," Barnon argued.

"Which is why I didn't burn the place down, but if that boy is stupid enough to try to escape, he deserves anything he gets. He is not the Prince of Trulin."

Boy? Fayela thought. Anga was Tohmas' elder. Tohmas was starting to sound like his uncles.

"He is the heir of Trulin," Sol's steady voice added, siding with his younger brother. As usual, sticking together, she mused. The sons of Zayban always stood by each other. They had supported Habal marrying her despite their father's opposition. Without the brothers, Habal and Fayela would never have been able to sneak into the temple to be married. Fayela still loved them for the gesture.

"But right now, he is just the heir," Tohmas replied in a firm voice. "I am doing him every courtesy by letting him live. If he challenges me, he dies. I cannot have the enemy coming up behind us as we march on Cainton. The Rydans will keep him pinned."

"If he sallies out—"

"Then he is a fool! He knows he is trapped, so let him stay trapped until we are done in Trulin. I am showing him more kindness than I owe him."

She expected to hear them argue further, but silence followed. After a dozen heartbeats, Tohmas gave them a quiet dismissal, and they heeded it without comment.

Stepping aside, she watched the people leave too absorbed in conversation to notice her. Once it seemed empty, she gathered her courage and finally entered the tent.

Tohmas sat at his father's table, his eyes distant in thought. He was tall like his father, but she saw little else of her husband in him. His beard, now proud and thick, had come in shaded red, unlike Habal's prominent blond, and his eyes were a strong blue, unlike the entrapping cloudy grey of Habal's. He wore the green and silver tunic, the fibers stretched over his broad shoulders. The garment had been padded to provide some protection and warmth. Because of their limited time together, he seemed a stranger even as he sat with something flipping over his fingers.

If she looked closely, she could see some of her family in him. Her father had born the red-tinged beard, for instance. But his mannerisms and voice were strange, no matter whom she compared them to. She had never heard any son of Zayban be mild, and Fayela's father had been known to sell wares across the city without leaving his front door. Being accustomed to that bluster meant she did not know what to do about her son's softness.

Carsh—the Rydan who had come to Wayburn after Habal's death— was perched on a chair next to Tohmas. Prime Protector Carsh was still a mystery to her despite Tohmas' attempted explanations. They were friends, she understood, and she did not begrudge her son the company he had found among the savage lands in the south, but Carsh frightened her. He was, like the lands that had spawned him, untamed. She did not like the influence the Rydan had on her son: Carsh and the land he came from, she reminded herself.

While he often concealed it well, or so Vallant claimed, Tohmas had civilized himself by force upon his arrival to Wayburn. Fitting in with Esparan traditions was not easy for him. From Vallant's reports, it was rare that Tohmas' upbringing in the Outlands slipped through.

She took a long breath and then smiled. Perhaps she could help him adjust. It was her duty, in memory of Habal, to try.

"Are you busy?" she asked from the door.

When he lifted his head, his hand was already on a weapon. She blamed the habitual gesture on Rydan paranoia. His brow creased in thought as he looked her over. When he hit upon the answer, he jumped to his feet.

"Lady—" He winced and corrected himself. "Mother!" He ushered her in and offered a chair. "I was not expecting you!"

She removed the heavy cloak from her shoulders, feeling taller with the weight lifted. "No, I know you were not. It was Vallant's idea, but I had wanted to visit for some time, Tohmas, so do not blame him, please."

She lowered herself into the seat when he took her traveling cloak and delicately folded her long ivy-green dress over her knees, so it settled without a crease. Some habits, enforced by the proper ladies of the prince's courts, were not easily forgotten. Her feet chilled quickly, her leggings exposed without the cloak to insulate them.

"I think I will have words with Kingsman Vallant. I disapprove of him putting my Lady Mother in danger," Tohmas said after draping the cloak from a post's peg next to his fur-lined cape. A large puddle had formed below it, showing how often he had been outside despite the stationary army and weather.

Carsh raised an eyebrow at Tohmas from his perch on the chair, then tilted his head toward the door. It was not hard to see the question.

Tohmas did not immediately answer his companion. The two men had been inseparable in Wayburn, which Fayela had attributed to her son's need for a friendly face among the strangers of Galanth, but she had not expected it to persist this long.

But Tohmas tilted his head in acceptance, and Prime Protector Carsh, with a swift head-bobbing bow to her, left at a brisk pace.

"Will you be staying long?" her son asked as he retrieved a bottle and cups from a nearby chest. He settled on a weak northern wine like the one he had shared with her over lunches in Wayburn.

"However long is needed," she replied. Seeing his confused expression, she smiled. "Do not worry. I know the perils of war. I traveled with your father often enough."

He paused, considering over her comment.

She laughed aloud. "You are confused."

"I am surprised he allowed it," Tohmas confessed.

When they had been reunited after his fifteen years of absence, Fayela had worried she would have to earn Tohmas' trust. Instead, he had opened up quickly. He had told her she was the only mother he had ever known. They had been close in his childhood, but he never spoke about those times. She could not blame him: much of his life had been overshadowed by his experience in the Outlands.

He had not spoken of that either. All their discussions had been about family, histories of Espar, or current policies he had to deal with. She advised him on Galanth but had not discussed his missing fifteen years. She wanted to give him time to settle before asking, but then he had marched out.

She shrugged, smiling to hear his protectiveness, again reminiscent of Habal. "I got used to it, if only because the alternative was to be parted from him."

His baffled expression remained.

"You did not know your father well," Fayela said, "but he was a wonderful person, Tohmas. Even the Rydan wives follow their men. Did Chief Tamv not have a wife?"

He was shaking his head before she finished her sentence. The shake suddenly stopped, and he frowned. "Chief..." His posture tightened, his fingers flicking as if wishing for a blade. It was subtle, but she was sure she had startled him. His reaction to uncertainty always seemed to be to search for a knife. Another habit from the Outlands, she assumed.

"You did not realize I knew," she said as he put down the bottle. "You never talked about it, so I avoided the topic, but Habal told me, Tohmas. He and I alone knew about the trade with Chief Tamv and the Second Clan's war that trapped you. Honestly, I am very impressed by everything the Chief taught you. I had thought it would be a miracle if you even spoke Esparan, yet here you have come among us so well trained, even your men do not know that you were raised Rydan."

She patted him on the arm with a weathered hand. It was hard not to notice the many scars on his hands. Anger and fear rose to see them, reminders of the many people who had come close to killing her son.

"No one else knows," she comforted him. "Keeping your location secret was vital to keeping it from our enemies. Still, Habal and I loved each other: there was nothing we kept from the other."

He rose to finish pouring the cups, muttering "love" in scoff.

She took the cup, laughing. "You have not known love, Tohmas, not like Habal and me! There are no words for it! A love so complete, it overruled everything, a trust that knew no exceptions, and a passion that knew no bounds!"

It was easy to slip into those memories. She had never considered herself beautiful—she had always been too tall for boys her age—until one of the middle sons of Prince Zayban had noticed her. She had been selling biscuits at a festival, and he had stopped to talk with her. After buying a dozen biscuits to justify distracting her, he had come to call at the bakery every day for the next mooncycle. Within days, it had been clear that they were meant to be together forever.

They had survived threats and deceptions, all aimed at keeping them apart. When Prince Zayban had finally made it clear that his son would never marry a woman so below his stature, Fayela had been heartbroken. She wept all the way to the temple. Her tears prevented her from recognizing what was happening until she stood before a Celebrant of Ocea with Habal swearing a marriage oath to her.

Many said the wedding day should be the happiest day of one's life, but Fayela liked to think every day had been better.

She shook her head and sipped the wine. "What is the Rydan word for 'love'?"

Tohmas answered promptly, "There are six."

"Six? Six words for love when I see so little of it among them!"

Tohmas shrugged. "In Esparan, 'love' can mean affection for anything, or anyone, to any degree, but the Rydan have different kinds, different degrees, of love."

"I would love to hear them," she joked, resting a hand on his.

His smile was somewhat bemused, but he did not pull his hand away. Accommodating her in a manner no other enjoyed, he said, "Well, the word tinluv means a weak love, like for things. You could say a woman tinluvs beads or a man tinluvs his weapon or..."

"...his horse?" she guessed, but he shook his head.

"Horses are more valuable, and there is more attachment, so you would never tinluv a horse. Instead, you would use faluv, which means love, loyalty, and trust. It describes the relationship between Follower and Leader; the horse is viewed as a Follower. With the trust comes obedience, so it also implies a willingness to serve or to lead."

She changed her terminology to reflect the current circumstances. "So, your kingsmen would faluv you," she checked.

"And I, them," he confirmed to her thoughtful nod. "Faluv is still weaker than famluv or claluv, which is love and loyalty to one's family and one's clan. The most important of these is claluv, to one's clan, which is expected to dominate any other. For claluv, men will die."

She took that to be a love of one's princedom—province, she corrected. She had seen many die for the safety of their land.

"But what of a man and a woman? What of the matters of the heart?" she asked, feeling the most important aspect of love had been overlooked.

"Both loves for women are weak and not to be trusted. Laluv is lust. A man may laluv a woman and seek to claim her, but he is not loyal to her, and it does not imply fidelity. It also does not mean trust."

To this, she was indignant. "How can a man be said to love a woman if he does not trust her?"

"The woman's only hope for power is through their husband and the connections he allows her to make. They will try to control other men however they can. How can you trust that?"

Galanth was on the border to the Outlands; she'd heard plenty of stories about the wild men and women of the south. Fayela had not put much stock in them, thinking it rumors. Now, she reconsidered.

She'd heard a Rydan woman could be traded between men, so long as her husband permitted or if he could not object because of his rank. Women also had no right of ownership. The worst stories said a woman could be killed for the slightest insult, including bearing a girl instead of a son. The way Tohmas described their view of love seemed to support this.

What he described was not what love should be. It was not what she wanted for him.

"What of the other love?"

Tohmas snorted and made a face. "Foluv is translated as 'foolish love.' It is a curse; it clouds a man's judgment, even making him turn against his family or clan. A man in foluv will think of nothing else until the woman has been... claimed is not the right word. The men under the spell of foluv are weak to their women. They will be swayed easily, dangerously so. It is..."

His words trailed off. He cocked his head at her bemused smile.

"A man will do anything for the woman he foluvs?" she clarified, and he nodded. "Then you have found what I shared with Habal."

"It is a bad thing," he tried, evidently thinking he had been unclear.

"It is a blessing," she corrected. "Think of it, my dear. What if you had someone you knew you could trust to be there for you always? Hard days are shared. Everything you give is returned to you tenfold. Imagine having someone with you whose very life is committed to making you happy. Imagine..."

She could tell she was losing him in her dream. There had to be a way to explain it to him in terms he would understand.

"May I see your sword, Tohmas?"

Without worry—she wouldn't be able to use the blade anyway—he drew SoulBurner and placed the glowing sword into her hand. She smiled in memory once more, the weight familiar in her hands. Habal had taught her how to care for a sword properly, which later endeared her to her father-in-law. Sharpening and oiling a blade was as familiar as weaving for her.

This was a spectacular blade, and she knew she had never seen its equal at once. She also knew there was more to the weapon than was immediately evident, for she had heard Vallant's account of Tohmas receiving the blade from a burning waggon. The light vanished when Tohmas released the grip.

"This blade was a gift, correct?" she asked, and he nodded. "You may have worked for it, but you paid no coin for it. I imagine it was far more than you ever expected to receive too." She twisted the blade, and the candlelight slid along the smooth surface. It flickered on the writing etched in the metal.

"Now you have this wonderful sword, and it will never leave you. It will always be sharp, always be ready, always be strong. You know your blade will stand with you no matter how dire the situation. You can count on it."

He again nodded.

"Would you question the loyalty of your sword?" she asked. "Would you be jealous should another hold it briefly? Of course not! You know the blade is yours and yours alone. No other touch will make it glow as you do. Just as it brings out the best in you, you bring out the best in it."

Cocking her head now and lifting the blade, she pressed, "Imagine for a moment that this sword has a personality, a voice, and a body. That is what your woman will be like. Somewhere out there, my dearest, is a woman who can bring out the best of you, just as you will bring out the best of her. You will treasure her as you do the blade—no, more so—and you will love her more than anything, clan, family, Followers, and horses all. When you marry, Tohmas, you will know the happiness I found with your father, and you will finally know a trust that cannot be shaken. You must love your wife as fully as I loved Habal. Never let anyone come between you."

For a long moment, he looked at her with glazed eyes. She waited. Then, with a shiver, he seemed to come out of some deep thought and focused on her, his expression warm.

The sword in her hand pulsed with power, and she thought she saw a red aura flash up her arm. She heard words whispered although she could not understand them.

Surprised, she dropped the blade to clatter onto the table. The sound was jarring, making her heart skip and her words fail.

Picking up SoulBurner, Tohmas sheathed the sword and gave her a patient smile. "I will have a tent set for you. Or perhaps a vardo would be more appropriate. I presume you plan to travel with us. You will need somewhere to dry off."

Maybel slammed the door behind her, then leaned against it as if to keep the bad luck from following her in.

"Trouble, dear Maybel?" Tostig asked banally.

Her initial reply was a deep-throated growl that should have accompanied tearing out hair, but her appearance was too valuable. Her fists hit the door behind her instead.

"Wizards!" she said as if the word was a curse. "Useless! Kitable considers me no more interesting than last night's weather! I do not think he likes anyone! I tried! I asked around and came up with precisely the right character, and he still dismissed me like a botched summon spell!"

The wizard's continual rejection of her offers unnerved Maybel more because she feared Tostig would doubt her sincerity. It was not her fault it was not working! Nothing she did these days seemed to work.

Tostig's smile was from ear to ear as he sat down at the table, a steaming mug in hand. "What did you learn?"

Maybel heaved herself off the door. She was missing something. He had a glimmer in his eyes.

"Well, Kitable has no friends," she said. "Celebrant Calanor and Celebrant Corolys come around every second day, but their talks are professional. They're helping him with research."

"You are as daft as ever, my little sprite," Tostig said with a shake of his head. He insisted, "What else?" before she could be either offended or curious.

"The neighbors admit a Northlander visits sometimes, but I have not seen him."

"What of the waggon driver?" Tostig prompted, proving that he already knew the answer to all of his questions.

"Fine!" Maybel threw up her hands. "Yes! He has one friend. Apparently, he picked that idiot out of Galanth and cleared the man of a theft charge. He is deaf, Tostig, but can understand words enough for Sendings to be of use, which is what Kitable does. The waggon driver carries a stone with a permanent Sending on it, so anyone who holds it can..."

He placed his tea down and waved her off. "Sufficient," he said.

"What?" she barked, loud enough to make her grateful for the Wind Barrier that covered the waggon. "I have done my part, best I could, and failed. Are you not mad? I didn't win Kitable over at all!"

At first, she thought she had erred, for Tostig was notorious for hoarding information, but today his mood was too lifted. With a vindictive grin, he patted the pillow beside him at the lowered table. She begrudgingly lowered herself into the seat but crossed her arms to ensure he knew she was still mad.

"Dear Maybel, you have confirmed what I suspected."

"Why did I have to confirm it? It's embarrassing to be dismissed like that! This whole place has me shaken, and you are still sending me out like a walking stick testing the path! I do not like—"

He patted patting her knee in comfort. His voice remained smooth. "I needed to know our opponent. Now I have everything I need."

If she demanded he tell her, he would refuse, even laugh at her presumption that she deserved anything more than what he offered. However, if she were careful not to interrupt, his ego would fill in far more details than she would glean otherwise.

A flicker of silence was all it took.

"Master Kitable," Tostig said, "is incorruptible. Every Princedom in Espar has tried to win him over. None of them have succeeded. Money is no incentive. Princes have offered him three times his current salary to no avail. His loyalty to Galanth is solid.

"I thought," the Double Blade leader went on, "about trying to destroy his reputation, but again, he cannot be unseated. He is already considered rude, anti-social, and arrogant, so the respect he maintains is based solely on power. I could only tarnish his reputation by making him appear a fool, but that is beyond even me under these circumstances. I considered framing him and labeling him a traitor, but even that would not work! Prince—King, whatever—Tohmas trusts him. Tohmas would believe Kitable and the prince is the court. Ironically, that led me to consider framing Kitable for Tohmas' murder. However, even if I had every drop of evidence pointing to our dear Master Kitable, all of Galanth would still turn to the master wizard for advice. They love that demon-kissing wizard!" Tostig laughed aloud. "He is all but untouchable!"

There were days when talking to Tostig was like being the butt of a perpetual joke. He seemed exceedingly pleased with himself, yet all the information had been bad. Maybel did not understand. After an evening of humiliation, she could not handle the mystery anymore.

"Then what are we going to do?" She slapped the table, making her rings dig into her fingers painfully. "You cannot match him, I cannot distract him, and Mapan's weapons would never get through his shields!"

"Untouchable! Oh, you do not get it! Not just to be unable to touch, but truly untouchable!"

She paused to gather her thoughts. After a fair bit of mental searching, she finally dug up the word. "You mean people who can't do magic?"

He sneered at her. "Very few people can do magic, you filly! Untouchables are the antithesis of wizards! Their very touch destroys magic, and no spell can, as the name implies, touch them. As impossible as it seems, there are two untouchables in this march, and by your account, he only knows one of them!"

She kept her silence, encouraging the rant to continue.

"Both are celebrants," Tostig went on, "One, Celebrant Calanor of Totho, he often meets, as you said. Apparently, Calanor can project his

powers, and Master Kitable is investigating this phenomenon. But while he watches Celebrant Calanor, a second untouchable goes unnoticed. He never meets with Celebrant Loni, and because he never attends services, he fails to recognize the danger! Now you, dear Maybel, will fit in perfectly with Loni's whores! We will sow discontent between the wizard and the harlot. When they clash, we will be there to take advantage of his weakness. All of Prince Kelland's soldiers will join us!"

She had never seen Tostig so animated. The enthusiasm snuck through her animosity, and she caught herself smiling. If it could be so simple, the job would be done, and they would all walk away wealthy. It was enough of an incentive to keep her working on the assassination.

Besides, if they succeeded, she would get revenge against the man who had rejected her.

Chapter 10

Shimmer's expectations for her Rydan performers were simple. If the camp stayed in one location, they had to attend rehearsal before the midday meal. If the camp was on the move, they reported to her as soon as they stopped for the night, which gave her only a candle or two to train them before the shows started. It took, surprisingly, a quarter-cycle before she was happy enough to let them perform, although she stubbornly refused to dance with them directly until they improved. As a novelty, the audience would be forgiving of their imperfections. She was not as accommodating.

Being strict with them worked well. They complained, but they promptly did everything she told them to and kept most of their moaning out of her earshot, where she could ostensibly ignore it. She even thought she detected a tease in their whining when they knew she could hear them.

The march slowed to a trickle early on the ninth of the 3rd monocycle. The forces crossed the fjord at the mouth of Rimy Lake. Although shallow, the river IceSerpent Run was a long crossing only a few waggons could make at a time. Shimmer had watched Master Kitable smooth the river floor to aid the waggons, but the currents and depth meant they still required aid. Soldiers who had already crossed left their belongings and pushed the waggons through until they were too cold and wet to continue, then traded off with their friends at the campfires on the far bank. The camp was forming properly on the far side, Fixer City piled in a jumble waiting for their turns.

Shimmer would take her turn under lamplight. To pass the time, she had initiated a practice with the Rydans in the ruins of a burned-out village by the mouth of the river. The rubble and debris could have been Darknim DoomDragon's work from the years preceding his alliance with Tohmas, but the years since the destruction had buried clues. Still, it provided a cleared field for practice.

When Darcina broke from the other Rydans, Shimmer sat up from where she had been mixing herbs for her father. The women had been practicing a difficult flip-turn and had not perfected it. The leave of absence was unacceptable.

Darcina still frightened Shimmer, but they had, Shimmer believed, come to an understanding. Darcina heeded her when she discussed dancing, and Shimmer deferred to the Rydan in direct dealings with the other women. They spoke respectfully to each other. Despite the woman's overbearing attitude, Shimmer was starting to like Darcina. Under her persona of power, she was an intelligent woman, and Shimmer enjoyed talking to her.

"I did not say stop," Shimmer objected, standing to give her presence the weight it needed.

Darcina closed the gap between them wordlessly. Once at Shimmer's low table, the Rydan drew a dried plant from her belt.

"I be nee'in mo," she said, dropping the plant onto the table. Shimmer noticed the Rydan positioned herself to shield the plant from the view of the other women.

Franx flower, Shimmer recognized. Distilled, it was deadly. Dried, as this was, it would make someone ill if they ate it.

Shimmer frowned. "It is poison. I will not sell poisons without a damn good reason."

The woman hesitated, the usual response Shimmer got when she made that assertion to buyers. She had accepted losing sales for her policy about poisons and dangerous herbs years ago. But it let her sleep better at night.

When the Rydan did not storm off, Shimmer reconsidered. This was that important.

Darcina's voice was soft. "Naw baybe."

Shimmer's imagined assassinations vanished in a blink. Franx flower was also abortive. Realization dawned; Darcina wanted the herb so she could poison herself.

The leaves on her table would be just enough, she estimated, to make one woman sick enough to destroy any child within her. But only once.

Shimmer went cold.

Darcina, like every Rydan woman in the camp, was the wife of one of the Rydan fighters serving Tohmas. Shimmer had assumed her husband was Burlotak, the Leader acting on behalf of Chief Tamv for the Rydans away from home. At the least, Darcina was the highest-ranked woman within the Rydan forces abroad.

Did Darcina's husband know she was trying to stop pregnancy?

"Why?" Shimmer choked out, aware that she had lost the strength in her voice, but she could not bring it back.

"Naw safe," Darcina said in the best Esparan she could manage. "Ee naw trud me baybe be 'is."

"I have seen you swap partners," Shimmer protested. "Why would he care if you carried a child and he couldn't know he was the father? None of you seem to know!"

Darcina was already shaking her head.

"I be forbih," she insisted, which Shimmer translated as "forbidden." Darcina gathered away her frustration and confessed, "Enn' ee' ave enemy, maynie enemy. Me baybe die."

He has enemies, Shimmer translated. *Many enemies. My baby will die.*

In Shimmer's limited understanding of Rydan customs, Darcina had just committed a grave crime; she had flatly confessed that she did not trust her husband would be able to protect their child. Had Burlotak known, he would have been gravely insulted.

Childbirth was dangerous, and if her child had a very low chance of surviving, then it seemed prudent to keep any child from entering the world in the first place. The difficulty of a planned miscarriage would be less than the heartbreak of losing a child, no?

Shimmer's father had taught her to respect and love life from her earliest memories. The husband must not have known what was happening, or he would have stopped her.

Shimmer could tell Burlotak that he was being denied a child. She would save the unborn child.

CHAPTER 10

To what end? So that he could make the Rydan woman bear a child she neither wanted nor could keep safe? Would Burlotak force a child on Darcina when bringing it into the world would question her fidelity and put the child at risk? And would Darcina even love her child? Would the child live knowing it had been unwanted?

At that thought, Shimmer smiled to herself and made up her mind. She knew a woman who had endured precisely that. Shimmer knew all too well the hurt of having a mother who wanted nothing to do with her child.

"Franx flower," Shimmer said as she scooped up the plant, "is a dangerous one to play with for abortion." Before Darcina could do more than just frown, Shimmer added, "But I can get you something that will do the job just as well without making you ill."

The Rydan nodded back wordlessly. Although she said nothing, Shimmer saw the gratitude in the woman's eyes.

It was surprisingly easy to infiltrate Celebrant Loni's gathering by the fire. Maybel was welcomed fondly, and her tales of failed employments and desperate days lacking food were met with sympathy. She almost wished she had used the truth. There were enough similarities between her and these girls to make a genuine bond, but the last thing Maybel wanted was friends. Her lies sufficed.

She was beautiful enough to attract plenty of attention, and that too eventually got her what she wanted: Celebrant Loni's affection. The celebrant was unexpectedly approachable, particularly to her girls. Once Maybel had been given a red candle of the Gathering of Inac, she could access the celebrant whenever she wanted. Not wanting to push it, she kept her visits short and, as always, humble. Soon she was being doted on like an only child.

On the third day, Tostig initiated the final stages.

Tostig left the waggon, Maybel knew, simply because he could not stand to watch. He could have landed the blows for the bruises they needed, but the little caster proved to have a weak stomach. Maybel took it to mean he was fond of her and did not want to see her come to harm.

Thankfully, they had Mapan.

At first, he would not do it. But after nearly six years with the man, Maybel knew all the places to push. She quickly had him angry. Even after the first blow landed, she kept insulting him until he finally recoiled in disgust. He had not done any permanent damage—she would never have allowed him to—but her blackened eye, bruised arms, and scratched breast all testified to his temper. Leaving him to his drink, Maybel sought Celebrant Loni's gathering.

She played the part as if she was on the grand stage in Leviathan. Once in the comforting arms of her fellow women, she sobbed and shook and behaved like a pathetic, traumatized animal until they brought Loni to her. Even then, like the proper cowed child that she was meant to be, she refused to name her attacker. They guessed most of the story, and Maybel did not correct them.

After enough comforting words, warm pats, and soothing strokes, she caved and told them, "You cannot do anything! He is too powerful!"

The mere suggestion that she was not strong enough to defend her gathering had Celebrant Loni in a tizzy in a blink. Although Maybel had never noticed the knife before, a long blade was suddenly held in the celebrant's scarred hand. It glimmered in the firelight menacingly.

"I will not have any man harm my gathering!" the Celebrant of Inac declared and, for all her fury and ferociousness, Maybel believed it. "Give me his name!"

It would have been hard to disobey the woman even if Maybel had wanted to.

Maybel still made sure her voice trembled as she told her celebrant, "Wisavi Kitable," in the smallest voice she could manage.

The celebrant was off like a slingshot stone. Maybel scrambled to follow, knowing Tostig would need her. That, and she wanted to see Kitable's reaction.

Loni found him at his campfire, resting between bouts of casting to smooth the path across IceSerpent Run. Had she been given a choice, Maybel would have liked Celebrant Loni to catch Master Kitable in his vardo, where she could have destroyed the magic of his enchanted home. And that would have cornered him, preventing escape.

There had always been the question of whether Master Kitable had known that Celebrant Loni was untouchable, but Kitable was on his feet and putting the fire between them as soon as he saw the crazed woman. He knew. Colt's cart driver rose with him, but he did not scramble clear like the wisavi did.

"Bastard!" Loni screeched. "How dare you harm my girl!"

The knife came up as she lunged, but a quick word activated an alteration spell that gave Kitable the extra speed he needed to dodge around the attack.

"Crazy bitch!" Kitable replied. "What are you talking about?" Kitable again put the fire between them, making fast circles to keep his distance.

Narrowing his eyes, the waggon driver glanced between the two people, perplexed. He made a hesitant step toward the enraged woman, then abruptly stopped. Although Maybel could see no cause, she suspected magic had intervened.

Tostig was nearby, after all.

"How dare you!" Loni cried, lunging through the fire, her dagger arching ahead of her.

Kitable cast something with muttered words as he darted aside. A purple light curved away from them, reaching for a distant target. It winked out after it cleared the top of the waggon, destroyed.

Tostig's work, Maybel thought as she leaned back to put her weight against the waggon beside her. Doing so hit one of her bruises, but the pain only made her smile. She had played her part, and now she got to see the fruits of her labor.

Kitable was not going to be fast enough to dodge Loni forever, and the moment they touched, Kitable's defenses would fall. Tostig was ready.

And then their contract with Prince Kelland of Trulin would be fulfilled.

Tostig was not surprised when it took an extra candle for Loni to appear, for he had expected Maybel to elaborate her story. He resented it but remained hidden only a few dozen paces from Master Kitable's waggon, hoping he would remain undetected. He would scold Maybel later.

On the one hand, Tostig was disappointed when Kitable reacted immediately to the Celebrant of Inac, for that meant the man recognized the danger. On the other hand, he rather enjoyed the expression of panic on the wizard's face.

Master Kitable of Galanth, the most powerful caster in all Espar, was standing instantly and magically boosted a moment later with a Speed spell. When the waggon driver tried to intervene, Tostig activated a magic charm and snuck a force spell through the earth, anchoring the waggon driver's ankle to the ground. In his hasty withdrawal from the enraged celebrant, Tostig figured that Kitable had not even noticed that his waggon driver was not coming to his aid.

While Kitable tried to verbally discourage the woman—futile, certainly—Tostig saw the formation of another spell. A call for assistance.

I can't have that...

Tostig countered. The spell died, cutting Kitable off from aid.

"Loni! Get a hold of yourself!" the wisavi shouted as he dodged another leap. Even from his hidden place, Tostig could tell the wizard was looking for solutions that did not involve targeting the celebrant. Not wanting Master Kitable to have the luxury of being able to think and knowing he could not attack the wizard without having to break down too many defenses, Tostig aimed for the waggon driver instead. The more pressure on Kitable, the better.

He made it as obvious as possible, even adding an illusion over the spell so everyone around the fire could see it coming. More likely, when the master wizard spun around, he was responding to the sensation of the magic, not the colors, but at least the illusion gave him a very clear target.

Kitable reacted with a force disc, which deflected the blast Tostig had aimed at Colt into the next waggon over.

Realization dawned on his face. His expression changed from panicked to alert.

Yes, you know it's not a coincidence, Tostig thought. *That's right; you're in a duel, and you didn't even know it.*

In that distracted moment, Celebrant Loni lunged with her knife. The shields deflected the stab, the blade being iron, but the woman herself landed on his back.

Every last spell the master wizard had hovering or bound to him blinked out of existence.

CHAPTER 10

This was the moment Tostig had dreamed of since taking the contract from Prince Kelland to rid the world of Master Kitable, but he could not take it. Celebrant Loni's lunge had ended with the woman's arms around Kitable's neck, making Kitable impossible to target magically. Even if he had fired a targeted spell, Tostig did not know what effect the untouchable would have on the spell if she was still in contact with the target.

Well, the way she's turning her blade toward Kitable's throat may solve the problem. And if it did not, Tostig was ready.

The struggle was fascinating. Celebrant Loni had worked in service to the Warrior Queen aspect of her goddess, and she was a dancer who kept fit for her performances both around the fire and in the waggons afterward. Her strength was impressive for one of her size. Master Kitable was a true wizard, which meant years of practice and discipline. More importantly, it also meant physical strength, for magic was demanding on the body. When he held Loni's wrist, keeping the knife at bay, even Celebrant Loni could not move it forward.

With surprisingly speed and agility, the wizard suddenly dropped, twisted, and swung in one motion, throwing Loni like a load of stones cleared from a miner's shoulder. She landed in the short grasses.

Tostig sat up in readiness, but he paused. Kitable staggered a step instead of immediately casting.

Celebrant Loni still had her blade in hand, but Tostig saw now that she had been doubly armed. A second knife—shorter and bone-handled—was now sticking out of Kitable's back.

It did not stop the wizard. With the celebrant off him, his magical trinkets were again free to bestow their gifts upon him. He wasted no more time.

"Colt! Get in the waggon!"

Tostig sneered at the command. Firstly, the man was deaf. Secondly, the driver was still bound by the tendril under the ground. Kitable was wasting precious time in trying to get...

A word from Kitable activated an item, and the dispel hit the waggon driver in the chest. The binding that Tostig had so carefully attached and concealed was destroyed.

Tostig did not try to block it, for his Spell Sight revealed the number of defenses on the Eight-layered Dispel Kitable used. It must have been a costly spell to cast, he mused, which explained why the wizard had enchanted an item to hold it instead of making it part of his general hovering spells. Using an item also meant the versatile spell was available even if the wizard had been dispelled.

Not waiting for the celebrant to stand, Tostig threw his dart spell.

But the dispel was not the only emergency trinket on Kitable. By the time the dart spell reached its target, Kitable had broken a chain on his belt, and two defensive spells were protecting him. The dart spell hit a Missile Deflector and was wasted.

"Colt!" Kitable shouted, and the waggon driver was up the stairs and behind enchanted doors before Tostig could even decide on a new spell in light of the defenses. He still had his quarry on the run.

The defenses were weak. One was against physical attacks, the other against missiles. That meant magic targeted directly, which would be conjured, would suffice.

Celebrant Loni attacked again, but Kitable managed to duck clear of her, and impressing Tostig mildly, he did so while casting.

The leader of the Double Blades could see what the spell would be, and he thought it clever. Better still, as it was aimed at the celebrant, it would give Tostig enough time to form a perfect spell combination to end the Master Wizard of Galanth here and now.

They finished their castings at the same time. The earth destruction spell that Kitable used appeared directly under the untouchable's feet and dropped Loni into a pit. Tostig's spells, meanwhile, knocked aside Kitable's last defenses, froze every muscle in his body, and slapped a Vox on the man.

Overall, Tostig thought he had come out better in the exchange.

Ah, the mighty Kitable, he snickered as he moved out from behind the waggon he had been using to hide the aura of his Camouflage spell, *how mighty are you now? Unable to cast, unable to move—*

The answer to his question came in the form of a flying body that knocked Tostig to the ground.

He had defenses up to protect him, but the force of what he recognized as a tackle still knocked him prone and pinned him under the enraged waggon driver and his knife. Once his Molded Shield had turned aside the stab, Tostig recovered sufficiently to shout an activation word that tossed the assailant back.

He rolled out from under Colt in time to see Master Kitable getting up.

Part of him wanted to know how the man had gotten out of the holding spell, but the rest of him wanted to focus solely on the fact that the wizard was now up and lifting an item—a wand?—toward him.

Tostig's shields would defend him against any projectile, magic or mundane, and he had spells up to counter bindings. He still had time to respond, and he was the only one of the two who still had their hovering spell. Further, he could see that the Vox was still bound to Kitable, so if the item had an activation word, he would be unable—

Something else acted as the trigger for the item, for the Vox did not stop Master Kitable.

Color flooded Tostig's vision as a waterfall of magic flowed down over him. For a moment, it seemed harmless, but when something sharp and burning slapped into his shoulder, he reconsidered.

Firstly, it hurt, and Tostig was not accustomed to pain. Secondly, there was a burn to the attack that was getting progressively stronger with each sting. Thirdly, and this one took him a dozen stings to realize, he was losing his spells. With each sting, a hovering spell was destroyed. He was rapidly being made helpless.

He did not know what had hit him or how to stop it. Without a second thought, he pulled off the ring on his left hand. A Relocation spell flared. He was suddenly in his waggon.

For a long moment, he could not move through the burning ache of his muscles. As he lay there in agony, he started recognizing the sensation.

As an enchanter of things, Tostig seldom experienced Spell Burn, but he had known it well enough in his youth. Indeed, in all his life, he had never experienced a burn so complete. There was usually a slight burn in his morning casting sessions, but he was a careful caster and a meticulous enchanter, so the feelings were weak and typically short-lived. He never drew enough magic to leave the remnants to burn him. Not like this!

He sought his hovering spells through the ache and found them all dispelled. Instead of invoking a pre-cast spell, he had to cast the Pain Destruction spell from memory, and it took him a long time to get it right. Once the spell took effect, and the pain was destroyed from his mind, he opened his eyes to find Mapan looking down at him like an inquisitive puppy.

"Why are you red?"

"Get the mules," Tostig snapped as he sat up and rushed for the door. "We go, now!"

Putting his hand on the lever that would open the door made him realize that the bodyguard's question had been valid: his skin was lobster red. Although the Pain Destruction spell had cured him of the most obvious result of whatever spell Kitable had attacked him with, he was still stuck with an odd side effect. He looked severely sunburned.

"Maybel?" Mapan interrupted Tostig's thoughts to ask.

"She should be here shortly," Tostig insisted, shaking his hand as if to dismiss the color change, "and if she is not, we leave without her."

He pushed the strange tint of his skin out of his mind to focus on what they had to do now to survive. It would have to be enough. He had left the master wizard dispelled and badly wounded. He had done his duty and disabled Kitable.

Prince Kelland's attack would be hitting soon. Tostig had to prepare for retaliation.

Once Shimmer headed for her waggon to get the herbal mix she promised would keep pregnancy at bay, Darcina let out a long breath. She had been running desperately low on the plant called *baban*, and there had been nowhere to get more this far north. Likely, others had stores, but access to these would require her to admit she had been using it. She would be shamed by that admission, at the least. If, however, word reached her husband, he would kill her. The others could blackmail her if they knew.

Because of this stigma, she had approached Shimmer without the others present, but she was doubly thankful for their absence. When they danced, they all knew that the Esparan was the teacher because she was the better dancer, so they allowed her to yell corrections, even insults, at them, but that was as far as Darcina dared let it go publicly. Esparans were weak and stupid. Rydans could deal with Esparans, but it should never be taken too seriously.

Chapter 10

Shimmer Weaver did not fit anyone's expectations of an Esparan. If the girl had stood up to Darcina in ignorance, Darcina would have, like the others, rolled her eyes and played along while snickering behind the girl's back, but Darcina had been challenged by guile and strength. Shimmer Weaver may have been at least five years Darcina's junior, but she was the clear master of the gathering that followed the Hand's army. Fixer City was hers to command.

That realization had struck Darcina the day she met the dancer face to face, but it had been reinforced several times since. No one, not even the girl's father, told Shimmer what to do. Shimmer took what she wanted without giving anything in return. The dancer taunted men, and yet no man had ever claimed her. No one could claim her, and Darcina envied her for it.

It had taken only a day for Darcina's envy to change to respect. She could not allow others to see the respect, but it was still there, and if she looked carefully, it seemed to be mutual.

She was grateful for the Shimmer's aid and was considering some way of repaying the girl—Esparans had a fondness for metal discs, but her friend had plenty of those—when there was a shout. Although Darcina did not understand the harried Esparan words, she understood their meaning: fear.

Horns replied. It annoyed Darcina to be so blind, but she had not learned the Esparan version of the signals. She had to presume the defending Esparans were sounding an alarm.

The nearby soldiers rushed through the dancing and formed up on the west of Fixer City. The Rydans had crossed the fjord, as had most of the Hand's forces. The enemy was known to be to the east, on the other side of the river. Who, then, were these riders charging Fixer City from the west?

The green-clad Esparans scrambled to form a defensive line, with the other soldiers appearing between the waggons. It was futile; Darcina could see the impressive horses and their riders rushing across the abandoned farmland. The horses would trample these meager defenders. An enemy would soon be among them.

People screamed until the ring of the horns was almost inaudible. Everyone fled to the cover of the waggons.

Would the wooden walls protect them from the attackers? For now, possibly. But there was always fire…

Darcina's women were above panicking. They were the wives of warriors, and had each lived through many attacks. There was only one weapon a woman could carry, a *shanye*. By the time the women had rushed to Darcina, every last one of them had their short, double-edged knives in hand. There was not much to the little weapons, but Rydans came from a place with few resources. They knew how to make every little thing count.

The women formed a block, then spread into a broken line designed to deal with horse riders.

The enemy lifted weapons, the thunder of hooves rumbling the earth below Darcina's feet. Spear-throwing was a well-practiced art in the Outlands, but these spears were tiny—hardly the length of a man's arm—and they were not thrown: they were propelled by a tool. Third Clan had once been known for using leather thongs to fling their spears greater distances, little good it had done them once the First Clan eliminated them. But the tool the Esparans used now moved the small spear far better and, she rapidly saw, with better accuracy.

She had heard the men discussing these tools and weapons. They had called them *flypas*.

All the women dropped into a crouched, angled position to make themselves the smallest possible target. It worked for big spears; it should work for the *flypas* too.

She had expected to have time, to be able to charge the horses as soon as they were within range with their weapons, but the flypas arched through the air farther than any she had ever seen and plunged to earth among the waggons while the horsemen were still far away. Most sunk into the wood of various waggons, but those that found flesh made the gathering cry out in pain.

None of the women were good enough to be *turnabots*, who could catch the spears, and they all knew there were too many *flypas* to dodge them all. Still, once this volley passed, the riders should be close enough to attack. There was no fear from her women, not a one of them. Knowing the spears brought death, they waited.

But the riders came to a halt instead of plunging through the defensive line. They were close enough to see now; they were Esparans wearing the brown and white of the enemy. And their weapons were rising again, this time aimed obviously at the Rydans who stood outside the protection of the waggons.

The weapons let loose their cloud of death, and Darcina sank into her position. The cover of the waggons was too far away. Once they survived this, she would call her women into the shelter of Fixer City and force the enemy to come close enough for her *shanye* to be effective. She had misjudged these strange tools.

Seeing the many *flypas* sailing toward them, Darcina was suddenly unsure how many women would remain to join her.

In the instant before the *flypas* fell upon them, a strong voice called, "*Daforn*!"

Every last one of the *flypas* clattered against an invisible force, ricocheting off and falling to the ground a dozen paces before the Rydans.

Shimmer was now among the Rydans, standing firm with her hand held up as if to stop someone, her bracelets and bangles glittering in the low light. She kept the position as she shouted, "Get among the waggons!"

A new cloud of *flypas* soared in from the attackers, but again each bounced away. This time, Darcina saw they had hit something hard and flat, for the light twisted with each impact and made the invisible wall briefly flicker.

Magic, she realized. Her skin went cold, gooseflesh covering her.

A flyer was nearby.

Darcina had seen Shimmer flinch with the impact of the *flypas* against the magic wall.

Darcina forgot about the horse riders. She was not a knife dancer, but she hated magic with a fervor shared by every Rydan. She would slay the caster if it was within her power, and she was not alone.

Shimmer kept one hand raised to stop the spears when she looked at Darcina. "Do not give me that look, Darcina!" she snapped. "You know me! You know—"

Words could be spells, and Darcina was unwilling to let another spell be cast, particularly on her or her Followers. She darted in, leading with her *shanye*.

The strike never landed. Something much like the wall between her and the horses stopped Darcina's attack abruptly enough to jar her arm and make her joints tingle painfully. Another one of the women tried the same from the other side, with the same result.

"If I drop this wall," Shimmer said without moving her position, except to flinch again when another volley of *flypas* was stopped, "you will all be killed. Please! Get among the waggons! I am not the enemy!"

The magic around the Shimmer contradicted her insistence of innocence. Darcina swung harder.

The blow knocked the girl hard enough that her feet shifted this time. Shimmer stumbled. With a curse, Shimmer dropped her hand and ducked low.

"Darcina," she said in final plea, her empty hands out, "you know me! I can help! I—"

Darcina felt like a fool. How could she have been so blind to trust this woman, this flyer, with her secrets? She had thought Shimmer strong, but now the truth was obvious; the flyer ruled Fixer City because she used vile magic. She was a flyer, an evil soul, and she had to be slain.

Knowing the flyer could be jarred, Darcina flung herself into the brightly clad dancer. They both toppled to the ground as the *flypas*, no longer blocked by the magic wall, landed among them. Several Rydan women cried out in alarm, struck by the iron tips.

Although they were both down, Darcina's blade failed to pierce the face of the flyer, blocked by magic once more.

When the dancer next pushed back, Darcina was genuinely surprised by the strength. With startling speed, the flyer twisted out of Darcina's grasp. A final *flypas* came close to the caster, only to be slapped aside in a flash of blue light.

"I am sorry," was the last thing Darcina heard Shimmer say before, in front of the keen eyes of the Rydan, the flyer vanished.

The curse at having lost sight of the flyer had not even formed on Darcina's lips when a shout from one of her women pulled Darcina's attention back to the Esparan horse riders. The *flypas* were falling at a speed she thought impossible for any throwing arm, and they were not slowing.

Knowing a flyer was working for the Esparans and feeling the sting of her gullibility, Darcina wanted nothing more to do with any of them. Three of her Followers had been hit, one of them badly, and she wanted

CHAPTER 10

to get them home. She would have to get help to deal with the flyer. For now, it was time to leave.

Once they had retreated to the waggons, Darcina saw the enemy's horses kick up into a charge, but she did not care. She would leave the Esparans to fight their own battles. They could all die under the hooves of their enemy's horses.

Shimmer could have blasted Darcina back to the Outlands, but compassion overruled. All she could bring herself to do was drop a Concealment on herself and flee. The spell was far from perfect, but the continued fall of arrows from the Trullers provided the distraction she needed to sneak away. Once she was around a corner and holding still, the camouflage became perfect, and she was all but invisible.

It was surprisingly painful to run from the Rydan. Although the knives had never pierced her Molded Shield, Shimmer felt a real ache in her chest. Through all the faked disapproval and double-faced conversations, she had liked Darcina, and she had thought the feeling mutual. It hurt to see that friendship destroyed so easily.

There was nothing she could do, and that made her pain shift to frustration. Shimmer had grown accustomed to controlling every aspect of her life, and the realization that nothing she did would bridge the gap of hatred the Rydans had for casters enraged her. Now that they knew she was a caster, she would never be able to deal with Rydans again.

Her frustration lasted only until her next thought. Fixer City was under attack. That required her immediate attention. She couldn't fix the situation with Darcina, but she would make the Trullers pay for forcing her to reveal her magic to the Rydans.

Arrows did not concern her, for she had activated a Missile Deflector spell as soon as the threat had materialized, and she still had her Molded Shield as a backup. But she feared for the rest of Fixer City. The Galanth defenders were taking too long to mobilize. The last time she had looked, they had been forced apart by volleys of arrows. Shimmer's Force Wall had dropped when Darcina had knocked her over; nothing stopped the arrows now. There was no shelter except for the waggons. The soldiers made a rough line using those waggons, but they were ill-prepared for horse riders. The nearest soldiers had sounded the alarm, and horns were blaring responses, but for the fyrd assembling between Fixer City and the attackers, help was not coming fast enough.

Flystead's fyrd, unlucky enough to be on duty as peacekeepers in Fixer City and now called to defend it, could never hold against a charge of warhorses. Once the Trullers were through that line, they would burn all the people who had hidden in their waggons.

Fixer City would die.

Shimmer climbed onto the waggon she had so recently been working beside, perching atop the roof. Camouflaged as she was, there was little fear of discovery, and her shields kept her safe from rogue arrows as she surveyed the scene.

With their stances firm and their shield high, King Tohmas' soldiers in green stood between the Trullers and the innocents of Fixer City. A new horn went up, and Shimmer's stomach dropped. The riders had stowed their bows, swapping to long spears. They lowered these for the charge.

The line of Trullers moved as one toward the Galanth green.

Without thinking, Shimmer activated her second Force Wall, followed by two Extension spells. They had caused enough trouble. This ended now.

She heard her father call. He was on the waggon in the next instant, his typically green eyes glowing in a multitude of colors. In the flicker it took him to identify the spell she held, she interrupted, "Don't you dare Boost me!"

"You can't hold this alone!" he protested.

The Boost was part of both their hovering spells and would tie their energies together. It would also share the impact against the Force Wall—which was about to be thirty warhorses—between them.

"If we both go down, we both die, Papa." Someone had to get Fixer City moving. Someone had to get her down from the waggon and inside so they could join the rest of the army across the river.

"But..."

She had argued long enough. The riders reached her wall.

She collapsed under the force of thirty horses at full gallop.

Chapter II

There was nothing.

For as far as Tril could see, the darkness was empty. The ground, if it could be called that, was smooth underfoot yet never slippery, even for his aging feet.

Initially, the vast, shapeless space had terrified Tril. But once he had walked its shores for long enough, he had come to see the place as the exact reverse of his homeland and, for reasons he did not understand, that made it less intimidating.

Where his fields of snow would have been bright, these spaces were dark, and no amount of light could make a shadow. At home, the wind blew a chill through skin and bones, but here the air was still and tepid. In the north, the sun burned white. Here, a spiral of colors rotated above without casting light.

Here, Tril could walk forever. In that way, he found it faintly like the open tundra he had left behind. In the Ice Fields, the horizon was a great stretch along the Ice Ocean that had never been conquered. Here, the horizon was a great blackness that tried tirelessly to smother the only light.

He could walk along the edge of this ocean and feel but not see its shore. There was a great gap between him and the giant spiral of colors that twisted silently in the darkness. He felt its presence like shifting ice under his heels. Like him, the wolf that shared his mind knew the danger. Defensively, she walked between Tril and the plunge that would toss his mind from this world.

When he first discovered the dark place where light cast no shadow and sound could not travel, he had been nearly dragged over the edge he now patrolled. Magic had driven him mad for a time, and this place had been his asylum. The powers of the wolf, his aspect, had rescued him many times, but these days she was needed only as a companion. After mooncycles of patient work, Tril controlled the visions sufficiently to keep his mind on this side of the gap.

He had a new purpose for his casual stroll in the dark. Visions had shown him a girl in the dark place of magic. She would fall if he did not catch her. He did not know why she was going to fall, not yet, but he knew she would if he did not interfere, and that was enough to see him pace the gap in search of her.

As the time of the vision approached, other possible futures circled him, making his wolf growl. Most visions fled from her, but the strong ones remained, and what he saw now explained much.

Trullers were attacking Fixer City. Tril felt he should warn King Tohmas or perhaps contact Master Kitable. A vision of Kitable caught his attention next. The master wizard was otherwise occupied. He could possibly warn King Tohmas.

But if he left to bring aid to Fixer City, Shimmer Weaver would fall.

His choice to stay was easy. Shimmer had provided the medicine that kept the Voice of the Raven, Elder Ela, alive, and Shimmer had helped the Circle fight Master Terant. Further, Tril was one of the few who knew whose hand had freed Master Kitable—Tril's friend—from Terant's deadly spells.

Lastly, and far more importantly, Tril knew that without Shimmer Weaver, Kitable was doomed for entirely different reasons.

Tril left the soldiers to deal with the fighting. His purpose was in the blackness.

The time approached and the visions he was monitoring gained strength. There was still the chance she would not make the choice that would throw her into oblivion, but that path distanced with every passing moment. Her heart, he knew, was gentle. He was confident she would throw herself into the magic, giving more than she had to help the people around her. Without him, it would kill her.

The darkness offered no landmarks except the gap to the light. How was he to find where she would fall?

Once the visions were strong enough, he sought the one that showed him catching Shimmer. Monitoring it, he broke into a run.

There were only two ways to go: left or right along the chasm. Tril chose right, and the vision gained strength. He moved to a sprint. There were still many visions of his failure, of the girl spiraling off into the darkness, leaving only a scrap of colorful cloth in his hand, but he focused on the ones that showed success and brought all his energy to bear. With every action, he increased the likelihood of that future, of Shimmer's survival.

He had seen the disaster that would befall Espar without Shimmer. His fear drove his run until even the wolf had to work to keep up.

Without light and shadow, it was hard to say how he saw her, but there was no mistaking the brightly clad girl as she was pulled toward the ditch by the thread of magic she was still channeling.

Tril never considered himself old when among the Northlander Circle, as he was the youngest member, but he felt his age now. She was moving too fast for his stiff legs to reach in time. Visions of failure surrounded him, gaining strength, while the vision of success grew weaker.

Kitable died in many of the visions. Tril died in others. In one, there was blood on the hands of a man with red hair. In another, blood flowed from King Tohmas' hundred wounds.

No, he protested. *I can't let that happen.*

The wolf answered. With a howl, they surged in unison. He felt he had four limbs instead of two, and his speed increased. He saw his quarry through the wolf's eyes.

Like a diving hawk, he soared after the girl and her magic thread. Soon, he could see her face well enough to see her confusion and fear. In the next flicker, the wolf pounced.

The wolf caught the ribbons of her dress in her teeth and pulled Shimmer back from the edge of oblivion. The magic thread she held dropped. She stumbled back into Tril's arms.

She peered at him with wide eyes, her fear clear. He tried to speak, but there was no sound in this place, so the words went unheard. Around him, the visions flared, then receded, and what he saw allowed him to release his breath in relief. There were still plenty of possible disasters, but this one had been averted.

He turned, seeking his wolf, but she was gone for now. *No, not gone,* Tril realized as he saw his furred arms. *One.* And he was not even winded by his sprint.

Leading her silently back to her mind, Tril hoped Kitable had fared so well.

The king, predictably, was annoyed. A flurry of activity followed the attack. He summoned Kitable formally. When he arrived, Kitable heard the exact words being repeated all over camp.

"No one attacks Fixer City!"

"Kelland does," came the king's calm reply. It was oddly soothing to hear Tohmas' firm statement answer the continuous denial. "Switch the Fyrds of Boro and Arrow, and have Sol pick one of his to take over from Flystead. They're too few to hold the post until they recover. Get long spears from the waggons too. Carsh, we need Burlotak at first light for some new training; no one can take down a horse like a Rydan. I just wish I had given Flystead's fyrd the spears."

He still had not raised his voice over a normal volume.

Runners rushed off to give written orders, and Tohmas tossed them each his token on their way out. Except for Carsh and Sabian, the tent was empty when the king finally turned to where Kitable was patiently waiting and asked, "What happened?"

Kitable's first reaction was to recite everything he knew about the Truller assault on Fixer City, but by the time he opened his mouth, he realized the king's question had been personal.

"How could you tell?"

The king cracked one of his legendary smiles. "First, Carsh thinks you're wearing fewer spells. Second, you are slouching. Third, you left a smudge of blood on the tent flap, and you weren't near the fighting. I can't see where the blood came from, but you're wounded." How Carsh had communicated the concern to Tohmas without words, Kitable did not know.

Tohmas was a man who appreciated bluntness; Kitable wasted no time.

"Celebrant Loni attacked me for a crime I did not commit. The moment I was dispelled, someone tried to kill me."

Tohmas lifted one eyebrow. "How bad?"

His back felt as if it had been briskly rubbed with a lit torch, for it had been stabbed, cleaned, reformed, and stitched, all within the last candle. For Kitable, the pain was a necessary evil. His enemy had seen him wounded badly enough to form a scar. If they knew what that scar looked like, they could use it to define and target him from a distance. He had made Colt open the wound further to make the shape something that would not be recognizable.

"I am slouching," Kitable replied.

"Bad," Tohmas correctly interpreted. "Thoughts on who?"

"I will know more once I ask Elder Tril, but my divination has identified a three-member mercenary band called the Double Blades. They fled ahead of us once I fended them off. They travel with a waggon, but they are using magical speed. You can't catch them."

"You got all that from divination?" Tohmas asked, his voice mildly impressed.

Kitable nodded, then winced. His back sharply stung. "Tril could have gotten the color of their nose hairs, but I thought I should talk to you first."

"I appreciate it. I have a few problems of my own, and I need your advice, Wisavi."

With the use of the title, it became official. Kitable sat at the table, and Carsh presented him with the customary cup of wine.

It was good, Kitable considered, that the king had not asked what had happened to Celebrant Loni, for Kitable had no answer. As much as he despised her, he had no desire to see the woman dead, so he had called the woman's keeper, Celebrant Sedgan, to get her out of the magical hole. The celebrant had argued, but Kitable had pointed out that it was Sedgan's duty to control the celebrant of Fixer City since his involvement in the cleansing fires of Inac that had killed two celebrants and their acolytes. His secret known, Sedgan had accepted his punishment.

If Loni was lucky, Sedgan would help her out of the pit. If the rest of the camp was lucky, he would leave her there.

"You heard about the attack," the king interrupted Kitable's musings, but it was not a question and required no reply. "As near as we can tell, it ended by magical means, and since you have confessed no involvement…"

"Weavers," Kitable concluded. "Fixer City is their home."

The king had his cup now and, in respect for Kitable, had chosen to share the drink of wine. The prime protector remained standing but joined them through his skin of wildwater. Sabian did not seem to mind being excluded.

"Apparently," Tohmas went on, "the charge tripped on something, and most of the Trullers either fell off their horses or had their horses fall on them. Flystead's fyrd took care of as many as they could before the rest ran off, so we can call ourselves victors in that one. I want to know how those apothecaries pulled that off, but no one has been able to find them, and to be honest, that worries me."

"For a pair who makes their career out of being noticed, it is indeed strange. I will look into it," Kitable promised. He shifted his weight to rise, but the king continued.

"That's the least of my problems." Tohmas tossed a carved wooden token onto the table between them. It spun twice, then landed face up.

Kitable recognized the anvil symbol. "Lour?" Tokens were used to confirm the source of messages, but he could not think of any reason for the Kingsman of Lour to be contacting them now.

"An earthquake hit StoneTop. He's got massive cave-ins. What few soldiers he has locally are trapped or dead. Pillaging is getting bad. He has requested aid."

Kitable knew exactly what Tohmas had promised in his treaty; if Kingsman Loritat requested aid, Tohmas had sworn to provide it.

Kitable grimaced.

"Personally," the king said with a frown, "I think Kelland is tricking us, but I cannot afford to be wrong, not this early in things. I must send aid to Lour, but I dare not weaken myself here, else Kelland's odds improve."

CHAPTER 11

Kitable picked up the token and turned it over in his hand. From the woven border to the tiny letters spelling the princedom's motto "Strength of heart, strength of hands" on the edge, it was accurate.

Of course, there was another option.

"Any chance Kingsman Loritat is the one lying to us?"

It was surprising to see Tohmas start back wearing an expression that suggested his waggon horse was composing poetry while his back was turned.

"He swore the oath."

There were several possible arguments to the statement, but none warranted pursuit. If Tohmas was confident, then Kitable would try to be confident too.

"So we need to investigate the claim," Kitable decided into his half cup of wine, "without weakening ourselves to the Double Blades. SoulBurner will protect you, but I fear they are working with Kelland. They were coordinated with the attack on Fixer City."

"Sabian."

The word from Carsh was so unexpected that Kitable spilled his wine in his jump. Carsh seldom spoke, and usually the few words he did mutter were aimed at insulting Kitable, the Esparans, or both. Hearing a helpful comment, even a possible suggestion, from the Rydan was shocking.

Tohmas took it in stride. Without blinking, he faced the Vait boy.

"You willing to hunt flyers, Sabian?" Both Prime Protector Carsh and his Follower tensed at the word "flyer," and the pale eyes of the Esparan knife thrower narrowed dangerously. Kitable shivered to hear the chill in the voice that answered.

"Gladly."

Bloodlust, Kitable mused, *is evidently contagious.*

"If he joins you on the chase for the Double Blades, then you will be free to go to Lour, Kitable. If they are in trouble, then help or send to us for more men. If not, get back here as quickly as possible."

Kitable's attention was still on the young man with the knives who was to join him. "Perhaps the Pack Runner would be better suited as an ally."

As much as Kitable did not want to offend Sabian, there was something profoundly wrong with sending what had once been a boy making his way by betting on throwing games to hunt casters like a trained dog. The Pack Runner was already a beast.

To Kitable's dismay, the king shook his head.

"Laorn's given birth, or will in the next few days. Honestly, he would probably still go, but she cannot hunt and would die before accepting our aid. I will not force him to make that choice."

Kitable had to nod, despite his misgivings. For the sake of a child, another child would be lost. By the look in Sabian's eyes, however, Kitable thought the Vait boy likely was already gone anyway.

"We go at first light," Kitable informed Sabian, and the knife thrower nodded in acknowledgment.

Tohmas puffed his cheeks as he sat back. "And I need to talk to Lance. He knows the Trullers better than anyone."

The protectors' duty was to keep the king safe; everyone knew that. A protector's word was law for any lesser rank; it was unusual to see any protector arguing with anyone, let alone a broad Rydan woman with a long woven hairstyle. But as Lance, called in his role as guardian, arrived at Tohmas' tent, that sight met him. Her insistence was frantic, and although the protectors tried to be patient with her, it was about to come to blows.

Most of her words made little sense to Lance, but he caught one of note.

He worked his way around the conflict and stuck his head into the tent to see Tohmas and Carsh talking quietly at the table.

"Carsh, a Rydan woman outside is saying something about flyers. She seems to want—"

The prime protector was pushing past Lance before he finished his sentence. Tohmas was slower, joining Lance at the entrance as the woman shouted in frustration and reached for her blade. Again, the only word Lance understood was "flyer."

Carsh dove in, dodging the woman's blow fluidly and catching her by the throat. She pulled on his grip with both hands, but when he released, it had nothing to do with her efforts. He tossed her aside and

CHAPTER 11

turned away as if the encounter was over. He had her knife in his hand already. The protectors backed off.

From her place on the ground, she shouted, *"Sha be flya! Nye's danca kill!"*

Time with Sori was paying off; Lance understood that she was identifying some woman as a flyer and asking Carsh, a knife dancer, to kill the caster.

"Naw be flya!" Carsh retorted, and it shocked Lance. Carsh had never hesitated when asked to kill someone, and Lance knew how deeply a Rydan's hatred for casters went. Carsh refusing to kill a suspected caster was unprecedented.

Carsh met Tohmas' eyes and explained with one word: "Weava."

Lance's heart skipped. Shimmer Weaver had been recognized as a caster. This Rydan wanted her dead.

"Sha be flya!" the Rydan woman insisted as she clamored to her feet. *"Ya be cowa! Fee' ard! Fee' ard!"*

Although Lance had no idea what *"fee' ard"* meant, it was an insult based on the effect on Carsh. The knife dancer was instantly in front of the woman. His strike knocked her again off her feet.

At least Carsh used his open hand. One blow was often all the prime protector needed to kill, and he was armed.

But the Rydan was tougher than Lance had expected. Even from her prone place in the dirt outside the tent, she repeated, *"Fee' ard!"*

Carsh went after her, landing more blows as she covered her head in the mud. She was at his mercy but did not cry out when he pinned her to the ground. Her brow showed bruising already, her face flushed from a strike, and her lip was split, but Carsh did not seem to be slowing.

Concerned, Lance turned to the only person Carsh ever listened to. "Gods, Tohmas, don't let him kill her!"

As he often did when overseeing Rydan affairs, Tohmas stared ahead with a painfully blank expression and a hard look in his eyes.

"He can if he wants to, Lance," Tohmas replied evenly. "She has insulted him badly. He has every right to retaliate."

Lance turned back to see the prime protector scoop up the beaten woman. The viciousness of the attack and the disturbing fire in the Rydan's eyes as he carried the woman down the hill had Lance looking away.

The woman did not move as Carsh carted her off. *Did she give up or lose consciousness?*

Once Carsh had vanished down the slope, Tohmas' tension released, and he sighed. "He will not kill her, Lance," he said as he turned back to his tent without his prime protector.

"How can you be sure?" Lance demanded, following Tohmas in, his heart still in his throat. He wanted to chase after Carsh, but what could he do? Fight Carsh? He was no match.

"He loves her," Tohmas muttered, shaking his head as if the conclusion had only just dawned upon him. "He will never admit it, but he always has."

"Demon shit!" Lance objected at twice his intended volume, stepping into Tohmas' path. The larger, younger man's expression was mild. He wasn't angry or even upset. Lance dropped his voice to normal levels. "You cannot hurt people you love like that," he reasoned.

Tohmas finally smiled away some of the tension. He pulled out a chair. "You can if you know the one you love will die if you do not."

Lance could not find an answer but stood numb by the table. The lump in his throat was letting go, but he was too lost to make sense of the explanation. Thankfully, Tohmas continued without prompting.

"Darcina was the eldest daughter of the Chief of the Second Clan."

"Second Clan?" Lance's voice caught. "Sori's Second Clan."

"No, she's not. If she's Second Clan, then the First Clan wants her dead. You'd best call her clanless."

Lance nodded, not wanting to draw attention to the girl who still made Lance dinner most nights. He found a chair and lowered himself into a seat. "She said she didn't have a home, so I guess clanless is right." He swallowed hard. "What happened to the Second Clan?"

"First Clan wiped them out," Tohmas answered, giving Lance a sidelong glance. "But you knew that, Lance. Are you trying to see if I have a different version?"

Lance shrugged without committing to anything. "If there's no Second Clan, why is Darcina alive?"

"Because Carsh has her under control," Tohmas replied. "If that control slips or is perceived to slip, she dies. If he wants her alive, he must keep his authority absolute." He paused, his eyes narrowed. "You have Sori under control?"

"Of course not!" Lance replied instantly. "She's a wildcat. No one controls her!"

The moment the words left his mouth, he regretted them. Although she was sometimes trying and demanding, he was fond of Sori. Unlike most Esparans, Lance knew Tohmas' ties to the Rydans were tight, and the only Rydans here were First Clan. Had he damned Sori?

He had fought to protect Tanuka. Would he have to fight for Sori too? Would he have to fight Tohmas?

Lance met the stare across the table, keenly aware of the sword he wore. SoulBurner was at Tohmas' side, and Tohmas was the better fighter by ten-fold, yet Lance knew he would stand his ground if it became necessary. It was simply the right thing to do.

But Tohmas did not rise. His stare distant in thought, he considered their exchange. At length, he said, "Best call her clanless."

Lance finally swallowed. "I'll remember that. Now, you wanted to see me?"

As Tohmas pulled a map of Trulin out and discussed the position of the Trulin defenders, Lance wondered if the conversation would have turned out differently if Carsh had been present. How close were the ties to the Outlander?

The thought of where the Rydan prime protector was soured Lance's relief. At least the woman would survive. But was that enough? And how long would she fight for?

How about Valia? Would she fight? And for how long? He had abandoned the woman he loved in Gaidol by taking a new oath. Her father would undoubtedly seek a husband for her as quickly as he could. What choice did she have?

He tried to focus on Tohmas' questions, reviewing Trulin lands in his memory. But his mind followed the rolling hills and forests south and over the BrokenFall River separating Trulin from Gaidol. Valia was beyond, trapped in the Manor of SwordWood and surrounded by people who only cared about her father's approval.

"Lance?" Tohmas voice cut in.

Lance shook his head. "Thinking," he said. This part of Trulin was riddled with rivers. Their route was vulnerable over various bridges unless he found a way around.

He cleared his throat. "I hope Darcina keeps fighting," he confessed.

Tohmas' stare was harsh over the map. He visibly clenched his jaw initially, cutting off a reply. *Cutting off the Rydan response*, Lance assumed.

But once the moment passed, Tohmas nodded. His voice lowered. "I hope so too. The pain of defeat is more tolerable than the agony of surrender."

Their conversation turned to Trulin.

Chapter 12

Kitable tracked the waggon containing his assailants despite the enchanted defenses that were bound to it. By the time the dawn rose, he was ready for them. With Sabian, he Relocated to a position ahead of the fleeing waggon. The Vait boy took a quiet place at his side as he set up the wooded part of the road he had chosen to use as an ambush.

"There are three of them," Kitable reminded Sabian. "Help how you can, but the smallest of them is mine."

"I can—"

"Stay out of his way, Sabian. The caster Tostig is dangerous." His throbbing back reinforced the statement.

Sabian nodded as if he did not trust his voice. It was good enough for Kitable.

The waggon had set a quick but not reckless speed upon its departure from Fixer City, and it did not change that as it rounded the corner in the woods. The thin forest provided minimal cover, but Kitable had selected a place where a sharp bend provided some concealment. Seeing the waggon, Sabian vanished into the trees as if he had used a Camouflage spell.

Turning his attention to the waggon, Kitable started by using a destruction spell to essentially poke a hole through the defenses protecting the floor of the waggon. He slid a Fire Blast into the gap next.

Shields worked both ways. In this case, the spell trapped the entire strength of the Fire Blast inside the waggon.

The juggler bodyguard, who was driving, came off the driver's seat in an acrobat leap that had him landing on his hands, ducking into a roll, then jumping to his feet. The jolt of the spell contained by the waggon defenses spooked the mules, and the harness snapped instantly, to Kitable's surprise. The horse tethered to the back of the waggon was just as lucky; it yanked on its tether the moment flames exploded from the waggon and broke the head collar, freeing itself to run.

The juggler only had enough time to watch the horse run away with a look of slight disappointment before Kitable's next spell put two lines of force across his throat. The man froze.

If he moved, Kitable would snap his neck. He was out of the fight.

Kitable turned his attention to the waggon just as the spells finally fell, and the fire erupted in all directions, driving pieces of the waggon ahead of it in a blinding flash. A few blinks cleared the spots from his eyes. Tostig stood at the center of the now-extinguished remnants of the waggon. The pale-haired woman dashed to the far side of the road, and Kitable let her go. Sabian could handle that.

Tostig raised a wand and shot a poorly-aimed Eight Layer Dispel at Kitable's defenses. The attack was pitiful, especially as Kitable included, as most wizards did, protections from Eight-layered Dispels in his usual repertoire. That the Double Blades leader expected to dispel him was laughable.

Kitable retaliated with a three-way alteration that protected a more potent destruction. The reward for his efforts was a pleasant reduction in the number of auras surrounding the enemy caster.

On the edge of his vision, Kitable saw the blond woman stop by the tree line. She raised her hand as a knife slashed at her throat, using a trinket to defend against the attack. She wouldn't be able to keep the Rydan-trained knife dancer back for long with measly trinkets when full wizards had failed, Kitable was certain.

He fired another spell at Tostig, breaking through three more shields and opening a direct path in. One of the defenses had belonged to a trinket; Tostig's belt buckle shattered as the destruction spell hit. Tostig triggered another trinket, and a Force Wall appeared between them. Kitable efficiently targeted the open thread and snapped it, dispelling the wall. *A pitiful attempt at defending*. But then, this caster had not faced a master wizard before. He would not be skilled at duels.

In the pause, the juggler, Mapan, lurched forward as if to join the fray. With a thought, Kitable's brought the lines of force across each other. He broke the man's neck. Mapan collapsed instantly.

The distraction cost Kitable time for a spell against his real target: Tostig. The caster had shot a spell, although Kitable's defenses handily defused it. Still, the delay had been dangerous. *Should have killed the juggler right away,* he scolded himself. *At least it's done now.*

Disintegration was a five-way alteration that targeted the principal elements of the human body and changed them each into tiny particles, essentially ending everything that made up a person. With the path clear, Kitable aimed the spell at the bald little person.

Tostig desperately threw up a Decoy, but as soon as Kitable saw the ball of elements, he conjured an additional dispel atop it, setting off the Decoy and wasting it. The unobstructed Disintegration struck Tostig's chest.

The man was instantly gone.

Silence reigned for a moment as Kitable surveyed the scene. The waggon fragments smoldered, some dozens of paces deep into the forest. The juggler lay in an unmoving heap. Fine dust wafted from where Kitable had destroyed Tostig. The remaining hovering spells blinked out, lacking anchors without a living caster.

On the edge of the road, the woman had climbed a tree. Like a treed cat, she stood on a branch above Sabian's head, and like the hound, the boy circled the trunk. There were no lower branches, which left Kitable wondering how she had gotten into the tree in the first place, but the Vait native still could have killed her with his knives from that distance. Clearly, he intended to capture her instead, although Kitable chose not to think about why.

Kitable checked out the pile of dust that had once been a man before concluding that their job was done.

"Leave her!" Kitable commanded. "She was just a subordinate of his anyway."

When he moved to stand under the woman's tree, Kitable could not tell who was glaring at him worse, Sabian at having his prize stolen or the woman for letting her be the prize in the first place. Her face was crimson over her scandalous blue dress.

Even knowing that she had tricked Loni into attacking him, Kitable did not want to end her life. The sight of the bruises on her face made him stop. He had no use for her, and alone, she was harmless.

"We're leaving, Sabian," he informed Carsh's Follower. Turning his angry, colorful eyes to her, Kitable added, "and if you ever get in my way again, little bird, I will kill you."

He could tell Sabian wanted to object as they Relocated back to the Galanth army, but he did not speak. Instead, Sabian ultimately accepted that their duty was done and left.

Kitable reported his success to the king and then returned to his waggon, where he started planning his trip to Lour.

Interrupting him, the dull ache on his back changed to a sharp pain that felt like Loni's knife was again between his shoulder blades. He fell, coming to leaning over his bed, the pain reducing but not gone.

He inhaled raggedly and peeled his robe off his sore shoulder. He couldn't see the wound, but the stain on his robe made it clear he had pulled his stitches. It had bled through the bandage.

He packed it anew and covered it with fresh bandages. Sitting on the bed, trying to find a position that didn't hurt, he packed a bag for Lour. Then, realizing he had unfinished business, he sought the Weavers.

Maybel waited another full quartercandle in the tree before descending to be sure they had gone. Although she knew it was useless, she checked on Mapan. Sure enough, his broken neck was beyond even magical assistance. She was still kneeling beside him when Tostig arrived.

"We need the mules," he said.

She glared at him. "Mapan is dead!" she snapped, pulling her arm from his touch. "Not all of us have a spoon quite as nice as yours! Such an elaborate illusion! So convincing! Where was Mapan's?"

Without looking back, he moved to where the waggon lay in pieces. Although she did not feel the magic, she was certain he was dismissing all the illusions he had layered around the remains.

"And we will be too if we do not get moving. I got a curse on Kitable, but I will not count on him failing to notice."

"How could you let him—"

"Maybel," Tostig interrupted, "go get the mules. They will not have gone far tethered together like that, and if we do not make it out of this war zone by nightfall, we will be caught in the crossfire. Stop whining. Get the mules."

When she rose, she had closed the dead man's eyes, emptied his pockets, and removed his shoes. There was no point in wasting things. Still, the vision of Mapan lying by the road, unburied, stuck with Maybel as she climbed up next to Tostig on the waggon's driver seat.

With the magic of the waggon keeping it from getting stuck or weighing down the mules more than minimally, they made exceptional time on the road toward Cainton. Tostig took time to cast while Maybel drove, using magic to check on the army they had left behind. He told her what he had seen, his voice softer than she had ever heard. Prince Kelland's attack had been of minimal effect, stopped by Shimmer Weaver. The Galanth forces were still advancing into Trulin.

At dusk, horse riders appeared on the eastern horizon.

He appeared initially excited by the prospect of conflict. Maybel couldn't blame him; she wanted to hit something too. But the situation changed when their waggon's lanterns illuminated the banner's colors.

Another performance, Maybel admitted. She pushed out her chest, checked her hair, and put on a fake smile.

"Thinking of getting away from me?" the lead rider said with a laugh once the horsemen had surrounded the waggon needlessly.

"If I was trying to avoid you, my prince," Tostig said, scoffing in a similar performance, "I would not have been going toward Cainton, now would I? Besides, I want to get paid eventually."

Prince Kelland of Trulin nodded but then paused. "Paid?" the prince wondered aloud like a child saying the word for the first time. "You were hired to stop Kitable from interfering during my raid."

"Which we did!" Tostig snapped.

"I lost fifty-eight Riders, mercenary, so stand silent," Prince Kelland returned. Being on the run was wearing on Tostig, Maybel decided. She'd never seen him accept chastisement before. If the illusions of his death had failed, Kitable could be right behind them. She was too afraid to even look over her shoulder; perhaps he felt it too.

"My riders were stopped by a magic wall, Tostig. If Kitable—"

"It was the Weavers," Maybel interrupted, standing on the driving seat of the waggon to draw their attention. She felt her bruises, which had not had enough time to fade, giving her presence extra weight.

"Oh?" The Prince of Trulin's attention was snagged instantly, and Maybel adjusted her golden locks again to hold it. The news would be better received from her.

She smiled soothingly. "Two casters of Fixer City defended against your raid, not Kitable. Master Kitable was completely disabled, as promised. Based on what we determined, Shimmer Weaver is likely dead for her efforts against you. The magic she used was far beyond her. We saw her collapse. She will not repeat the feat."

"And what of Kitable?" Prince Kelland mused.

It was a trick, Maybel knew. The Prince of Trulin was asking solely to hear if they would lie to him. She knew that was a death sentence.

"He was badly wounded in combat and retired to his waggon before the battle began, where he remained. He attacked us after, but we deceived him. For now, he is unaware of us. And he is cursed," she hastily added. She didn't know the full ramifications of the curse, but she would leave that to Tostig to explain.

The news that Master Kitable was as of yet at large, and possibly aimed against him, did not surprise or seem to concern the prince. He cracked a smile.

"He has left the camp," he said. "He's heading for Lour, baited out of the area. I need you again. Turn your waggon around and come with us now."

Maybel opened her mouth, but the prince immediately confirmed, "Your regular fees, I presume."

Tostig nodded, and Maybel smiled at the prince. "Always at your pleasure, good prince."

The way she spoke the words let the man read it as much as he wanted. Traveling on the road would be lonely, after all.

It was unusually warm in the waggon when Shimmer finally dragged herself into semi-consciousness. Her first hesitant steps back to her mind were met with racking pain, and she withdrew to the darkness of the place she had never known existed instead of fighting the pain. The wolf and its owner were gone, but the darkness was a curious place to explore. She did not miss consciousness.

After enough time, she decided she wanted to know what was going on and wandered forward to stand between the magic place and her mind. The pain was less, but she heard voices this time.

"How long has she been out?" said a familiarly disgruntled voice.

"Over a day," Dust replied. Shimmer felt something cool brush against her forehead. The chill lessened the ache she had been avoiding. "How long were you out when—"

"Different circumstances," Kitable's voice corrected.

"About twelve candles," a new voice said, answering Dust's question. It took Shimmer a few heartbeats to recognize it, but once she had, she easily envisioned the Northlander elder standing in the doorway between the bookcases. She could even see Kitable roll his eyes.

"I was magically driven to the edge, Tril. She voluntarily drove herself there."

"She also came much closer to going over than you did," Tril replied. "She is allowed to be unconscious for longer."

Spell burn, Shimmer recognized. Her father was trying to soothe the pain of severe spell burn. The cold thing was moving down her arm now: ment ointment.

There was a pause, but Shimmer did not know how long it persisted in the distant black. They seemed to be continuing a different conversation when she next heard the wisavi's voice.

"What treatments?"

"Same as we did for you," Dust replied, and Shimmer envisioned Kitable flushing in memory. He had been vulnerable then. She had saved him. "Aloe and vinegar, followed by ment. Just trying to cool it down. How long were you red for?"

"Nearly a quartercycle."

"You hid it well," her father replied.

"I had to."

Silence came again, but the burn was not paining her as much, so she ventured hesitantly forward.

At first, there was no change, but as she put one foot in front of the other along the smooth ground she could not see, she felt the world materialize around her. First came the burn she could not ignore. Second came the feel of the hammock around her. Third was the sway of the moving waggon.

When she heard voices, they seemed closer.

"I have already told you what I know, Wisavi."

"I have run out of time, Weaver. My duty calls me away, and if your daughter refuses to—"

"Shimmer," she corrected. "My name is Shimmer."

Her face hurt as she used the muscles, but the soothing tingle of the ointment her father had applied lingered and eased the flare.

The pause seemed short.

"So you are conscious, Miss Weaver, or is that a reflexive correction?"

She smiled despite the pain. "Might as well be for the number of times I have to say it." She pried her tired and surprisingly painful eyes open.

In the blurriness that was slowly clearing, she saw his face, and for an instant so brief a blink could have made her miss it, she thought she spotted the barest twitch of a smile on his face. Her heart, seemingly the only non-burning place in her body, warmed to see it.

She gathered her strength. "What do you want, Wisavi?"

Standing by her head, Dust offered her a pill, which she immediately swallowed. It would help the pain further.

Kitable's face became strict, but it was expected and did not bother her. "What happened?" he demanded.

Indeed, what did happen? Leaving him standing at the foot of her hammock for much longer than she would have liked, Shimmer pulled her memory slowly together. When she had sorted through reality and dream, she said, "I cast a Force Wall."

He scoffed in evident disbelief. "A Force Wall that blocked sixty-odd charging Trullers? Not big enough."

"Three Extensions."

His scowl changed to a frown. "Force Walls are open spells, Miss Weaver. What you did was extremely stupid."

"We're all here. I'm guessing it worked," she objected. Either the pill was taking effect, or her indignation was overruling the pain. She sat up.

"It nearly—" he snapped before stopping himself. Prying his fingers off the hammock string he had grabbed in frustration, he stood straight and immediately demanded, "What did you see? What do you remember after the invaders hit the wall?"

"I was unconscious," she pointed out as she too settled back from the argument, this time by falling back into the hammock. She had to adjust the light sheet her father had covered her with, but somewhat surprisingly, Kitable did not seem to notice, focused on the answer he sought. "But do you remember? Did you dream?"

"I seldom dream," she said. She was not often shy, but if it happened, it inevitably involved Kitable. His power alternated between amazing and intimidating her. He already thought her stupid. Would further explanations confirm or dispel that belief?

"Most wizards do not," he softly said.

She was so startled by his reply that she momentarily forgot her trepidation. "They don't?"

Kitable crossed his arms and sidled back. "Fact of magic. It probably has to do with how people cannot be targeted when they sleep or why spells often drop off people overnight, except if that person is a wizard. Hells, maybe it has something to do with untouchables, but that is all speculation. The point is—"

"When did you last dream, Wisavi?" she asked.

His scowl returned. "Not the issue at hand," he refused.

She laughed, only to discover that her chest muscles were just as unhappy as the rest of her. Still, she pressed, "You answer my question, and I will answer yours."

She expected him to snort and turn away to avoid the personal question, but when he instead stood his ground, she knew she had him.

Something about her forced slumber was important enough for him to accommodate her this once.

"I was thirteen," he said emotionlessly. "Your turn."

She wanted to know what the dream had been about, why he remembered it so accurately, or how he had figured out that casters rarely dreamt, but she figured she was probably pushing her luck. It was better to savor her minor victory and move on.

"In my dream," she said, "I was flying through a place of great darkness. There was light, but the light would not travel, as if contained. I remember holding on to a tendril of light because I knew people would die if I did not, but it dragged me toward the lights, toward danger. I remember feeling the surface give way under my feet and falling."

She could not help herself: she shivered in memory and let the tale trail off.

His hand again on the rope of her hammock, it seemed clear the wisavi did not want to press her, but once the silence had gone on for many breaths, he softly asked, "Did you fall?"

She shook her head. "Tell me why," she demanded. "If I tell you what happened, you must tell me what you know. I will not say another word unless you explain it." She knew the tendril was the pull of power that had held the Force Wall, but nothing else of the dream made sense.

He stepped back and shook his head.

"She deserves to know, Kitable," a new voice pointed out firmly from the door. "She has endured as much as you have in that place. She has the right to know why."

With the logic presented by one of the very few people Shimmer knew could call Kitable "friend," the wisavi pressed his lips and reconsidered. The firmness of Elder Tril's words made the choice clear.

"I will explain what I can," Kitable conceded. "Tell me what you saw."

Unable to see the Northlander by the door, Shimmer sent Elder Tril a smile in spirit, but she felt confident he had seen it.

Shimmer took a long breath in. Knowing it sounded mad, she confessed, "I saw a wolf. A white wolf caught me by my skirt and pulled me back. We walked. It left me on the edge of the darkness, on the edge of my consciousness."

The lack of ridicule in Kitable's expression gave her confidence.

He considered her words, chewing his lip absently and tapping his fingers against the rope of her hammock. Figuring it would be prudent to let him think uninterrupted, she gingerly started testing the extent of the Spell Burn by wiggling her toes. She quickly made a mental note to avoid doing that again.

The wisavi turned as if to leave, but a tsking noise from the elder in the doorway made him pause. The voice was quiet now, but Shimmer still heard it invite, "Tell her."

When Kitable faced her, his expression was only half present. It reminded her of the time she had watched him cast a Scry with his eyes open, only instead of having his vision on something distant, his eyes were turned inward in thought. It was surprisingly exciting to be part of his discoveries.

"Very well. I will explain. I believe the spiral of light you saw is the source of all magic, which we draw into this world as tendrils of a given element. The darkness is our side: no magic exists here. The gap keeps us from the magic side. Wizards reach across for their power."

She nodded once to say she was listening but let his ramble continue instead of commenting. It was nice to hear him speaking to her without sounding like he was lecturing.

"You have probably heard of wizards dying by pulling in too much power, which is what I think you just attempted to do," he continued, "only Tril caught you before you fell in the ditch. The result of that is your Spell Burn. Where else could the magic go if it was to be kept from returning to the spiral?"

"This happened to you too."

Shimmer had wanted to ask about that, but she had not dared draw his attention lest he remember she was listening. Hearing the question from the Northlander made her smile again. *Wasn't it Ela who read minds?*

The confession was made particularly small voice, most unbecoming of the most powerful wizard in Espar.

"I was hit by a spell that amplified, then un-cast my spells, forming a tendril to the spiral too strong for me to control. Thankfully, the spell targeted binding spells, so once I dispelled binding, I was safe. I stopped before the edge, but I too burned."

Kitable straightened himself pointedly and regained his firm voice. "I needed to know if your description of the space in between matched what I have seen myself."

"And it does?" she asked hopefully.

"It does," he admitted. "Thus, we can conclude it is, in fact, a place where only one's mind can venture. I will have to think on this."

"You are leaving?" The prospect of his absence made her realize just how much she had enjoyed his presence. His rants intrigued her. She wanted to know more.

"Very astute, Weaver."

"Shimmer!" she corrected as he turned away.

"Good day, Miss Weaver," was the last thing he said before pushing his way out the door and into the daylight.

Elder Tril had to step outside to let the wizard out. Now sitting up to watch Kitable leave, Shimmer saw the Northlander. Shimmer's eyes were drawn to the wolf skin on the man's shoulders. *Is that a smile?*

"Thank you," she said to Tril with sincerity in each word.

The man joined his beast in its grin. "How could I do less? You are needed, Shimmer Weaver."

"Needed? Why? Needed for what?" She shot her father an accusatory stare. "What have we agreed to?"

Dust gestured soothingly, giving her a fatherly smile. "Nothing, nothing."

She settled back and released her fiery muscles to recover from the effort of sitting up, still concerned.

Elder Tril sighed, glancing down the path Kitable had taken. When he fixed his stare on Shimmer, a chill as cold as an arctic wind came over her. "Kitable is a delicate soul, Shimmer Weaver. He is my friend, and I know he would be angry to hear me say these things, but I want you to understand. Truly, I fear to see him break. If we are not careful, that is exactly what will happen."

Shimmer had been around her share of fortune tellers, and she had dabbled with divination herself, but nothing had ever matched the weight of Elder Tril's words. Divinations were always only possible, not definite. How could he know with such certainty?

Or was Elder Tril, Kitable's friend, not the Northlander elder who made these assertions? Just looking at Master Kitable's life provided enough confidence that he walked a fine line.

She swallowed hard. "He needs you more than he needs me. You are his friend. Colt too, and King Tohmas. If any of you fail him…"

She didn't finish her sentence. It was obvious: it would be the end. Master Kitable trusted so few people in his life, if that trust was ever betrayed, she doubted even Elder Tril would be able to find a future for the man.

The smile on the elder's face became sad. "You are better at divination than you think, but you do your role too little credit. You are more important than I am."

He left and closed the doors behind him, leaving Shimmer feeling crushed under the weight of his words. Dust methodically went around replacing the defensive wards.

She had nothing to say about the conversation with the magic men. Instead, she closed her eyes again, reviewing the memory of the attack and the Force Wall.

Darcina came to mind.

"Papa, I need to hide for a bit."

"I can stick an illusion over your red skin, Shim."

She wanted to shake her head, but it would hurt too much. "More than that, Papa. Darcina saw me cast and now wants me dead." She tried to keep the disappointment out of her voice.

Despite the calm tone he manifested, she heard the concern in his voice. "Want to leave?"

"No." The word was out of her mouth before she thought it through. *Kitable is here. I have to stay.* "But I need to be invisible for a while."

"I know a kind heart we can contact."

She fell into a dreamless slumber, content.

Lour was Kitable's least favorite place in the world.

He had not mentioned that hatred to Tohmas for the same reason he avoided speaking with a Lourite accent: he did not want people to know where he came from. There were many things in Lour worth avoiding. His past was one of them.

Because of the sick feeling in his stomach, he intended to make his visit as short as possible. Thus, when he Relocated to the main hall, he did so with no time wasted on subterfuge. He appeared in the middle of the hall, right in front of the kingsman and all his sharded soldiers.

Officially, Kingsman Loritat was now required to change the ranking system of Lour to match that of Galanth, with protectors and guardians, but they still wore triangles of metal across their chests to indicate rank. Not enough time to convert, Kitable assumed. At least, he hoped so. It was encouraging that Loritat himself wore a colored rank braid, even if none of the others did.

Predictably the heart guards, recognized by their golden shards, attacked him as soon as he appeared. He quickly shoved them against the walls under force magic.

"Call them off, Kingsman," Kitable half requested and half demanded. "If I wanted you dead, you would already be dead."

There was a long pause, during which Kingsman Loritat appeared to recognize Kitable. The kingman's voice boomed out the stand-down command. Kitable dropped his force spells without warning. The six heart guards fell onto the floor.

"King Tohmas sends his regards," Kitable said as the warriors returned to their positions. "I am here to fix your problems."

The kingsman raised thick grey eyebrows. "You're fast," he commented dryly. "I had not expected much of a reply and certainly not so rapidly. King Tohmas made many promises, but I think very few would have been surprised if he had shirked them."

Kitable raised an eyebrow back at the man. "Presumptuous of you to make such declarations in front of a rather obvious ally to the king. You may offend one of us."

The leader of the mines of StonePeak laughed as he stood. "We are all allies, are we not? Tohmas insisted he appreciated honesty, so you can tell him what I told you, in all honesty. Besides, if that offends the king, we are all doomed."

"You are rather light-hearted for the seriousness of your situation," Kitable remarked. "Did you request aid solely to test the king?"

Loritat's smile vanished. When the kingsman stepped down from his raised seat to stand eye-to-eye with Kitable, the room was powerfully silent. "I have people trapped, Wisavi. I have even more dead. I call upon the king because his aid may limit the number of trapped people who become dead people. I would not request assistance without believing I needed it."

Kitable cut off his preferred snipe and instead said, "The king requested I offer what aid I can or fetch others if you require it. He is at your service in your time of need." It was the best he could do, considering his little experience speaking eloquently.

Chapter 12

"Then we are content. Whether we need additional aid depends on how much you can accomplish, Wisavi Kitable."

"Shall I start by releasing your trapped people?" Kitable asked with as much indifference as he could. He remembered the feeling of being enclosed by stone. He wished it upon no other.

The kingsman pursed his lips. "Can you?"

Kitable nodded solemnly. "I am strangely proficient at digging."

Chapter 13

They held the camp on the east bank of BleakWater River to deal with the wounded. Tohmas was restless as they waited. Although the Rydans had celebrated properly, the first significant engagement of this war had been losses. Tohmas worried the Rydan tradition, which claimed the war ended as it began, would doom him now. He had to find a way to change his fortune.

Just before camp broke on the morning of the 16th of the 3rd mooncycle, a horn call drew him from his tent. Rydans arrived, shouting and waving weapons in victory. They were his Followers; he insisted the protectors let the crew through. They dismounted hastily, and Krahr presented Tohmas with a severed head proudly.

Anga must have fought expertly, he reflected. Only a truly magnificent enemy would be honored in this manner.

Beside him, kingsmen Sol and Barnon made faces.

"Gruesome," one of the brothers said.

The Rydans were waiting for Tohmas' reply, which he gave with a single word: "Goh."

They leaped to their feet in excitement, mounted their horses, and were down the hill in a blink, ready to spread the word of their victory. Tonight, the Rydan camp would be thunderous.

"Is… is that Lord Anga?" the youngest son of Zayban asked once he had stared at the bloated head for long enough.

CHAPTER 13

"Was," Tohmas confirmed. "He left the fort, apparently, and the Rydans saw him fight so well, they wanted to honor him."

"Honor?" The word came out choked.

"Presenting it to me is honoring him. Leave it where it stands. We need to get moving."

Although Tohmas returned to the tent, the two kingsmen remained to stare at the head for long moments more. Eventually, Sol returned to the table and asked, "How long until Kelland knows?"

"If he does not already know, he will by the time we break camp."

They seemed mildly unconvinced, but since leaving the camp and the head behind meant they would not have to see it again, they were content to obey.

A heart guard named Tekton led Kitable down long corridors of stone that looked and smelled too familiar. Tekton was a deceptively small heart guard, young to his post and unassuming in comportment. Kitable assumed his position had depended at least partly on connections and familial ties; he'd spent enough time around fighters to recognize someone who wasn't one. But the young man could handle escorting Kitable well enough; he seemed to know the tunnels of StonePeak well.

Kitable heard the work before he saw the cave-in. The clatter of metal pickaxes and the crack of stone on stone reached his ears. A pony-drawn cart trundled by, the cart loaded with rocks just big enough to lift. The wheels tilted over the rubble.

They've already cleared this...

The light was alchemical nearest the tunnel's end, a phosphorescent lamp casting a white-green glow over the workers. Although they worked shoulder to shoulder, smashing the stones into pieces small enough to load and remove, their expressions were worn. They had no hope.

"How deep does it go?" Kitable asked Tekton.

The man pursed his upper lip as if bristling a mustache although he seemed too young to have more than a light fuzz. "There's a cavern at the end of this corridor about a hundred paces farther down, but we don't know if that has caved too or—"

"It's caved," a worker interrupted. The guard shot the woman a dark look, but the worker held the stare easily and continued, "The people trapped say they're caught in an area between two collapses. We're not going to get them out before they starve. At least with the vents, they have air."

StonePeak's network of corridors and caverns had been outfitted with plenty of air holes, Kitable knew. They let the smoke of the lamps out and provided plenty of hiding places for someone small enough. Many corridors had long stretches of vents, so it was unlikely a single cave-in would hit them all.

Kitable stopped listening and turned his sight inward. With a minor Scry, he detached his vision and sent it through the tiny cracks between the stones. When it went dark, he added a light. Although unnatural, it matched the phosphorescent well in hue.

After a long course of weaving between stones, he spotted a child of seven or eight peering down a hole at his Scry. He headed toward the child, who retreated, mouth open in awe.

Other people came into view with the light in the enclosed space. They spoke, but Kitable's ears were too far away to hear. He used the Scry to bind a wind alteration spell and heard the finishing, "...is it?"

They were more than a hundred paces buried. An extended Dig spell could reach maybe twenty-five paces, but that meant four spells, plus the Extensions. But the Dig spell was a destructive earth spell: if anyone got in the way, it would kill them. He could cast the first three with impunity. Once he got close, he would have to be much more careful.

He moved the vision to leave, but the child grabbed at the light and called, "Don't go! Don't let it go dark! No!" with such force, Kitable felt the vibrations of the cry despite being a hundred paces distant.

Although he had meant to pull his vision back along the path to double-check the distance, the fear in the voice changed his mind.

Leaving the light, he cast an Extension on it, then dropped the Scry. He was suddenly back in the corridor in front of the rubble.

The eyes of every last worker were on him when he regained his vision, most of them with their mouths gaping open as the child had done. *Must have spoken,* he mused. They were all looking as if he had changed color.

He checked in case he had. It had happened before.

Once satisfied that their awe was merely because of a display of magic, he faced Tekton.

"They're buried deep, but I can remove the stone. Get your people here clear."

Without hesitation, the workers rushed away from the rubble. A crowd had formed behind him, he recognized, and Tekton seemed to lack the clout to move them. Kitable glanced at the outspoken worker and asked, "Can you clear the area?"

"Get back!" she shouted, lifting her pickaxe as if she would personally enforce the command with it. "I won't have anyone getting in the way! We got lives on the line! Get back!!"

It was potently effective. The corridor behind him was soon empty for a dozen paces except for the worker and Tekton. In the distance, the crowd peered on tiptoes to get a view.

Kitable ignored them and started casting.

Two Dig spells and their Extensions were hovering spells requiring only activation. The third Dig took a full cast. At each release of the spell, which eliminated the predicted twenty-five strides of stone in approximately the same course the corridor would have taken, there was an audible gasp behind him. They were accustomed to halls of stone built with pickaxe and shovel, although legends claimed a wizard had built StonePeak. What could these have accomplished with a wizard among them again?

With three down, Kitable paused. Another cast would kill anyone it hit, and they were close enough that it was a danger. He advanced down the newly opened space, stopping when he reached the final wall of stone. Voices were now easily heard through the barricade, excited cries and fearful outcries. The crowd followed Kitable, although they kept a respectful dozen paces distant.

Inspired by faint light visible through the cracks, Kitable altered his lingering light spell into a line, then slowly advanced it until it was visible on his side of the stones. With an exact distance measured, he tied his next Dig spell, again a full cast, to the light.

"Tell them to get back from the light," he instructed. "Anyone between me and the end of this string of light dies when I cast again."

Although his focus was on the spell, Kitable saw Tekton blanch. He froze in amazement instead of doing as he was asked.

The worker sighed. Her pickaxe still over her shoulder, she strode ahead of Kitable fearlessly, raised her booming voice, and gave the trapped people their directions. She tromped back to Kitable's side, cautiously taking a position behind his line of light, and grunted, "Do it."

Kitable fired his held Dig spell.

At first, there was a collective sigh of relief to see the faces of the imprisoned people huddled together in the cleared area. But before anyone could move, the ceiling above the people shifted.

There was no time to think about what he was doing. With the support of the caved-in areas gone, the one place that had been spared was coming straight down, and it was Kitable's fault.

He intuitively slammed up a Force Wall spell, angled it to deflect the stones away from everyone, and braced himself.

The weight of a ceiling landed on him, knocking him to his knees. Defiant, his arms went up against the ache of torn muscles. The stones were held against the invisible wall for a moment.

"Get ... them ...." was all he could say under the pressure. Tekton and the worker rushed in, either unaware of the instability of the spell holding the avalanche or uncaring.

Not all trapped people were mobile enough to take advantage of the opening. Even with assistance, it took time to move them clear.

The cut on Kitable's back felt like it was ripping its way down to his tailbone and erupting into flames as it went. With the entire weight of the ceiling on his shoulders, he felt like he was sinking into the ground. Kitable saw the stars behind his eyes.

It took every bit of concentration he had to keep the spell up against the weight of the cave-in. He knew he had stopped breathing. His arms were shaking, but he would not let them drop until...

"We're clear!" someone shouted, and unable to see, Kitable took them at their word. Although it would have been nice to tilt the spell and lower the stones gently, the only thing his remaining strength allowed him to do was to drop the Force Wall.

The rumble that followed shamed thunder. For a moment, Kitable feared more of the tunnel he had just created would collapse, but the magic had dug through solid rock in many places and was not easily disrupted. Despite an impressive grumble, the rest of the construction held.

Taking deep breaths slowly, Kitable did not move for moments more. After enough time, his vision returned. He had lost consciousness, he realized.

"Wisavi...?" Tekton's voice was a squeak.

At length, Kitable made his legs respond. He gingerly stood. "I will need somewhere to rest."

"This way," was the immediate response.

There was nothing he or the hounds could do for Laorn; she would have the child and live, or she would die. The one thing Crawthran could do for his mate was to make sure she had fresh meat to sustain her.

Crawthran left the rest of the Rydans and went hunting.

The great mass of humans frightened much of the game. Still, he found tracks—cows—and followed them to an empty settlement late in the dusk. Three of the hounds—Beast, Bristle, and Valley—tracked with him, with the young Valley dashing forward and back twice as often as the others and messing up the tracks in her eagerness. The older hounds watched her with disapproving grunts.

Valley had been born the fall before. Already, she was showing great speed and a love for the hunt many of the elders had lost. They all still obeyed him, but only Valley seemed eager to do so of this trio.

With her running back and forth, Valley was the first to catch scent; she ducked her head low and examined the scent with intensity. The others put their noses to the ground. Beast gave the appropriate response: a deep-throated growl reserved for intruders, not prey. That, Crawthran knew, meant humans.

He was not bothered. Deer, horse, dog, and human were all good meat for a mate and pup. He had not set a preference when leaving the other Rydans. If any man had failed to retreat from this hostile land, he was glad to correct the error.

Together, the four pursued their meal. Valley fell behind to follow the older dogs, watching for lessons. Crawthran came last, knowing the sight of a dog frightened men less than the appearance of a Rydan with blades.

The settlement, with its huge *shellas* of stone and wood, seemed empty, but the hounds persisted. It was not until Beast aimed himself at an entrance that Crawthran looked in.

There was a family of them, but no female. They sat around a low-burning fire, ducked and silent as if hiding. He wondered for only a moment what they might be hiding from.

"You!" someone shouted, followed by Valley's alarm bark. Another human had appeared from another *shella*. The man got as far as to add, "A scou—" before Crawthran's knife hit his throat, and he was silenced.

It was too late. More enemies appeared at each *shella*. The family he had tracked had not been alone. Now more men than Crawthran had ever seen in a single settlement emerged, bearing weapons and hard skins.

Beast struck and tore out one enemy's throat when it approached. The hound sprang off the downed man to avoid the next blade, and the wielder's one chance for revenge was missed. Crawthran's knife caught the attacker in the heart, tossing the dead man through the doorway. Crawthran followed him down, wanting to limit the number of attackers.

The hounds and their master emptied the building rapidly. But the enemies clambered through the doorway.

Crawthran left by the window. A spear came after them. Valley jumped aside at the last moment, then followed the pack out. He tossed a blade at the next enemy he saw. Bristle's attack kept another from coming around the other side of the *shella*. They seemed able to hold until a yelp made him look over his shoulder.

Beast's left hind limb had been cleanly cut off. The hound fell.

Crawthran threw his knife, taking the enemy in the chest as Valley did her best to get through the back of the man's neck. The intruder was dead twice before he hit the ground, but the damage was done.

Bristle rushed to cover the gap, leaving Crawthran alone defending the approach.

Horses arrived, the enemies on their backs covered in metal scales and carrying long swords.

CHAPTER 13

Fear was a sign of weakness that had been banished from Crawthran's life. Flyers insulted him, but he did not fear them. Men could not hurt him. Even the beasts of the wild knew to avoid him.

But Crawthran was afraid. He could not kill the enemies surrounding him fast enough. He worried even for a moment about Bristle and Valley, for Beast was already dead, before making a decision he had never made before.

He whistled, calling the hounds off. Usually, it was a command to clear the way for Crawthran or his mate. For the first time in his life, Crawthran heeded the order. His blades cut a path through the riders, and he ran.

After two days of marching under blue skies and warm wind, Tohmas was back in the tent sitting in contemplation in the evening. His Lady Mother had finally come to visit him after several days of nothing but confirmations of her wellbeing. In-person, she confirmed her desire to remain in Fixer City. Tohmas reminded her that Kelland had already attacked Fixer City, whereupon she reminded him that Kelland was unlikely to repeat the ploy now that Tohmas had put Fixer City closer to the center of his forces. The matter was laid to rest.

Religion snuck its way into the conversations, and she pressed him to make an appearance at some of the other services besides Inac's. She had been impressed by Celebrant Corolys evidentially and thought the "young" woman would be a good influence.

Celebrant Corolys was several years his senior, he recalled. Although he occasionally pondered on wives and children, he had nothing to say to the Celebrant of Ocea. Corolys seemed happy now that she was with Calanor anyway.

Another example of giving up something for the sake of love. He did not know precisely what she had given up, only that she had surrendered it all to be with Calanor. There seemed to be an increasing number of examples of this glorified *foluv* his mother spoke about.

He was trying to dismiss the notion from his mind and focus on finding Kelland, who did not appear to be in Cainton, when a protector stuck his head through the flap.

"A Rydan woman wants to see you and seems not to understand when we say no. Would you rather we fetch Prime Protector Carsh?"

"Carsh would be tricky to find," Tohmas said with a laugh. When Fayela visited, Carsh often quietly requested to leave. When Tohmas freed him, there was only one place Carsh would go.

Tohmas smiled. Carsh's *foluv* was different than Fayela's, but there was no other way to describe the infinite patience the second son of Tamv had for Darcina. Had she been anyone else, Carsh would have long-since killed her.

No, Carsh was not around to be called, but that meant Darcina was not the woman outside. There was no other Rydan who would come to call on him on the Galanth side of camp.

Curious, Tohmas said, "Let her in. I'll deal with it."

That Laorn was walking must have been a miracle from Ocea herself. Despite still having a swollen belly, the woman had recently given birth. Although it was not as bad as Layla's birthing, the Rydan was still blood-soaked and had done very little to clean herself. Her health had seeped out with the blood. The hair hung limp, and her body was now thin and freckled. She'd remembered to don sparse garments; a simple double wrap over her chest and a Rydan's parted skirt, all of hide.

The protector raised an eyebrow at Tohmas, asking if he wanted to change his mind. Tohmas waved Protector Linco off, curious to see what the Pack Runner's mate carried wrapped in furs.

The eyes had lost none of their awareness, and even as he saw the weakness of her body, Tohmas was acutely aware of the strength that still existed in the woman. She had given birth recently, for there had not even been time for the blood to dry or wash away, but she had walked here. She must have nursed the child, for it lay quiet in her embrace.

Once alone, she extended the child to him.

"Take," was all she said.

The weight of the command made Tohmas hesitate.

Must be a girl, he thought. The Pack Runner had no time for girl-children. Traditionally, the Pack gave any female child to the chief. Since Chief Tamv was distant, Tohmas was the appropriate substitute. Tohmas had seen her first three children, all girls, in the Outlands.

But when he took the child, it was a son.

CHAPTER 13

He considered the sleeping baby, saw that he was a good weight and a good color, and extended him back to Laorn. "*Crawthran be prow.*"

She crossed her arms, stepped back, and spat. "Take," she said once more. "*Vanaw boy.' Ee vanaw' ave boy!*"

Tohmas froze with his arms extended, shocked by her blatant admission. *Never a boy. He will never have a boy.*

The infant stirred in his arms, and Tohmas reluctantly pulled him against his chest, if only to buy time.

"*Ya be goh man,*" Laorn told him softly. "*I be seein' ya oft, ann ya goh man. Ya 'elp 'im. Ya keep 'im.*"

Without a son, the legacy of the Pack Runner died with Crawthran.

Looking at Laorn answered Tohmas' uncertainty. In a blink, he remembered her screams when Crawthran had chosen her as the Pack Runner's mate. She had fought him. They had all known about it and done nothing. There had been nothing to do.

The woman he had seen among the hounds of the Pack was nothing like the confident girl he had watched be dragged into the woods. He'd thought her half-dead. Now, he reconsidered.

She was fighting, he realized. No other girl would be taken from their friends and broken against fists and starvation. The greatest fighter of Espar, Outlands, and Northlands could not compete with the Pack Runner, but the legend would die at her hands.

He looked at the infant in his arms, easily seeing Crawthran in the tiny face. But he did not see a monster. The child, like Laorn, did not deserve a fate of hunger and perpetual hunt. There was a chance to save the child.

He had disobeyed Chief Tamv either unknowingly or unwillingly before, but he knew what he was doing this time. He could do an old friend this one favor so long as no one ever knew.

To her, he nodded once. He would take the child, and Crawthran would never know he had sired a son. The Pack Runner would remain without an heir.

Laorn was immediately gone.

"Runnah! Get me Celebrant Corolys," Tohmas called.

In many ways, Arnika Trulin was glad she had passed her seventeenth birthday that spring. As an unmarried woman of full age, she rode with her father's soldiers as part of the joats with her cousin Altana.

Among the spinsters and maidens of the joats, she was just another servant to the army. She spent her time fixing weapons and tunics, cooking, and bandaging wounds, just the same as all the rest. Her father's army was distilled down to only what was needed to limit the risk of discovery.

When Anga's head was found, a gruesome display worthy of the conquering beast that was invading her homeland, her father initially intended to send Arnika and Altana back to Cainton, but Tohmas' forces were too close. Arnika was grateful; she was the eldest female relative to the Prince of Trulin. She had to be present for the fire talks. Altana seemed less keen, but she knew her place and said nothing to the prince or her cousin.

When the warriors left these hiding places to corner Tohmas against the walls of Cainton, the joats would remain in the town of LandWater and only join the army once it was safe. They were helpers, not fighters.

She sat on her stool overseeing the fire talks as those plans were brought into question.

It was tradition that the closest female relative of the prince be present at all fire talks, although if anyone knew the actual reason behind the convention, they had never told Arnika. Some said it was for luck, while others said it gave the women stories to tell the next generation. Her favorite reason was that the tradition had risen from a time when women had fought alongside their men, with the chief's closest female relative at their head.

In her formal role, Arnika was present to hear of a single Rydan and three dogs coming into LandWater.

"That would be the Pack Runner," Prince Kelland confirmed. "He's not a scout. I believe it was a mistake."

"Should we be moving?" a charger asked.

The prince shook his head. "For Tohmas to get anything from the beast, the Pack Runner would have to return to camp without dying of his injuries, which were numerous by all reports, then decide not to hide and nurse his wounds like the dog he is. He'd have to seek out an

CHAPTER 13

Esparan he hardly knows and barely obeys to report. Besides, Rydans can't count!"

There was little doubt the mood of the room lightened.

"Besides," the prince finished, "even if we thought he had reported us, there is nowhere better for us to be. We will watch for Tohmas. If needed, we will engage him here instead of at Cainton."

Arnika knew the Galanth army was within two days of Cainton and LandWater. They had no room to adjust their plans now. Her hands were unsteady as she stitched a leather tie onto the chain link shirt her father would wear.

"What about Kitable?" The same question was asked at every fire talk. No warrior could fight a caster. Trulin relied on the Double Blades, but they were merely hired help.

Fyes turned to Tostig, who sat on a stool among the crowd of chargers. He had been cleaning his nails with a strangely shaped knife, but at the acknowledgment, he smiled his lop-sided grin and palmed the blade. "We're ready for Kitable, don't worry, but he's still in Lour right now, and the trinket he left for Prince Tohmas is no longer functioning. He cannot call for his pet wizard now. My finest illusion is at your disposal, my prince."

Tostig's answer left out details Arnika wanted to hear, but the others did not ask questions. She did not speak up.

"Then be prepared; we will engage within the next two days. If Kitable is paying attention, we will need you."

Tostig shrugged. "We have our share of surprises for him, I assure you."

Prince Kelland snorted. "The bounty is worth it, I assume. Let us all get some sleep. The conquest of Espar ends here."

Arnika watched the chargers depart but lingered behind to tie the last stitch on the armor. Proudly, she handed the fixed garment to her father. He smiled at her softly as only a father could.

"You know," he said as he donned the armor he would test fully in a few days, "you are quieter than your mother was."

She paused tying the straps of the armor. It was uncommon for him to mention her mother even in good times, and he avoided the topic fervently when things were rough as if her mother's memory was reserved for joyous times. There was little need to make mention of his third wife, reputedly his favorite, when curses or prayers to either the first or second would suffice. Arnika liked to think his silence was reverence.

She resumed assisting him with the armor with a wordless smile.

He chuckled. "See? I would like to hear more from you, Nika. I always listened to your mother's advice. You might not have had her experience, but you have her spirit. If you have something to add, please do."

"Watch the south," she heard her voice say.

His white eyebrows rise into his wrinkled brow. "South?" he wondered aloud.

When he faced her, she tried to make herself taller, to add artificial experience or weight to her words. The unspoken "why?" still threw her confidence, and she let her eyes drop. As much as she would have liked to embody her mother, there was too little of the determined woman in her to break through the polished child who had spent her life in manors, weighted on and generally pampered.

"Nika," the prince's official voice pressed, spurring her loyalty into speaking even when her timidity prevented her.

She chose her words carefully. "When I first met Prince Tohmas, I noticed his ability to get the results he wanted without appearing to. He likes doing the unexpected almost as much as he likes doing the impossible. But he..." She was not making her point, but she could not find a way to explain the impression she had of the traitor to Espar. "He does not ride straight! He will not come at you as you expect. I thought south would be the least likely, so that is where he will be."

The eyebrows lowered to unite over a perplexed stare. "You think he knows about us in LandWater," he interpreted, and she nodded. "How?"

"He..." As ridiculous as it sounded, she had to say, "He always knows. He sees things, and he hears things. He..."

She trailed off, seeing him shake his head in disappointment. Her face flushed, and her heart sagged. "He is just a man, Nika. Never forget that. Judge your enemy by what you see, not what you fear."

She nodded and tried to smile, but it faded quickly when he patted her head as if she was six again, complimented the repair, and left. Watching him walk away so full of strength made her heart sink further. She wanted to follow his example, but her heart trembled at the thought of battle.

CHAPTER 13

Celebrant Corolys took the child, although Tohmas was reasonably certain he had not succeeded in convincing her that the child was not, in fact, his. Bound by oaths to keep the children of her goddess safe, she gave up on having him raise the child himself and took it to find a wet mother.

Of all the people, Tohmas thought himself the most dangerous to care for the child. He was one of the few people Crawthran may deal with in the Galanth camp. If Crawthran discovered Tohmas' crime, one of them would die. As confident as he was with his weapons, he could not slay the Pack Runner. Deception was better.

The following day, making no mention of the baby, Laorn came to Carsh and delivered the news; Crawthran had found the enemy in a village they had expected to pass.

Tohmas split the army, changing his goal from Cainton to a small village on a stream southwest of the capital. He sent off those who had fared best at the raids immediately, with directions to follow the river down and cut back across the stream to take the south of the city. This gave his wounded soldiers an extra day to recover before they struck at the village's north.

It would have to be swift. He had already sent the Rydans farther north in anticipation of Lord Tandar's attack from Cainton, but Tohmas would be happy if that proved unnecessary. If he could destroy the village and its concealed forces before Cainton knew it was happening, it would simplify the entire war.

And capture Prince Kelland, he reminded himself. As much as his Rydan mentality insisted Kelland was an enemy to be vanquished, he knew the kingsmen wanted as much of their old ways to survive as possible. Although he hated the words, that meant that princes did not kill princes. The lancers, riders, and chargers were fair game, but the prince would not be harmed.

There is still hope, Tohmas tried to convince himself as he left behind the morning spars to ride to the village. Perhaps Kelland would see reason. He had once spoken of unity. Maybe now he would see its full potential and be convinced.

Tohmas would have to speak with the man when the fighting ended.

Chapter 14

Covered in crusted blood and trailed by two hounds, the Pack Runner stumbled up the slope. The protectors followed him in a wide, respectful circle. Tohmas met him on the rise and kept his distance. The man looked half dead, but he still clutched a knife, his expression feral. Tohmas was unsure if the beast would recognize allies at all.

It wouldn't be hard for the protectors to cut down the legend now. Thinking back to Laorn, Tohmas wondered if he should command it. The savagery of the tradition gnawed at him anew. Had Laorn not rebelled and given him the child, another young boy would have been damned to live wild at the chief's call. This monster was an unabashed killer. He could end it.

The Rydans would hear of such a betrayal, and Chief Tamv would be furious. Tohmas knew better than to offend the most powerful man in the Outlander.

He waited, wondering if the knife would fly for his throat. *If he knows... if Laorn betrayed me...*

He'd made his choice. The child was safely with Celebrant Corolys. In his own way, he was helping end the tradition.

The Pack Runner's words came out as grunts. "*Nemy.*" He pointed. "*Shellas.*"

Tohmas followed the gesture, trying to match what he saw with the maps he had been staring at. The Rydan wasn't pointing at Cainton.

CHAPTER 14

There was a village that way, already checked and deemed abandoned. He couldn't remember its name.

The Pack Runner turned and left, passing between the protectors without looking up. The dogs followed him, glancing back, their ears flat to their heads. There was blood on their muzzles.

Once the Pack Runner reached the cover of trees and vanished, Tohmas let himself breathe. It would be a long while before he felt safe, he realized. If Crawthran found out Tohmas had helped Laorn deny him an heir, he'd put a knife in Tohmas' back. He feared few men in the world, but Crawthran was undoubtedly one of them.

Carsh came up on his left, and Tohmas tried to shake off his fear. By Carsh's tension, the prime protector had detected Tohmas' unease. He might not know the source, but he was ready for trouble.

The map became clearer in Tohmas' memory. "LandWater," he said, turning to face the direction Crawthran had pointed. "He thinks there are enemies in LandWater."

"'Ee knows," Carsh replied. It made sense; this was no guess. The Pack Runner had been confronted and nearly slain. That meant there were a great number of enemies.

They had assumed Kelland had taken his riders into his capital, but Tohmas had no spies reporting to him from Cainton. Besides, fighting in the streets limited their greatest strength: their horses. If Kelland had hidden, would the fields outside the capital not make for a good footing for a charge aimed at crushing Tohmas' forces against Cainton's walls? It made sense.

It sounds like something I would do if I were in his position.

Decided, Tohmas called for his guardians. Even if he was wrong, going wide would take a few more days. He could still march on Cainton after. And it seemed an excellent opportunity for a trick.

The green and silver standards appeared on the horizon.

"Send the runners to ready everyone," Kelland commanded. "This ends today."

He had no time to curse the beast man who had undoubtedly given the warning and identified the forces in LandWater. But he was not helpless. So the battle would be at LandWater. With Tandar bringing Cainton's forces in from behind, they would crush this so-called king just as surely.

"Tostig! Tell Tandar to get down here with his soldiers!"

The small man nodded, his ringed fingers flashing as he pulled out a bullhorn. He spoke the message and then blew the words into the sky. Kelland imagined he saw the streak of magic heading north through the summer's sky.

"Any sign of Kitable?" Kelland asked the caster.

Tostig shook his head, his grin ear to ear. "He's in Lour still, pleasantly oblivious. Would you like the illusions to assist you here?" The bullhorn stowed, Tostig now held a clay figure in his grip, painted red with superb details in each scale.

Although the little village had no walls, the defenses were set long before Tohmas was within sight, but additional surprises for their enemy were always welcome. "On my command," Kelland replied.

Tohmas' green standard flew over the middle of the forces, well protected, as they advanced on LandWater. Assembled in a heartbeat, Kelland's horsemen formed a line. The ruse was over. It was time they showed the glory of the warhorses they rode.

Dusk was approaching, but it did not matter. He could still see the green banner among the forces in the gloom, and Tohmas would not stop for the darkness; the charging horses would overrun his camp if he tried.

Cut the head from the snake, and the body dies, Kelland reminded himself. That banner was his target. He and Stormbreaker would clear the way if they had to, but he and Tohmas would meet and end the conflict here and now.

The enemy's riders kicked into a charge, and Kelland called for the Trullers to match them; let them see the power of a true warhorse! It was not until they were nearly atop each other that Kelland recognized something was wrong.

The enemy's horses were massive, larger than any Galanth steeds. The riders were not Esparan at all; the green tabards seen in the dim light were paints on bare skin. One held a banner, that was true, but the carrier discarded it as soon as the forces met.

Rydans.

CHAPTER 14

It was too late; they were atop each other.

Kelland's soldiers had fought from atop their warhorses for lifetimes; they made good. Despite the southerner's ferocity, the discipline of years of battle won the charge. Horses crashed and skidded, but Kelland's line held. Spears and swords entered the fray. The armored Trullers, working as a unit, pushed back the disorganized Rydans.

"Behind us! Look! The light!"

Kelland pivoted at the call from one of his chargers and was surprised to see a red light within the village. The red light, according to the legends, followed Tohmas alone. That meant the self-declared King of Espar was in the one place Kelland did not want him: LandWater.

Before he could formulate a response, a joat arrived at his side, pulling up her pony expertly. It was not Arnika, he was pleased to see. He would have been furious if the joats had allowed his daughter into the messy battlefield. For now, he still had a region cleared around him, his riders engaged with Rydans throughout the field. "The Galanth forces coming in from the south!" the joat reported. She had a small sword in hand, and her eyes were wide as she surveyed the scene around her. The Rydans were losing ground, although the toll was growing. And, worse, this was a diversion. The main forces, and Tohmas himself, were not here.

"Pull back!" Kelland called. "Tostig! Your turn!"

A dragon soared overhead low, the Double Blades making good on their contract. Although Kelland's horse snorted and kicked, the bit kept the warhorse in check. The Rydan's horses, while not necessarily frightened by the dragon overhead, were certainly distracted, and it provided cover for his riders to retreat. They had defenses to pull back to. He could hold overnight if he had to. Running would be deadly, but once Cainton's additional forces arrived...

He sent a thought to Arnika as he passed back into the streets of LandWater. She had been right: Tohmas indeed did not ride straight, damn him.

With Kelland's main riders chasing green-painted Rydans, Tohmas and his forces made their way through the river south of LandWater. They were in the streets by the time they met resistance. Alarms sounded. Tohmas drew SoulBurner.

"Eyes up! Enemy in the sky!" a protector shouted.

A red dragon flew in on brown wings, its heat making the air shimmer above him. Tohmas' stomach dropped. The Red was perhaps smaller than the Black he had faced, but he had not felled that great beast; DoomDragon had. And the ax that could cut dragon scale had been destroyed. His other option—Wisavi Kitable—was most painfully absent.

Knowing SoulBurner upset Kitable's spells, he sheathed the enchanted blade for a moment and said, "Kit, I could use your help."

Nothing happened. There was no sudden appearance of the wizard. He waited again, wondering if SoulBurner had damaged the spell. Kitable had always heard him before.

Fine, he decided. SoulBurner could get through the scale, he was certain, but how would he get close enough to the beast without being burned? His legend said he was immune to fire, but he had not yet begun believing the tales.

"Tohmas!" boomed DoomDragon's voice far to his left. "Yellow! It is an illusion!"

Darknim was closer to magic than Tohmas could ever hope to be, and Tohmas knew it. While Kitable used spells to see magic auras with enchanted eyes, DoomDragon achieved the same by looking. It was faint, he claimed, but wizard magic glowed under his grey-eyed stare.

Tohmas' hesitation vanished. Illusionary fire could not burn him. Illusionary teeth could not hurt him. SoulBurner was now infinitely stronger: the aura would dispel the magic.

The beast had circled back from scattering the Rydans in the north but abruptly rose over Tohmas' region, remaining out of reach. Tohmas had to frown. He had been hoping to get SoulBurner out as the dragon flew above him and destroy it in Inac's glory, but the illusionist seemed to know already to avoid the sword.

Behind Tohmas, the beast let loose a blast of fire that made his fighters shout in pain. Were there spells within the illusion that truly caused pain? It didn't matter so long as he brought the beast down.

A dozen arrows, fired from protectors as the beast passed, missed or went through the vision. They fell onto his fighters. He was in the

middle of cursing when a roar shook the ground beneath him, and a new shadow soared over his head. He ducked despite the buildings around him would prevent the new dragon from hitting his head

Before the red dragon could turn, the new glittering gold dragon loosed its fire. In the approaching darkness, it lit up like a bonfire against the cool blue, so bright he couldn't see if the illusion reacted.

"Greetings, King Tohmas!" a man's voice shouted from behind the lines of protectors. "You've got some magic problem, I see! Can I be of assistance?"

The green-clad protectors parted to admit Dust Weaver and his daughter. The apothecary's eyes remained on the sky as he held one hand up and tilted it slightly. The gold dragon above swooped to its left.

"Very impressive gold dragon, Master Weaver. How long can you hold it?" Tohmas asked.

The red-haired man harrumphed and waved his hand grandly in demonstration. Above, the gold dragon performed a delicate spin, lit by the light of the flames pouring from it. "Longer than our enemy can!" he said.

The red dragon turned its teeth onto the gold, and the two illusions clashed above.

"Oh, and I have something for you," Shimmer Weaver added. She lifted a decanter bottle. To his confusion, it was empty.

"Bad time for a drink," he said.

With a grin, she removed the stopper and words echoed: "Your father commands your immediate departure from Cainton with full forces to his position at LandWater. An engagement is imminent. Hurry."

The words dissipated as they were spoken. Tohmas was left blinking at the empty decanter.

"I caught their message," Shimmer explained. "Didn't think you wanted more people joining this dinner party."

Now, Tohmas could join her in smiling. If Kelland was expecting reinforcements...

Before giving his guardians their commands, he raised an eyebrow at Shimmer. "You didn't catch another message, did you?" He had been expecting Kitable, but the wisavi was still notably missing.

She shook her long red hair.

So be it, he thought with a sigh. With Dust keeping the dragon at bay, it seemed an even fight now. *Good enough.*

"Darknim! I need your hunters; they are fastest on foot!"

The Northlander gave a toothy grin, his smaller axes in hand. The grin grew as Tohmas explained his idea.

Kelland's fighters did their best to press forces cornered in LandWater, but Kelland could not get close to the red light. No matter how he maneuvered, Galanth fighters always kept him back.

Well, I can play this game too. He needed to buy time, and the easiest way was to use Tohmas' trick against him.

Sending his banner north, Kelland headed south. He had not gone far before he came across several green-coated enemies on horseback. They quickly attacked, not recognizing the prowess of his entourage and taking due caution as they would have had they seen his banner. Although the fighters were unremarkable, many of them rode undeniably Trulin-bred warhorses. The sight of something so precious in his enemy's hands made his vision blur.

The horses met furiously.

They were good, but Kelland's riders were better. Two Galanth fell to each of the Trullers injured. Finally, Kelland found their leader: a mustached man wearing the red rank rope. They set their eyes on each other. Dropping his blow low, Kelland struck hard, throwing the retaliating strike wide. While Kelland's sword cut deep into the enemy's hip, Kelland only took a knock against his helmet. It was hard enough to break the leather ties, but he kept both his seat and his helmet as he rode on.

He expected no pursuit with the guardian so injured, and he was proven right once he reached the village square unopposed. Two dragons wrestled overhead. *Tostig is battling the enemy wizard*, Kelland assumed. *So long as Kitable is busy.*

Soon he was eagerly pushing the Galanth back, their blood thick under his horse's hooves. Somewhere in the melee, his helmet came loose and was lost, but Kelland still fought his way to the rear of the

CHAPTER 14

lines. He set his riders at the city's core, defended and secured. The joats were safe here. He could hold until Tandar arrived.

Finally, as midnight loomed, a joat reported the forces coming from the north. His soldiers cheered as the Rydans, still active on the north field, scattered. To Kelland's relief, the reinforcements beat a path into LandWater.

He rode out to greet his nephew and the army that would drive out the enemy of Espar. He did not know which side had more soldiers remaining now, so many had fallen, but with Tandar's fresh forces...

Something dug into his back between the bottoms of his shoulder blades. He paused, confused. There were no enemies here. Tohmas and his warriors were still in the south of the city, kept at bay. The dragons were gone from the skies.

But the warrior came into the light of the torches. Fur-clad and thickly-muscled, there were not the Truller footmen Kelland had expected. These were Northlanders.

"Back to the defenses!" he called, turning Stormbreaker with his knees so he could swing at the brute before him as he retreated with his riders. A trick! Another damned trick! This was despite...

The pain in his back pitched him forward onto Stormbreaker's neck. The ax in his back shifted deeper.

Darkness fell in an instant. It was cold, and then Kelland saw no more.

Chapter 15

Every time Kitable rested, the bleeding restarted. A Scry on his own back—a somewhat disconcerting view—revealed the infection was spreading. His wound became a raised shade of purple and red with dark bruising, and it hurt fiercely and constantly. No medicine or salve he tried helped.

He ran their errands, hiding his wound and the pain. Three extended Earth Destructions finished the job of clearing the largest collapsed tunnel. He dug out other collapsed areas and then cleaned away debris. For days, he dug and fixed everything they pointed him at.

Rumors held that the tunnel of StonePeak had been made by wizards in the years before, but no wizard had ever claimed credit for the feat. It was not difficult to shape or destroy stone, but the very scope of the network made for long days. By the end of the day, he could hardly move.

Using minor spells, Kitable cleaned the wound once more and applied a new dressing, but it still ached enough to make him move delicately as he returned to a collapsed region. In defeat, he wore a Pain Destruction spell. Nothing else allowed him to stand straight.

Kingsman Loritat met him with a broad grin and a basic breakfast. "Another day?" he asked.

Kitable did not dare shrug. "I suppose," he said. He accepted the oatmeal, impressed that the kingsman had found early strawberries somewhere in Lour to top the bland meal.

"I am grateful," the man said. "Think of the lives you have already saved! And how prompt you were in answering me! I was shocked it took only two days. I am delighted! If I can assist in your work, please let me know. If only we had a wizard of our own!"

Kitable had not been listening, being too busy eating the cool oatmeal, knowing he would need the strength. But one line of Loritat's rambles snagged his attention.

"Two ... days? You mean two days from when we received your message?" he asked.

"No, two days from our sending it, my dear man."

Tohmas' army was many days east of Lour. No rider, without magic aid, could have traversed that distance in two days.

"I thought you said you had no caster among you."

Loritat laughed. "Our princedom has not had one in over twenty years."

Since Master Sylas was killed by one of his apprentices, Kitable finished mentally. It may not have been true, but it was undoubtedly what the then-prince would have been told.

A sinking feeling pulled Kitable's stomach so far down that even the strawberries could not recover his appetite. "If there was no magical assistance, we received your call for help five days before it could have arrived." The implications made him balk. "What caused these cave-ins?"

Loritat shrugged. "Minor earthquake, maybe. Hit a few separate areas, but I do not recall feeling any..."

The disaster had been staged and the message sent early. Kitable had been tricked into leaving Tohmas' side.

As much as he wanted to rant at the man, it seemed futile.

"Since there are no longer immediate lives in danger," Kitable quickly said, handing the kingsman back the bowl, "I must be on my way. We can arrange reconstruction another time. I must check on the king."

Kitable locked onto his waggon anchor and activated the Relocation spell before the kingsman could form a reply. He left him holding the oatmeal in the light of torches.

Kitable landed in the camp to find it chaotic. Colt wasn't at the vardo, and there was no visible banner. Instead, he had to find a protector to take him to the king. Somehow, the defenders always knew where Tohmas was.

Bit by bit, he pieced together the story; a battle had taken place. It was ending.

Kitable had never seen such disarray. He was accustomed to surrender, treaties, and organized retreats. War had become, under the control of the princes, strangely civilized. Even Northlanders had been coordinated under DoomDragon and had battled with some semblance of order.

But the forces here were scattered. Some broke and fled while others surrendered. Others just lost interest and managed to get themselves killed in combat. No one seemed to know what they were meant to be doing and ended up doing everything and nothing at once. The results were decidedly in Tohmas' favor.

The protector brought him to the king in the village square. He was still atop his warhorse and covered in blood but sorted through prisoners and final pockets of enemies in the dawn.

"Why didn't you call me?" Kitable snapped, scanning the area, then checking the skies. Old auras lingered, but nothing was active. The king's forces seemed to be winning. That was fortunate. His hovering spells were not designed for battle.

Tohmas cocked his head from atop Schlavarai. "I did. You took your time, it seems."

Kitable straightened, blinking up at his patron. His heart skipped. "You did?"

"Clearly, you didn't hear me. Well, Shimmer trapped their message. Maybe yours was intercepted as well."

His throat dry, Kitable nodded. *Me? Intercepted?* He couldn't believe it. The implications were far-reaching. How much did his enemy know about his spells? They had circumvented at least one. What about others? And were they responsible for the destruction in Lour?

"Are you all right, Wisavi?" Tohmas interrupted his thoughts.

"Just plotting who I have to kill," he answered. "Have you need of me now?"

Tohmas shook his head and waved on the group of prisoners, all riders by their attire. They were carted away. "I think we're under control. But if you can keep an eye out for the caster, please do. His illusion vanished somewhere around midnight. The Weavers were good to their word; they matched him. But we didn't catch whomever it was. I still haven't found Kelland either. We're still flushing out pockets of Trullers, but if the prince is still among them, he's not made himself known. And no one seems to be in charge!"

Kitable mutely nodded, perplexed. How many casters were there this time? He'd finished the Double Blades, so who was casting here?

As Tohmas was called to the side, Kitable leaned against a wall to wait. A feeling of profound disappointment lingered in his gut. He wasn't accustomed to failure, yet here it was. He had missed the call. He'd been tricked into being away from Tohmas when the king needed him. And who had done it?

He was leaning on his wound, he realized abruptly. He straightened. The Pain Destruction spell was keeping him from feeling anything. But damaging his injury further was probably not wise.

Distracting him, a line of women was escorted past. It remained to be seen what Tohmas would do with the joats. As much as they had no desire to slaughter women, their lives would be easier if Cainton did not have the support of the healers and helpers during the siege.

The lowered head of one young woman caught Kitable's attention. How could he recognize any woman of Trulin?

"Wait!" he commanded, and the lines of soldiers paused immediately. Kitable left the wall and stood before the group of women. They crowded around the face of interest, obscuring her in a shield of skirts and shawls, but the shy stare peeked out, and Kitable recognized it further. And when he checked, he spotted Lady Altana as well. He had met both women at a dinner in Forsinth during the early march.

They had captured Kelland's daughter, Lady Arnika Trulin, and her cousin, Lady Altana Oranon.

He glanced around, but Tohmas had moved onto something else and was not in the square.

"Prime Warden! I need a runner to fetch—"

The young woman burst from her companions and fell onto her knees before him. His words dropped in shock.

Her voice tight; her words were swift but soft. "Master Kitable! Our lands are strong, and our wealth great. I swear, I will give you anything you want! Please! Do not turn me over to that monster!"

Having a woman beg him on her knees shook Kitable enough to make his words lag. He had to hope his uncertainty was not seen as considering her offer.

There was no question: he handed a runner one of his tokens and told the man to get the king to him as fast as possible. The runner looked a little concerned over the tone of the summons, but he left at a sprint. Only then did Kitable look back to the woman peering up at him with cold blue eyes.

"He is not—"

"He is an invader, a thief, and a murderer!" Her voice rose as she stood. She'd skinned her knuckles in kneeling, he saw. An empty knife sheath sat on her belt. "Think of what he will do to me! To them! Have you no heart, wizard? Have you not seen—"

"I *have* seen," Kitable snapped back. "I have seen more than you can guess. I tell you now, he is not going to harm you."

"Then why call him?" Lady Arnika insisted from among her entourage. "If I am meaningless, why separate me? Why draw his attention to me at all?"

"I never said *you* were meaningless."

"He has invaded my family's land, butchered our people, stolen our horses, and even now makes plans to conquer all of Espar! What kind of man is that!? What—"

Shouts and hoofbeats interrupted, and Lady Arnika shrank from the confrontation. Pressing her lips as if to stop the words physically, she hid among the joats once more.

A moment later, Tohmas arrived on his enormous warhorse. He loomed over Kitable. "The runner who delivered your summons, Wisavi, delivered it in the smallest voice I have ever heard. For some reason, he seemed to think I would resent having you order my presence, but I assume you have a damn good reason for—"

When the sentence paused, Kitable knew he had spotted Lady Arnika.

For a long moment, no one moved. Now in the king's more formidable presence, Lady Arnika said nothing, her bravery depleted.

Tohmas' voice lightened. "Lady Arnika, how unexpected." He nodded to her politely. Turning ever so slightly to his waiting wizard, he added, "Thank you, Kitable."

Kitable could only shrug and step back, willing to pass off the confrontation now.

Clearly not believing anything Kitable had said, one of the women in the crowd shouted, "You will not lay a hand on her!"

Unbothered by the malice in the voice, Tohmas lightly smiled. "I assure you, I mean her no harm."

One of the older women, with white streaks in her pale hair, pointed out, "Your definition of harm may vary from ours, beast. We will not allow—"

No one is letting anyone finish their sentences today, Kitable reflected.

"I gladly swear by the Flame that I will not lay an unpermitted hand on her except in self-defense." Seeking her stare among the accusatory glares of the other women, Tohmas added for the Lady alone, "I request only to speak with you."

More than one woman added their opinions, quickly rendering each other incomprehensible, but the firm voice of the youngest among them cut through: "You will not harm them."

It was the second order Tohmas had received today, but he was no more offended by Lady Arnika's insistence than he had been by Kitable's. She pressed, "You will release all of these ladies, alive and well, to my cousin Tandar in Cainton."

"If you remain, I will gladly return these women to your cousin," he countered immediately.

"Alive!" she insisted with a flare of her modest dress and the elegant cloak that failed to let her quite blend in.

"Fair Lady," Tohmas immediately appeased, "all the joats will be returned alive and well to Cainton by the most direct route, so long as you remain. Are we agreed?"

It was surprising to see him extend his fist for the agreement, as Kitable would never have expected a woman to be held to the old gesture. The knocking of fists had come from cutting across the fists of the agreeing parties with a knife. The matching scars proved that both parties had initially agreed to the terms if the agreement was squelched. Now, the gesture was nothing but a knock of one fist on the other, but people had not expected women to participate when mutilation had been the mainstay, and they did not expect it now.

"Nika, no!" Lady Altana objected as she tried to pull her cousin back.

Arnika Trulin stepped up and knocked her fist against the king's fist. The size difference between her and the large man made her hand childlike. "We are agreed," she said softly, "but the gods will hold you to your oath."

He smiled at the threat. "I never expect otherwise."

A guardian was assigned to escort the joats to Cainton immediately. Tohmas chose a protector who had overheard the conversation, presumably because he would know the oath that had been made.

"Take Lady Arnika to the Healing waggon," he added to another protector. "Her knuckles need treatment."

Kitable moved to leave. Briefly, he caught Tohmas' eye and received a nod of thanks, but the wizard was too tired to reply. Instead of being sore, his back felt weak. He needed to think.

The moment he was in his vardo, everything came crashing down. Renewed pain shot the length of his body, sending his vision into dizzying spins. He may have stumbled, but all Kitable remembered was falling onto the bed before he lost consciousness.

The promise made, Arnika tried to come up with something to say, but her mouth was dry and her throat thick. Too rapidly, the joats were gone, and she was left with Galanth protectors. She heard the commands Tohmas gave for their safe deliverance, and her heart was satisfied that the women would live to fight the invader again. The joy of that victory was fleeting in the uncertainty of her fate.

He would betray his oath surely. She knew, with terror in her gut, that she was trapped.

Escorted away by two protectors, she took only steps around the corner of one of the houses of LandWater before, desperate to slow events down, she stopped.

"A stone," she said to the protector, lifting her foot. She went through the motions of investigating her leather-soled riding shoe, trying to give herself time to think.

She could escape, perhaps, but was now the time?

The words "found dead" interrupted her thoughts. From back the way she had come, she heard reports being delivered to Tohmas. She lingered with her shoe, prodding deeper as if the stone eluded her.

"Demons," the so-called king replied with vehemence in his voice. "You're sure?"

"We had five men confirm it independently. He was nowhere near his banner and was missing his plumed helm. No one would have been able to recognize him."

Her hopeful heart stopped in her chest, and she went cold. There was only one man who carried a banner in Trulin.

"Demon shit," Tohmas cursed. "I never wanted him dead."

There was a pause, and another voice chipped in, "Guardian Caraway mentioned meeting the man but recognized him by the helm. Said they exchanged blows, and Lance took a blow through the hip that nearly castrated him. He's in Healing Mother Gracie's waggon."

More silence followed. One of Arnika's protectors offered to help with her shoe, but she muttered something about a crack in the sole, and the excuse bought her time to hear, "Set up a pyre; Prince Kelland deserves it. I had better tell his daughter. I would rather she hear it from me."

When it seemed they might disperse, she slid her shoe on and immediately started walking. The protectors followed, leading her to the Healing waggons.

She held back tears during the walk, but the moment she saw the blood-covered so-called king in silver and green, she fell apart. Held by the foreign Pari celebrant, she wept.

Some part of her heard Prince Tohmas' words of comfort, but she did not answer him, and at length, he saw to the others in the waggon. She overheard conversations about the battle, including an account of a battle with her father, but nothing penetrated her sorrow. For candles, she hid among the arms of strangers and sobbed.

It had always been a possibility too remote to be considered. Tohmas had to be stopped. Her father had taken that risk to protect Trulin. Pride and loyalty had guided him straight to his death.

She could not eat and did not sleep. At dawn, they lit the pyre.

Flanked by Galanth protectors, she watched her father and her hope for Trulin burn away. People spoke to her, but she did not hear them. Despair threatened her in the bright noon sun when the fires burned out, and she did not chase it off.

More strange faces came to her. The Celebrants of Inac who had lit the fire offered her condolences, and the woman swore more glory to the Goddess for her father's great strength in battle. Then a man dressed in white and a woman wearing blue approached her with a child between them. The last of the fires were reducing to embers behind them as they spoke.

The woman embraced her. "The Goddess weeps with you this day."

Finding her voice for the first time since hearing the news, Arnika scoffed. "Why would you weep for him? You were his enemy."

At this, the comely woman smiled, and Arnika, for a brief instant, saw an echo of another face. Although her mother had died years ago, Arnika saw a mother's love in her soft smile.

"The Goddess weeps not for him, for he is done and rests. We weep for you, Lady. We weep for every child who is lost."

"Lost?" Arnika echoed in confusion.

A man's voice answered, although there was no sound. *Grown up,* it said.

The family left.

Arnika stood alone again, her mind too muddled to hear the condolences offered by more strangers. The two words that had come to her mind, not her ears, lingered with her. Who had spoken? Were, as the woman said, the gods weeping for her? Were their voices reaching out? Or had it been her father? At his pyre, had the ghost spoken to her?

Every possibility meant the words had been important, and Arnika considered the conversation again as dusk fell. Grown up? She was seventeen, but she was unmarried and had no children. A woman was not grown until she had wed, surely! Her father's death made her feel more like a child than ever, a lonely child.

But the love and certainty of her mother, seen briefly in the Celebrant of Ocea, stayed with her. Like a ghostly whisper, she heard her father's voice: *You have her spirit.*

He had seen the spirit; it had to be there. She would find it. As the celebrants had said, she was going to grow up. She was alone, but she could be strong. Could she help her people from her position among the enemy?

CHAPTER 15

She drew her hair over her shoulder and braided it quickly. Turning to the nearest protector, she requested his knife.

The man apologetically refused but offered, if she desired, to cut the braid for her.

Unable to speak to him, she nodded and stood silently as the knife cut unevenly above the braid.

Approaching the embers where her father's ashes lay, she placed the hair on the fire as a final farewell.

As she turned from the embers, she faced Prince Tohmas. He had not moved from his place by the fires since the celebrants had lit them. Although people had spoken to him, he had hardly responded. A strip of brown cloth wrapped around his arm, but she sensed he was trying to converse with the fires more than grieve over them. Now, he stood and called over the protector who had cut her hair. She expected a rebuttal, but instead, she heard, "Take her to my tent."

The child in her shrank back and wept, but her mother's spirit stretched its wings. Breaking his oath would see him damned even more than he already was. He did not frighten her, not anymore.

Her shoulders feeling as light as the lack of hair made her head, she met his stare as she was led away, but his eyes seemed only sad.

Watching the flames helped him get closer to Inac, for she had not visited for more than a mooncycle, and Tohmas felt he needed her. Plans for Trulin were confused. If they took much longer to fix Trulin's support, Gaidol would be able to move against Solta or Tohmas' forces with Polthian. That large of a force meant bloodshed. Even if Tohmas won, there might not be sufficient forces remaining to stop Damoria from invading Galanth. The logic had him going in circles. He alternated between cursing Kelland and respectfully wishing him well.

Another prince was dead. So far, that meant five princes had died over the last two years despite their continual insistence that princes did not kill princes. Tohmas' hand had killed two, and his orders had killed another two. The fifth one, ironically the first prince to die of the five, puzzled Tohmas the most. Seeing Arnika lose her father brought that memory back.

He had not meant Prince Habal harm. In fact, Tohmas had slain his father's killer. Still, he could not pretend he had done so in the name of justice. Bragn had attacked Tohmas when he had shown uncertainly between loyalty to the father he had only just met and the conditioning of fifteen years to obey the Rydan chief. Trained by too many battles, Tohmas had killed Bragn by accident, for nothing Rydans did was ever gentle.

Although Bragn had killed Habal, Tohmas had accepted and aided the subsequent deception, coached by Bragn's wisavis. Why the cutters had not noticed the gut wound that bled Prince Habal dry, Tohmas did not know, but he had not questioned it. If Galanth had known of the murder, suspicion would have been cast on Tohmas.

Someone was dead once more, and he was guilty.

There is hope, he thought as Arnika Trulin walked to the pyre. Although he had failed to convince Kelland, if he convinced the descendent of the prince, perhaps she could sway the princedom. Having her lead the Trullers instead of her cousin Tandar, who would undoubtedly fight Tohmas for every step he made into the princedom, was preferred. And if he wished to deal with her as a representative of Trulin, he had to treat her like one.

When she moved to leave, he called over the protector and instructed that she be taken to his tent. To a runner, he added, "Ask my Lady Mother to meet me outside my tent in a candle, please." The runner left at a sprint.

More problems, he thought. The fire was done, and he had just given himself a timeline. As frustrating as it was, it was time to go.

Sending runners to set up a new tent for himself, he belatedly recognized he had just given up his altar. Tonight, as the sun vanished, he would have to go to the Temple waggon to pay homage. Presumably, he could get Sedgan to empty the waggon.

Carsh followed as Tohmas wandered to the Temple waggon circle and, for a moment, contemplated the four waggons around the camp circle.

There were four again, which was good. Immediately after Celebrant Corolys had joined, Tohmas had bought her a waggon and given her the funds to prepare it as she saw fit. The result was a decor of shells and dolphin mosaics along both walls, with seaweed-like curtains banking the entrance. She'd collected a gaggle of girls somehow, but they were likely in bed by this time. Only worshippers of Inac were in the campfire circle tonight, spilling out from a full Temple waggon.

Celebrant Loni was visiting, Tohmas noted idly. She hailed him as the Champion, and he had to tell them to stop kneeling to him. When one acolyte was isolated, Tohmas realized he had stumbled into an ordainment. This acolyte had, by this candle exactly, become a full celebrant.

He congratulated the now-celebrant and wished him well in Inac's work, which had the man blushing, bowing, and repeatedly kneeling before eventually returning to Loni's side. The look they shared made it clear what congratulation the celebrant would offer soon, but Tohmas let that pass.

Rather than interrupt, he instead turned to the other waggons and went to visit Totho.

Since the arrival of the Rydans to the forces, Carsh often left Tohmas during the early hours of the evenings, when Tohmas usually was at his altar. Now, Carsh paused outside the waggon of Totho, and Tohmas realized that his brother had been avoiding the prayers. Tohmas knew Carsh did not understand Esparan religion, despite the similarity of the gods between the races. Still, he had not really noticed his brother's unease with the Esparan waggons before.

Given the choice through Tohmas' shrug, the Rydan stayed outside.

Hammocks had once filled the front area of the Temple waggon of Wind for the acolytes, but only one hammock remained now. Timon was asleep as Tohmas entered. The celebrant, however, was not.

Having avoided Totho's Temple waggon for a very long time because of his association with the dead, Tohmas felt out of place. Totho was also called the Guardian of Secrets, and for a moment, the implications of that made him hesitate. He held many secrets, most of them revolving around death. Abruptly, he felt entering the waggon had been a bad idea.

Before he could excuse himself, he met the white-robed celebrant's stormy grey stare, and the mute man's mystic powers flooded over him.

He had experienced the holy powers before, but those had been individual thoughts given to his mind. This time, Tohmas' own thoughts came to the front of his mind, and what he saw made him regret entering the Temple waggon even more.

Every memory of the deaths he had caused, from Habal's to Kelland's, returned to him in their entirety. Within a blink, he was again standing over Prince Habal's deathbed, silently wondering why the cutters were not treating the gut wound. He heard the voices of the two Rydan wis-avis who had helped him hide Bragn's death promise compassion from the Chief. Tohmas would be Prince of Galanth, and he would conquer the world, one princedom at a time, in the name of Tamv.

The rest of the deaths followed in quick order: Rairn, fading away with fever and shakes because of the poison Tohmas placed in his water; Dragal, collapsing into Tohmas' arms, blood pooling around the arrow Tohmas had driven into his back; Marfaie's jaw shattered to keep the secret, then handing him to two vengeful brothers. He was left to starve, tied to a post.

All the secrets were exposed in the blink of an eye.

Deception and death, came the clear thoughts from the holy man. *Murderer!*

"Calanor..." Tohmas began, but before he could form an argument, the celebrant's thoughts again jabbed, like a bright burst of light, in his mind.

They trust you, and you deceive them, not once but five times! Five murders on your hands, all of them trusted. Murderer!

Tohmas saw the moments again, and he was brought to his knees by the intensity of the visions. First came his inaction at Habal's assault; he stood confused beside the bedside, watching the color fade from the unconscious man as he bled out. In the next blink, Tohmas saw his own hand pull the soaked Tarol root from tainted water, then place the water beside Rairn. With each sip the healers gave, the man's fever worsened. The Prince of Barlaby never regained consciousness.

Dragal had asked for death, but Calanor did not show that memory. With perfect clarity, Tohmas instead saw himself take the arrow from Carsh, grasp it behind the tip, and drive it deep into the back of his "uncle." With Carsh's help, all the blame fell to a fabricated shooter across a courtyard.

Marfaie's death was two words that now echoed through his mind. Tohmas said, "He is yours," to the two brothers after they had been told Marfaie had killed their eldest brother.

You feared Marfaie because he knew what you kept from us! Calanor accused.

In his mind, Tohmas heard Marfaie's voice. "You are doing this for conquest! You are obeying Tamv!" Tohmas' concern had been to silence the man before he spread his discovery, taken from Carsh's mind by magic, to others. There was no denying the memory.

They would question you rightly, and you will not allow it. How dare you presume to take that choice from them!

"I do this—" Tohmas said, but the wind whipped over him and took the air from his lungs.

You do this because a southern voice has told you to! the celebrant insisted. *Then he placed a spy in your shadow to keep you to your purpose! When it is finished, you will hand us over to Tamv like a meat offering! You lie to us because you know we would not follow if we knew!*

Tohmas' thoughts went to SoulBurner, but there was no way to pull the blade through the powers that held him on his knees. Had he had breath, he would have whistled for Carsh, but the air would not come into his lungs. Even Tohmas' strength could not force its way through the magic he did not understand.

Unable to make a sound, he sought instead to focus his thoughts. Getting through Espar had been an obstacle fought with words, not swords. He had conquered half of Espar with treaties and promises. He did not need his sword.

I do this to see peace in Espar! Tohmas repeated in his mind.

The narrowing of the grey eyes visible over the grey scarf made it clear that the celebrant had heard Tohmas' answer.

Peace! Celebrant Calanor scoffed, the sound a grunt because of his missing tongue. *You rule! You conquer! What peace?*

Before Tamv, Tohmas thought as clearly as he could, *there was nothing but war in the south. Now, all three clans are united, and there is peace. I want that peace for Espar!*

There had still been no breath with which to form words. Tohmas' lungs begin to insist he breathe.

Peace through deception and violence!

Only when peace fails do I follow war.

"Calanor, beloved, wait, please."

The female voice had a soothing effect on them both. For Tohmas, the greatest relief was the sudden release in his chest. Air flooded into his lungs. Finally able to breathe, he tried again to move, but whatever spell the celebrant used had not released entirely. Still, the stars behind his eyes went out.

Celebrant Corolys stood near the entrance to a curtained area of the waggon, wearing a shift of pale blue and nothing else. For the first time since Tohmas had met her, she was painfully undecorated, except for a single bracelet around her right wrist signifying her marriage to Calanor. Somewhere under his sleeves, the Celebrant of Totho was probably wearing a matching one.

As she entered, her expression became distant. Her face remained calm. But at length, she blinked and seemed to focus.

"I see, beloved," she said to Calanor, clearly having "heard" something from him. Tohmas groaned. "But I saw more in those visions. You are being too harsh."

Coming forward, she laid a soft hand on her lover's cloaked shoulder. "Rairn was a traitor. He should have had a trial by Esparan rule, but Tohmas was using the only law he understood, that of the Outlands. Dragal asked for death, and his dying words were thanks for the gesture. Marfaie was a traitor to his class. Even if he was not responsible for Dragal's death, he was certainly guilty of crimes against Sol." The woman advanced to lean over Tohmas and met his stare. He was still frozen, permitted only the rise and fall of his sore chest.

"Most importantly," she finished, "did you feel his sorrow, my love? Did you hear how he regrets Kelland's fall? How these deaths have broken his hope for a bloodless conquest?"

Her tender hand touched Tohmas' shoulder. "I believe him when he says he wants peace. I know he fights for another's purpose, but his cause is more than that. I do not know Tamv, but I will certainly make sure I do when it comes to making any meat offerings. If this Rydan thinks he can take Espar from the Esparans without a fight, he is mistaken. Tohmas, after all, has just spent the last two years teaching us how to fight together."

The cold of the wind pressed against him, Calanor delving into his mind for his reaction. Tohmas was surprised by his thoughts.

CHAPTER 15

He had unified Espar to conquer it. At the time, his concern had been the Rydans, who had a tradition of following only leaders, but as he considered the woman's words of warning, he realized he had made a mistake.

All the plans had been based on a single assumption: Esparans were weak. But if, as he had proven, they could be brought together, even be good enough to become his Followers, why would they accept Tamv? Just as no Rydan would accept an Esparan leader, the Esparans would never accept a Rydan one.

Tohmas had told Kelland that only he could hold the alliance together. That had not changed.

The two celebrants seemed to follow his thoughts to their conclusion. The woman smiled to see his confusion.

He had done this for Tamv, but it would not work. He could not hand them over. He had made Espar into so much more.

"You see the problem," Corolys said. "Do you still seek peace, knowing this?"

The wind pulled away from him, allowing Tohmas to nod. SoulBurner pulsed on his hip, heat cutting through the chill wind. He was sure that the words *A blade for the war that brings peace to Espar* were burning nearby.

Is this Inac's will as well?

Celebrant Corolys stared at him, and he feared her power for the first time. There was something penetrating to her stare, as if lies would be made evident.

"Prove it," she challenged.

The wind dropped. Tohmas landed on his hands and knees, shivering.

Part of him wanted SoulBurner to cut down the celebrants, but he rejected that Rydan instinct. Firstly, these celebrants were close to their gods, and since Tohmas believed in those gods wholeheartedly, he did not dare lay a hand on them. How did he know that it was not Totho and Ocea who confronted him? With the powers Celebrant Calanor often demonstrated, it was hard to draw a line between the celebrant and the god.

Secondly, Tohmas had already lived through a broken circle of celebrants and knew that to be an ill omen he did not wish on his camp right now. He needed the balance of the four to achieve his goals.

Thirdly, Tohmas did not think the celebrants had truly been as out of line as his Rydan sensibilities believed. He had indeed murdered five princes in a world where princes did not kill princes, and he had been concealing that. The gods had called him on the deception. He had been judged and found guilty. They were offering a challenge in retribution.

"How can I prove it?" he whispered.

They conversed without an audible word. At length, Calanor stepped back, carrying his wind with him. Celebrant Corolys gave Tohmas a soft smile. "End this war with Trulin peacefully," she said.

He would have been more optimistic had she asked him to raise the level of the Ice Ocean.

"I just killed the Prince of Trulin," he said, the confession feeling wrong as it left his mouth. "I don't think Trulin will follow me without bloodshed."

She crouched before him and placed her hand back onto his shoulder. She squeezed gently. "You will figure it out."

The sight of the Celebrant of Ocea's bracelet caught his attention. The husband's bracelet was always made from the hair of the wife, and vice-versa. Seeing it now made him think of the braid of hair the daughter of Kelland had lain in the fire.

If he convinced Lady Arnika, she could help with the rest of the princedom. A marriage between them...

With that thought, Tohmas' world changed.

...treasure her... know the happiness I found ... know a trust that cannot be shaken.

The flare from SoulBurner forced the last of Totho's presence from Tohmas' mind, and he stood firm with the burn of the fire. He had his solution from the memory of his mother's words, spoken with a blade in hand:

You must love your wife, as I have loved Habal, and never let anyone get between you.

"I will bring Trulin to me without another drop of blood spilled," he swore.

He had his path.

Chapter 16

Fayela waited outside the green tent impatiently for her son. The battle in LandWater had left her energized by anxiousness. Being called out without explanation thickened her fears. She could only imagine him calling for aid if he was half dead, and the thought terrified her.

Seeing Tohmas arrive without a scratch on him lightened her heart considerably.

"I had thought you were wounded when your men called for me," she confessed after a brief embrace, something she had never attempted before.

He received her concerned affections warmly. "I am perfectly well," he confirmed. "Better than I have ever been before, even. I asked you because Lady Arnika is waiting within, and I think she will be less nervous if a woman is present."

Although she had thought she knew Tohmas well, uncertainty flared in Fayela, and she frowned. "I'll not help you if you mean her ill—"

"I have already sworn not to lay a hand on her, Mother…" he interrupted, and her heart skipped. He had never called her "Mother" before, not directly. The best they had ever come had been "Lady Mother" in referring to her. She had not been called "Mother" in more than fifteen years. "…and I'll keep that oath," he carried on, oblivious to her start. "I merely wish to speak without having her panic."

Feeling mildly sheepish at her suspicions, Fayela squared her shoulders. "I will gladly attend."

"If it helps, there is a brazier and pot you can use to make some tea. Just use the light off the altar, assuming she's not put it out."

She was still wondering what kind of tea he had lying around his tent when he gestured to the opening, asking her to lead on.

She was familiar with the tent already and found the expected table, chairs, cot, and chests all in their places. The notable difference was the presence of the unknown girl.

The petite girl by the table in Tohmas' tent had to be several years shy of twenty. Her clothing was modest, but a few trinkets of silver and brown held a cloak and circled her wrists. The strangest thing about the girl was her hair, which had been cut roughly. Wind or hands had ruffled the remnants, which only reached her ears now. It left her head looking a bit like a hedgehog nest.

Fayela paused at the door, hoping to let the girl calm before intruding, but Tohmas' arrival dismissed any hope she had of easing the girl into their company.

Everything about Lady Arnika hardened. Her face darkened, her shoulders stiffened, and her arms crossed. The latter Fayela interpreted as fear.

Although she spotted the bronze brazier, Fayela turned to her son and asked, "Have you scissors, Tohmas?"

His attention on his guest, Tohmas blindly gestured toward a chest. A quick search found scissors at the bottom. When she turned back to them, neither Tohmas nor the Truller had flinched.

Fayela held up the scissors, drawing the girl's attention. "Shall I even out that haircut? You two can talk as I—"

"I have nothing to say to him," the girl replied shakily. Her eyes finally lowered.

"Hear me out, please, Lady Arnika. Hear what I offer with your own ears, then make up your mind."

The offer was so sincere that Fayela reassessed Tohmas. He had wanted to talk, he claimed. But this was more than a treaty. Something was off. *Is he ... nervous?*

CHAPTER 16

When the Truller sat at the table, she sat with great dignity, but it was still only because she had no choice. "You did not convince my father your purposes were pure," she informed Tohmas coldly.

He took the chair opposite her, putting the width of the table between them. "Your father was a very smart man," Tohmas replied with a respectful nod, "but he had lived through too much squabbling to believe people could be different. I ask you to see this with new eyes, open eyes. I pray you see the possibilities and the good that can come of it."

Fayela raised an eyebrow. She had never heard any son of Zayban speak so eloquently, and she had not thought them capable of it. It was hard to believe a Rydan had taught her son such beautiful Esparan.

Lady Arnika released her frown slowly. In a gentle, searching voice, she addressed Fayela. "I would be grateful if you would trim it. I would hate to look unkempt."

Has the girl ever looked unkempt in her life? Fayela would have been surprised, but she obliged the child with a smile as warm as she could make it considering the tension. She took to trimming the uneven hair.

Lady Arnika looked back to Tohmas, her face becoming stern once more. Her hands were clutched on the table, yet they still trembled slightly. "Say whatever you came to say, please, Prince Tohmas, then leave me to my grief."

Fayela had conversed with Tohmas during trying times before, including through plans for wars that rivaled any that had ever taken place in all of Espar's history. Yet she had never seen her son so anxious. It did not surprise her that he started off-topic.

"How has the harvest been in Nothor of late?"

Lady Arnika frowned at him. "Not good, I have heard."

It was too casual a conversation for Fayela; she almost laughed. Were they talking about the weather while at the local bakery? Although she wondered what Tohmas was up to, she tried to focus on the hair.

"And did Trulin increase their sales in Nothor to fill to void?"

The girl, forgetting the scissors, shook her head, but Fayela got the blades clear without clipping her ears. Her dangling gemmed earring nearly caught instead. Fayela muttered apologies, but no one seemed to notice.

"We don't trade with Nothor."

"And why is that? You had a perfect chance to change your excess harvest into other goods, maybe ships, and you wasted it."

"We are at war with Gaidol."

"And where Gaidol goes," Tohmas rightly filled in, "Nothor follows. So because of that, you missed an opportunity for trade. Why are you at war with Gaidol?"

Lady Arnika bit her lip in hesitation before choosing her words. "They argue over our claims to Nero and Galvay."

"Border cities," Tohmas interpreted, and the girl weakly nodded. "Who owns them?"

"Currently, Gaidol has Nero; we hold Galvay."

"And next year?" She pressed her lips again. "Maybe the year after that?" he continued. "When all the Gaidolons have been chased out and murdered, will you take it back? And the year after that, will more Gaidolons come? How do you know it belongs to you at all? Was Trulin the original conqueror, perhaps?"

She flushed, her folded hands tightening on her lap. It was a good habit, one Fayela had also picked up. When confronted, it wouldn't do to lose one's temper.

"It's our land," Lady Arnika said firmly.

"If Prince Dorakon was sitting there, do you think he would say differently?"

From her position over the girl's shoulder, trying to cut straight despite the girl's movement, Fayela saw Lady Arnika's jaw flex as she clenched her teeth. She had cut herself off.

Instead, the Truller took a shaky breath. Her voice softened. "None of us disagree that a world without constant battle would be a good thing, Prince Tohmas. We all like peace, but we are unwilling to live as your servants, even if it is during peace."

Seated as they were, Tohmas' overwhelming height was not as apparent. When he leaned forward, their stares were level. With his fingers tapping the table's surface, he considered her for a moment, then smiled.

"You know," he said, his softened voice matching hers, "when your father asked me to choose another, I tried every combination I could think of. If we are to be unified from mountain to sea, I alone can do it."

"If we all agreed with that, you would not be fighting through Espar," Lady Arnika replied coolly.

Fayela was impressed.

"Some people do the right thing because it's the right thing to do," Tohmas replied. "Others will only do the right thing when given no choice."

Firmly pressing her lips, the lady did not reply.

"Fair Lady," Tohmas continued, pulling a vellum sheet from within his shift and sliding across to her. "I am not talking about leaving things the way they are and just putting my name atop it. I am looking for continued cooperation between every participant. Just last quartercycle, Galanth assisted Lour in freeing injured people from cave-ins and re-securing StonePeak in the face of riots. Without us, they would have taken mooncycles more to clean the mess. That is the sort of cooperation I want to promote."

Lady Arnika let a small smile surface.

Tohmas did not miss it. "Of course, we eventually realized those cave-ins had been sabotage by Trulin." The lady's smile was gone, her secret known. "My oath," Tohmas pressed, "was to aid them when they asked for it. I kept my oath despite the disadvantage to my forces here. I would do the same for any of my kingsmen, including Trulin. Can you see the advantage of what I offer?"

Stubbornly, she avoided his stare by examining the table. With the table's contemporary life in the army camp, its surface had become roughened, scratched, and stained. There were plenty of things to distract herself with, even if just in show.

Refusing to carry the conversation alone, Tohmas let the silence continue.

"I see it," Lady Arnika admitted at length. Glancing up and fixing a determined glare on her captor, she added, "but I see the disadvantages as well: tithes, taxes, being forced to pay more for distant goods while receiving less for our own, losing our surpluses, and answering to the whims of a single, supercilious individual who, alone, stands without accountability."

Withdrawing the scissors and giving her handiwork a final check, Fayela chuckled. "Well said," she commended, which earned her a smile from her son and a mildly startled expression from the lady. "Your hair is as even as I can get it. Looks quite fetching. Shall I make some tea?"

Without pausing for an answer, Fayela went to the brazier and lit the coals. The pot sitting beside it already had water in it.

"Thank you," the girl mumbled, abruptly self-conscious, but it was hard to say if it had been a response to her compliment or her offer of tea.

Tohmas also seemed to appreciate Lady Arnika's assessment of the situation; he was smiling. When Lady Arnika looked back at the king, Tohmas removed his delight from his face.

"This," he gestured, "is the same agreement the others have marked and the same one I presented to your father at Narsol. You should see, close to the bottom, the extent of the accountability I have endeavored to put in place."

The lady left it on the table in front of her. "I imagine it's a little late for that in Trulin."

Tohmas straightened in his seat. "It's not. I still have hope."

With nothing else to do as water boiled, Fayela sought tea leaves. She found an unlabeled pile and went through them by scent to find a good variety.

"Hope?" the girl echoed in a small voice, but the repetition of the word seemed to inspire Tohmas. He leaned forward, this time with his hands on the table and a bright look in his eyes.

"I ask you to read the agreement yourself. If you think there is any chance ... if you think Trulin would take a kingsman ... then I ask you..."

He seemed to run out of words and let out a sigh Fayela thought sounded worried. His eyes dropped to his hands as he gathered his strength. Then, with a resolute nod to himself, he brought his stare up and finished, "I ask you to marry me."

In a distinctly un-lady-like manner, Lady Arnika's jaw dropped. In the moment of silence that shock provided, Tohmas added, "I beg you not to answer before you have had a chance to think it through. You are welcome to this tent for however long that takes. You are free to ask anything you would of me, anything you think may help you decide. My oath stands. No one will touch you except by your permission."

The lady's gaping jaw managed to shut by the end of his invitations, but no sound escaped.

CHAPTER 16

"I have given you much to think on," Tohmas said, excusing himself, "and I know messengers are waiting outside by now. Call upon me whenever you wish, day or night, fair Lady. I am at your service."

He ducked through the tent flap before Lady Arnika could recover. *This,* Fayela mused, *has just become interesting.*

It took another dozen heartbeats after Prince Tohmas' departure for Arnika's heart to resume beating. With a deep breath, she tried to steady her nerves, but failing, she found herself rising from her seat and slamming the vellum onto the table. Behind her, the chair toppled.

"Of all the ridiculous, dim-witted ideas!" she half-shouted with barely enough volume to be heard by someone in the tent. Making a shout soft was a skill she had developed after learning no proper girl could throw a fit without being disciplined. The therapeutic, if occasional, tantrum was a necessity.

"Best political move I have seen him make," the Galanth woman responded as she pulled the boiling water off the coals and placed the pot on the ground. Having forgotten about the additional visitor, Arnika spun on her heels. The woman merely smiled at her and stirred tea leaves into the pot.

Despite the green and silver attire that marked the woman as proudly Galanth, Arnika did not know what to make of the stranger. She seemed friendly and had even supported Arnika against Prince Tohmas. The prince had not even seemed offended.

"If you consider it," the older woman said, "your support could bring him the rest of the princedom without another death on his conscience. Besides that, he is twenty-four, unwed, lonely and, if I read him right, smitten with you."

Arnika's jaw dropped. "Smitten?" she echoed, aghast.

The woman sat and placed one filled mug in front of her and the second mug in front of an empty chair. Feeling too stunned to stand, Arnika ignored her toppled seat and fell into the empty one.

"That boy does not trip on his words lightly," the woman said.

Arnika had not noticed how the prince had hesitated or the slight stutter he had made, but having it pointed out made it obvious.

"That boy," Arnika snorted in disdain, "is trying to take over the world."

"That boy," the woman corrected, "is succeeding in taking over the world."

Arnika wrapped her hands around the mug of tea and fell silent again.

"Child," the woman said with a soft smile, "I know you would see me as an extension of the enemy here, so I can hardly expect you to trust me, but I would like to offer a few suggestions. You can do whatever you want with the advice."

Arnika nodded. It would be easier just to let the woman talk. The more time Arnika had to think, the better.

"Push him," the stranger advised, surprising Arnika. "Take him up on his offers and challenge him. I first suggest summoning a confidante, someone you can talk to in earnest and without fear. Second, have him bring some of your belongings out. Best you feel more at home; it will give your confidence. After that, please find a way to answer every question you have about this war and its players. If that means learning his strategy, then so be it. Take your time. Make him earn you."

There was little doubt that the King of Espar, as he had declared himself, would not be happy with Arnika's answer to his proposition. Once she refused him, he would have no further need of her. Her life would be forfeit.

But as long as he thought her answer might be "yes," he had said he would wait. How long could she delay the army? How much time could she give Tandar and others who opposed the invasion?

Can I weaken him? Distract him in catering to me? She would have to be careful—too much of an inconvenience, and he would lose patience—but if she could keep him hoping...

The woman was sitting back enjoying her tea when Arnika again looked up.

"Who are you?" she asked. Everything about the woman labeled her as Galanth, but her words were almost treasonous. Either she was lying, perhaps to win Arnika over, or Tohmas' trust in her was mislaid. Was she a possible ally to Trulin?

The woman chuckled. "I am someone who has spent her life trying to understand the human heart, only to find she understands the least about her own." With a distracted, reminiscent smile, she finished, "I am his mother."

Arnika spilled her tea. It hit the corner of the vellum Tohmas had given her, and she moved quickly to pull it away before the tea washed away the words.

Lady Fayela Galanth, Arnika identified, the widow of Prince Habal of Galanth.

"Then why help me?" Arnika exclaimed.

Lady Fayela put down the mug and gently laid her hand on Arnika's hand in encouragement. "Because I believe love needs to be challenged. If it doesn't survive, then it was not worthwhile. And because I think you can challenge him more than all the forces of Espar have to date."

When Tohmas left the tent, he found dozens of people waiting for him. He dealt with each one at a time, reorganizing the camp to last two or three days, sorting the location for the remnants of Fixer City that now joined the forces in and around LandWater, and excusing himself from a temple service by necessity. Following that, he arranged a new tent for himself. It would be small, but right now, all he needed was a cot and a roof. Through it all, his mind remained on the woman in his tent and the proposition he had made.

After those duties, he sent runners to each guardian to inform them of his relocation; Lady Arnika now occupied his tent. The beautiful, spirited Arnika...

He leaned against a supply waggon and slunk into a sitting position.

In a single conversation, he had been completely exhausted. *Declaring my dominance over Espar to a room full of princes was less stressful! How can one woman be so...*

He had no words to finish the thought. He didn't know what to think. He wasn't even sure what he felt. Was he impressed? Worried? Perhaps both?

Tohmas sat against the waggon, silently counting breaths for a long time. Finally, sometime before midnight, movement at the tent opening attracted his attention.

When his Lady Mother's pale eyes adjusted to the dimness, she raised an eyebrow at him in the torchlight.

"Have you been sitting there the entire time?"

"Had some things to think about," he admitted. "Did she say...?"

"She has a request," the Galanth matron interrupted factually, and Tohmas unwittingly released a sigh of relief. If Lady Arnika asked for something, she had delayed making a decision. At that moment, that felt very important.

"Anything she wishes," he confirmed.

His mother frowned slightly but lifted two folded, sealed, vellum sheets. They were of the finer kind, cut uniformly as if for binding, and thin enough to be easily folded.

"She would have these delivered to Cainton. One is a request for her cousin Altana to join her as a handmaiden and friend. She will also bring along some of her belongings. You are to open neither of them, Tohmas."

Although she extended the letters to him, he raised his hand and called over a protector instead.

"Eight of you ride to Cainton and deliver this directly to Lord Tandar Oranon. Do not leave until you have a reply."

Instead of the typical, "Yes, my prince," the protector placed one gloved hand into the other in Rydan salute by way of confirmation.

Tohmas had his mother hand the letters directly to the protector. As much as he wanted to know what the second letter contained, he dared not let them pass into his hands. The protector was gone before he could reconsider.

Lady Fayela nodded thoughtfully as they left. As she turned to leave, Tohmas said, "Thank you. Your presence was a great help."

The woman gave him a wry smile. "Don't thank me yet, Tohmas. You don't know half the things I said."

Chapter 17

He no longer had to sit on the stool. Tandar's place was wherever he wanted it to be.

Prince. In one fell swoop, he was Prince of Trulin. Nausea had still not left his stomach. *Anga dead. Kelland dead. Arnika captured.*

Is Inac laughing at us now?

He could not sit in the chair, so he stood by the mantle of the fireplace, where his uncle's white-bristled helmet had been placed in tribute. Standing by the fire put him near the window over the courtyard, where he could watch the messengers who had brought him his cousin's letter.

The room contained the people best suited to advising Tandar on the issue: those who had fought with Tohmas Galanth. Charger Grandon who had led the attack on Fixer City stood by the window, unwilling to sit or perhaps finding his leather armor uncomfortable to sit in. By the fire, Altana frowned and fidgeted on the stool once occupied by Arnika. The Double Blades, now only consisting of Tostig and his companion Maybel, sat on the plush couch. While Maybel preened silently, Tostig picked at a plate of strawberries, ostensibly ignoring the statue on the mantle.

If not for the statue, a secret Prince Kelland had thankfully shared with Tandar, Tandar would never have allowed himself to be in the same room as any caster, including Tostig. Although no one had told Tostig how his powers had been negated, the way he rolled his eyes at the golden statue made it clear he knew. Thankfully, there was nothing the man could do about it. For now, they were safe from magic, whether Tostig's or Kitable's. Casters were perhaps necessary, but magic made Tandar nervous.

Below the window, four protectors of Galanth stood where he had left them: at the center of the courtyard with their hands at their sides and their eyes straight ahead. The other four protectors who had come to Cainton were outside the city, holding the weapons of the four who had been given access to the city under the sanctity of messengers. The ones outside had made camp, but the four in the courtyard had not moved a muscle despite a persistent drizzle.

"Do you think he is trying to scare us?" Tandar asked.

Charger Grandon leaned over, made a face at the view, and leaned back.

"I know about his battle techniques, not his political strategies. You dined with him, my prince. What do you think?" Cold winds had brought in the rain, and Tandar could feel the dampness cutting through his leather as he stood by the window. If the four below felt the wet, they did not show it.

"That was before he was a conqueror of Espar," Tandar pointed out. He glanced at Altana, but she only shrugged. She had been at that dinner as well. That interaction had been polite and even favorable. *To think, I'd liked the man then.*

There was no one else to prompt discussion. If he did not speak, it seemed no one would.

"Even then," Tandar said, "I would not put it past him. Having four men stand for fourteen candles without eating or drinking in the middle of the capital is not doing good things for the people's confidence. These protectors are frightening."

"By all accounts, they're worse in battle," Charger Grandon conceded with a grimace that dropped his beard low. "Tohmas and his men fight as one body, from the first charge to final withdrawal. The protectors fight like demons with holy men on their tails, and their devotion is fanatic, as this proves. Makes no difference, does it, my prince?"

Tandar regretted flinching at the title, but he could not stop himself. He hoped he would be over instinctually cringing whenever someone called him "my prince" by the time Tohmas Galanth was at Cainton's gate.

He made his voice strong, as his uncle had taught him. "No, it changes nothing. We will still stand and bring Gaidol in behind him."

Altana perked up. "Have we heard from Gaidol directly yet?" she asked, her voice uncharacteristically optimistic.

Tandar leaned away from the window. His hands were too chilled to clench. "No. If they are acting, they are doing so silently."

Hostilities between the two princedoms were decades in the making. No Truller would ever trust a Gaidolon. Tandar had to presume the reciprocal was probably also true. It seemed more likely that Gaidol was simply not telling Trulin what it was up to, but he had no doubt they were mobilizing. "Prince Dorakon hates Tohmas. He will not work with us directly, but we have the same goal."

A glance at Altana on the stool by the fire got Tandar a nod.

"So the question then comes back to what reply to send," Tandar concluded. They could not have four Galanth protectors standing in their courtyard. Detaining them was unacceptable, as they had thus far been nothing but messengers. But the protectors insisted they would not depart until they had a reply, and the defenders of Cainton had yet to decide upon one.

Playing at conversations would give them time. Tohmas had not advanced on Cainton yet. That was good.

Proving he was not the only one considering buying time, Charger Grandon added, "The most obvious reply would be to accept your cousin's request. You are, after all, certain it was her writing."

"No doubt," Altana insisted.

Tandar nodded. "I know her hand."

"Then the only doubt we have is whether she had been enchanted," the charger finished.

They all turned their stare onto the Double Blades.

Tostig snickered and tossed aside a strawberry top. "No chance. Master Kitable is incapacitated. My curse will hold him for days yet. He should be dead by then."

"Should be?" Tandar pressed.

The miniature man's face crunched up like a raisin. "The Sapping Curse on him has rendered him unconscious, and he has retreated to his waggon. There is no one there to feed him or bring him water. He ought to be dead by tomorrow with the blood he has lost, and the curse will outlast that easily!"

By the end of his rant, the caster was grinning at Tandar. Sensing the reason for his delight, Tandar again made his voice as official as he could.

"You get nothing further until we have him confirmed to be dead," Tandar said.

The mercenary's grin waned. "I have been observing—"

"Then I expect you will be watching when he dies," Tandar responded. "Nothing until then."

The little man sunk back into his seat with a frown.

"So we expect she wrote it with her own mind and hand," Charger Grandon continued. "Perhaps she wrote it with a sword at her throat."

"At the least, she thought they would read it," Tandar agreed. He picked up the first page of the letter from the mantle where he had laid it. "What she wrote was vague. I think ... I think she is trying to slow them down."

It was hard to see what Arnika, separated from her joats and hand-maidens, could do against the conqueror of the north, but the letter had indeed hinted at something. The seal had been unbroken; he wasn't sure if the enemy had read it at all.

"So we send her belongings?"

Tandar did not like the answer, but he saw no alternative. The course was evident, and only his heart opposed it. He had been head of the Oranon family since thirteen and hated the thought of putting his family in harm's way.

But it was what the Prince of Trulin had to do.

"Altana will go," Tandar agreed in a flat, un-brotherly voice that made Altana look up and press her lips in concern. "Tohmas will likely be more willing to let her come and go than Arnika, so we may be able to understand better what is going on."

Charger Grandon and Tostig helped by nodding agreement. Tandar waited, but neither had any opposition to the idea.

Tandar looked to Tostig next.

"I am officially offering ten gold wheels to any man who slays Tohmas Galanth of Galanth."

CHAPTER 17

The leader of the Double Blades sat up as if he had been kicked. "That's twice what we were offered for Master Kitable!" Even his companion's eyes went wide.

"Make sure you tell your friends, Tostig," Tandar finished, turning to face the fireplace in dismissal. "If we can free Arnika, all the better. If not, our priority is to bring down Prince Tohmas of Galanth by any means."

His stomach clenched into a fist, but the nausea was gone as he stared at the helm with the white plume, wishing someone else would wear it into battle in a few days' time but knowing there was no way out.

With the messages sent, Tohmas set up his new home. For now, most of his belongings could be left in Lady Arnika's possession. He could not arrange for an altar that satisfied him, so he surrendered to making trips to the Temple waggons. In the end, it benefitted him further: he had an excuse to go to each of the waggons and spread his devotions. There was no doubt that Inac still held his heart, but he could see the use of the other deities with each visit he made. He both delighted and terrified the celebrants with each visit.

It would take the protectors only half a day or so of straight riding to reach Cainton with their message. Still, it could take several days to get a response, particularly if the answer was a "yes" to Lady Arnika's request for company and effects. Traveling with someone and their belongings would slow the protectors down considerably. He was rather glad when the first full day passed with no response; his protectors had not simply been refused.

On the second day, a waggon surprised him by coming from the south, not the north, and what they brought with them surprised him even more. Lord Garmont, a steadfast ally of Prince Neillen, would not be far from the Gaidolon/Nothor forces, Tohmas was certain. But the man's presence and the seal on the letter handed to him were the first sign he had seen of Nothor in the conflict to date.

A scout arrived in Lord Garmont's shadow; the two must have practically run their horses side by side.

Seeing no reason to separate the two, Tohmas asked for the report from the scout with Lord Garmont in attendance.

"Six days out," the scout reported as Tohmas popped the seal on the letter open. "Gaidol and Nothor both in full colors. The count is between ten and twelve thousand."

Tohmas nodded; it confirmed what Garmont's presence had implied. The letter in hand would make it official; Nothor and Gaidol stood against him in force.

"Give your details to your guardian," Tohmas instructed the scout. "Then take rest."

The lean man saluted in a Rydan fashion, then turned. He made a face at Garmont's back as he left, making it hard for Tohmas to keep a straight face. Beside him, Carsh snickered. His knives passed from one hand to the other, movement visible out of the corner of Tohmas' eye. He had both blades out, throwing blades. Garmont would be an easy kill; he had come without armor.

"Spying on us?" the Nothor Lord in green and gold grumbled once the scout was gone. "Not a very princely thing to do."

"Scouting is not spying," Tohmas corrected mildly. "My *spies*, on the other hand, tell me the numbers are twelve thousand and five hundred, with six thousand horses and machines of war from Nothor. They also say ships keep the men supplied as they move up Serpent River and that Prince Neillen is in the march. Dorakon appears to be holding back for now." He favored Lord Garmont with a grin. "Don't tell me you have no spies among us. I know of four, and I'm certain I'm missing some!"

Lord Garmont sneered, looking down his hooked nose at Tohmas as he remained in his seat, one hand on a cup of wildwater. As if presenting to a crowd that was not present, Garmont drew himself up and declared, "I have been sent by Prince Neillen Lodaton of Nothor, wearing my blade on my right as a sign of peace, to make known our intentions. Nothor demands that your war on Espar cease. If you return to Galanth immediately, no pursuit will be made."

Carsh burst into laughter, but Tohmas kept his face straight. It was true that once, on his way into Nothor, he had switched his blade to sit on his right hip, but it had not been a sign of peace. At the time, Tohmas had worn his sword for a right-handed draw, concealing his natural preference for his left. Going into Nothor alone to discuss passage for his army, he had swapped it to make his weapon more readily available. Ironically, it had been to make himself more dangerous.

"I appreciate Prince Neillen's forthrightness," Tohmas answered formally. "Most others have tried to skirt around the edges of loyalties and official standing. To know exactly where you stand and what you require of me is a pleasant change. Unfortunately, as I imagine you guessed, I will not return to Galanth. Nothor may be kind, but I expect no kindness from Damoria, Trulin, or Gaidol at the moment."

Tohmas had liked Prince Neillen during their one meeting enough to quietly send Rydans to annoy Polthian's borders and take some of the pressure off Nothor. It was probably best that Nothor was still unaware of Tohmas' assistance.

Tohmas sought two cups and poured wine. Initially, it seemed to confuse the man, but he eventually accepted the cup and the seat Tohmas offered. He sat on the very edge of the chair, ready for action, and put the cup onto the table without drinking.

"Nor should you expect it," Garmont confirmed.

"I was impressed with Prince Neillen when I met him," Tohmas said. "Even now, I am grateful for his courtesy. I cannot change my course now, but his consideration is most polite. Unexpected, but pleasant. I would—"

The flare of blue robes entering the tent stopped him. While Tohmas raised an eyebrow at the arrival of the Celebrants of Ocea and her pearl-ladened clothing, Lord Garmont stood so quickly that his hand knocked the cup into the dirt. Carsh skipped up to avoid the spray hitting his feet. "Corolys! What—"

"Aran," Celebrant Corolys interrupted, "you will stop this nonsense. Return to your prince and tell him he is to withdraw his support from Gaidol."

Into the awkward silence, Tohmas blinked in confusion. "I take it you two know each other," he said.

A protector followed in, but Tohmas raised a hand to keep him out. There was no threat, he was certain. This promised to be interesting.

Garmont spun on his heels, his face flushed. "Of course, I know her! But ... you..." Garmont pivoted again, his wrinkled brow dropping low and his eyes on Celebrant Corolys alone. "You did not..." He trailed off.

The Celebrant of Ocea's voice was still as ice. "He does not know. I never told him."

Garmont glanced back, quick decisions passing over his eyes. His shock choked him into silence.

Tohmas came to his feet as he put pieces together. "Celebrant Corolys, am I to assume you are from Nothor?" She nodded, her pearls clinking softly. "I assumed you had been the celebrant for a princedom, but I never guessed which. It never mattered," Tohmas realized.

"For which I am grateful," the celebrant said, squaring herself proudly. "Lord Garmont…" Faced by the holy woman, the man blanched slightly. "…tell Prince Neillen that King Tohmas rides with the gods on his side. He will not be stopped by any mortal force. For the sake of your people, retreat to Nothor. Consider again the treaty he has offered you."

Garmont gathered his fine clothes around himself, his expression like an indignant child scolded by a parent.

"If the prince is wise, he will refuse you this!" he said, his voice a whine. "You cannot—"

She had gestured, Tohmas realized, with her right hand. In doing so, she had shown her bracelet.

"You…" he first stammered, giving Corolys and Tohmas time to brace for the full realization. "You are married!"

Incensed now, Celebrant Corolys seemed twice her normal height. "Of course I am!" she snapped. "I am a Celebrant of Ocea, the Loving Mother! Why should I be denied marriage or family?"

"Family?" Lord Garmont shouted back. "Family? How can you speak of family when you have not told your sister that you are married?"

Everything came together in Tohmas' head in a flicker. In Narsol, Tohmas had learned that Lord Garmont had been courting Prince Neillen's sister-in-law. No one had told him she was a celebrant. Had he stolen the High Celebrant of Nothor and the prince's sister-in-law?

"Demons," he grumbled.

"You want to be loyal to family," Garmont pressed, oblivious to Tohmas' cursing. "Then come home, now."

"I am not leaving." Corolys crossed her arms. "My family is here." With great emphasis, she added, "My *son* is here."

More infuriated than Tohmas would have guessed from his outward appearance, Lord Garmont recklessly grabbed the celebrant's arm and pulled her forward a step. "You are coming with—"

"Garmont!" Tohmas snapped. He came to his feet, one hand out to stop Carsh. The Rydan knew Tohmas was going to object, and to the Rydan, the easiest way to object was with a blade.

The man, still holding the arm of the celebrant, started back a step. Tohmas moved into the space, using his bulk to distance the lord from the celebrant. "If you want to leave, leave. You will not be taking her anywhere she does not wish to go."

Though flustered, Garmont stuttered, "She is the High Celebrant of Nothor, and her prince, through me, calls her to service. You have no right—"

"She is the Celebrant of Ocea for Galanth," Tohmas interrupted. "That makes me her patron. As such, I have every right to threaten to remove your head if you lay another hand on her."

Carsh stalked forward, just in case they got to carry through on the threat.

Lord Garmont's grip fell immediately from Corolys' arm, and the celebrant stalked to the king's side. Once she was beyond the reach of the Nothorian, her voice of ice spoke again.

"I forsook Nothor. I serve Ocea for Galanth now."

For a brief moment, Tohmas wondered if the man's fury would overrule his senses, but the last shred of reason helped him, red-faced and fists clenched at his side, make no attack.

"Give Nothor our messages," Tohmas ordered. "There is nothing further for us to discuss."

He debated it, Tohmas was disappointed to see, but after some muttered farewells Tohmas did not acknowledge, he left.

It was still another dozen heartbeats before any of them moved. Once he was gone, and she could be sure he was not returning, Corolys sighed in relief.

"Thank you," she said as Tohmas returned to his seat.

"I am your patron," he replied, "and you have aided me many times, Celebrant. I did nothing unexpected."

At this, her smile broadened. Her hand found Tohmas' arm. There was a red mark, Tohmas was angry to see, where the Nothorian had grabbed her.

"You are one of the few I would indeed expect such things from." A kiss found his cheek.

"You know you can call on me if you require anything, Celebrant. That was our agreement. Thank you for your words here."

Her nodding smile said that this was completely understood and always had been.

Pushing back the strands of her perfectly combed hair that had come loose in her fury, she sighed again. "I thought to do you a service, but I fear I have filled him with too much ire for our message to be properly received."

"But I appreciate your support regardless of what he does or does not do. When I last spoke to Prince Neillen, I thought him a good man. Hopefully, he will see past this."

She headed for the entrance, shaking her head. The strands came loose once more. "He will see only the anger my marriage has caused for both Garmont and my sister. I wish I could see her and clarify things, but I..."

Once she was gone, the implications of her words settled in. She'd said "son." And she was married. If she was indeed related to Prince Neillen, what claim did she and her son have on Neillen's position? Neillen had no children, and Tohmas was hard-pressed to name a closer relative.

It didn't matter. If all went well, he had no intention of replacing Neillen. He wanted the prince converted, not dead.

Corolys left the waggon behind, her heart torn. She'd meant to help but had no doubt made things worse. Emotions threatened to overwhelm her. Garmont reminded her too much of Nothor and her family there: a sister who had once loved her but then grown jealous of her love and her child; a brother-in-law who tried to be gentle but couldn't understand the call of religion; a gathering of faithful she had abandoned.

Garmont's waggon drew away through the mud, flying the colors of Nothor proudly as it rolled through the tracks. Corolys wondered if she would ever see those colors without tears coming to her eyes.

But Calanor and the other celebrants were outside the tent, ready to comfort her. She'd left their conference in a hurry when she'd heard of the visitor and was grateful they had followed. However, as she reached for Calanor, Corolys noticed a strange expression on Sedgan's face.

"Celebrant?" she asked. He'd not understood her concerns, being oblivious to her heritage.

"Loni," Sedgan replied, the word spoken partially to himself and partially as if calling after the waggon in a whisper. "Demons, Loni..."

Corolys knew the name; Loni was a fanatical, eccentric Celebrant of Inac who worked out of Fixer City. Because the woman seldom came to the Temple waggons, Corolys knew nothing else about her.

The fearful expressions on the other celebrants seemed to say there was more.

"Where?" Darak chirped. He searched the surrounding area anxiously. Corolys thought it likely that, should he spot the bright dress of Celebrant Loni, he would flee.

Sedgan's eyes remained on the departing waggon. "I knew she had followed me, but since she did not interfere, I did not worry over it! Demons!"

The waggon, Calanor said to them in answer. Whether he was reading thoughts or just guessing, Corolys was uncertain.

Sedgan finally glanced at the other celebrants. "She's on the waggon. Gods only know what she has done! Or where she has gone! Demon piss! That woman..."

If she believes Lord Garmont means Tohmas ill, she will seek to enlighten him, Calanor warned. *Shall I follow?*

Corolys had no idea if he meant in person or somehow by magic, but he seemed confident he could catch the waggon.

Sedgan swallowed hard but nodded. "I would appreciate it. I'm going to have to keep closer track of her."

Corolys raised a skeptical eyebrow at the Inac follower when she heard fear in his voice.

"She is that dangerous?"

Although he briefly debated his response, Sedgan eventually nodded. "She doesn't follow reason and grows restless without battle. I acknowledge her as a celebrant but also as a madwoman needing to be carefully watched. She has her uses, but she must be controlled or her fire may consume us all."

Visions of fires filled her mind with the smell of smoke. She saw lines of torch-bearing attackers corner acolytes as Temple waggons to Earth and Water burned. Only Wind had escaped because Calanor had discovered the attackers prematurely.

These, she knew, were the memories Calanor had collected from the fires that night. He had seen into Sedgan's mind, too, she recognized. The visions included her hands, although they were callused and thick, securing the barrier across Ocea's door to lock the celebrant and her followers in. Corolys recognized Sedgan's gold and ruby ring on the finger.

Is there no one who does not have blood on their hands?

The following thoughts to fill her mind were panicked ones. Again in Sedgan's memories, her head pounded, and her body shook as she learned she had been drugged. Sedgan had known who the poisoner was. The ache of betrayal filled the memory.

Although Corolys had not knowingly closed her eyes, she had to open them once the thoughts had passed. She found Celebrant Sedgan waiting for her.

He had been drugged and used. Now he kept Loni chaperoned to make amends, trying to stop other crimes to undo his own.

"She has her uses, but she cannot be trusted," Sedgan finalized.

"Wise words," Corolys said as the memories left her. Calanor was gone. She prayed he would stop a disaster.

Shayne walked the streets, and no one dared get in his way. Even the riders of the city, dressed in brown uniforms and carrying polearms, subtly skittered aside as Shayne traveled.

His face was not known, but no man alive could look down at Shayne, and he filled his walk with enough purpose to push others aside. Even when he found Broker, the squirrelly man tucked in the corner of a market with a handful of eavesdropping mercenaries, Shayne did not pause. He stood before Broker, and every other customer quickly decided to be elsewhere.

"You do know how to make an entrance, Shayne," Broker said, craning his neck up to meet the mercenary's stare. "Scared off my clientele."

Chapter 17

"Heard there was a high-priced offer," Shayne answered, his words sloppy and thick. His Esparan never sounded right, no matter how much he practiced it. His tongue didn't seem to work the same way as theirs.

Broker nodded a bit too eagerly. "Not an easy prize, but worth ten gold wheels to the taker. Enough to retire by, I dare say. And you've got permission to make it messy if you can catch the man."

Shayne cocked his head, and Broker flinched.

"Messy's easier," Shayne said. Sadly, in his line of work, it was also seldom convenient.

Broker squared himself up before Shayne, making him look at Shayne's chest. "I thought you'd like it. The more impressive, the better. This one's going down in history."

"Who?" Shayne demanded.

With a wry smile that probably was trying to be ironic, Broker said, "The King of Espar."

"I don't know that word," Shayne said. Despite his foreign origins, he had gotten good at Esparan. Still, his curiosity was irrelevant. He didn't care what "king" was.

"He used to be Prince Tohmas," Broker clarified. Shayne shrugged with indifference. Killing people was easy, no matter who they were. "Don't let your ego get in the way," Broker warned as Shayne turned to walk away. "He's protected by damn good soldiers, and he's pretty good himself. Plus, he's got magical back up."

Shayne stiffened at the word "magic."

"Trinkets?" he asked, casting a dark look over his shoulder.

Broker shrank back under the cover of his canopy as if the look was enough to hurt him physically. It was tempting, Shayne considered. He *could* make a glare hurt, maybe show the man his red eyes and watch him really squirm.

"A magic sword that makes wizards stop working," Broker stuttered. "And then there's Kitable. Master Kitable? Heard of him? A master wizard, the best in Espar."

"Interesting," Shayne answered, flicking his tongue over the sharp edge of his concealed teeth. Wizards were a problem. Wizards were dangerous.

"So?" Broker interrupted, peeking his head tentatively into the light. "You want to take the job?"

"Why wouldn't I?" Shayne asked.

"You suddenly look nervous," Broker justified.

"Don't overthink things," Shayne said. "I'll take Tohmas out. Simple."

"Simple?" Broker echoed. "Right, as simple as walking through a few hundred trained bodyguards and getting a knife into a man rumored to be good enough to beat most, if not all, of his own protectors. Oh, and then there's the prime protector, who can knife you three times before he sees you." Broker held out his hand. "But hey, you said you'd take it. My fee?"

Once this job was done, Shayne might need another, so Broker remained potentially useful.

Shayne placed a tiny copper table coin in the man's palm.

It was high time a mark this big fell to him. Notoriety would be nice. And if a prince ended up dead, maybe there would be an opening. He had always thought the title of "prince" would suit him.

Steely grey clouds dominated the north horizon, but the balcony Tricks occupied lay in the light of the setting sun. The air hung heavy and did not stir, as if watching with rapt attention for the arrival of the dark grey clouds and the storm they heralded. The view from the balcony reached over the city walls and onto the distant fields, making it an ideal position from which to watch the incoming travelers.

Most were refugees fleeing the army that was fast approaching. With Prince Tohmas of Galanth in Trulin, the better-informed and more paranoid citizens had already taken refuge. Now the rest packed their households into large waggons and trundled down the uneven paths toward the sanctuary of Cainton like ants returning to their hill.

A step sounded behind Tricks. "Will there be anything else, Lady Dora?" the servant asked in a suitably monotone voice.

Keeping her reply short, Tricks said only, "No." The steps retreated through the large balcony doors and then through the room. Only once she had heard the hall door latch did Tricks turn from her position at the railing and glance into the decadent room behind her. Certain now she was alone, Tricks let her cloak fall open.

The opulent gown and fur shawl of Lady Dora faded with the release of the illusion, and the cloak, once clinging to her to create the folds of the dress, shifted back to its tattered brown. Tricks let out a sigh at being able to release the concentration required to maintain the illusion.

Selecting a shadowed white beech chair, Tricks settled in to wait, her feet on the railing.

The lowering of the sun cast longer shadows as she watched the weary people, their steps swift in a fight to beat the night and subsequent burglars. A golden flash caught her attention at the main gate as the sun became crimson on the horizon. Tricks sat up. The flash materialized into a person garbed in gold and silver. Gold dragon scale covered the chest and legs, and his helm was shaped from two silver dragon scales, making it impenetrable. Her current employer had claimed the use of scale armor would make him impossible to kill, but once Tricks got a good view of him, she yawned in disappointment.

The man's face was open.

While the golden man made his steady way into the streets below Trick's balcony, Tricks pulled her long knife. After a pause to consider the plan, she swapped the long knife for a cheap, stocky flint blade.

Dragon scale was uncommon and required justification. Tricks wondered what lie the man told at the gate. Would he claim to be a renowned dragon hunter, perhaps? Would the guards below know the scales were older than their wearer and recognize he was nothing but a treasure hunter and thief? A thief who made many enemies and was now worth a considerable bounty?

As the target swung his gaze through the streets, he turned to look up at the balcony. *Thieves always looked up,* she thought.

Tricks tucked her cloak against herself. She focused on the doors behind her, becoming invisible.

"You take some of the fun out of these jobs," a voice said behind her.

Refusing to rise to the bait, Tricks did not turn her attention from her camouflage. "Bannock," she said, "you damn well better be hidden right now."

"I can't compare to your fairy dragon cloak, my dear Tricks, but none of the louts below are aware of me, have no fear."

The grey sky had crept toward them and now hovered over the house. A single drop fell onto the railing.

The golden thief below continued his sweep of the streets, then kicked his horse on, not even bothering to walk it despite how thick the roads were.

Tricks held her grip loose on the blade she had tucked against her chest under the cloak. "Get to business, Bannock. If you think you'll steal this contract, I'll knife you now."

The Lourite man chuckled. The laugh itself seemed to have a northern accent.

"I would never dream of it. I'm here to watch your back."

"Not get me on my back?"

He came forward, crouched below the railing. As thin as he was, he crept into the shadow of a single pillar and remained in it as he sat, back to the post, and looked up at her. Several ill-advised fistfights had left him with only seven teeth, most of them in the back, but all were visible when he grinned. "Maybe later."

"So what do you really want?" The bounty would soon pass under her.

"After he dies, I have a job for you." He eyed her skeptically. "You are paying close attention to your target, right? I'm not distracting you, am I?"

"Better talk fast, Bannock," she replied, moving onto the railing while holding close focus on her cloak's camouflage. She stood exposed to the world, but not one of the refugees below could see through the hiding powers of the cloak.

The rain began.

"A new bounty's out," Bannock said.

Tricks made a face, despite knowing he would never see it through the cloak's magic. "I don't care what they're offering; I am not going after Kitable."

The bounty below paused, trapped by the crowds momentary. He cursed and kicked at the people until they gave way.

Bannock put out his hands in mock surrender, the leather wrappings on his wrists making the hands look disproportionately small. "You've got a magic touch, Tricks, but if anyone's going to get Kitable, it'll be a grunt. You don't fight magic with magic. You fight mundane with magic, and magic with mundane."

"Then you go after him. Time's up, Bannock," she said, crouching low on the railing in readiness.

"I'll make it worth your while," he quickly added as Tricks jumped.

Her leap landed her on the back of the horse, behind the man in dragon scales. The horse kicked, throwing them both forward and adding momentum to the flint knife Tricks positioned just in front of the man's face.

Tricks felt the enchanted flint pierce skin then bone. Blood spurted over her hand and arm as she released the blade and left it.

It was done in the blink of an eye. By the time the city guards heard the horse's cry or the man's surprised squawk, the knife was already buried to the hilt in flesh and skull. And Tricks, her bloody arm tucked under the magic of her cloak, pushed off the horse, caught the balcony above, and pulled herself back into hiding.

The clouds opened further, and the downpour fell.

She joined Bannock beneath the railing and focused on keeping herself invisible as the rain beat down on her cloak. She noticed that her fellow bounty hunter looked mildly pale.

A warning bell tolled, and the shouts of angry soldiers answered. The crowd below screamed and panicked away from the man with a knife in his face as he toppled from his horse.

"So what's the job?" Tricks asked Bannock softly.

Seeming to choke slightly to her casual inquiry, made while the street below screamed and the skies dropped a torrent onto her, the word sounded glottal as Bannock said, "Tohmas."

"What about him? He's marching toward Trulin, but I can't say I care. I go where the work—" When realization struck her, the powers of the cloak faltered, and for a moment, Tricks worried she had seen between the pillars. She closed her eyes and focused. The magic answered. She still had to wait two breaths before trusting herself to speak.

"The prince? There's a bounty on Prince Tohmas?"

Bannock nodded. "The new Prince of Trulin, Tandar Oranon, has commissioned it."

"Princes don't kill princes!" Tricks shot back, raising her voice over the pound of rain.

"Then it's fortunate that Prince Tohmas has named himself king. Apparently, kings kill princes, so this prince is looking to kill the king. You in?"

Tricks hesitated. She knew little about the Prince of Galanth except that he was now the leader of the largest army in Espar. Rumors said he was a superb fighter. He'd already survived multiple assassination attempts.

But Tricks appreciated a challenge.

Before she could answer Bannock's query, Tricks felt the alarm she had set on the stairs go off. A second followed. Then a third and many more. Tricks lost track of the number of people who were rushing toward her.

She wiped her arm onto the inside of her cloak and, making a face at Bannock, changed.

The ratty cloak wrapped itself around her once more, and the silk curves of Lady Dora's gown formed. Tricks snuck toward the balcony doors to be beyond the sights of the streets below before rising.

"That's just creepy," Bannock said. "The outfit is one thing, but the face, the hair, the..." His eyes drifted lower. "She does have a nice arse, though. Hey! You're not wet!"

"Shut up, Bannock," Tricks threatened, drawing herself into the proper straight-backed posture of a woman of the higher society who had been hiding under the house's awning.

"The voice needs work," Bannock commented.

Through the lattice of the doors to the balcony, Tricks saw the inner door open and admit the servant she had previously duped into allowing her to access the balcony room. Behind him came a dozen household guards.

Bannock saw the movement and slunk further into the pillar's shadow. He had been soaked by the rain, lending his dark cloak a midnight shade.

One eye on the approaching guards, Bannock said, "One job, and you're set for life, Tricks. I'll take the Galanth side. You take Trulin. We meet in the middle and split it. We never work another job so long as we live. Now throw an appropriate tantrum and keep them from coming out here, would you?"

CHAPTER 17

She dared not glance back to the assassin by the railing but instead tossed open both balcony doors and stormed into the room.

"Gruesome! Such terrible, terrible monstrosities! Send a dozen men out there at once! Find the assassin who dares perform such dastardly deeds upon my doorstep! Where is my husband? Find him! And get me a celebrant! Gods, see how shaken I am! Get me Celebrant Austin at once! I would hear..."

Behind her, the shadow of a pillar slunk away, leaving a wet trail.

Chapter 18

Seeing Altana made Arnika's heart both heavier and lighter at once. As the prince's Lady Mother had said, Arnika needed someone to talk to, but knowing she had just brought her cousin into dangerous circumstances made her feel guilty. She had hoped Tandar would object or have a better plan, but the appearance of her cousin on the morning of the thirty-first made it clear that her idea had been the best one.

By the time she stopped hugging her cousin, the protectors had set down the trunk, opened it, and started searching it.

Deciding to see how far her host's good graces would extend, Arnika interrupted. "You brutes, stop that!" To her amazement, they paused. "Get me Tohmas."

One of the men who had been guarding the tent immediately snapped to attention. He bowed his head as he said, "Yes, fair lady." He left at a run.

Into the silence, Altana's voice was hushed. "Why did that…?"

"Their prince," Arnika informed her cousin in a resolute voice while keeping her stern stare on the three offending protectors by the trunk, "has promised to tend to my every wish and has given me the freedom to call him whenever I choose. I choose now."

Stoically, she held the gazes of the protectors but, to her disappointment, most of them simply appeared bemused.

Prince Tohmas arrived a short time later, either having put away his armor or not yet donned it. His tunic was still green, but the shorter sleeves exposed the thick arms crisscrossed with old injuries like a blind painter's work. Despite this half-dress, he wore SoulBurner on his hip across from a decorated dagger.

Altana squealed and hid behind Arnika at the sight of him. For a long moment, Arnika lost her voice, fearing that she had overreached. Although he was willing to wait on her, he would grow weary eventually and withdraw his offer. She dared not push him there too soon.

But when he stood by the entrance, he did not seem angry. "What might I do for you, fair lady?" His voice was surprisingly mellifluous.

"Your men are disrupting my belongings," Arnika forced herself to say.

He still did not seem angry when he turned to his protectors and said, "Leave off, boys."

They pulled away from the chest, but their eyes went meaningfully to the prime protector behind the king.

The Rydan rolled his eyes but said, "Naw safe."

Arnika had her answer: Tohmas would make himself foolishly vulnerable, but those closest to him were protecting him. But he was the prince, or king, whatever that meant. Tohmas had the final word on any argument. She had to convince him, then keep him far enough from his friends to prevent them from interfering.

One surprisingly bold protector with crossed arms added, "That's reckless. Someone has to look it over. If she doesn't want things disrupted, then ask Master Kitable to take a look."

"No!" Altana interrupted, and everyone jumped to the sharpness of her voice. Seeing she had attracted the room's attention, Arnika's cousin shrank further behind her and muttered, "I..."

"Altana," Arnika quickly filled in, "has been bruised by your wizard's disregard for her attentions. I do not want him upsetting her."

Although Altana had certainly discussed a crush on the wizard after their initial meeting in Polthian, it was hard to believe that was the cause of her cousin's outburst. There had to be either something essential in the chest or some reason Altana wanted to avoid Kitable. Arnika did not care which it was.

Suddenly hitting on a solution, Arnika blurted, "These things are personal. I do not want a man rifling through them. Have your Lady Mother search it."

After a moment in consideration, Prince Tohmas nodded. "I am not in the habit of ordering my Lady Mother to do anything, but I will pass on your request. Is this acceptable?"

Everyone nodded stiffly.

Lady Fayela arrived shortly afterward and shooed the men out of the room. Arnika could not help but smile to see the legendary Champion of Inac and his deadly Rydan shooed away like mischievous schoolboys.

The lady apologetically sorted the trunk's contents and helped Arnika find a place for everything. As soon as she was done, she smiled at both girls and invited them to call on her whenever they needed. She did not remember to call back in the protectors, allowing them privacy.

The moment they were alone, Altana revealed news from Cainton at a dizzying pace.

The plan, Arnika heard, was to send Altana back to Cainton in a few days to report under the guise of fetching more belongings. They were working on a way to free Arnika or kill Tohmas, whichever was easiest, which included a significant bounty on Tohmas' head.

Equally of interest was learning that Master Kitable was only a few days from the five hells, explaining why Altana had objected to Kitable's involvement. If possible, Arnika had to keep Tohmas and his allies away from Master Kitable until the man had the decency to die.

For a brief moment, Arnika's heart panged for the dying man. By Altana's account, the caster was dying alone, and no one had noticed. He had not seemed like a terrible person when they last spoke, and it upset her to think of him suffering.

But it was war, whether the King of Espar wanted it to be or not, and so she would do nothing and pray that whatever end the wizard found was swift enough.

By the time Fayela left her son's tent, dusk had fallen, and people were returning from evening meals. Her stomach was silent as she returned to her waggon. She took one of the longest routes possible to give herself time to think.

The visit to the girl she may eventually call her daughter-in-law held minor significance to Fayela. For the first time, she had seen Tohmas with bare arms, and what she had seen had confused her so entirely that she nearly got lost on the way back to her waggon.

He was scarred. A mosaic of lines covered most of his arms. His face was clear, as was his neck, but otherwise, he was marked profoundly. He had always worn long sleeves, she realized, during their time in Wayburn. He had hidden the scars.

At first, the scars had not alarmed her. In idle musing, Fayela wondered about the memories in those marks. Most had been very long and seemed more like whip marks than sword cuts, but she had reminded herself that Rydans used long spears that were very different from Esparan versions and blamed that. Each of those, she pondered, would hold some memory to him. One of them, she had smiled to remember, they shared.

But when she had looked to the right arm where he had once fallen off a horse and snapped the bones of his arm, then lived through mooncycles of bandage changes and cutter work, she did not see the X-shaped scar she had tended. He had been only six then, but she could not make out even the faintest hint of it.

It was not possible! An illusion? A trick of the light? No, she had looked quite closely, but why was there no scar?

One question led to a hundred more.

Why did he never talk about life in Wayburn or the people he had spent the first eight years with? Why were there no references to the moments they had shared, like the picnics to the river or the rides out to Hallow to see the old bakery? Why, indeed, did he know nothing about Esparan folklore or anything social like dancing? Why did he listen to Esparan music as if deciphering it?

Why could she see so little of Habal in him when everyone had said, from the very start, that Tohmas inherited so much of the line of Zayban?

Had this man ever broken his arm? Where was his scar?

Thousands of men had red-tinged beards, and Tohmas' upbringing could account for his size and strength, even if there was no other inheritance from Zayban. His eyes matched neither hers nor Habal's. How was that possible?

She surprised her protectors by sitting down on the steps to her waggon instead of going in, but they all took their guard positions to avoid interrupting her apparent pondering.

There were, she concluded, four men alive who could answer her questions. One was Tohmas himself, but she worried about confronting him. The second was Carsh, but Carsh terrified her, and Fayela could not imagine making any accusations to the Rydan. The third was Chief Tamv himself, who was made inaccessible by his distance. She might have found him intimidating but didn't know him well enough.

The fourth was someone present who had been with Tohmas since his return and could, unlike anyone else, seek the answers if he did not already have them.

She would seek Master Kitable. Tohmas was her son, she told herself firmly, and she just needed Kitable to confirm it. That was all.

As she cleaned her hands and picked at her dinner, her thoughts remained in tumult. She did not even finish the meal before rising and going back out.

"I need to find Master Kitable," she informed the protectors, but they shrugged. Like her, these protectors had spent their last while in Wayburn. And Kitable often did not make finding him easy.

She turned to her newest handmaiden, who had lived in Fixer City.

"I know where to find him," Seraph confirmed. "He may not appreciate the interruption. He never does."

"I need to talk to him immediately," Fayela insisted. "Please, Seraph, if you know the way..."

The grinning girl bowed her scarf-covered head. "Of course, my lady. This way."

As much as Tostig resented hiding under the waggon, it remained the best position for watching the Wisavi Kitable's waggon. There was always the danger of being discovered, especially by the wary, unfriendly waggon driver. Still, sufficient defenses and concealments had Tostig as happy as he could be in his position. A combination of spells let him look through the defenses and the walls to see right into the waggon, where Kitable lay cursed and dying.

Chapter 18

He would have liked, if only to avoid more waiting, to finish the job and leave, but the defenses his Scry let him see through were not going to let him get into the waggon without retaliation. Several of the defenses were offensive if challenged, and there was a genuine danger the actual threat hid under the obvious ones. Kitable was too good at layering spells for Tostig to be confident he'd survive an attempt to break into the vardo.

Waiting would do. Even now, the Galanth wizard looked unlikely to survive the night.

Having finished his dinner, Tostig lay back and watched the strained breathing of the man in the waggon. Kitable was having nightmares. *How apt.*

Two women entered the campfire circle. One was clearly a woman of importance, walking with her head a stride above anyone else and wearing the green and silver of Galanth. The waggon driver bowed deeply to her, clearly recognizing her. Lady Fayela Galanth, Tostig surmised.

Despite what could be a lovely face, the second woman was very plain. Her attire marked her as far less auspicious. As Lady Fayela of Galanth was known never to own slaves, the modest younger woman had to be a handmaiden. The women appeared to be traveling without protectors, which was strange but rather opportune.

Recognizing the woman's status, the waggon driver was heading toward Kitable's door, and Tostig sprung up. *Not now!* Of all the times for a disruption, the eve of his enemy's death was most unfortunate! He had to stop them!

The easiest solution was a Fire Blast spell that would kill all three people. Thanks to its defenses, the waggon would be spared, but he was certain it'd kill the people present. Prince Tandar might even reward him for slaying both Kitable's friend and Prince Tohmas' mother.

Tostig almost felt bad for the handmaiden, but it was her fault for being in the wrong place at the wrong time. He did not dwell on it.

It was a hovering spell, activated by a single word. He had not even bothered to activate Spell Sight to track its progress, but he regretted that the moment the handmaiden moved.

With an unexpected shout, the servant leaped into the path of the spell, threw her arms wide, and activated a spell of her own. The Fire Blast exploded, but when the light cleared, the campfire was scattered, the dirt flattened, and the stairs of the vardo were gone, but all three people were unharmed.

It had been a mistake, Tostig frowned, to think the mother of the Galanth prince would walk around unprotected. The handmaiden had to be a bodyguard. *Probably*, he thought with a sneer, *trained by Kitable to help defend the family. More misfortune!*

Bringing Spell Sight to bear, he could now see the layers of spells on the girl. None of the spells looked like anything capable of stopping the blast he had just conjured. Had she used up her only major defense, or were there spells hidden from Spell Sight among her hovering spells?

One way to find out.

The five-way alteration hit and destroyed the girl's Molded Shield, but that did not seem to concern her. With her back to Tostig, she cast protective spells on Lady Fayela; a Concealment spell that Tostig, given his current Spell Sight, could see through.

The waggon driver was gone the next moment, but his escape was not magical. At a surprising sprint, the small man bolted from the area. Tostig shot a Tracker after him. To his disappointment, the spell slipped off the man and failed.

Kitable gave the man defenses since the last time we fought. Now Tostig could not follow the man or stop him from seeking assistance.

But what assistance could they bring? Would Tohmas come to rescue his mother? If not the prince, then soldiers? How many could Tostig defeat?

I'll have to finish Kitable tonight after all, he decided. The only thing in his way was the pesky bodyguard.

Activating a trinket, Tostig fired a destruction spell at the caster's back. This time Tostig's fear about the defenses proved true: a concealed spell took out his attack before it landed. He had only just decided to target the mother when the yellow silhouette representing the concealed Lady Fayela stood and ran.

Within the first step, the yellow aura split into two people, who ran in different directions. In the next step, both auras split again. In two steps, eight silhouettes were present, and all were fleeing in different directions.

He could not target Tohmas' mother. But he could still try to get to Kitable.

With her charge safe, the bodyguard spun to face the source of the assaults and brought her attacks to bear. It was a weak dispel aimed at discovering his whereabouts. Catching and destroying the spell before it exploded, as it was an area spell, prevented that.

He came out from under the waggon anyway, and he could tell by her narrowed eyes that she had seen the movement that had only been partially hidden by his Concealment. The ring on his left pinkie flared in answer to his command, shooting out a binding spell.

She threw up a counter, and the spell's strength made it clear she had limited options remaining. The Eight-layered Dispel could have been far more effective as an attack but had now been wasted.

Tostig activated one final trinket. His own Eight-layered Dispel, hidden in a cage of smaller dispels, ate through her shields and struck her in the chest.

She was twice as fast as he had expected. The moment the spell struck, the girl ran. She was out of the clearing so fast, Tostig's surprised stutter almost cost him his Tracker. He still got it on her, but it only caught her ankle, as that was the only part of her visible by the time it went off. He'd not expected her to run! Wizards usually thought too highly of themselves to flee!

But the way was open. The disrupted campfire area was empty. It was just him and Kitable now.

Planning to keep it that way, he attached a binding to the Tracker spell he had on the bodyguard. Now the sprite who had just cost him his great secret could be dealt with easily. She, whoever she was, would die for getting in his way.

Connecting himself to the Tracker mentally, he chose a destructive spell and let it fly. He felt it go off and breathed a sigh of relief before turning his attention back to the waggon.

He had to finish this.

Hiding as Seraph, a handmaiden to Lady Fayela, should have been safe. Lady Fayela led a quiet life away from the main bustle, keeping Shimmer out of the way of Rydans. But in helping the Lady Mother find Kitable, Shimmer found herself suddenly in a duel.

She thought she fared pretty well, considering the circumstances. Indeed, she had been dispelled, but she had saved both the Lady Mother and Colt, and if she was lucky, Kitable would finish the job now. Whoever had attacked could no longer take anyone by surprise because of her. She was proud of herself.

When she fled the campfire circle, the feeling of magic on her foot was obvious. Instead of dispelling it and making her escape obvious, she cast a quick alteration and stuck the Tracker on a tent peg instead.

The targeted spell obliterated the peg and the rope attached to it, leaving an irate owner, but at least it meant the attacker was unaware that his true target had escaped.

But then, she didn't know if she had been the target or if the attacker had been after Lady Fayela. With that in mind, Shimmer followed her spell and located the woman behind crates of dried food. Shimmer recast her defensive spells as she walked, just in case it came up.

Shimmer found herself wrapped in a warm embrace.

"Thank you, Seraph," the Lady Mother said. "That explosion…"

"Consider it repayment for hiding me," Shimmer replied. It was odd, she considered, to be hugged without feeling it. The fresh Molded Shield kept the older woman's touch from landing, but the Galanth woman did not seem to notice.

"Will they come after you again? Who—?"

Shimmer shook her head. "The people after me don't have access to anything like that. That was something else. If the caster had known I was there, he would have dispelled me first, not wasting time on spells I could easily stop."

The word "easily" was deceptive. Although activating the defense had been simple, the spell was one of her more powerful spells. It was challenging to put together.

"Is Master Kitable in danger then?"

Shimmer had to shrug. "Is he ever not in danger? And what is danger to that man anyway? People have been trying to kill him for a long time." She shook her head to stop the musing. "But I would like to find out, my lady. It would be best if I went alone."

The grey-haired woman nodded. "I know my way back to—"

"Before you go, might I suggest you take my clothes? I'm rather non-descript and impossible to target magically, but your green and silver are distinctive. Take my skirt and blouse. I'll make do without."

Soon enough, Shimmer was dressed in her white underclothes and braiding her now-loose hair to get it out of the way. Although Shimmer's skirt reached only the lady's mid-shin, the blouse fit her nicely, and the shawl finished the disguise. No one would know the woman now, at least not until she returned to her waggon. Most importantly, the caster would be unable to define her.

Satisfied that she had adequately protected her father's friend, Shimmer headed to find out what had happened at Kitable's vardo.

One by one, Tostig broke down the defenses, sweat creeping over his skin as the effort took its toll. Layers upon layers of magic looked back at him still, but he made steady progress.

Tostig took a large step back when he saw white robes turning the corner into the clearing. Just behind the Celebrant of Totho came blue: his wife, the Celebrant of Ocea. And behind them came Colt.

Doesn't matter. They can't see me through my spells.

But when the celebrant's eyes, the only part of his face visible between the scarf and hood, narrowed on his exact position, Tostig reconsidered.

Untouchables, Tostig remembered. Apparently, that meant more than just dispelling magic. This one could see through illusions.

Without waiting to see the response, Tostig turned and ran. He knew the celebrant could project his strange untouchable power. Those powers would destroy his many precious trinkets and render him helpless.

Once he was out of sight and had breathed for many moments without being dispelled, Tostig crept back to the vardo. So long as Tostig stayed hidden, he would kill Kitable yet. If he could get through the...

Tostig felt a grin growing. As he spied around the neighbor's waggon, Colt pulled himself over the missing steps and knocked on the door. If no one answered, maybe he would get the celebrant to try. Then all the spells would drop instantly, and Tostig would have his moment.

But when the knock went unanswered, the waggon driver simply opened the door. The ease of it shocked Tostig, catching him unprepared.

There were still a dozen spells on that door! Kitable had given his waggon driver authority to bypass them! *If I had known sooner…*

Tostig cut short his frustrations. With the door open, he had his opportunity. He could make his attack now and curse mistakes later. Calanor had entered the waggon but stood to the side, not even obstructing his view.

The waggon driver knelt by the bed, clearly concerned for his master, who lay unresponsive. He said something to the celebrant about something "smelling wrong," but Tostig dismissed it and pressed on with his spell. He passed the magic between the onlookers and attached it to the defenseless wizard.

Got you. He had Kitable bound. He shot the final killing spell like a well-aimed arrow down the binding. Tostig leaned back, relieved that the job was done.

But before the final spell landed, Celebrant Calanor touched a careful hand onto Kitable's burning forehead in concern.

The bottom fell out of Tostig's stomach. "No!" he choked out despite himself.

The touch broke Tostig's binding, blocked the killing spell, and removed the Sapping curse instantly.

Free of the influence of the debilitating spell, the wizard sat up, rolled out of bed over Colt, and slammed the door shut. In a blink, all the defenses were again obstructing Tostig's view.

"Of all the demon-kissing timing!" Tostig cursed, his hands tightening into fists in the dirt at his feet. He checked his surroundings, making sure he had not been overheard. He didn't have the time, or the skill, to get through the defenses now. And Kitable was awake!

He abandoned the place under the cart and used an enchanted item to pull him home to his waggon. With Kitable partially recovered, the fight would soon be coming back at him, and he had to be ready.

Tostig set his next trap for Kitable, cursing all the while about missed opportunities.

CHAPTER 18

How Tril spent all his free time wandering in the empty darkness baffled Kitable. Very quickly, Kitable was fed up with the nondescript, dull emptiness with the light that cast no shadows and the ground that was both there and not. As much as he stared at the spiral, he never saw a pattern, and as far as he could see across the gap between him and the spiral, he never saw the other side. Every moment he spent there was a waste of time, but he had no choice.

The only option was to return to his body, which was now an avalanche of pain and fever. Here, away from the physical pains he was suffering, his mind could think clearly. He could almost forget that he was dying. Unfortunately, the length of time his body took to finally die left him sitting in the void for much longer than he liked.

It was hard to say if time was different in the place between worlds, for it seemed to take forever. Surely, his body was not that resilient. At one point, Kitable wondered if he had died and not noticed, but a quick look back to the conscious world had shown him how much pain he was in and convinced him that death had not yet come. People often said their lives flashed before their eyes when they were about to die. This did not seem to be occurring naturally, but a review of his life would at least be better than staring at the madly unhelpful spiral of magic across from him.

What was there to review? Life in Woodcutter's Retreat had been misery, but at least he had learned to read there. Master Syphilis had been abusive and useless, except that he had given Kitable access to books on magic. Then there had been the mess about Master Syphilis' debts and the old master wizard's murder. As far as Kitable knew, he was still wanted for that.

Then there was Prince Habal, who had taken him in when anyone else would have put him on trial and executed him. Days alone in his room had followed, but that had culminated in the development of the Contingency. That had led to dozens of duels as others had found him interesting enough to need to fight. Habal's campaigns to secure Galanth had filled the time between duels. Near the end of the battles, in a single day, Kitable had re-shaped magic by turning his secret loose, and life had been quieter. Occasional visits from Habal or Fayela had been his only interruptions. That had been simple.

Tohmas had destroyed that, but Kitable did not resent his new patron for that. Because of the march, Kitable had crafted a dozen new spells and learned the art of un-casting, which still had the potential for further exciting applications. The Weavers had not really helped him learn much, but at least he had finally met a caster he did not feel required to kill for his own safety. Then there had been the Double Blades.

Many oversights there, he had to admit. He should have looked into their dealings or watched them closer. He should have killed them sooner.

At least the troublesome group was dead. With perfect clarity, he remembered their leader Tostig standing in the ruins of his waggon with few defenses remaining. Kitable remembered launching the Disintegration and relived the man's dissolution into dust. It had been profoundly satisfying to finish the conflict.

The world seemed to pause on Tostig's death.

Kitable had a sudden urge to slap his forehead. "Not red!" he shouted to the darkness, although he made no sound. "He was not red!"

Before chasing the Double Blades, Kitable had struck him with a Full Reversal, one of the interesting new applications for the art of un-casting. The spell inflicted a Spell Burn so intense that the victim's skin was stained red by the effect for several days. But Tostig's skin had not been red. That meant, at the least, that there had been an illusion present to conceal the discoloration, but Kitable's augmented Spell Sight had not spotted any illusion auras. And if his vision had missed one illusion, it seemed very likely that it had missed other, more important ones.

Again, Kitable cursed the empty blackness, but this time for not having anything he could kick in his frustration.

He spent the next while pacing back and forth from his body to the empty black part of his magical mind. For a dozen paces, nothing seemed to change: the pain was constant, the silence absolute, and the body unresponsive.

Death was no longer acceptable. He'd not finished the job. The Double Blades were still a threat. He had to get back!

On one visit to his body, voices made him linger.

"He smells wrong!" It was Colt's voice, but Kitable could not see whom he was talking to.

CHAPTER 18

"Sick?" came a female's answer that Kitable could not place. If Colt was courting and had not told Kitable, Kitable would have been offended, but it seemed unlikely that the waggon driver would open Kitable's door just to let a girl visit.

"Bad magic," Colt replied, so whoever was speaking must have been holding Colt's stone and thus been heard. "Not his magic. Someone else's magic!"

How, and when, had Colt developed an ability to sense magic? And how could he tell it was someone else's magic?

Kitable's brain hiccupped.

What is someone else's magic?

"Not red!" he cursed again, and his mind stomped around in irritation. His body remained unresponsive.

If it was a spell that had made him so ill, he could counter it. Without his body to channel power, he had not been able to cast anything in the blackness, but he had to do something! Dying from a stab wound was acceptable but being defeated by a spell profoundly annoyed him.

How? How could he cast when the blackness did not create sound? How could he pull magic in when it remained far above and beyond the chasm? There had to be a way!

Before he could find a solution, the pain suddenly stopped.

The commands he had been screaming at the unresponsive body suddenly took hold; he was instantly sitting up and seeing through his own eyes. All at once, he was aware of the open waggon door, Colt's concerned and thankful smile, Celebrant Calanor's gentle touch, and the complete lack of defensive spells.

He leaped off the bed and slammed the waggon door closed. It might have been his paranoia, but he had the distinct feeling he was being watched.

"Not red," his broken, dry-throated voice grumbled once more. "He was not red."

The Double Blades were not finished.

Neither am I, Kitable decided.

Once the celebrants had been excused, Colt again repaired the knife injury on Kitable's back. With the curse gone, the spell-induced spoiling vanished, the edges of the wound came together nicely. It still hurt, and he realized it had always hurt, but the ache was so much less than it had been that he hardly noticed it.

There are things to do, Kitable decided as Colt finished the stitches. He had to find the Double Blades once more and repay them for this kindness. He would have to warn Tohmas first, but then he would deal with yet another enemy.

"Fayela wants to speak to you," Colt told him once it was clear his duties were finished, and he would be sent back out.

"When I have a moment," Kitable promised.

Colt shrugged and left. Kitable watched him go with a sigh of relief and gratitude. There were very few people he could trust in this world, but Colt represented one that had never let him down. He would have to find some way to repay the man who had saved his life.

Chapter 19

Tohmas had heard two accounts of the incident at his wizard's waggon by the following day when Kitable finally arrived at the new meeting tent in the dawn. Seeing him, Tohmas sent the rest of the people out. It was just Tohmas and Carsh when Kitable sat down.

"You're wearing an illusion," Tohmas commented as he handed Kitable a cup of wine, which the wisavi placed in front of him without drinking. There was a sour look on the otherwise flawless face.

"First Carsh can tell where I am by the hairs on the back of his neck, then the Northlander says magic shows up like a diluted rainbow to his eyes, then my waggon driver informs me that each caster has a distinctive scent to their spells and now you are detecting magic too? If you tell me I sound like a dancing tune, I think I may just become a hermit in the DragonTail mountains!"

The most amusing part of the tirade was imagining the dancing tunes Kitable had suggested. The wisavi would be one of the more lively tunes; he was so tense this morning, he was nigh on bouncing.

Tohmas waved the wisavi down and laughed. "I am as blind as ever, but you look five years younger than the last time I saw you. When was the last time you updated your illusion of yourself?"

Kitable raised one eyebrow. "I've never looked as good since that day," the wisavi confessed with a shrug. He finally reached for the wine, sipped it exactly once, and then replaced it. "Honestly, Tohmas, I look awful right now. The Double Blades are alive, and one of them cursed

"

me. I have only started shaking the effects off, but I wanted to warn you as soon as possible. I'm going to go after them again. I'll finish what I started."

"I have no doubt you will," Tohmas answered. "You know you can call upon me if you need anything."

The wizard shook his head. "I'll deal with them."

He was standing and heading for the door before Tohmas could even offer, "I hope you will have a chance to rest after that's done, Kitable. Things here are quiet. I think it will be safe."

The wizard shrugged again as he limped out, and Tohmas poured out the rest of the wine.

Fayela heard Kitable was visiting Tohmas and ambushed him. Having left Seraph behind, as Seraph claimed the master wizard would take offense to the handmaiden's presence, Fayela stood alone among protectors until Kitable left Tohmas' new command tent. Although he did not seem to see her at first, she chased him as he passed between two houses.

"Wisavi! A moment?"

He initially stiffened, but his posture softened when he recognized her. "Colt had told me you were looking for me, my lady." Kitable bowed his head and gave her a tired smile. It seemed to take great effort, making it all the sweeter to her.

"I need your council," she answered. The words felt odd. Kitable was more than twenty years her junior. She had watched him grow from a scared pre-teen into a powerful wizard. She had not expected ever to seek his advice.

"Is it urgent?" he replied. "I have an enemy wizard I need to see to."

She did not realize she had lowered her gaze until she noticed her vision was on the grass. Her voice was soft. "It's nothing that challenges Galanth's safety, Wisavi, just the peace of mind of an old woman."

Surprisingly, Kitable did not immediately turn away and go about his chores. When she looked up, he had not moved. Then, with a raise of his hand and a single word of command, he sealed the area with a twirling shield of wind that blew in a dome around them, separating them from the nearby buildings. A second word created a green light in the air between them.

"None will hear you through this barrier, and if any seek to eavesdrop, the light will change to red." Looking slightly embarrassed, he finished, "You seemed to want privacy."

He was, she had to admit, more attuned to people than he had been, and the show of concern disturbed her. With the discretion she had needed, she felt herself collapse. Before she had spoken a word, she had burst into tears.

"Oh, Kitable..."

Again showing that he had come a long way since his arrival to Galanth, Kitable placed comforting arms around her. The gesture destroyed any remaining hesitation, and she blurted, "He's not my son!"

All she could do was sob against his chest for the long silence that followed.

After giving her time to catch her breath and calm her tears, Kitable cleared his throat and said, "I presume you mean Tohmas."

"Yes. Tohmas is not my son." The words made her greatest fear too real.

Without Tohmas, Habal's death would have been unbearable, but now the son that represented the one thing she still had of her beloved husband was not real. She felt as if her heart was hearing of Habal's death once more, and this time there was no part of him to cling to.

The wizard, the only person within the entire Galanth camp she trusted enough to bring this secret to, seemed to know there was nothing to say. In silence, his arms held her gently as she found her voice.

"Tohmas fell from his horse when he was six, Kitable. His arm broke. The wound was grievous, yet now I see no mark of it on him."

"Tohmas has many scars," Kitable said.

Fayela shook her head. "I looked for it. It's not there! Besides," she continued as she pulled back and tried to push aside her tears, "have you not looked at him? Do you see Habal in him? Do you see me?"

"He has Habal's height."

"He is taller than Habal was," she corrected, "and taller than any member of my family! He is... he cannot be... he doesn't act..." Tears welled once more. The sentence dropped.

Kitable's voice remained mild. "He spent little time with the Esparans, so we expected him to fail to pick up Zayban's command style. Although he tries to conceal it, he has a great deal of Rydan in his way of thinking and…"

Her eyes widened. "You know!"

The wizard shrugged and then seemed to regret the gesture. With one hand massaging his right shoulder, he explained, "My Scry showed me, rather accidentally. I have seen Tohmas' life among the Rydans and so probably understand better than most."

"But Kitable, you know, in all his talks with me, he has never mentioned anything that happened before he left. No mention of the five puppies he raised from the mongrel under the stairs, or his favorite horses, or places to ride, or the games he played, or even the playmates! Two of his protectors were his best friends, and now he treats them like any other!"

Kitable pressed his lips and said nothing. Instead of the comfort she had been seeking, Fayela realized she had found something else: the truth. He knew more than he was letting on, she was sure.

Placing an arm around her and embracing her gently, Kitable proved her suspicions by saying, "Once I deal with the Double Blades, I will do some more reflections on the matter, my Lady. Perhaps I will be able to find where the scar you recall has gone."

She kissed his cheek. "I never meant to bother you, but I did not have anyone else to turn to. I know you find these family matters tedious."

To her shock, he trapped her hand gently and held it between his. "There is a woman in Lour who would give anything to have her son back, but instead, I am here. You have your son. I do not blame you for wanting to keep him."

It was still a few heartbeats before he could drop the spell that protected their privacy and let her go on her way.

Finding them had not been easy, but nor had it been too difficult. Tostig proved himself clever enough to mask himself from searches, and despite Kitable's precise definition, Kitable failed to locate the distinctive man. Maybel proved harder to define but easier to find.

He found her.

What he saw through the Scry, however, made him pause.

CHAPTER 19

Two men lay unmoving beside a campfire amid a spattering of scorch marks and burned grasses. Tostig lay across from them, equally prone and motionless, with Maybel draped over him as if she had flung herself over him. Old spells hovered, useless, and untethered. Their owner was dead.

It was, he knew, very likely an illusion. However, once a careful search of the area revealed nothing else dangerous, Kitable decided to investigate. He threw an anchor for his spell into the Scry.

Kitable had sent himself all over the world with Relocations and never found them disorienting. Today, however, his arrival in the camp had him briefly bewildered, and he instinctively threw up an extra defense in response. By the time he had gripped his emergency crystal pendant, thinking he should escape, his mind had settled.

He decided there were spells in the air, and one of these had thrown him off. He felt immense power nearby, but his Spell Sight revealed nothing in the surrounding area. The Double Blades were exactly where his Scry had shown them—on the ground looking dead—he took another moment to check his defenses. Something had changed. Three defensive spells were down. He had Relocated through a shield that had partially dispelled him. Was it a new or old spell cast on the camp itself?

Movement caught his eye, and Shimmer Weaver stepped into the wreck. Spell Sight showed all her hovering spells in detail. She had expanded her repertoire, he noted.

Dressed in her regular apothecary clothing, everything from Shimmer's ribcage to the top of her pelvis was exposed. Her many-layered skirt was the brightest yet, embroidered with beads and charms. Her hair, for a rare moment, was without bandana or braids and bounced over her shoulders like fine cloth. Somehow, her green eyes seemed even more brilliant, and her smile made them sparkle.

"What are you doing here, Weaver?"

"I followed you," she confessed with a shy smile that made his heart skip several beats and leave him weak.

He had to force the words out through his constricted throat. "I am certain I have told you specifically not to..." She gazed at him through long lashes while fiddling with one of the red curls that hung over her shoulder. "...do that," he barely managed to finish.

"Please don't be mad at me." The girl pouted as she advanced. "I was worried about you. I could not stand it if anything happened to you."

She was close enough now to reach out. One ringed finger touched his arm in plea, but the Molded Shield kept her touch at bay. Although it had always been one of his greatest defenses, Kitable cursed the shield. He would have liked to feel that touch on his skin.

"I could not be angry," he said, but the voice sounded very unlike his. It was true, but he had not expected to admit it.

"You don't trust me!" She pulled her hand away, frowning so profoundly that his heart physically ached.

He followed her movement, catching her arm and turning her back to him. The gap between his hand and her arm persisted. "I trust you, Shimmer," he confessed. "You have never betrayed me. I..."

He felt drunk. Had he been sober, he doubted he would ever have been able to admit how highly he thought of her. Still, every word was accurate, and now that they were alone together, without any chance of intrusion or eavesdropping, it seemed vital that he tell her. There had to be a chance.

"But you will not even let me touch you," she whispered. As proof, she ran a delicate hand over his face, where the Molded Shield continued to keep her skin from touching his. Where the finger passed, Kitable's skin tingled in anticipation, and his lungs forgot about breathing for a long moment.

They were alone, and the enemy was already defeated. Molded Shields were helpful but not irreplaceable. He did not need it.

He dropped the shield. The finger that had been kept from his skin landed gently on his cheek.

Everything from his throat to his knees went into a knot to feel the press of her warm skin. It tightened when her hand cupped the side of his face.

For her smile, he would have dropped any spell. With her, he did not need them anyway.

She lifted herself on her toes and kissed his mouth tenderly.

His first kiss stole his breath. She smelled of sweet spray herbs and tasted like honey. But as she pulled away, his eyes had trouble focusing, and his mind finally kicked out a coherent thought.

CHAPTER 19

Only a moment ago, he had observed a suspicious setup and told himself that it was likely illusionary. He had known that before he had Relocated. When had he forgotten it?

Dizziness intensified, and he stumbled back from the woman he had kissed. Was her hair auburn, or was there blonde in it? Three of his shields had been dispelled. Which had those been? The ones protecting against thought magic?

His legs shook, and it had nothing to do with desire. As he staggered back, the magic came undone, and he recognized Maybel. At that exact moment, he knew he had been trapped. Worse, how the world was keeling around made him highly suspicious that he had just been poisoned.

"Finally," came Tostig's voice. "Finally he..."

As unresponsive as his body seemed, he had trained himself to go for his crystal pendant when threatened. Kitable's right hand found the pendant and, the instant before he blacked out, crushed the crystal into his hand.

He was not conscious enough to feel the spell whisk him away.

Kitable, the all-powerful Master Wizard of Galanth, lay unconscious under Arnika's table, and she did not know what to do.

"I still think we should smother him," Altana said.

Arnika pressed her lips together and unfolded her arms. Backing away from the body on the floor hid the green and silver robes in the shadows, but she could not push its presence from her mind quite as easily. They had to do something.

"What if it's a trap? He's a wizard! He will not be without defenses. What if we try something and fail?" Worrying about deception was easier than admitting she did not want to kill Master Kitable. The wizard had been kind. Somehow, the way he lay prone seemed to disconnect him from the war.

"But he's the enemy," Altana replied. She had selected a pillow from the beds at the back of the tent and clutched her weapon to her chest determinedly. "Think of the advantage we could give Tandar! Without Kitable—"

"What if he wakes up?" Arnika objected. "Even if he doesn't kill us, Tohmas will. They could be testing us!"

It seemed, she had to admit, unlikely, but no reason she could devise for the master wizard to be unconscious beneath the table seemed likely. She was unwilling to be fooled. She was also reluctant to smother the vulnerable man just because he had sworn loyalty to the wrong side.

"We could be—"

Unable to withstand more of Altana's arguments, Arnika interrupted her cousin. "Protectors! One of you! Either of you! Come here, please!"

One enormous man with a green braid on his shoulder stuck his head into the tent. He had to be the largest one she had seen yet, but he did not look particularly dangerous or angry.

"I..." she commanded with little strength, "...I need Prince Tohmas. I want him to come see me."

The behemoth raised a thick, blond eyebrow. "When would you like to see him, fair Lady?"

"Now!" she snapped with an unwitting glance to where the most powerful caster in Espar lay under her table. "Immediately!"

He bowed his head and rushed out.

"I still say—" Altana began.

"Gods, keep your voice down!" Arnika chastised her. "If they think—"

"We should kill him, Nika," Altana whispered. "We could say he appeared dead, and no one would know otherwise. Think about it! Without their magic support..."

When the green and silver-clad man entered, Altana jumped back and dropped her pillow. Scrambling to pick it up, Altana snapped, "Gods' sakes! Knock before barging into a lady's quarters!"

She was, Arnika laughed to see, most concerned that Prince Tohmas had seen her with the pillow and would suspect her purpose. Her fluster gave her courage enough to correct the Prince of Galanth.

The Prince of Galanth, taking the scolding well, bowed his head. "I apologize for the intrusion, Ladies. I did not mean to—" Initially, Arnika thought he had seen the body, for he paused, then straightened. But instead of rushing to the wizard, he glanced over his shoulder and said, "You are living in a tent. What exactly would you have me knock on?"

"Well, you should…" was as far as Altana got.

The prime protector barged into the tent. The Rydan was in, over the chairs, and standing on the table before Arnika could find her voice. Once perched high, Carsh spun in search of something, then dropped to the ground and found the body under the table.

He could not have seen the body from the door, let alone from outside the tent; something else had attracted the prime protector to the unconscious wizard. But Arnika did not dare ask what.

The Rydan stood and, with a subtle raise of his chin, brought Tohmas over. Prince Tohmas had drawn a blade in response to the prime protector's intrusion but now sheathed it.

Both men crouched beside the fallen caster. Carsh had two knives on hand still.

"What happened?" Tohmas asked as a hand sought a pulse on Kitable's neck, the neck Altana had suggested slitting.

"He…" Arnika stammered, ignoring the way Altana abandoned her to replace the pillow. Arnika's cousin distracted herself by making the beds yet again as if the pillow had been in her hands merely because she had been rearranging the sleeping area. "He just appeared. Is he dead?" Arnika asked.

Prince Tohmas shook his head as he pulled his hand from the pulse. He checked the wizard's forehead for fever. Less civilized, the prime protector poked the wizard with the hilt of his knife.

"He's not dead, but his defenses are down, and that's bad. Runnah!" Tohmas called. The same enormous protector responded. When he did so, it was by rushing into the room, instantly poised and ready.

"Get me Darak and the Weavers immediately. Geddit!"

The man was out the door in a stride. While they waited, Carsh did a circuit of the area, inspecting every angle of the tent. The king seemed to be looking for something on or around the wizard, pulling him out from under the table during his investigations. Despite finding nothing, they noticed that Tohmas' hands had blood on them. They could not see where it was from.

The first person to respond to the king's summons was a plainly-dressed woman of Arnika's age who carried a large canvas sack. The king had to squint, but once he had recognized her, he motioned her to where the caster was lying.

"Different, Miss Weaver," was all he said about whatever had made him pause.

Just as the woman moved from the entrance, the second respondent arrived, and this was a heavy-breathing, brown-clad celebrant that Arnika had seen at her father's funeral pyre. He had a sack and a vest of cutter tools in hand when he exclaimed, "Who's dying? You only ever call when someone's dying!"

Prince Tohmas gestured to the floor. "Over here, Darak."

Celebrant Darak rushed forward, muttering, "I hate being right." But once he saw his companion, the celebrant's face brightened, his annoyance forgotten. "Very modest, Miss Weaver. You look lovely."

As Miss Weaver did not look up, it was hard to tell if she enjoyed or resented the compliment.

The last summoned helper arrived next. The only thing brighter than the man's brilliant robes, trousers, and vest, was his red hair and goatee. A black cap balanced atop his head askew when he arrived just as breathless as the celebrant. He moved impossibly fast to join them at the body.

"What happened?" the new arrival asked.

"Just appeared," Prince Tohmas replied.

"He's wearing an illusion," Miss Weaver quietly reported.

Tohmas winced. "Demons, I'd forgotten that. That's probably why I didn't see where the blood came from." Tohmas showed the blood smeared on his hands. "I couldn't find any injury."

"Good pulse," Celebrant Darak said as he removed his fingers from the throat and checked the eyes. "Not dead yet."

"No defenses?" the red-haired man asked, and Miss Weaver shook her head. Like the man, the girl had dark red hair, but she had wrapped a cloth around whatever locks she boasted. A small curl snuck out.

Arnika, standing to the side, pressed her lips, trying to decide if she had done the right thing without looking like she was uncertain about either the prince or Altana. With Altana focused on the sleeping area, Arnika stood alone between the chests and the edge of the table where Kitable had been dragged, with Tohmas and Prime Protector Carsh between her and the best view. It was hard to see what was happening and harder still to make sense of what she was hearing.

She had not thought anyone had been paying attention to her until Tohmas motioned her forward. Cautiously, she stood to the prince's left as they looked down on the caster.

"*Helani*," Miss Weaver said.

She's a wizard? Arnika thought. She'd expected healers and cutters, not casters. And she'd not even known women could be wizards at all.

In a blink, Kitable looked ten years older. Scratches crossed the man's right hand, the source of the blood. Certain those marks had not been present when she had first discovered the body, she looked to the healers for an explanation.

Celebrant Darak lifted the hand out, inspecting it. "Thank you, Miss Weaver. It's so much easier to see without magic in the way. I've seen this before," Unconcerned, he dropped the hand.

"Doesn't explain why he's unconscious," the red-haired man replied.

Miss Weaver leaned over Kitable, her ear angled to the downed man's mouth. "Poisons perhaps? Would it..." Mid-sentence, the woman paused, turned her head, and looking briefly as if she might kiss Kitable, sniffed lightly. She sat back with her jaw agape.

The red-haired man repeated the investigation, but when he sat back, he was smiling and shaking his head. "Didn't see that one coming!" he said with a laugh. Miss Weaver riffled through her bag but at least the laughter brought relief. Surely, if Kitable were in danger, they would have been less eager to chuckle at their discovery.

It then fell to the celebrant to smell the wizard's breath. He pressed his lips and nodded sagely. "You have the counter?" he asked, and Miss Weaver nodded mutely. Of the three healers, only she seemed upset by their diagnosis.

"Explanations?" Had he not spoken, it would have been possible to forget Prince Tohmas was even present.

"Your wizard has become a victim of a good night kiss, my king," the celebrant reported, taking a small disc of something from Miss Weaver as he spoke. "Under the tongue?" he briefly checked, to which the woman mutely nodded. Celebrant Darak propped open the wizard's mouth and slipped the disc under his tongue.

"A what?" the prince asked, smiling cautiously.

"The good night kiss..." the red-haired man said as he stood. "...is a combination of two drugs used by con artists, thieves, and prostitutes.

The first drug knocks out the body's muscles, stopping the victim from fighting back. The second drug knocks out the brain, leaving the person unconscious. Beyond that, it's harmless. He may want to check his purse."

At the entrance, Miss Weaver kept her eyes downcast as she added, "He'll not want to see us here when he wakes. Celebrant Darak can deal with the cuts to his hand, if that's all, my king."

"Shimmer?" Tohmas called. "You—"

"We have things to deal with, King Tohmas," the red-haired man interrupted. "If that's all, we will be on our way."

It was apparent, even to Arnika, that the conversation the prince wanted was being refused, and to her surprise, Tohmas did not press it.

"Thank you very much for your help," he said instead. "I appreciate your aid, yet again." Both man and woman bowed their heads to him and left.

Already Kitable was beginning to flinch at the celebrant's ministrations to his cut hand. By the time the final bit of what appeared to be glass had been picked out, Kitable had opened his eyes.

It took the confused wizard another dozen heartbeats to focus on the people around him. At length, he seemed to determine his location.

"You failed to mention visitors," Kitable said to Prince Tohmas. "Lady Arnika? Are you still here?"

Tohmas laughed in relief. "I think he'll be fine. I'll get him moved to a Healing waggon."

All Arnika could do was nod.

"Feel free," Tohmas added as he lifted the wizard to his feet and kept him standing with an arm around his shoulders, "to call for me any time you need anything. Thank you, fair ladies."

Although Celebrant Darak seemed to want to say something, he bowed to Arnika and chased his patient.

Tohmas cares. There was no doubt that the prince had genuinely been worried about finding his wizard injured. Because he was concerned about Kitable, or because he, like Altana, believed that the wizard was vital for his conquest? Would he have missed Kitable or the power Kitable represented?

"I still say we should have killed him," Altana said as she punched a pillow in demonstration.

CHAPTER 19

"No, Tana," Arnika answered. "Do you not see? We have done him a favor. He owes us."

For a long moment, Altana was silent. Then, her voice filled with awe at the possibilities, she asked, "What will you ask for?"

Arnika let herself smile once more, and she could feel confidence seeping in. "I'll ask for all his army's secrets," she told her cousin. "I'll ask for a tour of the camp. Then we will see how that golden tongue can wag, and you will carry everything we learn to Tandar the next day." She nodded to herself. "What I learn will be his undoing."

Knowing better than confronting Shimmer immediately, Dust took a long route to Match and Mixer. He did not know why he thought she would go there instead of back to Lady Fayela, but he was proven right.

Shimmer sat at the table casting. The spell ended the moment Dust arrived.

"He kissed her!" she cried, throwing herself into the cushion seats around the table with enough drama for the stage. "Gods above! He dropped his shield for her!"

As expected, she had cast Reflections to determine the source of Master Kitable's drugging. Since the lips were the most common means of administrating the drug, it had seemed inevitable that she would not like the answer.

Dust sat down beside her and ran a hand along her now-unwrapped head. The long red curls hid her tear-filled eyes, but he could hear the sorrow in her voice.

"I thought it was just him," Shimmer said. "If he wasn't interested in women, I could live with that, but that's not it! It's me, Papa!" She sniffled as she rolled over to put her head on his lap. "He hates me!"

"He doesn't hate you, Shim. He may have found someone who fit him a bit better, but—"

"Maybel?" she snapped, springing out of his lap and leaving his stroking hand mid-air. "A woman who represents everything I thought he disliked about me? How could I be so stupid? How? Oh, gods, what am I doing? What am I doing wrong?"

She punched a pillow, then collapsed onto her back among the seats and stared at the ceiling with her arm flung over her forehead.

The crush sparked when she had met Master Kitable had reached a critical threshold. They had been remaining primarily because of that infatuation. Now Shimmer's devotion had been betrayed.

"Shim," he finally said to her silence, "you cannot become Maybel."

She half whined and half groaned as she rolled over to bury her face in the pillows.

He continued, knowing she could have put a pillow over her ears. "You may be able to get him to love someone you are pretending to be, but he will never love you because of who you pretend to be. If you want to change, then change because you want to, but don't let the wants of a blind fool dictate how you run your life." With a final sigh, he finished, "If you can let him go, then that's what you need to do."

He counted in his mind for a dozen beats, then let himself smile. The passion awakened in Shimmer, one he had experienced before, was not going to be stopped by this or any other disaster.

"If, however," he pressed once she did not respond, "you find yourself unable to imagine a life without that blind fool in it, then please consider this: he may have let Maybel kiss him, but she poisoned him. He has been betrayed. All that demoness has done is proven Master Kitable is mortal. That opens things up for you."

When she rolled over and pursed her lips thoughtfully, she knew he was right.

Dust patted her leg. "So prove to him that he made a mistake. Show him what he is missing."

She was still sniffling, but at least she was sitting up. "No more hiding," she said.

The father in Dust protested before he could stop himself. "What about the Rydans?"

"I'll make peace with Darcina," Shimmer insisted.

Dust furrowed his brow. "How? Kitable may not hate you, Shim, but I'm rather certain that Rydan does."

Shimmer's eyes were raised, but Dust knew better than to think she had received divine inspiration. Her stare had landed on a hanging herb in the rafters. "In true Rydan fashion," she said, pulling the dried franx flower down. "I'll bargain with her. I'll blackmail her if I have to."

CHAPTER 19

Dust was satisfied he could leave that with her. He could trust Shimmer to keep herself safe.

Or, he mused, seeing the determination in his daughter's eyes, *at least keep herself as safe as I keep us.* Life was about living. If it got bumpy along the way, then the walk was all the more exciting.

This year promised to be very exciting.

Chapter 20

Arnika waited until late, hoping to catch Tohmas sleeping, to put him off guard. But when she finally demanded to be taken to the king at once, the protectors were nonplussed. He was at the Temple waggons. They happily offered to escort her.

Altana stayed behind because she had fallen asleep and because Arnika wanted to avoid distractions during this confrontation. It was easier to find her strength when there was less of an audience. Altana's fear of Tohmas was contagious.

The central fire burned low at the Temple waggons, and the people were sparse, but there was a noticeable gathering at the Fire waggon. The most obvious of these was the prime protector, who leaned against the waggon wall playing with a pair of knives. Celebrant Sedgan, the brand of his goddess on his chest, also stood by. They all came to attention as Arnika approached them.

One of her protectors said something softly to the prime protector, who pointed to the waggon with a nod.

"'Ee be alone," the prime protector warned. "Ya go, ya be alone wid 'im."

Until that moment, Arnika had not noticed how diligent the king had been in ensuring he had company whenever he visited her. The thought of meeting with him privately sent a shiver down her spine. She was not strong enough to fight him, not alone.

Chapter 20

But it's not like I have been surrounded by allies so far! Had he wanted to attack her, he could have done so with or without witnesses. Although his Lady Mother may have disapproved, she could not physically restrain her son. Arnika had been alone in principle in every confrontation thus far.

"I shall manage, thank you," she said, hardening her voice. Before her shaking stomach realized what was happening, her legs carried her into the waggon.

It was dark within, with dim lights from low-burning candles creating a red glow and deep shadows. As her eyes adjusted, the giant man rose from his place, kneeling in front of the altar.

He spun to face her. "What hap—" But as soon as he recognized her, the sentence fell off. He seemed to forget that he had been speaking.

For once informal in a simple cotton tunic and trousers, he held his sword and sheath in hand. He seemed less imposing than usual in the casual attire, alone in prayer.

She gathered her courage and inquired, "Whathap? Is that a Rydan greeting?"

His free hand ran through his hair sheepishly. "What hap," he said as he replaced the sheathed sword on the altar, "is the beginning of the sentence, 'What happened?' My men never bother me at this time of night unless it is an emergency. I expected the worst. I am becoming paranoid, perhaps."

He was long in releasing his grip on the blade, almost as if he thought it might not be there when he next reached for it. Eventually, he let his last finger drop off it.

The concern he showed for the altar and the flames there surprised her. "I never considered you a religious man," she said.

"A man who flaunts his faith is not spending enough time observing it," he replied. It sounded like a quote, but she could not place it. "Are you truly surprised to find me among Fire's holy light, even just as a worshipper?"

There were indeed a plethora of rumors concerning the so-called King of Espar. She'd heard him called "Champion of Inac," and the blade gifted to him by the goddess Inac was a popular legend. Arnika had put very little faith in those tales, thinking them propaganda.

"I had heard you called Champion of Fire before," she confessed, "but not even the Celebrants of Cainton knew what that meant."

"I used to deny it," he replied with a shrug, "but once I heard the Goddess speak it, I accepted."

It was hard to imagine when or where he had "heard the Goddess speak it." Only those devoted to the gods, the celebrants, could expect to know the will of the gods.

"I heard," she continued determinedly, "that you were branded by the Goddess. Might I see your foot?"

As he had been praying, he was already shoeless. Leaning on the altar, he lifted his left foot and turned the bottom to face her. It was callused but unmarked.

"I thought—"

"It's my right foot," he teased, shifting to show her the other foot, which revealed a pair of waving lines of a scar.

Seeing it, she felt herself flush.

"Like the celebrant outside. Is this a common thing in Galanth?"

Replacing the foot and standing tall, he shook his head. "Perhaps a theme with Inac these days, but it is not a deliberate act of man. All three of us—Celebrant Loni is also scarred—have come upon our scars independently. Celebrant Loni, the woman you met at the pyre, was pulled from a burning house when she was a child, and the only mark on her was the scar on her hand. Celebrant Sedgan woke branded after a night spent with a woman he had thought to be Celebrant Loni, only to discover that the celebrant had been ill and in a Healing waggon for several days."

When he did not continue, she pressed, "And you?"

There was a much longer pause before he replied, which made Arnika proud of herself. If he did not want to answer, he wanted to hide something. Perhaps it would help Trulin.

"When I was thirteen, I built a signal fire to the armies of the Outlands, who were at war. Later, I went to put it out and slipped. This scar was the result."

"They must have thought it a good sign," she remarked. The front of the altar was decorated in a golden double-S pattern that matched his foot. It was a well-known symbol.

CHAPTER 20

"Rydans don't use that symbol. It wasn't until my return to Espar that I realized what it meant."

It made her pause again. Prince Tohmas claimed to be the loyal servant of Inac but came off surprisingly modest in his faith. Was that because he did not want any more signs or because he did not need more?

"Have I upset you?"

Although it seemed apparent that his offers had to be self-serving, she found it hard to understand his motivations, especially when he was being kind to her. He seemed to genuinely think that soft words would sway her opinion of him and his quest for Espar, but that seemed too naive to be possible.

She straightened, aware she had gotten lost in thoughts. She shook her head and said, "I have a request to make of you."

"Ask whatever you wish," he replied immediately.

"I wish a tour of your camp," she declared, watching him carefully to see if she had overstepped.

"And when would you like to do this? Now?" No hint of suspicion crossed his face.

"Tomorrow." Knowing that he would let her wander around without warning in the dark was remembered for later use. "Daylight."

"Would you have me show you, fair Lady, or would you rather another?"

Again, his willingness to compromise his position surprised her, but it gave her the option she wanted, and she seized it.

"I would have you lead me."

This time, he bowed his head. It was a gesture she would not have expected of him even in the presence of princes. "I would be delighted. When would you have me call on you?"

She had no prepared answer, and her voice faltered. "When does your day begin, good prince?"

"I spar with Carsh before dawn, then meet the protectors at first light. That would be about the fifth or sixth candle of the morning. Slightly early for you, I would think."

"Not at all," she convinced herself to say. "I would see you and the prime protector spar. You will send a runner to fetch us the moment you rise." *Altana*, Arnika thought, *is going to hate me for this.* But it made the most sense. If she wanted to learn about him, following him all day was ideal.

"Very well," he agreed. "I will see you first thing tomorrow, fair Lady."

She had done all she had come to do and more, and if she was going to rise before dawn, she wanted to catch as much sleep as possible. He had not refused her request and seemed oblivious to the potential danger the day's prospect hailed, which suited her. She was ready to leave.

As she turned to leave, he spoke once more. "Thank you again for Kitable. I know he was your enemy. I am thankful you called us instead of trying to be rid of him."

For the briefest moment, she feared he had overheard Altana's insistences, but she forced her voice to sound light in denial of her fright. "Our meetings were always pleasant. I am fond of him."

She left before anything further could be said, fearing what he might say.

Shimmer tested the outskirts of the Rydan camp before committing herself and learned rapidly that the Rydans still recognized her face and bright clothing. Surprisingly, she was not accosted. In the very early morning, the men welcomed her with sly smiles and oblique references to her dancing that, without a Translation spell up, she could barely decipher. Once, however, she saw the women's reaction, especially the few she recognized from the dancing lessons, she decided to be more subtle.

It did not require magic for her to hide. Growing up, life rewarded her for being inconspicuous occasionally, and she found it easy to slip back into those patterns. All it took was patience. Although she was anxious not to miss Kitable's revenge against the Double Blades, it was more important for her to see things straightened between her and Darcina.

It took more than two candles, but investing the necessary time to get into the heart of the Rydan camp unnoticed paid off when eavesdropping eventually revealed Darcina's fire. Darcina was a name spoken with reverence. The largest hide shelter was hers.

CHAPTER 20

After enough patience, she found the woman alone in her shelter, repairing the short knife that had been a constant accessory on her hip since the first day they had met. The shelter was decorated with beads and bones, but it seemed evident that the weapon was the thing of most value.

Stepping out brought her into the Rydan's line of vision and the hands, which seemed to have been going through the motions of the repair without thought, paused.

Shimmer tossed the franx flower onto the floor in front of the woman pre-emptively. "I come to make peace," she informed the Rydan.

Darcina's pale eyes dropped onto the weed on the ground. If she believed in hope for a moment, it even looked like Darcina had less venom in her eyes.

"I know," Shimmer pressed on as she pulled a string of pills from her pouch next, "your people want nothing to do with me, but you knew me best, Darcina. You know I'm no monster. I want to help you."

Darcina's hands resumed their work with the knife as her cold eyes fixed on Shimmer.

"*Nye's danca be sayin' ya naw be flya,*" the strong voice whispered in clear fear of being overheard. Having justified her acceptance, Darcina scooped up the franx flower and hid it under a blanket. Both hands were on the knife in the next instant.

By Shimmer's limited understanding of Rydan, *nye's danca* meant "knife dancer," and that meant one of two people: Carsh or the Pack Runner. Figuring the Pack Runner had no reason to defend her, she guessed Darcina was referring to Carsh. Knife dancers, she understood, were trained to kill flyers, but Carsh had come to accept that some magic users were not the monster of the Outlands.

"Your knife dancer is wise."

"'*Ee be sayin' ya be frienh o'. And's wisavi.*" Most of the sentence was incomprehensible, but Shimmer got the reference to Wisavi Kitable and nodded.

"Yes, I'm an ally to Tohmas and his wisavi." With her string of pills still in one hand, she made the salute she, like many of the Galanth men, had learned the Rydans associated with Tohmas. Fist into the palm, she confirmed her friendship with the king.

The Rydan woman finally half-smiled. "*Ya be goh.*" The words somehow sounded like an apology and thanks in one.

Shimmer passed over the string of pills. Each pill was colored in a pattern of blue or green to emulate a necklace.

"You said your husband was not often home," she explained. "If you swallow one of these pills, your bleeds will come, regardless of whether you are pregnant. It must be after he has bedded you—within three days—but it will not make you sick as the franx flower did. Since he is not home often, you will not need to take very many."

The Rydan released her grip on her knife and accepted the token. Like admiring a jewel, she fingered the various patterns on the surface. They were Esparan patterns, but Shimmer had no other molds.

"I can make them in any shape you want," she offered, but the woman shrugged off the offer and threaded off a pill instead. She swallowed it promptly.

"He is here then?" she asked, and the Rydan miserably nodded. She then showed her a series of bruises along her ribs and neck by evidence.

"'*Ee be' ere.*"

"I should go then." Visions of an angry Rydan husband filled her head. Thanks to her father's at-time careless courtships, she had dealt with her share of angry husbands, but she had no desire to add a Rydan version to her repertoire.

Darcina stood, picked a necklace from her collection, and offered it to Shimmer. They had no understanding of coins, only trade. Shimmer was to be paid for her gift.

The necklace was spun silver, with a delicate engraved bone clasp and beads of delicately carved jade. It was, without a doubt, worth a fortune.

She almost refused it, but the Rydan woman had already sat down and resumed the knife repair, and Shimmer feared she would offend the woman if she rejected the gift. Instead, she hid the necklace in her bag and snuck out without another word. Words, she remembered, were few among Rydans. All good things were never said, just implied, and Shimmer thought a huge compliment had just been implied.

When she snuck out of the Rydan camp, dusk was approaching, and she started smiling. For the first time in a halfcycle, she could dance without fear. First, she reminded herself, she would check on Kitable's progress against the Double Blades, and then, if it was not too late, she would don her dancing clothes and once more make the night shine in Fixer City.

Dearest cousin,

I hope this note finds you without tampering, but Altana will be able to attest to that. As she will no doubt tell you, I am well enough, as the care of the Prince of Galanth has been generous thus far, and his oath keeps him from harming me. He has put me in his tent, although he now sleeps and converses elsewhere. I mention this so you may know my whereabouts.

On the pages attached, you will find as much information as I could gather about the camp at LandWater. Unless the man deceived me, you might believe all the total counts listed below, for they come from the prince. May you find them more useful than I have.

I was given a full tour of the camp in Prince Tohmas' company. I hope you will find enclosed some valuable information for your later assaults.

He begins the day at the fifth candle and engages in spars with his prime protector, the Rydan Carsh. Altana will be able to give a good description of him, so I will not make much mention of this except to say that his skills are terrifying. I pray you find him less intimidating.

The next stage of the morning is spars with his protectors, where he fights with his right hand until his defeat, then switches to his left to near victory. The protectors say Tohmas wins the matches some days, but they insist they do not let him win deliberately and seem concerned that he may never believe that to be the case.

After this, his day varies. On the day he gave me the tour, he led me through each of the three parts of the army, Northlander, Esparan, and Rydan. Among the Northlanders, we met Darknim DoomDragon, the Dragon of the Northlanders. He was nothing like the stories would imply. He is old. He has also become a father of late and introduced us to his two children. Tohmas knew the girl-child immediately and knew enough Northlander to ask after the mother in their language, but the baby boy seemed to be a surprise to him. DoomDragon insisted the prince had met the babe before. Eventually, Tohmas confessed that he did know the child. Tohmas would only say that the child's mother would be pleased, that the father did not know where the child was, and that it was for the best. If your spies know of this, perhaps it would warrant further investigation. I do not entirely believe his story about the father. Could it be that he has sired a child?

Among the Esparans, messengers are sent by runners, not riders, and we were followed by a good number of these boys in green as we went. One of them brought out a scout rider before we reached the end of the Esparan camp, who reported that Gaidol's colors had been spotted to the south. They seem to believe they have four days, but the kingsmen and guardians are concerned.

Tohmas remains impossible to read, as I have seen him sad but never angry, a strange thing for any son of Zayban. I once saw him worry over his ill wizard, but danger does not concern him.

I hope you find word of Gaidol's approach encouraging. I certainly have.

Although he tried to distract me with Rydan horses, I managed to over-hear some upset about prisoners. Six Trulin prisoners had attempted escape and killed a Galanth companion. When I confronted him, the prince confessed that he would see to the execution of the Trullers to discourage others from attempting the same. When I asked about other prisoners, he insisted he was treating many of the wounded, but that whole men could join the ranks of slaves or soldiers, depending on their willingness to forsake their oath to Trulin. He says he has over a hundred who have joined him since the fall of LandWater.

I met the Rydan horses in the end although I will not try to put words to them, for my words could go on for pages. He introduced me to his magnificent mare and said they run in herds among the Rydan camp. Without tethers and gates, would it be possible to scatter these steeds? Rydans without their horses are considerably less terrifying.

My trip into Rydan forces was uneventful, for these grassmen don't speak and seem to revere Tohmas and Carsh both. If they have a leader, we did not meet him.

Upon our return, we met a Gaidolon man named Lance Carraway. I mention him for two reasons, the first being that he is the last man who saw my father alive. I am pleased to say he also took a stab at his hip during the confrontation. Despite a splint and apparently, a complete lack of sensation in the hip and most of the limb, Tohmas has not replaced the man as leader of Arrow's fyrd. You may wish to seek that weakness in battle. The second reason I mention him is to say again that he is Gaidolon. If you speak to Prince Dorakon, perhaps it would be useful to inquire about the man. He has evident training, which did not come from Galanth. Prince Dorakon may find information on Guardian Carraway helpful.

Tandar, I don't know what to make of most of this or the following pages, but I know you, and I know you always did well during father's trials. I think I can hold Tohmas in LandWater for another few days, at least until you respond. Thus far, he has been willing to appease me. If you need anything, please tell me so I might assist you further.

Gods keep you, cousin, in all you do,

Arnika Trulin

Chapter 21

It took Kitable a day of scrying to find Tostig sitting on a stool in a tavern on the far side of Trulin. The place was quiet in the noon, but for once, the caster seemed to be without his blond companion. Kitable analyzed the region thoroughly, broke down what defenses he needed to, and cast Relocation into the Scry.

He was ready this time.

The moment he arrived, the entire room got to its feet. Now present in person, it was easy to sense the enchanted trinkets each thug had worn to hide them from the Scry. Snatching up weapons from under their tables, the mob in the inn set upon him.

Knowing direct targeting had probably been defended against, Kitable put up two parallel Force Walls in the middle of the room and slid each out to the walls. The result was a sweeping effect that gathered every man, chair, table, candle, and piece of dust against the walls. Tostig's trinkets on the various people in the room failed to defend against the general power adequately.

Only Tostig himself remained, his defenses considerably more complicated and thus effective. The half-bald dwarf lost his stool in the spell but held on to his drink. His expression was dejected and depressed.

Kitable raised his voice. "Every person here is in the unfortunate position of being in my way. I can and will kill you if you continue to obstruct me. Alternatively, you have until the count of five to get out of here. Anyone left in this room when I finish counting or anyone who returns will die."

He dropped the Force Walls and watched them scramble. One man, one of the first to be freed from the spell, lifted a weapon, but Kitable's attack hit him so quickly that the sword was only half raised by the time the man hit the floor. To keep others from following the example, he had chosen an earth destruction spell with enough layers to bypass the defensive trinket. The man's head vanished, leaving a spurting mess behind.

The room emptied without another hesitation.

Kitable's Eight-layered Dispel, modified and molded, enveloped Tostig.

"Can't find good help these days," Tostig grumbled. "Took you long enough. I'm easily twice as drunk as I could have ever hoped!"

Kitable tightened the open dispel around the caster, destroying each spell around the man one by one. He renewed each lost element as it was used up and locked a linger on each item the magic took out. It was elegant and precise, a spell to be proud of.

But Tostig didn't fight it, making it seem excessive for the circumstances.

The caster laughed as he finished the drink instead of attempting to counter Kitable's attack.

"I spent all my time underestimating you, and now I finally overdid it! That must be why you were worth so much! So unpredictable! So adaptive! So ... so ..." Disgusted, Tostig threw the mug sloppily. It was knocked aside by a Missile Deflector. "So annoying!"

Kitable had expected a duel on top traps, but Tostig seemed out of tricks. Drunk as he was, his words were slurring almost too much for full casting to be possible, although trinkets were obviously present. But he had not sought to activate any.

Kitable added one last dispel, this one designed to eradicate illusions. Nothing changed, and Kitable finally started having confidence in what he saw.

Tostig slumped down against the bar. "I almost had it all," he muttered. "I was so close. But dead men don't pay." He gazed up at Kitable, his expression cynical. "Can you be sure this is it? How will you know?"

Kitable drew the long knife he had brought.

Tostig nodded in understanding. "But can you do it?"

Killing with magic was detached and simple, but a living blade offered no buffer between him and the murder. *I do what is necessary.* It was not the first time he had killed someone with his hand.

With a linger on every trinket, the area dispelled, and Tostig now held by a Nahon's Lock spell, Kitable finally closed the distance between them.

He crouched in front of the man. His gaze glistened with tears, but Kitable ignored them. The man smelled like ale powerfully.

"You will not go after her, will you? Blame me, kill me, but leave her alone, please."

Kitable hesitated. But every person he had killed had been a son or daughter to someone, and most of them had had families they longed to see or children they wanted to have. Tostig's concern for Maybel was only unusual because he had taken his last breath to voice it.

Words not used in casting during duels were wasted, but the plea touched Kitable's heart, and he felt he could only give one response.

"No, I will not seek her," Kitable promised.

Although his body was locked, Tostig smiled. He did not speak another word.

Kitable positioned the knife perfectly, angling it beside the sternum but aiming for the heart. No defenses remained to stop him. For all his certainty, his will slackened as he held the long dagger poised, feeling strangely weak.

The ache of his back and the memories of the blackness he could not escape spurred him on. He slid the knife forward.

The heart stopped, Tostig dead.

Magic flared.

A single Contingency that had somehow survived every attempt at breaking its binding or destroying it, flared and brought what felt like the wrath of the gods down on the empty building.

At first, Kitable feared little from the fires that erupted, for his shields protected him from heat and flame, but dispels were woven into the winds and flames of the blaze. His hovering spells were assaulted.

It was random. Hovering spells were being cut and destroyed, and his shields were becoming as porous as beggars' robes. *If one hits my fire protection....*

The answer seemed evident. For the second time in as many days, he crushed the crystal pendant into his palm and waited for the magic to take him away.

The heat intensified. His spell had struck a Seal. Worse, there was a barrier around the building that his Spell Sight could not quite make sense of. He thought he should be impressed with the number of spells hidden from him, but he didn't have time to think about that.

He was trapped, and his spells were being destroyed at an alarming rate. He did not know which were still present to be called upon or if they would hit other surprises.

There was little choice. He pointed at the wall, knowing at least some of the spells needed the gesture, and started testing them.

"*Eganti*!" The earth and force destruction spell did not answer. "*Henaim*," he tried, but the five-way dispel was missing, and "*Enbau*" did not activate the Tunnel he could have used to push through the wall and spell both. "*Unathan*" equally failed to puncture the Seal spell, despite a correct somatic component.

It was not until he tried "*Grantant*" that a spell responded. It was a molding spell, open-ended and flexible, but it had not been designed to destroy walls. It managed to cut a hole in the barrier.

Kitable put his elbow through the window, then kicked through the slivers of wood. He pulled himself through the opening, a blast of fire at his back.

He landed and rolled from the fires he felt cutting through his defenses. Kitable rose to his feet, smoldering. Before he could determine the status of his remaining spells, he realized he was not alone.

It felt like the entire city had come out to watch. In addition to the thugs he had cowed into leaving, the crowd included a group of armed, brown, and white-clad riders. Kitable felt like a deer among hounds.

He was no more willing to let this crowd see him panic than to show Tostig his compassion for Maybel. Facing the threat, he squared his shoulders and, despite being below them, looked down on the riders.

"I spared your lives once," he bluffed. "Are you going to ask me to do it again, or will you get out of my way?"

Part of his mind was sorting through his spells, but the findings were difficult to interpret. There were hovering spells, and he could identify some of the elements or the associated domains, but he could not tell which spells they were. Without knowing exactly which spell he was calling upon and which version of any given spell it was, he had no way of knowing which command word to use. It was very likely any activation he attempted would fail, and he could not afford that uncertainty now.

His bluff had more effect with each flare of fire through the window behind him, and even the men with their horsehair-plumed helmets seemed reluctant. Finally, a man with a brown and black plume stammered, "Who... who are you?"

The green and silver of his robes were charred to black and brown, but Kitable knew he would be recognized by those who had fled earlier. *What is the point of hiding it?*

"I?" he declared indignantly. "I am Wisavi Kitable of Galanth, you idiots. Who else could I be?"

Is there a Relocation spell remaining? He could try. There had been three of them, but successfully casting it would require him to place an anchor first, and he still did not know if he had one of those.

"You have come a long way, Galanth," the rider replied.

Kitable waved them aside. "My business is done. The Double Blades and their leader are dead. I have no interest in any of you." He stared up at the rider meaningfully. "For now."

Shields? If one of those riders fires their bow, do I have any defenses against the arrow? After a mental check, he was certain the answer was "no."

"Then..." the man hesitantly ventured, "...then why don't you leave?"

Under his breath, Kitable tried one of the anchor spells, but it seemed to be absent. At times like this, he wished he was a more faithful man. Cursing gods was more satisfying when one believed they existed.

"I suppose I will," Kitable said, wracking his brain for a suitable, swift spell to get him out. Concealments might work, but they were notoriously incomplete, and he did not want to give these people any reason to doubt he was going. "I just feel," he continued to buy a little bit more time for his singed head to figure something out, "the need to point something out to you all." A Relocation would be best, but it would require an anchor. He could do a shortened Relocation and ask the magic to set an anchor as part of it. He had developed the spell for his crystal pendant to prevent his escapes from being predictable. He would have to increase the minimum distance of the spell to ensure he was clear of the city, but that seemed simplest.

"What I have done to that man in there," he informed the crowd, "I could very easily do to this city or even Cainton. I wanted you all to know that I have not, and will not, perform such feats against you only because of one thing: King Tohmas does not want me to. Remember when you see the green and silver on your doorsteps."

It took fifty-six words to get the spell to move him out of the city, but none of the onlookers interrupted his cast. Once he was sitting on a hill somewhere outside the village, where he could still see the glare of the contained fire, he allowed himself to breathe and sit down. Once the shaking had subsided, he replaced the vital missing spells.

Tostig's final words lingered in his mind until Kitable promised to Vox further victims, pushed it out of his mind one last time, and cast Relocation.

Maybel watched the inn burn from a distance and tried to keep her tears from being obvious. There had been a slim chance that Kitable would not find Tostig this time, but neither of them had put much faith in that hope. If Tostig's spell had gone off, then he was dead.

As much as she wanted to stop the master wizard as he escaped from the burning building, nothing she possessed could effectively oppose him, and she dared not try. If he was particularly vengeful, she would be seeing him soon, and there was nothing she could do about that either.

The game had been well played by both sides. Despite several victorious battles, Tostig had lost the war. There would be no claim to the bounty. Kitable had escaped even Tostig's final, desperate revenge. The Double Blades was dead.

Night fell without Kitable's appearance, and Maybel started scouring the streets to find company for the night. To her surprise, she spotted a fair face she knew.

Maybel had a few trinkets to fend off abusive partners, but she did not think they would be any match for Shimmer. The doom hovering over Maybel flared one final time, and she sank against the nearest wall.

"You here to finish what he started?" she asked the dancer wearily.

In the dusk, Shimmer Weaver sat into one hip and weakly smiled. "You know, I thought I was, but now that I'm here, I don't think that's what needs doing."

Strength returned to Maybel's legs. "Then why are you here?" she asked. She would not cast aside her dread without being sure she was not being played. It had been Shimmer's image that they had so recently used conjured by the wizard's thoughts to seduce and poison Kitable. Knowing that the Weaver was particularly fond of the wisavi, Shimmer could be seeking revenge. She was an actress. Deception seemed plausible

But Shimmer had no way of knowing that Kitable had "seen" her, Maybel realized. She might have recognized the Heart's Desire spell, but unless Kitable had told her, Shimmer would not know what Kitable had seen.

Moving up, Shimmer took her turn crossing her arms and leaning against the building as if ready for a long conversation.

"You have nothing right now, Maybel. Kitable has denied you the bounty for his head. Without something, you'll start walking down a path that will spiral and never let you out."

The description seemed overly dramatic. Maybel could get by well with her looks and charm. Moving from bed to bed was a pleasant enough way to survive. At least she would never be cold.

"Come back with me, Maybel," Shimmer surprised Maybel by offering. "Come work in Fixer City. We have no place for you to sleep, but you could dance and earn some honest money, or we could use your help at Match and Mixer."

Pity was not something Maybel had expected. She did not need anyone's mercy, donations, or help, nor did she want them. Pity was for those who could not survive on their own. Maybel did not need it.

The girl, Maybel knew, had never been where Maybel was going. Or perhaps she had tried and failed. *To be expected.* Shimmer had spent her life protected by her father and provided for by their trade as apothecaries. Dancing had been fun, not survival, and there had never been starvation. How could anyone expect her to understand these matters? She was a child still!

CHAPTER 21

She was a dangerous child with her magic. Had she learned from Kitable? That made her an ally of the man who had killed the Double Blades. She had, by proxy, ruined Maybel's stable life.

And Maybel knew that Kitable was lusting after this red-haired beauty. In the cold hands of the slighted dancer, this knowledge was power.

She would never get the reward from Prince Tandar, but she could still destroy the Wisavi of Galanth. She found the opportunity in the offered pity.

She deliberately shifted her body language to show relief and surrender. She used a small voice when she admitted, "I never need a place to sleep. I'll manage. I think..." She made her voice shake a little as if in uncertainty. "...I think I would do well to try something new."

Shimmer grinned like a proud mother and put a gentle arm over Maybel's now-slumped shoulders.

"Come on then! A good life awaits!"

Indeed. Maybel smiled as she followed the girl out, let her cast her spells, and was taken back to Fixer City.

After sharing an afternoon of tea with Lady Arnika, Tohmas' mother sent a short message.

"She's lonely. Visit."

Deferring other duties, Tohmas carefully approached the tent, feeling out of place.

"*Yadder, yadder?*" Carsh asked. For the first time, Tohmas thought the tent seemed both imposing and all too small. What would he say to her anyway? Lady Altana had gone to Cainton to fetch a few more effects. Lady Arnika had asked for nothing since the tour. What, then, was there to discuss?

But he had to try.

Tohmas paused outside the entrance and stared at the flap. "Probably," he admitted to Carsh. He was about to tell the Rydan to remain outside, as he knew his presence upset Lady Arnika, when he caught sight of a plank of wood against a wall nearby and hit upon an idea.

He found a stake, firmly nailed the board to it, and drove the stake deep into the ground beside the entrance. After returning the tools he had borrowed, he knocked on the board.

"Come..." Sensing that the sentence had been incomplete, he waited until Lady Arnika threw open the flap to regard his rough invention. She lifted an eyebrow at him in inquiry.

"I was told to knock in the future. Now I can!"

To his delight, she smiled as if restraining a laugh, and the light in her eyes made his grin stronger.

"You may enter," she said before disappearing back into the tent and letting the flap fall shut.

"*Sta*," was all it took to keep Carsh out. He presumed she would prefer meeting him in private to having Carsh as the only witness.

The teacups were still on the table from his mother's visit. What Lady Arnika had been doing in the time since he could not guess.

"I just stopped in to see how you were faring," he said, noting acutely she had put the table between them and was even now clutching the back of a chair as if ready to hurl it at him. Although it was difficult, he tried to make himself look smaller.

"I am lucky to have had visitors recently," she replied with a gesture to the cups.

"And how did you get on with Lady Fayela?"

The smile, this time, did not light her eyes as brightly. "Your Lady Mother has different ideas than mine regarding a lady's comportment."

Tohmas laughed. "It is common knowledge in Galanth that my Lady Mother was the daughter of the owner of Ready Bakers—that is, a completely boring, poor, and un-prestigious baker in the village of Hallow. Some thought her rise to the position as a prince's wife quite the scandal."

The girl pressed her lips. As if suddenly aware of her smile, she removed the amusement from her expression. Strangely, although she continued to be exceptionally beautiful, she did not seem quite as glowing as she had only a moment prior.

"I did not know your mother's heritage," she said softly.

"Does it offend you?"

The lovely head shook, short locks and all, before he even finished the question.

"She is a kind woman regardless," Lady Arnika insisted, her stare on where a pushed-out chair stood vacant in front of an empty tea cup as if envisioning the woman in the place she had occupied recently.

As he had entered the tent with nothing to say, he ran out of things to discuss. He could make further meaningless conversation, but he felt wrong wasting her time. He had just decided to take his leave when, surprising him further, she pulled out the chair she had been gripping.

"Would you like a cup of tea?" An instant later, she hesitated with a shy glance and added, "Assuming you drink tea. It's not usual—"

"You forget that it is my tea," he said. "I would gladly join you now if you wish."

For a blink, it seemed she would change her mind, but the decision was in his favor. She gave a half smile of approval and invited him to sit.

She must have boiled more water, for she had hot water to refill the pot immediately. It had been some time since he had tasted the tea Darknim had given him, but it worked well to calm his nerves and release some of the tension in his chest.

"We were trying to guess its origin," she commented as if he was one of her ladies joining him for a quick tea between weaving and baking. The thought made him smile. "I thought it was Damorian, but your Lady Mother said Galanth never bought anything from Damoria, and guessed it was Polthian. We both agreed the earthy flavor had to be southern."

Having already tested the tea to be certain of what his nose had suspected, it was easy to identify the tea. He only had two varieties.

"It's Northlander, a blend of dried reganin root and veshalan leaves." Seeing her face light to his commentary, he admitted, "Although I have no idea what any of that means."

She finally laughed. It was a soft chuckle, but the smile that went with it immediately made his chest crunch. He suddenly remembered why he had been keeping witnesses present for their meetings. Rydan ideas were surfacing, and it became very hard to keep them at bay.

"Oh!" she suddenly remembered, dropping her cup against the table and spilling it. "I wanted to ask you..." She was up and rushing to rifle through a nearby chest until, victorious in her investigations, she held up a wineskin. "What is this?"

When she passed him the skin, his fingers nearly brushed hers, and his oath made him move his hand. It still took him another dozen moments to remember he had been asked a question.

Although it was unnecessary, he removed the stopper and checked the contents. As much as he considered pouring himself a drink to calm his head and heart, he closed the wineskin and pushed the drink away. He needed to avoid Rydan influence. He could not just claim her in Rydan fashion, as much as he wanted to.

"Wildwater," he answered. "It hails from the Outlands. It's an ale, of sorts, made of…" The translation ran into confusion. "It's a plant that grows everywhere and is eaten by dragons. Rydans call it *dragopestin*."

"A weed?" she clarified, and he nodded. The word "weed" fit nicely. "Dragons eat it?"

"So I'm told, but I've only ever seen dragon steal sheep and horses, not raid gardens, so I'm not convinced. Still, dragon weed, as you call it, makes good rope and blankets, or clothes or…" He gestured to the wineskin. "…a drink that can be used to start campfires when the weather is bad."

Again, she laughed. The sound had more substance to it. "Why would you drink that? Rope? Clothes? As a drink?"

"It takes some getting used to," he confessed.

As her laughter subsided, she glanced around the tent, then down at her tea once more. "You bring these worlds together," she mused to herself. "They say you speak Rydan better than you speak Esparan."

"*Ya, fay 'ard. Der don be ma don,*" he replied. It seemed very unlikely that she would catch the compliment he had used, and with Carsh outside, he did not think he would be caught at it. "*Fay 'ard*" was a loving term, usually used only for a man's prized daughter or his best horse, but all it meant was that he favored her above others. It felt right.

The sound of Rydan strengthened her smile.

"And you spoke Northlander to Tiki yesterday?" she prompted.

He raised his hands in surrender. "I'm just learning it!"

"But you spoke so well!" she objected. "You sounded just like them."

Willing to do almost anything to keep her so animated and beautiful, he admitted, "I'm good with languages." Seeing the curious cock of her head, he demonstrated. "If I wanted," he said in a long-vowel Polthian accent, "I could be from the east. If I preferred…" He changed to a rough short-consonant Lourite style. "…I could be from the west. Clandac…" He mimicked his cousin's Clandacanese accent, which slurred words together and switched emphasis on occasion for some unfathomable reason. "…is in the middle, but a good place to visit."

Sitting down, she laughed again. "You sound just like a native!"

"Rydan," he finished, "or Northlander come easily if you know what to listen for." The last few words he finished in a Galanth accent.

She clapped as if applauding a show. "Amazing!"

He shrugged again. "A necessity. I learned Esparan from someone with an accent, who could only explain what the Galanth one sounded like, not speak it himself. I had to modify it when I set foot in Galanth, so I would not stand out."

He stopped, cursing himself. Life in the Outlands was not a casual topic to discuss over tea. Tamv would be furious that Tohmas had so lightly mentioned his training. He was not even drunk, and he knew the tea to be harmless, so what had come over him? Why could he even mention such things?

The smile seemed to have settled on her face. It held all the answers. To keep her happy, he would talk about anything.

The realization shook him. That was not right, not by any of his training, Galanth or Rydan. She was not an ally, not even a friend, and he should not be telling her details about Galanth or his life.

But he feared no treachery from her. He could not understand why, but he felt safe despite his shaky nerves. He was scared, but not because he feared an attack. How could a man who had survived by fearing attacks from every stranger and most allies simply stop worrying about it?

"You stand out," she said shyly, and she blushed, "no matter what you sound like."

Out, he decided. He had to get out before he further disobeyed Tamv or made a fool of himself or, most importantly, before he said something he would regret.

He swallowed the rest of the tea in a gulp. It burned the entire length of his throat.

"I should see how the guardians are doing. I never meant to intrude for so long."

As he stood, she mirrored him politely.

"No intrusion was made," she insisted. "I offered you your tea, after all." Now fully official, she added, "Please inform me the moment Altana arrives back. She and I have much to discuss."

He bowed, knowing all the while it was a sign of obedience that he should never have to make to any save a god, and used the time his head was down to close his eyes in search of focus. By the time he stood, he felt no better.

"Of course, fair Lady," he agreed. "Farewell."

He did not hear any reply, if one was made, so quickly did he depart.

Chapter 22

His two minor cuts were still bleeding as Tohmas found his way to a copse of trees beside LandWater, leaving his protectors at the bottom of the hill. Carsh had proven just how distracted Tohmas was by catching his skin twice during their sparring, and the mild ache was more a chiding than any words the Rydan could have strung together. Tohmas did not join the spars with the protectors but instead went to the hill, ordered the four following him to wait dutifully at the split in the path, and went to find a log to sit on.

The conversation with Lady Arnika the night before lingered. In frustrated desperation, he had grabbed one of Loni's followers overnight, but the morning dawned on more confusion and frustration, none of which had been diminished by the distraction. Everything he did brought him back to Arnika Trulin and the answer she had not yet given. He knew that far more critical things were happening in the world, but all others had lost their meaning.

"I'm intruding," a voice said as Tohmas paused on the edge of the woods to look down over the camp.

"Hardly fair, Lance," Tohmas replied with a glance to where the Gaidolon leaned against a tree, sitting on the sort of log Tohmas had been seeking. "You were here first."

Sitting as he was, it was almost possible to forget that Lance had lost the use of his left leg entirely. The only sign of the injury was the full-leg splint that kept the useless limb in a position to bear weight. Lance's cane stuck out of the ground like a new tree.

"How's the leg?" Tohmas asked.

Lance swung himself to sit forward. "Doesn't hurt, actually, and I'm not on pain pills. The celebrants say that's a bad sign, but who am I to complain?" He patted the wounded leg and gave Tohmas a weak smile. "Women trouble, Tohmas?"

Surprised, Tohmas raised an eyebrow. "What makes you think that?"

The Gaidolon smiled, knowing he was right. "If you were a normal man, you would be worrying about Gaidol and Nothor being two days off our asses, with Trulin to the north still undefeated and Damoria sending threats. But if you were worried about that, you would be in your tent, staring at maps. Since you are out here, I'm guessing you're not fretting about Gaidol or Trulin. If it helps, neither are we. Everyone assumes you have something planned." Taking a breath and fiddling with the leather straps of the brace, Lance finished, "Besides, there are few things that cause men nearly as much consternation as women do."

His eyes on the tent where she was resting, Tohmas had to agree. "That why you up here?" he asked.

Lance laughed. "Hells yes!"

In place of a log, Tohmas found a rock near an oak tree as a seat. Leaning back against the trunk, he stared at the tent and envisioned her lying in his cot, covered in furs, with her sliced locks a tangled mess around her head. Even in memory, she was beautiful.

"Me too."

Lance went back to leaning against his tree, his eyes on the south. "Not familiar territory for you, I guess," the Gaidolon commented idly.

Tohmas banged the back of his head against the trunk lightly. "I'm used to taking what I want, but I can't do that. *D'aems,* it makes no sense! Why can't I shake this?"

Lance chuckled from his place with his leg sticking out along the log. "It's a demon," he admitted. "Suddenly, life belongs to them, and it doesn't seem worth anything without them."

"Yours is in Gaidol, I presume?" Lance had denied ever touching the two Rydans who had adopted him, and Tohmas had never seen Lance with any other woman in camp, not even a whore of Fixer City. He sometimes had a bracelet in a pocket or worn on his arm, but it was

made of pearls, not hair, and did not seem to fit with the traditional Esparan symbol for marriage.

"Yeah."

"You left her to join me?"

Lance nodded this time, his expression longing. "There was no hope for us the way things were," he admitted, "so I had to change the game. Now I've made a promise I cannot keep and the idea of letting her down ... well ... has me climbing this ridiculous hill, in a splint no less, to stare out there wishing for a miracle. And I told Sori, so she's mad at me too. Pathetic, ain't it?"

"Anything I can do to help?" the Leader in Tohmas asked his Follower, but Lance shook his head.

"You?" Lance asked back, and it was Tohmas' turn to shake his head.

"That's the part I hate. I can't do anything."

"Well," Lance said, rolling to his feet and collecting his cane, "if it helps, at least you have her close. I presume you're not going to tell me her name?"

Tohmas closed his eyes with his head against the bark and shook his head. Lance chuckled again.

"You?" he asked, and the laugh developed further.

"Naw," the Gaidolon said in Rydan as he tapped his cane against the log to shake off the leaves and dirt it had collected. With a final sigh, he added, "Tohmas, any woman would be mad to turn you down, so why not just ask? No one expects you to marry a prince's daughter. You can do whatever you think is best." The man was hobbling back down the path when he added, "And just remember that I envy you for every moment."

"I have asked," Tohmas grumbled as Lance staggered down the hill. "I just fear the answer."

How many days would it take her to decide? And if Gaidol came between now and then? He could hold against them, as their camp at LandWater had become just as secure as the hill fort they had defended over the winter the year before, but he did not want to do it. It would be better to move south, but he could only do that if the north was safe. He'd promised the celebrants that this would be ended peacefully. He had done his part.

Why did it hurt?

The time for pondering on a hill was rapidly passing. Gaidol was coming quickly up from the south. Lady Altana could be expected soon from Cainton, which meant news from Trulin for Lady Arnika. Likely, Prince Tandar was nicely fortified by now. They knew they had the time and numbers as soon as Gaidol reached them.

If he moved swiftly, he could take Trulin, but the thought of causing Lady Arnika more pain made his stomach turn.

"D'aems," he cursed again, punching a fist into the rock and regretting it.

It was time to start down that path, whether he liked it or not. Time would sort out the rest.

Days were preparations and plans, and Tandar was kept busy. He collapsed each night, asleep when his head touched the pillow. He had not changed his quarters to move into Prince Kelland's old room. In part, there had not been time, but more importantly, he did not want to.

The chargers were a great help, but they did not have the answers he needed. Gaidol would reach Tohmas shortly. What would Trulin do in response?

Altana had retaken her stool, but there was no weaving, and she seemed to be shaking too hard to attempt it. The day was bright outside, just the sort of day he would have enjoyed by taking a long ride through the countryside. Instead, his mind was on warhorses and how to best organize the superior steeds to challenge the troublesome Rydans. Or could they scatter their herds?

His best advisors had taken apart Arnika's letter. Counts of the soldiers and their spread among the defenses had been helpful. He and the chargers had pinpointed the weakest spot for their main attack. Ironically, one of the points of egress was commanded by Arrow's fyrd, who had the cripple guardian, which made it doubly tempting.

LandWater was fortified, and that meant relying on the horses and their superior numbers. Magic was out as the Double Blades had disappeared. Thus far, Master Kitable had only ever participated in battles when wizards were present. If they avoided magic, would he get involved? What plans did Gaidol have for dealing with the wizard?

Lancers at the door admitted a breathless scout as Tandar went over the maps of LandWater again. For a moment, Tandar closed his eyes and wished the messenger had come to report someone had claimed the reward he had put on Tohmas' head, but when he opened his eyes, the scout was not nearly joyous enough for the news to be good.

"Nothor has broken!" the exhausted man declared as he collapsed into a couch.

One of the chargers was already pouring the man water and offering food. They all recognized the shakes of a man who had ridden for multiple days. The state of the horse would have been similar if it was alive. If it had made it this far, it would survive.

"What do you mean, 'broken?'" Tandar asked once the man had swallowed a gulp of water, then leaned back to pant some more.

"Gone!" he said, spilling his cup in his shaking. "A waggon in Nothor's colors returned from the Galanth camp, and they immediately split the army into green and gold and blue and white. That was it! The green and gold marched off! South!"

Charger Kanon, sitting beside the scout and slowly edging away from the sweaty man, raised an eyebrow to Tandar and asked, "Splitting forces?"

Tandar's eyes were on the map. "There is no clear path from the south. He should be sending them east, not south."

What is Nothor doing? Trying to corner Tohmas? How? Or is this a genuine retreat? What could Tohmas have said to Nothor to get them to pull away?

"It gets worse," the scout said.

"Not what I want to hear," Tandar grumbled, slapping a pile of tokens that had been organized on his table. He had over two hundred leave requests and stories of a magical attack that has shaken people. He had sent the conscription to the last of the cities, and reports kept coming that the counts were short.

He regretted his outburst when he saw the scout's panicked face. There was more bad news, and someone had to tell him.

"What is it?" he prompted, rubbing his temples to clear his mounting headache.

"They took Galvay."

For a moment, he was not even sure who "they" were. Had Tohmas moved, despite Arnika's insistence that she would hold him in LandWater? But the city of Galvay was on the border with Gaidol. If Tohmas was in Galvay, then he was behind Gaidol's army. The alternative "they" was no more comforting.

"Gaidol took Galvay," Tandar repeated aloud.

Two chargers cursed aloud.

"They didn't kill anyone but forced all our people out. The refugees are not far behind me but had to swing wide to avoid Galanth's forces. We did not have a chance against Gaidol."

"They were on orders to let Gaidol through and would have been facing the entire army if they opposed the invasion. I would not expect anyone to throw their lives away like that," Tandar comforted. At long last, the scout felt good enough to swallow some food.

Feeling his legs were becoming as unstable as the scout's, Tandar sought the seat closest to the fireplace and looked at the dying embers.

"Tohmas was right," he cursed at the fire. "All that talk about men wanting to fight because they always have fought. We could have an alliance through a common enemy, but we are betrayed!"

He pounded his fists against the armrests, but they did not help him find his answer.

Nothor possibly gone from their side, magic that was reaching days ahead of the army, men flocking to the green and silver over the brown and silver, and Gaidol seizing the opportunity to continue the war that had maintained them all these years...

His eyes found the glimmer of silver and brown on the mantle over the fire, and he pushed himself up.

"Tana," he decided, "take this news to Arnika at once. Five scouts will ride in your shadow. You have to get her out of there before Gaidol strikes. When Gaidol reaches him, we will be attacking, and I don't want her caught in the fighting."

Standing now but tugging her sleeves in anxiousness, Altana nodded to accept the orders. In finality, Tandar selected two daggers and extended them to his sister.

"You will take nothing else with you, so hide these well. One for you and one for Arnika. Use them to free yourselves or, if the opportunity present, to rid the world of this last demon."

CHAPTER 22

Her trembling hand took the blades from him.

"I will pray for your success," he finished.

Damp from the rain and grateful for the sunlight that had broken through the clouds, the small group of Trullers huddled together at the edge of the Galanth camp, surrounded by armed Galanth soldiers. The walk had mainly been dreary, although the company of neighbors had become fast friends. The group of neighbors had planned this confrontation along every step of their journey but found themselves unprepared now that it was upon them. Joney felt small surrounded by Galanth soldiers.

"They're not that bad," Ven muttered. "Kinda small, some of them."

"Bigger than you," Joney grumbled back. He was cold and missed his shop.

"Yeah, but I'm tiny," Ven replied.

"Just wait until you see the protectors," Ganton added from Ven's left. The street-maker unconsciously rubbed the bandage around his arm where one of these fearsome protectors had— they'd all heard the story—disarmed him with a single blow, then spared his life during the battle at LandWater. It seemed more likely the protector had seen Ganton fall and considered him dead, but no one had managed to convince Ganton of that. "Monsters, all of them! As strong as oxen and fast as snakes! You watch for those green ropes, then you'll understand."

More than one of their gathering was already rolling their eyes, but two others agreed with vigorous nods. The fact that those two were the only other two survivors from LandWater did not escape Joney's notice.

"You mean like them?" Ven gestured to a crowd of green-clad men with green braids looped around their right shoulders. Most of Joney's companions chuckled, but the three survivors went pale, and Ganton clutched his wounded arm.

They were not giant monsters Ganton claimed, but there was not one among them that could not have made Joney's hand hurt after a knock. Some were almost as short as Ven, but they all walked with a confidence that made them feel taller, and the wide berth the surrounding soldiers gave them doubled the effect.

At the head of the group came a man that made even the protectors give way. There, at last, was Ganton's monster. He stood the tallest and wore more knives than clothes. Slicked hair, a lack of armor, and grass bracelets identified the man as a Rydan. Still, the braid of green and silver rope tied around the man's upper arm, for there was no tunic to attach it to, identified the man as the prime protector of Prince Tohmas of Galanth.

The Galanth around Joney's party parted to let the protectors approach. The group split, exploring the Trullers with confidence.

Joney glanced around, but no one was moving. They knew they were being tolerated by the Galanth and were very unwelcome. They had to stay on good terms with these men if they wanted their offer to be taken seriously.

The prime protector walked the ranks as if inspecting animals for purchase at a fair, and none of the people on display went unnoticed. Joney got gooseflesh under the green-eyed stare, but the most significant effect was on the survivors. Ganton's legs had a definite shake, and he was not alone.

But the Rydan did not touch any of them. The worst he did was pause in front of Ven, wrinkle his nose as if smelling something unpleasant, then sneer.

"Ya be havin' magic." The Rydan lifted his grass-encircled hand, palm up. "Mine now."

"I..." was as far as Ven got in protest. The protectors had converged on the target their prime protector identified, and he was trapped. After only a blink, Ven pulled off his family signet ring and placed it in his hand.

The prime protector raised it to his face and scrutinized the copper piece before, with a dismissing grunt, spinning and tossing the trinket far into the grass. Joney lost track of it the moment it left the nimble hand.

"That was a family—"

"Naw magic!" the prime protectors snapped. "Ya be wandin' Tohmas. Ya naw be havin' magic!"

"It was harmless ma—"

"Give it up," a Galanth voice warned from over Ven's shoulder. "You'll just piss him off."

It was one of the regular soldiers assigned to keeping the Trullers under watch. The man who spoke was probably the most nondescript person Joney had ever seen, and he wore the same white rope over his right shoulder as any of the Galanth's low-ranking companions.

Hearing Ven make no further protests, Joney nodded to the stranger in thanks.

On the rise nearest the camp, another crowd of protectors appeared, this time surrounding a broad-chested warrior wearing light armor.

"That him?" Ven asked with his head turned to Ganton, but the older man squinted into the morning light and could not answer the question. Joney's eyes were better, and he could make out the silver braid on the new arrival's shoulder, but it still took him a moment to realize what that meant.

The braid ranking was universal to the sons of Zayban but had never included using a silver braid. Princes had marked themselves with black ropes. Did silver trump them all?

Regardless of the man's shoulder band, Ven's question seemed silly. Everyone deferred to the new arrival. The prime protector, the warden of the watchmen, and another protector all approached to deliver reports.

The man seemed to sort through all the information in the blink that followed. The moment his eyes were open, he delivered answers to each person around him.

The Trullers around Joney straightened further, and he thought he could hear them collectively swallow in apprehension. The glitter of an ornate sword made it clear; this was Prince— King?— Tohmas Galanth. He alone carried the magic sword SoulBurner.

"So," Prince Tohmas said, coming to a stop before Joney's group, "explain this once more to me."

No doubt Prince Tohmas had already been told everything, but if he wanted to hear it for himself, Joney would oblige him. He and Ven stepped forward.

"We represent the cities of Leven, Waterwind, and Hanven," Joney said. "We offer our services in exchange for protection for our cities."

The prince tilted his head, holding his hands behind his back comfortably. "A strange request. I would like to know why you make this offer."

Where others asked, the leader of the Galanth made his questions statements.

"Your wizard made it clear that your influence reaches the coast. Our families have no part in this conflict," Ven said.

Had he been sitting down, Joney had the impression the self-declared king would have sat back and stroked his chin. Without the luxury of a seat, the man dropped his hands and narrowed his eyes.

"My wizard..." Everyone knew the Wisavi of Galanth by name. Joney did not feel the need to clarify as the king turned aside. "I think I'm missing something."

No longer addressing the Trullers, Prince Tohmas faced the crowd of soldiers and runners behind him. "Someone fetch Wisavi Kitable for me, please."

Two runners left. Again the group of Galanth defenders closed in around Joney and his group. For a long while, they all stood in awkward silence.

Eventually, the prime protector flinched noticeably, and the wizard who had intruded upon Hanven made his way through the people.

"You bellowed?" the wizard asked in the same flat, cold voice that had threatened to destroy all opposition in Hanven. His clothing was somewhat less elegant than before, but there was no mistaking the sardonic stare that turned to the Trullers with only part interest. "Why is it I recognize some of this lot?"

Joney's legs weakened. Protectors and princes, even kings, did not bother him, but the powers that had ripped an inn apart from the inside unnerved him.

"Apparently, you went visiting," King Tohmas answered.

The caster frowned at the memory, looking flustered. "I didn't light the inn on fire! That was Tostig's doing!" He sounded like a schoolboy caught bullying the neighbors.

"There was an inn on fire?" King Tohmas exclaimed.

"Tostig had an extra Contingency. It triggered when I killed him. I did him the disservice of surviving it."

The king, clearly hearing the story for the first time, grit his teeth in anticipation of more bad news. "How many dead?"

CHAPTER 22

The wizard had to consider the reply as if the events were confused with many other similar ones. "Assuming no one else was in the inn, only two." The emphasis on the word "only" made Joney wince.

Prince Tohmas breathed a sigh of relief. "Well, that could have been worse."

"I thought so too," chirped the wizard from beside the prime protector, but even his smile made Joney's stomach tighten uneasily.

He had to look away briefly, and so he sent his stare to the second-most terrifying man present: the prime protector. To his surprise, he saw the prime protector place something in the wizard's hand. The nod Kitable gave the prime protector was almost imperceptible, but the Rydan acknowledged it by stepping back with a wink.

With his back to the pair, King Tohmas could not have seen the exchange, and his eyes were briefly shut once more in consideration. It took only a heartbeat for the decision to be made.

"Fine," he concluded, facing Kitable now. "No more traveling without telling me, Kitable."

The wizard stiffened and pouted. "As you say, my king."

None of the Trullers dared comment, for Kitable's eyes had changed from a steely grey to a moving rainbow that made them all feel as vulnerable as newborn children. Seeing how the order disappointed the wizard, Joney thanked the gods that King Tohmas had Kitable under control.

"You lot," the prince-turned-king said. "I am not in the habit of butchering cities, but as I have not come across any populated ones, I can hardly prove that to you. If you still wish to join us, set up camp there." He pointed to the dry ground outside the defenses. "I will have a guardian teach you the basics. In a halfcycle, if you can recite the oath without flaw, you will be incorporated into a fyrd of my choosing. Otherwise, go home."

"In a halfcycle," Ven said, "your fighting with Trulin will be done."

King Tohmas was already moving away when he replied over his shoulder, "Yes, that's the point."

The prime protector had not turned with his patron but instead was grinning at Ven once more. A lift of the chin indicated the man who, sensing the unwanted attention, shrunk back.

The Rydan tossed him a copper ring. With another wink, the prime protector was at his patron's side. The wizard followed them.

"Do you not fear leaving us at your back?" The words escaped Joney before he could stop himself. Keeping out of the battle meant the army would march without them, leaving them behind. Unfortunately, the question sounded like a threat.

But Prince Tohmas laughed. "When I leave here, the rear will be Fixer City and the Rydan women. I assume some of your friends will be able to tell you what happens when people attack Fixer City." Joney caught himself nodding. Although he had not been present, he had heard the stories about the magic that had defended the city. Many horses and their riders had been lost.

"I assume," King Tohmas continued with a darker glare, "that none present will know what happens when people attack Rydan women because all those who have ever done so are already dead."

The prime protector gave a snarling half-bark, half-cheer of agreement and seemed to enjoy how much it made the Trullers jump.

"So, no," Prince Tohmas finished, "I don't fear leaving you at my back. Attacking me is suicide. I don't think that's why you came all this way."

He headed down the path to the camp with the protectors closing around him.

"Prince Tohmas," a woman's voice called, stopping his departure. "I would speak with you."

They found the speaker on the edge of the soldiers and protectors, a protector on either side of her. Joney was one of the few who knew her face, but he was not the person who whispered, "Lady Arnika..." Her brown and silver attire was obvious.

Other whispers followed: "Alive?" "Is she...?"

Finding her in the crowd, Prince Tohmas seemed relieved. He even smiled before he replied, "At your service, fair Lady, as always."

"What does that mean?" Ven asked softly, but Joney had to shrug. *As always? Since when?* And was she indeed unharmed? Why was she in the camp? Better yet, why was she wandering around the camp with an escort of Galanth protectors?

The wall of protectors closed around the so-called king. The wave of green also swept the single brown and silver from his view.

CHAPTER 22

"Make your choice before dark," a lingering protector commanded. "Those left come morning can meet with Guardian Rant. Otherwise, go away."

Joney was torn. He had come expecting killers, but he did not believe these invaders would attack Hanven. His family was safe. The presence of the late prince's daughter in the army camp had tickled his curiosity but not enough to keep him here. He could go home. The only thing he knew for sure was that he did not want to be fighting *against* Prince Tohmas' forces, ever.

"We will bring some wood out," the Galanth man beside Ven offered in a voice low enough to fall short of his warden's ear. "The woods up there are mostly empty and will be too wet to burn anyway."

"Why would you help us?" Joney asked.

The man shrugged with a half-smile that seemed vaguely familiar. "I have a cousin in Hanven," he said. "We are, after all, just family."

He stopped protesting in light of the confession and, in the coming night, discovered at least three dozen men with friends or family in their villages. They ate well, and for one night, the doom of the coming confrontations seemed a little farther off. By morning, they were ready to hear what the guardian had to say.

Having wanted to inconvenience him, Arnika commanded the protectors let her seek out Tohmas, which they had begrudgingly allowed by insisting she have an escort of four protectors. She had learned to recognize their faces and knew two of the four by name.

She found Tohmas turning away from a group of evident Trullers although they were not dressed in the expected brown and white of the princedom. Despite wanting to deny deserters and traitors happened in war, Arnika knew there was no other reason for Trullers to be outside Tohmas' army. Answering her, Tohmas followed her back to her tent, all the while giving orders to various runners at a dizzying pace. She overheard Master Kitable, looking considerably better when last they had met, add, "You could have called me."

Tohmas shrugged and, seeming flustered and usually short, replied, "You didn't come the last time I tried that. Couldn't risk you losing face."

Kitable paused, looking hurt, but in his haste, Tohmas did not seem to notice as much as Arnika did. The wizard left silently.

It was possible that the strain of impending battle was wearing on Tohmas, but Arnika would have expected him to be eager for action, not drained by it. Instead, she blamed illness and wondered how best to use the knowledge. Furthering her suspicions, when they arrived at her tent, the protectors followed them in. The prime protector ran off, but Arnika did not miss the offensive Rydan.

The moment they were indoors, she faced Tohmas firmly. "I have been told Nothor has split from Gaidol," she scolded him. "Why was I not informed earlier?"

He hesitated, then said, "I have not conversed with you since hearing the news myself. I did not realize you wished to be kept informed."

Seeing him weakened, she pressed on, "Well, I do! What other news have you of the world outside this camp?"

As she had hoped, he told her far more than he should have: "Nothor split from Gaidol after Lord Garmont had a religious experience on his road home involving visions of Inac. Apparently, Garmont now insists that my purpose is sanctioned by the gods, for which I am grateful. Gaidol has stopped advancing and seeks assistance from Trulin, but we have stopped eight riders on their way to Cainton, and I don't think we missed any. Prince Tandar probably has not heard from them. Your cousin will, however, be well aware that Gaidol took the city of Galvay upon his crossing into Trulin; we let that scout through to deliver that news. Your cousin has been forced to use conscriptions, which have been avoided by four hundred and thirteen men thus far by my count, as they have either joined me or expressed an interest in doing so. The group you just saw outside increases that number by another thirty-six."

He paused for a breath.

"Kitable killed the Double Blades, which is a relief, but I have been the target of six separate assassinat—"

"Seven," a protector corrected over his shoulder, and Tohmas raised an eyebrow. "Caught one just now," the beaming protector explained.

Tohmas faced Arnika again. "I have been the target of *seven* separate assassinations attempts in the last quartercycle as I have a bounty on my head twice that offered for Kitable, by which, I may add, I am rather flattered. Have I missed anything?"

The protector cleared his throat noisily, then pointed at the ladies with a stare.

Tohmas sighed again. "Right, of course I have."

Arnika stood with her jaw slack when he, for the first time she could remember, took on a formal, cold tone.

"My protectors inform me that your cousin returned bearing two blades with her and that you both carry one now." Arnika's jaw dropped completely, but he continued as if not seeing her alarm. "Fair Lady, if you feel the blades will make you safer, I will not object, but if you still wish to harm me or my allies, then I'll simply assume your answer is 'no,' and you can begin your ride home today."

Had her jaw been able, it would have fallen farther, but she had reached her limit. She had to close it to stutter, "You would let me go?" in the smallest voice she had ever used.

Prince Tohmas' brow furrowed deeply at her words. "You expect me to harm you?" he finally guessed. "What sort of fool do you take me for?"

Altana had moved up beside Arnika when the knives were identified. Although whether her cousin had been hoping to hide the evidence or take the blame, Arnika did not know. Neither of them, however, had any response. With a sentence, he dismissed the fear that had haunted them since the moment the wizard had identified them among the joats.

"Right now, your land is divided. Some seek to join me while others fight me. If I release you, you may tell them I am a monster and unify them against me, but it would be based on lies. If I hurt you, I become the monster and unite all your lands against me." In a softer voice, he admitted, "Besides, I don't think I could ever hurt you."

She had nothing to say. Men of war were heartless; they had to be. Was this not the killer who had slain her brother? Was this not the invader? He was conquering Espar! He could not be meek like this!

"So," he asked apprehensively, "the knives?"

Her voice was lost among her thoughts. It took a while to form her reply, but he waited for it patiently. "They are for our protection when Gaidol attacks. I mean you no harm."

He let out his anxious breath, and a tired smile crossed his face. He usually smiled when he visited her, she realized. It had seemed odd to be missing that smile.

"Then you are welcome to keep them. Is there anything else I can do for you?"

The answer did not come. Nothor had left the fight, weakening Gaidol. Trulin's last magic defenses had been lost. The forces once commanded by her father were mostly destroyed, scattered, or converted. The potential alliance between Gaidol and Trulin was being held at bay by intercepted messengers and, most importantly, by Gaidol's taking of Galvay. Even this common enemy could not unite the traditional enemies. What hope was there for her homeland?

"Yes," she heard herself say.

He paused, waiting for her.

Will this last? Will he still drop everything to answer my call?

With his eyes on her expectantly, Arnika felt herself flushing, and she trembled slightly. Clutching her hands to keep them from showing her terror, she met his eyes and whispered, "Yes."

He blanched. "Yes?" he echoed.

Everything, for a moment, was anticipation. A word could have broken him, but the words she spoke were not the ones he seemed to fear.

"With conditions," she insisted, finding her mother's strength for a moment before her shy whisper finished, "but if they are met, yes, I will marry you."

Altana squeaked, one hand coming to her mouth.

"Name your terms," Tohmas said, seeming to fail in drawing breath.

To keep her quivering at bay, Arnika sank into one of the chairs at the table. Altana, blessedly, said nothing but took the seat beside her with one hand on Arnika's arm in comfort. King Tohmas pulled a chair away from the table and sat across from her on the edge of it, eager but uncertain.

She had to swallow a dozen times to clear her throat of the lump forming. "You will leave Trulin at once," she stated, but he was already nodding.

"Our path leads us south as it stands. I do not object."

The rest of her thought coalesced. "I will travel with you, and Altana will come with me." For her to track Tohmas and his activities, she would have to be close at hand, but if she left Trulin, she needed the support of her friend.

"Is the lady married, or should I worry about losing one of my soldiers to her at some point?"

His absolute willingness to meet her demands gave Arnika the strength to smile. "Worry about your soldiers, King Tohmas."

There, I've said it. King. After so much denial, she finally used the title.

Pressing on, she added, "We will be married at once." It was no good if he made the promise but then dismissed her before his oath to the gods bound him. It was hard to tell if the threat of divine disapproval would keep him, but it was the best hope she had.

"By at once, you mean within days?" he clarified. Once Arnika nodded, he relaxed. "I'll see it done."

By far, the most crucial point was to come. "Tandar will be Kingsman of Trulin."

Again, his hesitation was minimal. "He will have to swear the same oath as the others, but if you can convince him to take it, I'll gladly have him as a kingsman."

His easy acceptance lightened her spirit, but she knew it would be challenging to get Tandar to take that oath, and Arnika lost her smile. If she failed to convince her cousin, the bargain would be lost, and Trulin...

One thing at a time.

She had covered everything vital. Tohmas would leave Trulin and put Tandar in charge, and Arnika would remain close enough for her to exercise her minimal influence over the king. The last thing she required was purely her pride.

"I will not be made a mockery of. I will not be the wife while another is a mistress. If you take me, you will never take another in my place."

For the first time, he wavered. Altana snorted softly in disgust. Despite all pretenses, there was proof: he was just another man!

But when he explained, it was not what she had expected.

"Fair Lady, I will be loyal to you and no other willingly, but the world I am creating needs an heir, and I have sworn not to lay a hand on you, an oath I will keep until you release me. Everything I have built will fall apart if the kingsmen cannot see the potential for stability."

The words somehow escaped her before she could revise them. "I will bear you an heir."

Had there been no restrictions on him, she felt he would have embraced her in his joy. Like a boy promised a new horse, relief sent him back against the chair with an enormous grin.

"Then all your terms will be met gladly." Now possessing infinitely more energy, he pounced back to the front of the chair. "If Tandar joins…"

"I will ride today to meet him to discuss it," she agreed, to which Altana suddenly perked up. A brief smirk broke her horrified expression. She quickly erased it.

"Runnah!" Tohmas bellowed, jumping to his feet and nearly colliding with one of the two protectors who had followed him; they had not left. He seemed startled by their presence but only missed a moment before giving his orders. "Get me the eight protectors who rode to Trulin last quartercycle and fetch two fresh horses for the ladies! Geddit!"

Despite the confusion on each of their faces, both left without questioning Tohmas.

Spinning back to her enthusiastically, he almost reached a hand out to her before her invisible shield, made by his oath, stopped him. He clenched his hand instead and smiled. "They will be ready in less than a candle."

"I have to pack a few things," she lied, and he heeded the dismissal like a servant. He even bowed his head before leaving her with her shock.

"Nika…" was as far as she let Altana get.

"Let us get things cleaned up in here. We will have to do a hard ride, so we had best be ready."

"Nika—"

"Later, Tana." She had no answers for her cousin anyway. Arnika needed time to process her thoughts.

Ocea protect me, she prayed as she reached for her riding clothes. She had a terrible feeling she had just made the largest mistake of her life.

Chapter 23

Tandar heard the report only a few moments before Arnika walked in, giving him no time to prepare. With his sister on her tail, Arnika rushed forward breathlessly to be embraced.

Tandar already had his arms around her when he noticed the green and silver-garbed men standing in the doorway. Instantly, the riders formed a barrier between their prince and the Galanth protectors, but Tohmas' men did not answer with their blades as he expected.

"Leave them be," Arnika insisted, pulling away from Tandar, who tried in vain to keep her close. "They escorted me, nothing more."

Turning to address the eight men Tandar recognized from their earlier visit, she commanded, "You will wait here and only move in your own defense. I need to speak with my cousin in private."

The protector closest to Arnika spoke for the entire gathering. "Please be swift, fair Lady. Our king goes against Gaidol soon, and we would like to be there when he does."

Determined not to lose face in front of the protectors, Tandar did not let his jaw drop at hearing the Galanth accepting his cousin's orders, but it took effort. Initially, he thought she had somehow convinced these men to leave Tohmas for her sake, but hearing their continued concern for the king, he dismissed the notion.

Where were the scouts he had sent to rescue Arnika? He had not expected them to be so successful so quickly, but he had equally never expected Tohmas' men to assist!

She accepted the request with a regal nod, saying, "Of course," as if nothing else could be remotely feasible.

There was a brief smile from the protector, who then took charge of his companions and ordered them, "As the king would say, boys, 'sta.'"

All eight took the stance they had once held in the courtyard for candles on end, their eyes staring forward and their hands at their sides. Satisfied, Arnika left them behind, and Tandar followed in her wake. The moment they entered the sitting room, she selected a plush chair and sat delicately, as if sore. Altana threw herself across a lounging couch, her head back and her eyes closed. But she had a satisfied smirk on her face.

It was a full day's ride from the Galanth camp, and Tandar knew Altana had probably only arrived in LandWater that day. To reach Cainton so quickly, they must have left as soon as Altana had returned and run the horses hard the entire distance. They were expected to be tired.

"Did you not meet our riders?" Tandar had to ask as he closed the doors.

"We met them," Arnika said, "but we were on our way here anyway, so I saw no need for fighting."

Altana laughed but did not open her eyes. "The protectors were very defensive of her. She had a double escort the entire way!"

"Tohmas assigned them to me," Arnika explained, leaning back into the seat. "They obey him fanatically, Tandar. If he told them to find the demon cave entrance, they would die trying. When he told them to escort me, they would die to see me safely delivered."

"But you escaped!" Tandar pointed out. "We don't have to hurt them, just send them away."

At the word "escape," Altana laughed lightly and rolled over enough to face Tandar from her sprawling position on the couch. "You should have heard her! I think he believed her! Gods, that man will believe—"

Arnika let out a small sigh. "I did not lie," she said softly.

Altana tensed, and her face went pale to match the white leather of her riding boots.

Feeling left out, Tandar asked, "Lie about what?"

The next sigh was deep and seemed to lift Arnika up as she exhaled. Sitting forward now and opening her eyes, she stared at him as she answered.

"I told Tohmas I would marry him."

This time, there was no attempt at hiding his astonishment. His jaw dropped, and his heart skipped a dozen beats.

"Impossible!" he snapped when he could finally move. Coming to his senses, he grabbed her arm and pulled her to her feet, then to the fireplace. "Have you lost your mind?"

"Tandar," she tried more than once. "Tandar, listen to me. This is the best thing to do. I'm not mad! I have not been coerced, Tandar. You must see..." Every word she spoke was folly, and he did not respond.

He snatched the horse statue off the mantle and thrust it toward her. She knew what it was: a destroyer of magic.

"I have not been bewitched!" she objected with crossed arms.

Tandar found the voice of a prince at last. "Hold it, Nika," he demanded. "You want me to believe you, then hold it!"

With a frown at his distrust, she took the statue and, holding it in both hands, again informed him, "I'm not bewitched. I still think marrying him is the best thing for Trulin!"

The shock hit him a second time once the possibility of magical interference was negated. It had been easy to believe Master Kitable had enchanted, but now that she had been dispelled, it seemed impossible again.

Showing more determination than he had ever seen before, she replaced the statue and said, "Nothor has split from Gaidol, Tandar."

"I know!" He rotated away, finding a seat in the stuffy room. His legs didn't feel strong enough to hold him now.

"Do you know why? Did your spies tell you that?"

What would Prince Kelland have done? he wondered, his eyes on the helmet next to the statue. What was there to do? If she was not bewitched, then she believed what she was saying, but how could that be? Altana had been there. How had this happened?

Hearing no reply to her question, Arnika continued, "Lord Garmont had a vision of the Goddess, Tandar. Everyone with him saw Inac! The Goddess scared him into convincing Prince Neillen to withdraw. Do you not see? The gods are against us!"

Tandar felt his cheeks flush. "Everyone knows Inac is with Tohmas. That threat is hardly new! Prince Kelland knew it, and he stood against him then! Would you have—?"

"My father," Arnika corrected swiftly enough to startle Tandar back, "said that what Tohmas was doing was a good idea but refused to follow because the Prince of Galanth would not share his power. Well, now he is doing just that! If I marry him—"

"What makes you think he will share power with *you*?"

She flinched and pressed her lips together, the first sign of uncertainty he'd seen in her. He thought he had finally broken through her insanity.

"He listens to me, Tandar," she said softly. "I don't know why, but he wants to please me. I can keep Trulin strong through him."

We must have missed something. Tandar looked to Altana.

His sister shrugged pitifully. "It's true," she confessed. "He said he was at her service and did everything she said, every time."

"But will it last?" he asked.

Arnika pushed herself up and crossed the room. Earnestly, she wrapped her hands around his arm. "Tell me what you want him to do. I'll prove it to you."

There were many options. Could he get Tohmas alone? Could he claim the bounty?

"Have him come to Cainton," he tested.

Arnika grimaced. "His protectors will never let him go. Somewhere perhaps less dangerous?"

Before the joats had been trapped by Tohmas' attack on LandWater, Tandar had thought he knew Arnika well. With no mother of her own, Arnika had been raised as Tandar and Altana's sibling, but she now felt like a different person. He could not tell if Arnika was suggesting something less "dangerous" because she knew what he was planning and wanted to make it less obvious, or if she actually did not want to trap Tohmas.

"Fine," he conceded, "how about halfway? The crossroads to the South road."

She perked up. "Give me a day's head start, then ride. He will meet you there."

She turned for the door, but he caught her wrist.

CHAPTER 23

"You don't have to go yourself!" he objected.

She shook her head. Abruptly, he recognized that her hair was not tied back but shorn. It seemed so obvious now, he could not see how he had missed it earlier.

"I can convince him if someone tries to talk him out of it. One day, Tandar, then ride and bring this with you."

She handed him a piece of vellum, which he let go of her wrist to take. A quick read identified the contents.

He wanted to object more, but she was already at the door, a tired smile on her face. "I only agreed to marry him if he made you Kingsman of Trulin. Read it, please, Tandar. Look at what he can do for us, for Trulin. Think about what he did for Lour. Know that any oath this man gives is sacred and will be kept until the demons return."

She called to her eight protectors and disappeared down the corridor before he could form an answer.

"She has lost her mind," Altana muttered from beside Tandar. "Should I go?" By her tone, Altana was genuinely hoping the answer would be "no."

"Stay with me. I don't want to lose both of you," Tandar replied. He stared at the door she had left open in her haste. Her final words lingered with him. Doubt trickled into his heart.

What if she was not mad? Tohmas had indeed weakened himself to help Lour, just as he promised. Would he do the same for Trulin?

We will see, he decided. In one day, he would ride with his fighters and meet the king. He could bring half an army if he had to.

"Do you think he will come?" Tandar asked Altana.

"If she asks him to," she said, "I think he will."

"Quite a show of faith," Tandar said.

Altana shrugged and sunk deep into the couch. "He let her go, didn't he?"

It was rapidly becoming evident to Tandar that he did not understand this enemy. That would have to be remedied.

He sat down to read the treaty.

The main downside of his bulk was that Shayne could not blend in. Instead of trying to use crowds to get close to his target, the bounty hunter selected an inn between LandWater and Cainton and sat at a table. Sure enough, he spotted a shaggy group of fellow hunters in the corner. Their thoughts were jumbled and hasty but filled with the name Tohmas Galanth.

Without having to move from his table, Shayne listened in to their whispered conversation.

"Deovon and his boys got nailed," the first man said, his voice as tense as the straps on his shouldered longsword. He pulled on the green tabard he had used as a disguise as if the collar was currently tightening. "It was elegant; six guys, a lucky-hollow, and the Oustred maneuvered, but the protectors got every last one of them. They're just too tight. I can pretend to be a companion, and no one notices, but if I dare touch a colored rope, I'll be spotted and gutted. No one gets close to King Tohmas."

"That's how many? Six down?" A second man asked, checking with his companions. "This is too much for me. I'm out. Better that than dead."

Making his point, the man rose from the table and headed out into the drizzling night. The two other occupants of the table exchanged shrugs. Their similarity was strong; probably brothers, Shayne decided.

"He's right," said the younger of the two, the one wearing the green tabard. "Not worth it."

The older brother nodded. "Good going, kid," he said. "Let's get some sleep."

The two headed for their rooms.

Weak, Shayne thought. Weak men who gave in too quickly. They had missed the obvious opportunity that had walked through the inn earlier in the day; a pair of women had stopped for food with their defenders. With a bit of magic, Shayne had easily stolen their thoughts. He knew where Tohmas Galanth would be within a day or two. The opportunity was now.

All the better that the others gave up. He could claim the bounty easier without interference.

He headed up to his room, bending low under the door frame. The bed was too small and would probably crack under his weight, so he placed the bedroll on the floor. Against the dark brown material, silver thread formed letters no Esparan could read. Shayne crouched at the center of the pattern, breathed in the damp air slowly, and let his illusion drop.

Cocked on the balls of his feet, he touched none of the silver threads as he pulled energy from his core. The heat of the earth, buried deep under the granite, seeped up into him. He gathered it in the threads, feeding the symbols with each flicker of fire until the pattern glowed around him and warmed the air.

Channeling the magic, Shayne created his spell. When he opened his eyes, he stood in the shadows of an abandoned homestead. In the distance, two ranks of riders met. One of them was the King of Espar himself. He was, for once, traveling with only a handful of protectors to meet with a man wearing Trulin's crest. The day after tomorrow, they would meet in the night. He knew where he needed to be.

The spell slipped away, but when Shayne looked up, a bright beacon shone in his vision, pointing him west. The timing was perfect; he had to go at once.

He abandoned the room, leaving scorched symbols on the floor as he took his bedroll and headed into the damp night.

Tricks watched, sitting on the back of a stolen horse, as Prince Tandar and his soldiers rode through the dark streets. The dusk was deepening: her stolen tack could not be seen well enough to be recognized as not of official issue. The time was right.

Nearby, a slowly emptying sand bag finally let a stone fall from the roof onto a brass pan. The men started and every set of eyes turned toward the sound. And while their heads were turned, Tricks guided her horse into the ranks to join them, her cloak perfectly mimicking the brown and silver uniform from the boots to the horse-hair plumed helmet.

She rode with Prince Tandar's men as they left Cainton to meet up with a man worth ten golden wheels.

Chapter 24

To get away as Arnika requested, Tohmas had to go by night. That meant riding hard the moment the sun set and enduring the brief evening drizzle, but it got them to the crossroads before midnight.

Carsh went ahead and rapidly came back to report the location of thirty men, including the Prince of Trulin and several chargers. The rest of the area was clear.

Tohmas had left behind everyone he could sneak past, which had left him with only the dozen protectors who had spotted him leaving. The count meant Tohmas was severely outnumbered, and his horses were already fatigued, but with the Lady of Trulin half asleep on a new horse beside him, he still did not hesitate.

They dismounted and approached on foot.

"I'm rather surprised you came," Prince Tandar said, dismounting. He held Arnika's tea-stained treaty in hand.

Tohmas smiled. "She said you wanted to talk. As this is the only hope I have of avoiding more death, I thought it worth the risk."

Beside him, Schlavarai tossed her head and fixed the Trullers with an angry stare that Bashuran mimicked. Both horses had enough sense to recognize the threat of the soldiers around them, and both were ready to deal with it.

Wanting to keep the peace for as long as possible, Tohmas decided to pay Tandar a Rydan compliment.

CHAPTER 24

"Schlavarai," Tohmas introduced, "*dis be Tandar.*" Schlavarai immediately sighed and let her aggressive stance lower. Her eyes remained on the rest of the crowd with continual displeasure, but at least her ears perked upon hearing Tandar speak and did not immediately flatten in a threat to trample him.

Arnika smiled weakly from where she had been leaning on her horse to support her legs, which must have felt as substantial as mud. "You introduced him," she said. "Thank you."

She had heard the introduction once before, during their tour, and both the horse and the lady remembered it well. Schlavarai no longer saw Arnika as a threat.

"Introduced?" Tandar repeated with a curious raise of an eyebrow.

"To the horse, it means you are not an enemy," Arnika explained, stepping out to pat Schlavarai's neck. She leaned in unsteadily, and Schlavarai adjusted to support her smoothly.

It made Tohmas smile further. "It means she will not attack you without being asked to," Tohmas explained, "but her affection is not guaranteed. That's something she has unprecedentedly allowed for Lady Arnika."

If Schlavarai could read Tohmas' mind, he would not have been surprised, but it amazed him that the horse seemed to read his heart. While the introduction could declare a visitor as not an enemy, it could not designate them as friends. The horse had to make that choice.

Before Tandar could continue, Tohmas saw Arnika slump against the horse.

"Might you be able to convince the lady to lie down, Prince Tandar?" he asked. "She has ridden to and from Cainton twice in half as many days, but she will not listen to me."

"I'm fine," Arnika said from her place beside the mare, but her eyes were only half open. "I want to hear what you both say to each other."

Defeated again, Tohmas let her be.

Perhaps sensing he would not sway the stubborn lady, Prince Tandar turned to business instead of trying to convince his cousin to sit down. "I hear Nothor has left the fight," he said.

Tohmas shrugged. "Apparently, Lord Garmont was confronted by Inac on his way home. It is my understanding that Prince Neillen is not discussing it for fear of causing panic and more defections. But one of my celebrants—Celebrant Calanor—witnessed some of the affair." The more mention he made of celebrants and gods, the better the conversation would go, Tohmas was certain.

"I also hear you have Nothor's heir among your ranks," Prince Tandar said.

"You have excellent spies," Tohmas commended. "I was not even aware of that fact until recently. He is not a soldier; he is an acolyte. He serves Celebrant Calanor."

"Very popular man, this Cala…"

When Tohmas saw Arnika falling out of the corner of his eye, his first instinct was to catch her. By his oath, however, he could not touch her.

"Carsh!" he barked instead, and his brother leaped forward. The knife the Rydan had been playing with spun to point down when he caught and cushioned the Lady of Trulin as she collapsed.

She woke and blinked up at Carsh in the lamplight, bewildered.

"Oh," she muttered as Carsh replaced her, delicately, on her feet. "Sorry. I did not mean to…"

"Will you please lie down a while, fair Lady?" Tohmas begged. He pulled his traveling cloak from his shoulders, and three other protectors mimicked him. They laid their cloaks on the ground where she had almost fallen.

She shook her head. "I don't—"

"Nika," Tandar joined in, "take some rest. I promise to play nice while you sleep."

That was, Tohmas quickly realized, why she had been trying to stay awake; she wanted to be ready to interfere. The effort she was willing to go to make this agreement work made his heart lift.

He would make it work for her.

She finally lay down, and Tohmas, still without letting his fingers touch her, placed his cloak over her. It was a warm night, but sleeping outside on the ground would cool her quickly, and he wanted her to get as much rest as possible before she rode home.

He did not know which home she would ride to, and the thought that she might return with him made him smile.

Tohmas faced Prince Tandar and found the man scowling with his arms crossed.

"You would have let her fall," he accused, but he had dropped his voice to a whisper in acknowledgment of the sleeping woman.

"I swore an oath not to lay a hand on her," Tohmas protested. "I could not catch her myself without breaking that oath."

Prince Tandar's eyes narrowed. "Until you are married?"

So she hasn't told him, Tohmas realized. He had been wondering.

"If she chooses to lift it, then yes. Otherwise, I will honor it until she says otherwise. That was the promise I made."

She was sleeping already, one hand tucked under her head and the other holding onto his cloak. He could only imagine how sore she would be by morning.

Tandar stared accusatorially at him when Tohmas looked back at the prince. The man's voice was the softest whisper yet when he asked, "Are you in love with her?"

Tohmas felt a lump in his throat. The only answer he could manage was, "Why does that matter?"

The Truller let his arms fall and frowned deeper. "Do you remember the dinner in Forsinth?" Tandar asked. The dinner they had shared in one of the Zayban princedoms had been an entertaining encounter and the first time Tohmas had met any of the Trullers. Then, Prince Deiton of Forsinth had been courting Arnika. The determined courtship had been unwanted by Arnika, and Tohmas had helped distract his uncle away from the woman. Tohmas had heard no word of the proposed match since he had declared himself ruler of Espar. He had expected the talks to drop off when it was evident Deiton was on one side of the conflict and Kelland on the other.

"She did not appreciate your uncle's affection then," Tandar pointed out. "What makes you think she will be any more interested in yours?"

"Because, unlike him, I am not forcing anything on her," Tohmas replied evenly. "I asked her, Prince Tandar. I want her approval." He glanced at the sleeping woman and let his voice fall slightly. "I think I won it."

Prince Tandar leaned back as he considered the information, his eyes on the sleeping woman at the feet of the horses, his expression both concern and confusion. To Tohmas, it was apparent that Schlavarai was on guard over the lady, but he could not tell if Tandar would know the horse well enough to recognize the same.

"She said yes, so long as you become kingsman," Tohmas added. "I am asking you to become a kingsman, Tandar."

Tandar slowly unclenched his fist, freeing the treaty from his crumpling grip. He glanced at it half-heartedly.

"How many of our people have you killed so far, King Tohmas?"

"I can't say I know exact numbers, but it's a little under a thousand soldiers. Your attack on Fixer City was particularly regrettable."

"And how many have you lost?"

This time, thanks to meticulous tracking by the bookkeepers, he had an accurate answer. "One thousand and seventeen."

Overall, if only the numbers mattered, Trulin was winning, but Tohmas knew that was only half of the story. A prince should understand it better than any other.

"That said, I have over four hundred of your men sitting outside my door at the moment, asking to be invited in."

"Thanks to Master Kitable," the Prince of Trulin snorted in disgust.

Tohmas was glad he had not brought the wizard with him. He had considered it but then dismissed the notion when he had realized just how much of a sore point Kitable's visit to Hanven had been.

"He went seeking the Double Blades, your mercenary team," Tohmas explained. "They are, of course, now dead."

Tandar had known that, Tohmas guessed, and it was probably playing at least a partial role in the continued handling of the vellum. Tohmas had expected the treaty to be burned by now.

The Double Blades dead, Nothor estranged, his men switching sides...

The prince seemed to be thinking the same thing as he again considered the sheet in his hand.

"When you started this, you said the borders would be set as they stood. Does that mean now or when you..."

It was easy to see where the question was going. "I'll give you Galvay. Gaidol transgressed against you when they took it. It was yours when I made the treaty, so it will return to your hands."

I might be hopeful, he mused. It sounded like he was succeeding.

"You will offer us assistance against Gaidol and Nothor?"

"Once you are a kingsman, you have but to ask me, Tandar, and I'll give you as many men and resources as you require."

Tandar's eyes dropped back to his sleeping cousin, and he grimaced. However, when the Prince of Trulin closed his eyes, it was in defeat. "Fine," he said quietly. "Fine, I—"

Carsh moved forward into Tohmas' line of sight, but the Rydan's eyes were to the right. The shadow of an old building by the crossroads, missing a roof and one wall, was barely visible in that direction. Tohmas started back a step, tensed and ready as Carsh was. He saw nothing in the direction Carsh indicated, but his hair stood on end.

"Comin'," Carsh said. "Sometin' be comin'." Crash's bracelets rattled.

Tandar glanced at the farmhouse. "If this is some kind of...."

"We checked the farmhouse," a rider reported.

"As did we," Tohmas agreed. "But there's something amiss."

A flash of red light, too red to be fire, appeared in the window of the farmhouse, then went out.

"Forgive me, Prince Tandar," Tohmas said, "I am going to place a hand on SoulBurner. I mean no threat, I swear to you."

Tandar took a step back, and his chargers protectively flanked him, moving in like folding wings on a bird. Arms came to bear, but both sides pulled away instead of attacking.

Tohmas waited, teeth clenched, for permission. His instincts screamed at him that he was being watched and that the eyes were not friendly. He wanted his sword out and ready now. But he needed the treaty. And he'd promised Arnika.

Seeming to finally realize why Tohmas wasn't acting yet, Tandar said, "Very well."

Tohmas drew SoulBurner into the night. The bright aura went well beyond the lamps, illuminating at least a dozen paces around him temporarily. Once the flash was done, the circle of light stabilized around him.

A man, almost as tall as a house, was strolling toward them. The red light scattered shadows over immense oak-like arms, and a great hammer Tohmas thought should be carried by a troll. The stranger wore a torn tunic and breeches beneath fine Lourite solid coliron armor with barbs and spikes. It had to have been fashioned for him: it would be too large on any other.

Tohmas did not have to look up to meet the eyes of anyone in a very long time. This giant of a man stood taller than him by over a head, and he marched with absolute certainty.

The protectors formed a cage around Tohmas, Carsh beyond them in a snarling, pouncing position.

"Not my doing," Tandar said as his defenders moved into positions. Seeing the way the Truller chargers aggressively shielded him, Tohmas believed him.

"*D'aems,*" Tohmas grumbled. For possibly the first time in his life, he felt small.

His uncertainty lasted only a breath. It took only a glance to remind him that Carsh, also much shorter than the intruder and also a fraction of his bulk, had not wavered. It took only a blink to swap into a Rydan perspective.

Oh, look, a challenge.

"Get to the horses," a protector said. "He cannot keep up with—"

"No, Protector," Tohmas replied as he brought his knife to bear on his right, still holding the glowing SoulBurner in his left. "I am with you."

"It is our duty to—"

"If that brute means to disrupt this meeting, I will kill him," Tohmas replied flatly.

The protector recognized the resolution in his voice and gave only a final grumble of objection.

The giant man stopped at the edge of the red light. He seemed to sniff at the light before reaching out a tentative hand. It passed easily through the aura.

The stranger grinned broadly, showing teeth that would have been better suited to a cat. Tohmas realized the similarity was also in the eyes; the stranger's pupils were slits.

"I come for the king," the man said, his words mildly slurred. "The rest may stand aside." Each S seemed to slither into the next.

The Trullers stepped back, giving the man leave, but the protectors moved in. "Like hell we will!" a protector declared. "You want to die, you come on. If you're smart, you'll run back to—"

Faster than a firedrake, the colossal man charged. Carsh had to dive aside or risk being trampled, although the prime protector managed to throw his knife before leaping clear. The blade bounced harmlessly off the man's forehead.

Tohmas barely had time to balk at the sight. The knife had been perfect. The tip had struck center in the gap below the helm. Carsh kept his blades sharp; he knew which could cut bone and had to be aimed only at flesh. Why had it failed?

The attacker crashed his hammer down among the protectors, who broke to allow the hammer to hit the ground. Together, they surged back, ducking between the man and his weapon.

The hammer was on the move instantly, knocking two protectors from the side and throwing them nearly ten feet. Tohmas heard the crunch of bones breaking.

In the swing, the man's right side was open for attack. Both protectors who managed to strike had their blades bounce off both the armor and the flesh. One by one, they were struck and tossed aside by the swing of the huge hammer.

In a matter of moments, Tohmas' protectors lay sprawled, defeated, or dead.

Gripping SoulBurner firmly, Tohmas stared down the man with skin as tough as his armor.

The man paused to grin once more. The blood of the protectors ran down the handle of the monstrous weapon in the rock grip.

"You will not run from me?" the man asked.

Tohmas switched his grip on his sword to back, then the front. He gave himself a slight shake, warming up.

"I was about to say the same to you," he said, counting the heartbeats.

Sure enough, Carsh leaped up from behind. He thrust his long knife, double-handed, into the man's neck.

The blade touched the skin and snapped.

Undaunted, Tohmas charged while the man focused on the prime protector. Counting on SoulBurner to do damage when a mundane blade could not, he slashed the edge into the man's side, cutting through the metal.

Although the blade cut through the armor effortlessly, the flesh felt like he'd struck a tree. He did not stay to see how deep it would go. Using the momentum of the charge, Tohmas got himself out of the range of the hammer before turning to assess the damage.

A shallow cut. The blood seeped green.

Carsh was thrown off but ducked and rolled quickly back to his feet. He replaced the broken blade with new ones and joined Tohmas.

Tohmas glanced at SoulBurner to confirm what he could hardly believe. Sure enough, a trickle of green ran down the blade.

Not a man. Not magic or hidden armor. Not human at all.

"*Naw flya,*" Carsh said softly, his voice a hiss. "D'aems."

The word, used solely as a curse for all their lives, took on new meaning.

The creature paused to look at his wound as the many witnesses from Trulin collectively gasped. He seemed to consider the blood for only a moment before, in a strangely human fashion, the creature shrugged.

The man before them changed. The armor vanished as it moved, replaced by red scales as thick as a dragon's. The eyes lit red. The face lost discernible nose and ears but gained a sloping brow and two horns, each the size of a short sword. The body remained humanoid, but the legs shifted to run like a wolf's.

A call came up from the Trullers. Before Tohmas could move, a volley of arrows thumped into the demon. They did not so much as chip a scale.

The hammer arched toward them, and Carsh and Tohmas split to let it crash into the ground between them. Dirt sprayed, and under the shield of debris, both Tohmas and Carsh launched themselves at the enemy with renewed purpose.

Carsh led the way, sending several daggers toward the creature's eyes. When the demon deflected the knives rather than allow them to land, Tohmas thought they had identified a weakness, but one knife slipped through the hammer defense and struck, point first, the blinked eye. The blade shattered against the lids.

With the demon's attention on the knives, Tohmas was all but ignored. Aiming for where he hoped even a thin cut would hit something vital, he pulled his charge short and cut across the wrists as the demon crashed the hammer down. SoulBurner managed to cut through the scale but barely reached the flesh beneath. The monster did not seem even to notice the new thin line of green blood.

The demon's elbow crunched into Tohmas' side. Feeling like he had been rammed by a goat, Tohmas fell back several steps and landed at the feet of the Truller horses. Arnika now hid among them, guarded by Schlavarai. Tohmas heard the horse snort in query, but he did not call her out. What use were hooves here? She would be slain as surely as the protectors had been.

Prince Tandar's men had formed a defensive line and now looked down at Tohmas. As Tohmas turned, one rider, on the edge of the line, dropped suddenly from the horse and vanished. At first, Tohmas thought the soldier was fleeing, but the person was gone too; it had to be magic. The rider had been escaping SoulBurner's light. Tohmas had spotted a cloak. None of the other defenders wore cloaks.

More magic, Tohmas thought.

The demon with the hammer had tested SoulBurner's aura, he remembered. That had been the only hesitation it had made.

The demon stalked forward, and the line of horses above Tohmas retreated two perfectly controlled steps as if to reveal Tohmas as a sacrifice. Prince Tandar and his cousin moved with them, protected by the horses and lances, the archers spaced between them.

Tohmas pushed himself onto his knees and placed SoulBurner tip-first into the ground. Making sure he was far enough from the Trullers to avoid a knife in his back, Tohmas let go of the blade, and the light winked out. He spoke in a controlled voice he hoped sounded suitably urgent.

"I hope you're listening. Get out here, Kitable. I need your help."

The demon paused two strides away, a distance Tohmas had already seen him cross in the blink of an eye. "You bow to me? You want to surrender?"

Tohmas took a deep breath to steady his nerves and cracked a forced grin. "Surrender? Why? I'm winning, aren't I? You're the one bleeding." He grasped his sword once more and stood up, squaring himself for another exchange.

"I hit you, and you die," the demon pointed out calmly, a forked tongue flicking out between long fangs.

Tohmas heard the horses behind him shift uneasily. "All the more reason not to get hit," Tohmas replied. "I won't surrender, so you can forget about that. Either hit me or—"

A crack, like a lightning strike, interrupted. A green light flashed from among the Galanth bodies a dozen paces behind the demon. The demon pivoted, hissed, and for a second time, hesitated.

Kitable stepped out of the light, looking strangely spirited. "Creature," Kitable said in an unnaturally loud voice from the brow of the hill, "return to the caves! Be gone from our world!" The wizard lifted his arms, and golden light formed as bright as the sun at its zenith.

The creature's eyes fixated on the golden orb in Kitable's hands, seeming to forget about Tohmas entirely. The sphere flashed like a pulse. The demon watched, transfixed, as Kitable launched the spell.

Finally gaining some senses, the creature made to move, but Tohmas and Carsh were already behind it. *Veins be damned,* Tohmas thought. Bones and sinew held up any animal, and nowhere had less cover than the hamstring. Tohmas cut low. He sliced away less than a finger's breadth into the tendon, but it was enough to make the leg buckle.

The hobbled leg collapsed, bringing the demon to its knees. The orb struck the creature in the forehead.

It screeched like a stuck boar as the light encompassed it. The light, mimicking flame but without heat, followed the beast as it lurched to its feet and charged, arms flailing, toward Kitable. Tohmas leaned away and let the beast go.

The wizard did not seem to notice as he stood his ground with another spell building. Tohmas nearly laughed aloud; Kitable was looking unusually spry today. In fact, he looked almost ten years younger.

Sure enough, a voice called to him from where the wizard really stood, looking small, among Truller horses outside of SoulBurner's reach. "You don't think I'd stand in front of it, do you?" Kitable said. "Get them to fire a volley, my king; I'll enchant it. My spells are getting through, but the amount of power I'd need to kill it might kill you all."

Tohmas slapped SoulBurner away and faced the Trullers. "You heard him! Draw! You've got one shot."

The defenders checked with each other. While the flaming demon crashed into, then through, Kitable's illusion of himself atop the hill, the eyes of the defenders went to the prince they were defending.

Arnika stood beside her cousin's horse with Schlavarai on her other side. Tandar looked down at her first, and she met his questing stare with wide, pleading eyes. The howl of outrage from the demon sounded among the bodies of Galanth protectors.

"Bows at the ready!" Tandar snapped, facing his men. "On my call!"

The riders lifted their bows and trained them on the creature that had recognized the ruse and now turned, its red eyes flaring in light, to face them. It hissed, and fire bloomed from its mouth.

Tohmas looked for Kitable to find the wizard staring down the row of archers, whispering to himself incomprehensibly. Each arrow lit with a green glow.

"Loose!" Tandar shouted.

Streaks of emerald sailed through the night. Of the ten, eight hit their mark and buried themselves in the red scale of the demon. The demon was brought to its knees.

Carsh was suddenly there, holding out two knives toward Kitable, and the wizard gave a weary nod. Tohmas extended his knife, knowing SoulBurner could not participate with wizard magic. Once all three blades were glowing green, they let them fly.

Carsh's knives struck each eye. Tohmas' penetrated the base of the neck, cutting deep into the airways. The body of the demon, still gleaming emerald, fell.

The Rydan broke the shocked pause; ever pragmatic, he went to retrieve as many knives as he could from the mess. Tohmas looked to Kitable, but the wizard spoke first.

"What by the hells was that?" he demanded, his voice shrill. "Warn me before you call me in to deal with something like that! By the gods, Tohmas, what did you do? How the hells..."

"Thank you, Kit," Tohmas said. "Your timing was perfect."

"Why can't things ever be easy with you?" Kitable demanded, glancing around. "Damn it, I'd better see if anyone survived. Behave yourself!"

Flaring green robes, Kitable marched to join Carsh among the protectors, leaving Tohmas, for a moment, alone.

He looked for Arnika and was grateful to find her still with her cousin, beginning to look tired once more. The excitement was wearing off. They could...

A shadow shifted behind Tohmas, and he reached for his sword, only to find it gone, the belt-loop cut. His right hand went for his knife, but instead, he felt the prick of a dagger on his throat.

"On yer knees," the voice threatened. "Quiet now."

Tohmas lowered himself gently to the ground. He distantly heard Carsh and Kitable begin an argument about something found on the demon. Their bickering went on, unaware of the knife at Tohmas' throat.

"I claim the bounty," the voice behind Tohmas said, gaining femininity with each syllable. "Tell Prince Tandar."

The chargers closest to them passed whispers back, and soon Tandar came forward to stand before Tohmas. Tohmas had to look up to meet someone's eyes for the second time.

Licking his lips, Tohmas looked up at Tandar. "We had an agreement," Tohmas said.

The Prince of Trulin considered first Tohmas, then looked over Tohmas' shoulders. "Show yourself, hunter," the prince said.

Tohmas felt nothing change, but Tandar's expression shifted to surprise; he could now see whoever had positioned themselves behind Tohmas. The hand holding the knife, visible on the edge of his vision, was petite.

"Nothing's changed," Tohmas said. "Nothor and Gaidol still won't help you. Your soldiers are..."

The grip on Tohmas' shoulder tightened, and the knife moved closer. He felt the blade touch his skin coolly.

"Quiet, I said," the bounty hunter insisted. "Prince Tandar, I offer you him alive but should that be unsatisfactory, I could offer him dead instead."

"We had agreed," Tohmas reminded Tandar. "I leave it in your hands."

The opportunity to stop the conquest of Espar knelt before him, but Tandar could not take it.

The meeting had been a ruse to get the protectors to relax and give the king space. It had worked, as the protectors pulled back enough after Arnika's fall to let the Tandar and Tohmas speak in whispers that would not be overheard. Yet he'd not given the sign to cut Tohmas down. Too much doubt existed in his heart now, Arnika's pleas too raw. He had hesitated too long.

The demon confused matters; Tandar had been forced to think about his own survival. Now the monster lay dead, the king's defenders were dead or distracted, and a little bounty hunter, her cloak lending her surprising invisibility, offered Tandar the solution to all his problems. One last chance, one last opportunity.

Out of the corner of his eyes, Tandar saw Arnika step forward, one hand on an irate Rydan horse's shoulder. Her eyes were teary.

When he had asked Tohmas if he loved Arnika, Tohmas had denied or avoided it, but that was answer enough. Arnika was right; she could influence this so-called king. Tohmas Galanth had fallen in love.

This was a greater advantage than Tandar had ever dared dream of. With all other forces in this world aligned to stop him, Tandar seriously considered the offer. If Arnika could push the king to Trulin's favor, this conquest of Espar could ultimately be Trulin's conquest.

And if Tandar allowed the bounty hunter to kill the king now, what would the Rydan rifling through the bodies on the hill nearby do? The statue might protect Tandar initially from magic, but nothing could stop a set of well-aimed knives. And the horse? She would not attack without being commanded to do so. If Tohmas was dead...

I am not, Tandar decided, *surrendering, but I will stop fighting.* It might only be for a short time, but it would be a much-needed rest. Things were changing. It was time to keep up.

"I will pay the bounty," Tandar said. "Release him."

The bounty hunter did not move, as if uncertain she had heard the command correctly.

Into the pause, Tohmas burst into motion. His right hand flashed up, grabbing the crossguard of the knife. The king's left hand reached across, catching the small woman pulled over his shoulder and onto the ground at his knees.

After a twist, Tohmas held the knife at the bounty hunter's throat in threat.

"Good choice, Kingsman," Tohmas said to Tandar. To the woman before him, he added, "Hunter, I am impressed. If ever you want employment, talk to me. For now, I trust you see that no bounty is due—you could not have delivered me."

The king flipped the blade in his hand and offered the hilt to the woman. Taking it, the bounty hunter slowly got to her feet.

Tohmas held out his hand. "My sword?"

The green and silver scabbard appeared from under the cloak. Tohmas took back the blade and shoved it under his belt.

"Tohmas?" a voice called. "Warn me before playing with that thing!"

"I will, Kit," Tohmas shouted back.

Kitable, Tandar assumed, had been watching the entire time. He had to wonder what would have happened had he made the opposite decision or if the woman had tried to make good her threat and cut the king's throat.

Pivoting, the king extended a fist to Tandar. "Our agreement?"

Tandar gingerly lifted a hand. The tension in his gut finally released. He had done everything he could. He was relieved the responsibility was now gone.

As Tandar saw Arnika's slow, weary smile surface, he suddenly thought Tohmas' ambitious plans for Espar possible.

"I will swear the oath of a kingsman," Tandar agreed.

"And I'll swear one of patronship to you," Tohmas agreed with a final grin.

Tandar knocked his fist against Tohmas' scarred hand, and it was done.

The ride back to camp was a haze for Arnika, much like the rest of the night. She had vague nightmares in her slumber, something about deadly green arrows and a beast with horns, but nothing could rouse her once she was finally allowed comfortable rest.

She emerged from the green tent long after noon, moving stiffly as every muscle from her shoulder to her rump ached from so much riding. Lady Fayela ambushed her at once. As far as Arnika could tell, the Lady Mother had been waiting by the door since dawn.

Arnika found Fayela in her element.

They emptied the tent in part; the table, chairs, charts, and tokens were removed and put in King Tohmas' current tent so that the new wife would not have to put up with the guardians intruding at inopportune times to talk of battles and planning. A large area close to the Temple waggons was cleared for the wedding, with innumerable people recruited for flowers and candles. Sewists were waiting for her.

The first thing Lady Fayela did was embrace Arnika, making Arnika even more aware of the invisible barrier between her and Tohmas, for the king seemed to envy, from a distance, the luxury his mother took advantage of. She wondered if he'd slept but noticed his hair was askew and his clothing rumpled. Not only had he slept, but he had also done so without changing.

"Congratulations!" Fayela exclaimed, grabbing her son's hand and Arnika's as if bridging them.

Fayela was the first person to approach the topic with excitement, and Arnika found herself caught slightly off-guard by the enthusiasm. Tandar had acknowledged the marriage as a necessity, and Altana seemed to think it was a funeral, but Fayela was giddy with the prospects of having a daughter-in-law. If it were not for their earlier conversation over tea, in which the Lady of Galanth had professed a dislike for drink, Arnika would have thought her mother-in-law to be drunk.

"What color will you be married in, child?"

Arnika flushed. "White!" she snapped. Tradition dictated that only virgin brides wore white, and a wedding dress of any other color was considered a quiet confession of the bride's previous indiscretions. Arnika's mother and aunt both would have disowned her if she had ever lost the right to get married in white.

Seeing her aghast expression, the Lady Mother laughed and, with a wink, confessed, "No offense intended. I was married in blue."

Again seeming drunk, Fayela giggled at the shocked faces of the sewists around her, although the protectors did not even crack a smile. Tohmas either did not understand the meaning of the colors or did not care. The king seemed too distracted by the commotion of the dozen men it took to move the table out of the tent.

"I have a double cot on the way," the mother said, unabashedly poking her son, the king, in his navel, "so have them pull out your old one while they're at it."

"Mother…" was as far as Tohmas got in his objection. Arnika felt her stomach do somersaults at the thought of sleeping with the giant of a man snoring nearby, but she doubted anyone noticed.

"We have to get to Celebrant Corolys, dear," the woman interrupted. She waved Tohmas off dismissively, then snatched up Arnika's wrist. "I hear Altana's on her way! Don't worry!" The sewists had each taken a single measurement, but they had been wise enough to each take a different one, so they had no objections when Arnika was whisked away. "Go run your army," Fayela said. "We women will take care of this."

The king looked relieved, and it was enough to make Arnika smile slightly.

"Most little girls," Fayela said as she marched them off to the celebrant, "spend their lives planning their perfect wedding. If you have anything you want, child, ask for it now. Otherwise, I fear you may have to make do with whatever time allows."

Arnika had grown up thinking that weddings were only done one way: the traditional way. She needed a temple, a Celebrant of Ocea, a white dress, and a prestigious husband. That was all she had ever expected from any arranged marriage.

The year before, she'd feared Prince Deiton would stand beside the marriage table in the groom's position. But even now that King Tohmas was in his place, the vision looked pretty much the same.

"Just a traditional..." She paused. Once, years ago, a maid in Trulin had told her that her mother had worn no veil but instead had woven her hair with flowers. "I want flowers for my hair," Arnika said.

"Hair, indeed!" The Lady Mother chuckled, informally ruffling Arnika's shortened locks. "Name your flower, and I'll have it gathered. Actually," the woman carried on, "I was going to ask you about it! Traditionally, a husband and wife exchange bracelets of their hair as a bond, but with such short notice, and such short hair, I cannot see how that would be possible. What would you like to—"

"Horse hairs," Arnika said. "Let him use Schlavarai, and I'll use my mare from Cainton, Emerald Glory."

Already, the Lady Mother was nodding. "As I can imagine nothing more suiting, I agree!"

THE END.

Sneak Peek of Traitor

Traitor

Gannon sat forward and rubbed his eyes. The Scry in front of him kept perfect shape despite his distraction. He could sleep and hold the spell up, but who would watch what it saw if he slept? And it wouldn't do for the Watching Circle to catch him sleeping on the job.

He had to remind himself that being a part of the Watching Circle, one of only two Circles in all of Wanter, was a great honor. However, days of sitting and watching had removed much of the luster from the otherwise prestigious post.

The Tainted Circle was broken and had been since the spring before. Unlike the Circles of Wanter, the Tainted Circle did not appoint members; they seemed to hope for one to stumble into their gathering blindly. Years, if not decades, could pass between new members. A completed Circle was, as a result, rare. It might be another century before it reformed.

And he, with the rest of the Watching Circle, would sit and watch for it, just in case.

And he would be bored for every moment of the long and useless chore.

"Might be faster just to kill them all," Gannon grumbled to himself and the empty cavern. The other six members were already home in Wanter. With no Tainted Circle complete, they took turns keeping the Scry open. Of course, that meant the lowest rank had to watch the most. As far as Gannon knew, Rean, as the Voice of the Circle, was not even taking a turn.

But the danger of being caught not paying attention to the Scry kept Gannon honest. Here, an old woman in bird feathers. There, a man with a long beard and a white pelt over his shoulder. A thin man with a hooked nose and a hat of hawk feathers...

Six impossible disruptions to magic, somehow mixing their magic with Wanter's.

He was still staring at the Scry, moving it from Circle member to Circle member, by the time Yonny arrived through the portal from Wanter.

Like Gannon, Yonny had a focus gem set in his forehead and wore the ribbon robes of the Circle. They would earn another ribbon for every year they served. As the youngest, Gannon's robe had the fewest and thickest ribbons.

Gannon didn't trust even another member enough to let them through his shields. He anchored the Scry to a spot on the ground outside his defenses to allow Yonny to take over.

Letting go of the Scry was like finally closing his eyes after staring at the sun. The buzz of magic did not leave him—his spells were a constant comfort—but releasing the Scry at least allowed him to turn his gaze away and blink without feeling guilty.

Yonny took a seat on the cavern's rough ground with a self-satisfied grin, adjusting the cushion he had brought. Usually, the Seat of Divination in the Circle never wasted an opportunity to mock Gannon. *Has he not found a reason yet, or...*

Yonny's grin grew with each passing moment, and Gannon's curiosity would not allow him to leave without finding out why.

"Why exactly are you so pleased?"

Yonny would have to keep watch for twenty days now without rest. It was shorter than Gannon's twenty-five days but should not have been met with such enthusiasm.

"Can't read my mind?" Yonny replied.

With no patience remaining after his long vigil and having little when dealing with Yonny, even under good circumstances, Gannon narrowed his eyes onto the Seat of Divination. Most focus gems would change colors depending on the user's thoughts—a strange side effect no one understood—but Gannon was the Seat of Thought in the Circle, and he could control what thoughts the gem accessed. In this case, the gem stayed pure, brilliant blue, not showing his annoyance.

"I could if I wanted to," Gannon replied, his voice tense. "Of course, Rean might be mad if I yank your smug thoughts through your nostrils."

Yonny's smile vanished. Gannon felt more than one spell pulse nearby like the flexing of muscles.

But Yonny did not lash out. Instead, proving he was in a far better mood than Gannon had expected, Yonny's lip twitched only once as he turned back to the Scry. "You crude Shantanese," he grumbled. "Always about brute force. No finesse."

There was no point in trying to prove Yonny wrong. Thought magic, Gannon's strength by far, was all about finesse, but it could be used roughly to great effect, just like any element or domain of magic.

Feeling his question about Yonny's sanguine mood would go unanswered and was not worth the headache to chase, Gannon headed for the portal, only to pause at the sound of Yonny's laughter.

He refused to turn around but paused long enough to hear Yonny say, "My divinations say the time is coming. We will have to act before my watch is over. I alone will be witness to…"

Knowing every word was an attempt at goading his temper, Gannon forced his feet to carry him forward. The moment he was through the portal, Yonny's voice was too far away to be heard.

Gannon paused in the portal room on the other side, taking a moment to lean against one wall. If Yonny was right, which he usually was when it came to divinations, then the Tainted Circle would reform soon. The Watching Circle would be needed once more.

They could not allow the contaminated blood of Taint to stain their magic. Any who touched the powers had to be killed.

Would slaying one suffice? It had not taken long for the Tainting Circle to replace its missing member. Ganon thought he would push for the death of all Tainted Circle members should the situation arise. He had no desire to go tromping back to the world of Taint unnecessarily.

He decided to find somewhere to rest. He would need his energy for when the Watching Circle called him again.

Glossary

Barlaby: Far north princedom of Espar. Overrun by Northlander
    CURRENT PRINCE: Prince Lorian Rairn.
    COLORS: White and White.
    CREST: None

Calendar: Universal calendar pre-dates the Demon Wars. Roughly based on the moon's phases:
    YEAR: Eight mooncycles of forty days, and one mooncycle (the ninth) of a variable length, thirty-five or thirty-six days.
    MOONCYCLE: forty days.
    HALFCYCLE: twenty days.
    QUARTERCYCLE: ten days.

Celebrant: Esparan priest, traditionally assigned to a single deity of the four. Overseeing a group of Acolytes.

Clandac: Central Esparan princedom.
    CURRENT PRINCE: Prince Dragal Galanth. Eldest son of Zayban.
    COLORS: Blue with Gold.
    CREST: Scythe

Companion (Black rank rope): Esparan Companions are not soldiers by profession. They become soldiers when they are required, but have other occupations.

Currency (Esparan)

> LEG: Wedge-shaped copper coin with a hole in it for threading on a string.
>
> TABLE: Eight legs strung together.
>
> SLIVER: Wedge-shaped silver coin with a hole in it for threading on a string.
>
> SLICE: Eight slivers strung together.
>
> SPOKE: Wedge-shaped gold coin with a hole in it for threading on a string.
>
> WHEEL: Eight spokes strung together.

Damoria: South west princedom of Espar, corner of DragonTail mountains and Outlands. Enemy of Galanth.

> CURRENT PRINCE: Prince Wevan Damoria.
>
> COLORS: Red with Yellow.
>
> CREST: Dragon

Espar: The overall region north of DragonTail mountains.

Esparan (race): People of Espar. Pale skinned and featured peoples. Religion of four elemental gods.

Forsinth: Princedom of Espar, known for pottery and claywork. Close ally to sons of Zayban

> CURRENT PRINCE: Prince Deiton Darvin-Galanth. (Widower of Elinea Galanth)
>
> COLORS: Brown with Silver.
>
> CREST: wine pitcher

Galanth: Southern Esparan princedom on borders with Outlands.

> CURRENT PRINCE: Prince Tohmas Galanth. (Son to Habal Galanth)
>
> COLORS: Green with Silver.
>
> CREST: Tree

Gaidol: Princedom of Espar with prolific trading routes. Borders contentiously with Trulin. Close ally to Nothor.
> CURRENT PRINCE: Prince Dorakon Lodaton
> COLORS: White with blue.
> CREST: Shark

Guardians (Red rank rope): Each Esparan city had a single Guardian named by the Prince. A Guardian may or may not have a Prime status, depending on the size of the city.

Inac: Esparan fire god. Female. Also known as the Bitch Goddess, Dame Justice, Lady of Lust, Warrior Queen.

Knock: An Esparan gesture of agreement. Originally from a time of blood-bonds, where the two people would press their fists together and cut across the two hands to bind their words and spirits. More recently, no cut is used, just the knock of fists.

Lour: Western princedom of Espar along the Crescent and DragonTail mountains. Deep iron mines. Finest metalsmiths in Espar
> CURRENT PRINCE: Prince Loritat Naygan.
> COLORS: Gold with Grey.
> CREST: Anvil

Meloch: Far north princedom of Espar, currently overrun by Northlanders
> CURRENT PRINCE: Prince Garit Carnilan. Deceased.
> COLORS: Black with Red.
> CREST: Raven

Northlander (race): Race of the far north; a hardy people organized into clans but united by a Circle of the Raven, which comprises of magic-users. When the circle is complete (7 members), they name a DoomDragon (all clan leader).

Nothor: Eastern coastal Esparan Princedom. Known for shipping and mechanical innovation. Close ally to Gaidol.
>CURRENT PRINCE: Prince Neillen Lodaton.
>COLORS: Green with Gold
>CREST: Ship

Ocea: Esparan water god. Female. Also known as the Maiden, The Benevolent Mother, the Weeping Goddess.

Polthian: Esparan Princedom on southern border, close to Outlands.
>CURRENT PRINCE: Prince Emacen Polthian.
>COLORS: Blue with red.
>CREST: Eagle

Pari: Esparan earth god. Male. Also known as the Mountain King, The Beast Lord, The Traveler, Healing Presence.

Prime (single strand of silver in a rank rope): A distinguishing rank above the main associated one in Esparan ranking. For example, a Prime Protector would be one step above a protector and command them.

Protectors (Green rank rope): Bodyguards of a Prince of Espar. Commanded by a prime protector.

Rabarch: Esparan Princedom.
>CURRENT PRINCE: Prince Barnon Galanth (youngest son of Zayban Galanth)
>COLORS: white with red
>CREST: Dragon head

Rydan (race): Tribal people of the south Outlands, consisting of three clans (First, Second, Third), each ruled by a Chief. Primarily raiders and nomads, with a strong emphasis on horsemanship. Rydan horses are powerful warhorses, bound to a given master for life.

Solta: Central princedom of Espar, currently under siege by Northlanders.

> CURRENT PRINCE: Prince Sol Galanth (Second youngest son of Zayban)
> COLORS: Red with back
> CREST: Shield

Tanble: Northern Princedom of Espar, currently overrun by Northlanders.

> CURRENT PRINCE: Prince Vornan Marfaie (believed deceased)
> COLORS: Black with grey.
> CREST: Sword

Totho: Esparan wind god. Male. Also known as the Tempest, The Gust, North Star.

Trulin: North East Espar Princedom. Breeders of powerful warhorses.

> CURRENT PRINCE: Prince Kelland Trulin.
> COLORS: White and Brown.
> CREST: Horse

Wardens (Blue rank rope): Under the Guardians, these are permanent Esparan soldiers who guard the city and maintain the peace. The number of Wardens answering to a Guardian depends on the size of the city. If a call comes from the Prince, the Wardens become responsible for a company of ~20 companions.

Wisavi: A wise-man and advisor to a Rydan Chief.

Author Bio

At a young age, Deborah's rampant imagination kept her up, lending great detail to all the terrible things lurking in the night. In desperation, her mother suggested she invent her own stories to distract her brain. She has been doing that since, channeling her ideas into sword and sorcery-style fantasy novels and shorts.

In her other life, Deborah is a veterinarian. She lives in Sooke, BC, Canada with her husband of 13+ years, their two sons, and three demanding felines.

WWW.DLAMBERTAUTHOR.COM

INSTAGRAM: @dlambertauthor
TWITTER/X: @dlambertauthor
FACEBOOK.COM/DLAMBERT42

Book Club Questions

1. Although this is fictional, what real-life histories can you think of are similar to the politics or events depicted in "Esparan?"

2. What kinds of love did you see in the book? Do you think having more than one word for the nuances of love would be useful? If not, why not? If yes, in what ways?

3. How did you feel about Celebrant Corolys' choice to leave her oath for her child and lover? Do you think she made the right decision? Why or why not?

4. When is it reasonable to not "fight fair?" Do you feel either Kelland or Tohmas cheated?

5. How did Fayela's relationship with her son Tohmas change as she learned more about who he was?

6. Contrast the women of this book. How do Fayela and Arnika compare? What about Loni and Corolys? Shimmer and Darcina?

7. Does Tohmas truly love Arnika? Is it real love? How do you know?

8. Who is the noblest character in the book? Justify your answer with examples.

9. How does challenging love strength it?

10. Which character is your favorite? Why?

Discover more at
4HorsemenPublications.com

10% off using HORSEMEN10